ON
HER
OWN

ON HER OWN

Naomi Bliven

Grove Press
New York

Published by Grove Press
a division of Wheatland Corporation
841 Broadway
New York, N.Y. 10003

Library of Congress Cataloging-in-Publication Data

Bliven, Naomi.
 On her own / Naomi Bliven. — 1st ed.
  p.   cm.
  ISBN 0-8021-1130-0 (alk. paper)
  I. Title
PS3552.L54405   1989   89-1854
813′.54—dc19   CIP

Designed by Irving Perkins Associates

Manufactured in the United States of America

This book is printed on acid-free paper.

First Edition 1989

10   9   8   7   6   5   4   3   2   1

IN MEMORIAM

Anna
Emma
Tess

Contents

I

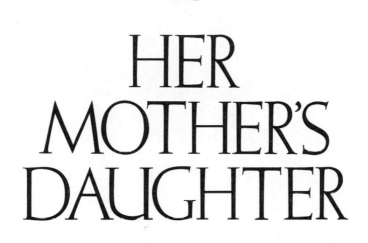

HER
MOTHER'S
DAUGHTER

Labor Day

"Ah, Mother," Alida cried, "you never understand me!"

This stale reproach erupted rather than was spoken, and then seemed to linger, suspended like smoke in the heavy summer-afternoon air in her mother's garden. Alida was humiliated by her words. Three months earlier, on the first of June, she had scooped up her child and fled from her unfaithful husband in California to her widowed mother in Connecticut. In so doing, she had acted like a child—literally, like her mother's daughter—and it was therefore all the more important never to *be* childish: dependent, disorganized, and, worst of all, whining. Yet here she was, bleating on her mother's terrace. She did not fully understand how she had reached this moment of simultaneous explosion and collapse. She sat and stared at the flagstones and then, amid the disorder of her feelings, her mind unexpectedly came to her defense and told her that every genuine statement of emotion—whatever human beings say spontaneously or incautiously—is inescapably banal: true feeling is never original. She thought of communicating her discovery to Hugo, for she realized it was what he had been trying to tell her when he used to complain that his writing suffered from too much wit, and that his greatest problem as a playwright was polishing his lines to sound unpolished. But why was she thinking of her husband? Her problem was to explain herself to herself so that she could explain herself to her mother.

Alida had waked early and, from the window of her bedroom in her mother's guest cottage, could see the heat already weighing on

3

the pretty scrap of landscape: the dew had evaporated, the great oaks had assumed their pose of patient self-pity under the sun, and three silent birds picked listlessly in the grass. Alida's stirrings roused her daughter Amelia, who slept in the next room, and who came into Alida's. They whispered so as not to wake May, Amelia's nursemaid, who slept in a room beside Amelia and ordinarily rose first and got breakfast. This morning Alida said, "We'll let May sleep as late as she likes and go to the club without her. It's a holiday—Labor Day."

They dressed quickly and quietly and tiptoed downstairs to the cottage sitting room, where Alida opened folding shutter doors concealing a tiny kitchenette that had been installed when the cottage was built, in 1938, and that had remained brand-new while becoming obsolete. She was irritated by the constricted space as she worked at the unfamiliar task of assembling breakfast, and wondered how May, who was bigger and clumsier than herself, managed in it.

Amelia mentioned the heat, and Alida said, "It's usually like this on Labor Day."

"Why?"

"End of summer, I think."

Alida often found it difficult to impart pure information, untainted by metaphor or personification, to her child. Alida had always imagined Labor Day as Summer's grand deathbed scene, when Summer showed her wrath at having to leave the stage, and, enraged that all her richness and lushness would go for nothing, gathered her forces for a last, furious demonstration of her power, muttering to herself, "They won't forget *me*." Alida told Amelia, "When I was a little girl, I used to think Summer was a fat lady who wanted to stay."

"Did you?" Amelia asked. "What a funny idea."

At nine-going-on-ten, Amelia did not want to hear about "little girls"; her daydreams dwelt on those godlike beings, teenagers.

After breakfast, Alida left a note for May and drove with Amelia to the Flat Rock Club to spend the hot morning in the swimming pool. At that hour—they were the first—it was a tranquil aquamarine rectangle embedded in green lawns behind the rambling white-clapboard clubhouse. Alida was delighted by Amelia's lithe, athletic body, so like her own. Amelia might grow taller than herself, and the girl's coloring was fairer than Alida's decided brunette, but all in all, Alida saw little of her husband in her child. Hugo was not

4

very athletic, while Amelia was already an accomplished swimmer. She showed off—"Watch me! Watch me!"—and competed—"Can you do this?" as she demonstrated a racing turn.

As the morning wore on, other swimmers interrupted their privacy. Mother and daughter got out of the pool and sat on its edge, idly splashing their legs and observing the newcomers. None of the other young children swam as well as Amelia, but Alida, who thought her daughter should make new friends, whether swimmers or splashers, asked, "Do you know that boy with red hair?" or "that girl in the blue suit?"

Amelia did not reply directly: she said, "I miss my own pool. I wish Grandma would put in a pool."

Her statement snapped the morning's charm for Alida, reminding her of complexities she preferred to forget, among them the fact that she had never told Amelia that the move to Connecticut was the beginning of the end of her parents' marriage. Alida had simply announced that they—just the two of them—were going to visit Grandma Waterman. Amelia asked, "What about May?"

So Alida took May.

Soon after they arrived, Alida had made a second announcement: they were going "to visit Miss Blossom at Mother's old school."

After that interview, Amelia understood she would attend Flat Rock Country Day School in the fall, yet she had asked no questions and Alida had told her no truths, thinking that divorce should be treated like the Facts of Life: a parent should wait until a child sought explanations. So far, no equivalent of a pregnant cat or a new baby had provoked Amelia's curiosity, and nobody had begun the process of enlightenment—not Hugo, though he wrote his daughter long, chatty letters twice a week and telephoned her every Sunday evening; not May, who had sulked through the summer complaining about Flat Rock; and not Grandma Waterman, who had scarcely discussed Alida's marital situation even with Alida. Amelia's longing for her California pool was the first intimation that by saying nothing, Alida had put them both in false positions. Yet she was unprepared for elucidations just now: she thought she needed advice—Miss Blossom, an experienced headmistress, might have some ideas about how to break such news. For the moment, Alida did not want to encourage her child to criticize her grandmother who, with both her children married (Alida had an older brother, Josiah), and both, until the past June, living in California, had had no reason to tear up her grounds, marring her

5

gardens and interrupting her vistas, to build a swimming pool for her grandchildren's occasional visits. On the other hand, Alida did not want the child, already discontented with her life in Connecticut, to long for losses, like a swimming pool, that could be made good. So Alida took refuge in the parents' tense, the indefinite future: "We'll see. Perhaps she'll put one in." And asked, "Shouldn't we have lunch?"

They had sandwiches behind the clubhouse, at a table overlooking the pool. Amelia, distrusting Alida's vagueness, clung to the subject of pools, saying things Alida wished she would not, such as "I liked our pool the best in all California."

Their conversation trailed off into a decision to go home and lie down; it was too hot to do anything else. As they were crossing the parking lot, Alida remembered that, upset by the unexpected concatenation of pools and truth-telling, she had never adequately praised Amelia's swimming, and said, "You're a wonderful swimmer, Amelia. Like a mermaid. Or a fish. A charming, graceful girl fish."

Amelia's face shone. "It might be fun to be a fish instead of a person."

"Don't forget, though, you'd always be in a school."

Amelia responded with the groan-giggle Alida expected to elicit, and while she was smiling down into her child's imitation-fish funny face, a man stepping backward to take something out of a car trunk bumped into her. He turned to apologize and said, "Why Alida, it's you. I would have phoned, but I've been away."

Alida did not recognize him; a floppy sun hat covered the upper part of his face and she could not think of anyone left at the Flat Rock Club nowadays who would talk to her so familiarly. She returned his greeting with a smile while mentally seeking his identity in every corner of her Flat Rock past. Club. Church. Games. Lessons. School. School—the tall, but not handsome, stranger was her onetime classmate, poor Eliot Jones. She had not thought of him in years. They had met in the kindergarten of Flat Rock Country Day School and gone through all its grades together: they had seen one another occasionally during boarding-school vacations, but after that very rarely. In those days poor Eliot was on the bottom of the Flat Rock heap. He seemed to have been born with eyeglasses, braces on his teeth, moist palms, and allergies that sometimes made him sniffle and sometimes covered him with hideous crimson rashes. He tried to be friendly, but he was hopelessly tactless. His

6

father was a liability, too, forever appearing at school to check on Eliot's progress, and contriving, by perpetual dissatisfaction, to make everything worse for the whole class. Whenever the charity of parents overruled the cruelty of children, so that Eliot was invited to a party, you could be sure Mr. Jones would invade the festivity to see that no liquor was served and that the chaperones were alert.

Time had not improved Eliot's address. He did not think of letting Alida move on out of the sun, but kept her standing in its blaze while he gave an involved answer to a question she had not asked, telling her that he had been on a long visit to his wife's family at their summer place in Canada, and that she was still there with the children, while he had come home to be ready for business after Labor Day. Alida feared he would never stop talking about his own uninteresting existence. Then he abruptly, amazingly, concluded, "Since we're both at loose ends, Alida, come out to dinner with me tonight."

Caught off guard, she accepted. She did not want to dine with Eliot, but his invitation was so unforeseen that she had no excuse ready. She was distracted by trying to guess how Eliot knew she was "at loose ends"—it would have been reasonable for him to assume that her husband, though not at her side, had come east with her—and she was afraid he would say something indiscreet in front of Amelia. The sun on her head addled her beyond her capacity to cope with a man who, awkward himself, had a gift for creating awkwardness around him. She took an indecisive half-step away, but he talked along—unpopular people like poor Eliot learn to keep conversations going with very little help—and produced several more complex, pointless sentences before his leavetaking: "I'll come for you at seven. I'll cheer you up. Poor Alida! Did you think your old Flat Rock friends would let you mope alone?"

Eliot's farewell staggered Alida. Did he know what he was saying? Did he know that, in pitying "poor Alida," poor Eliot had reversed their lifelong roles? Alas! His pity showed her to herself as a pitiable person—a rejected wife. It made her aware, too, that she looked pitiable—that the orange cotton slacks and coarsely embroidered yellow Mexican cotton shirt she had pulled on hastily that morning were rumpled, that their colors were too bright for her to wear without makeup, and that, since the rubber band that held her hair in a ponytail had disappeared in the water, her face was unbecomingly framed by damp, stringy locks: she must look like Medusa, both jellyfish and Gorgon.

7

"Who was that?" Amelia asked as they walked on to their car.

"Eliot Jones. I went to school with him," Alida said absently.

She was thinking about her hair. Its wet-mop reality was bad enough: worse, it served as an emblem—what was that figure of speech you learn in English, the part for the whole?—well, anyway, a symbol, of a very odd Alida. Alida, the normal Alida—Alida Waterman Kelly—had been a habituée of beauty salons from puberty on, tending her looks as intensively as her mother tended her land. The woman Eliot had just condescendingly invited to dinner had been washing her own hair in the shower, clipping and filing her own unpolished nails, forgetting lipstick—she had, in the common phrase, been "letting herself go," because, until poor Eliot had asked her to dinner, she had had no place to go. She could have found things to do and people to see, but she had not even troubled to go into New York City to talk over the legalities of her situation with Andrew Cameron, a lawyer who was one of her trustees. She had simply arranged, by telephone, for some of her income to be paid into a new account at the bank in Old Bridge, the town that served as Flat Rock's business district and shopping center. Of course—that must have been how Eliot guessed she had left Hugo! His father was chairman of the board of the Old Bridge bank, and Alida recalled that her mother had once mentioned in a letter that the old man had permitted his son to become a vice-president. She had doubtless appeared on his desk as "new business."

Driving home, with Amelia fidgeting and grumbling beside her, Alida began to recall the confidences she had received from wives who had left, or been left by, their husbands. They had all sketched schemes to resume interrupted careers, begin new ones, or return to school. Some had actually done these things. Others had had their faces lifted, their hair dyed, or had bought contact lenses. Alida had merely gone home to Mother to swim and play tennis at Mother's club, disguising her lethargy by physical activity, with the result that poor Eliot—who did not represent the possibility of a new social or sexual life, but who, as a man, could not help appraising her as a woman—pitied her. His pity stung the more because he was so unattractive. Alida Waterman had not been the belle of Flat Rock, a palm awarded to girls who were more outgoing, but Eliot, by every reckoning, had been its pariah. She would show him. She took it as a job, a task, a command laid upon her: this evening she would dazzle, defeat him, conquer him, and restore their former ranking. Her determination fixed itself upon her hair, her emblem-

8

atic, symbolical, metaphorical, messy hair. Hair had been a battle-
ground, hair had been a badge, for more than a decade, and that
wretched ponytail she had worn all summer identified a woman
who had renounced all hope of admiration. She had mislabeled
herself: she had lost Hugo, but she was not a loser, and by seven
p.m. everything about her, including her hair, would proclaim Alida
triumphant.

Once back at the cottage, she immediately went to her room and
reached up to the closet shelf for the satchel in which she carried her
hair-repair equipment—several hairpieces, along with rollers, clips,
and bobby pins. The rollers and pins were there, but her hairpieces
were missing. What could she have done with them? She tried to
visualize herself packing in California, hoping to conjure up a
gesture that would remind her where she had put them. She could
see her and Hugo's bedroom and her dressing room very clearly,
but at the memory of those rooms in that house, a knot of sadness
tied itself between her ribs and began to swell.

Would May know where those things were? Alida knocked on the
door of May's room, but the young woman, who had packed and
unpacked for herself and Amelia, could not remember seeing Mrs.
Kelly's hairpieces. Alida thought again and realized that, although
she believed she had been collected and methodical last June when
she had decided to leave Hugo, she must have been extremely
agitated: apparently she had not known what she was doing while
she was doing it. Was it possible that she had been half out of her
head without suspecting it? That thought was almost as disturbing
as Eliot's pity.

Never mind California last June. Here and now, in Connecticut on
Labor Day, with every hairdresser closed, she had to set her own
hair. The prospect daunted her. She had never done it. Her rollers
and hairpieces were for emergency repairs to sets coming undone—
like sewing on a button, not making a dress. She dithered in the
narrow upstairs hall, talking to herself. May grasped her practical
difficulty and said, "Let me help you with your hair, Mrs. Kelly.
Show me what you want."

May wore her own blonde hair straight and long, and had it
trimmed every few months by a unisex barber. She would need
more showing than Alida could show, but Alida accepted her offer
for the sake of a woman's company in a woman's struggle. May
followed her to her bedroom. Alida sat down at the small dressing
table and began to direct May to separate the strands of her hair.

May was tall and rawboned rather than delicate. Her strong fingers would tug a tress, drop it, and search for it again, while Alida, trying to give directions, was confused between right and left in the mirror and on her head. Her only clues came from pain when May pulled too hard.

May's fee for service was making Alida tell her about Eliot. "He's married?"

"Yes, of course, I told you. I've known him forever."

May kept returning to Eliot's marital status while Alida kept stressing the length of their acquaintance. May triumphed in extracting the admission that Alida did not know—had never met—was not an acquaintance of—the absent Mrs. Jones, and so not properly "a friend of the family." During cross-examination, May did manage to collect most of Alida's hair on rollers, and was stepping back to view her achievement when Amelia, who had been pretending to nap but was more interested in their hairdressing and conversation, came in.

"Your mother is going out tonight," May informed her, "and I am fixing her hair."

"I know all about it," Amelia said. "She met a man in the parking lot she went to school with. What does he do, Mom?"

That question struck Alida, who, since the morning's talk of pools had become sensitive to her daughter's transplantation, as a peculiarly show-business-child's question. She herself, as a child, would have asked, "Where are you going?" but her celebrity-conscious daughter wanted to know if any stranger was a celebrity.

"He is the vice-president of the Old Bridge bank," Alida said.

May demonstrated her contempt in an immense, theatrical shrug. She had come east out of attachment to Amelia and sympathy for Alida as the deceived wife, as well as curiosity about everyday life in the eastern United States—she had originally been imported as a nursemaid from Denmark to California, where she had always worked for families involved in the manufacture of entertainment. Alida's husband, Hugo Kelly, had been born in California, but Alida had met him in New York City, where she was living with her aunt and uncle and studying art history. He had had one play produced off Broadway, and after their marriage, one on. It had had no great run, but it sold to the movies, and he wrote the script and several more films after that, and then they had moved to California. By the time May came to work for the Kellys, Hugo had created a successful television series, *Galaxy Guards*, and the parents of Amelia's friends and the guests at the Kellys' house were people whose pictures appeared in fan magazines and whose names figured in gossip columns. Among them was Yvonne Taylor, the star of *Galaxy Guards,* an exceptionally pretty, exceptionally untalented actress who, Alida had learned last June, had become Hugo's mistress. Alida had given no thought to her nursemaid's appraisal of Flat Rock's industrialists, financiers, leaders of the bar, heirs, and philanthropists, and she was surprised to learn that May regarded the Flat Rock Club as an assortment of anonymous men, muscular women, snobbish nursemaids, and children who talked in a high-hat way. Alida told her these were important families, but they were not important to May. She said, "Old Bridge bank, hah," shrugged again, and bent over to screw little wisps of hair into pin curls at the nape of Alida's neck.

May was tickling Alida, but Alida was not laughing. As sometimes happens, misfortune was making her shrewd. She guessed that May, bored and lonely, had already decided to go, and had been waiting for an excuse that would sound plausible in an interview with a potential employer—an excuse that Alida herself was in the midst of providing: "Mrs. Kelly was just as bad as Mr. Kelly. Right away she started running around with married men."

All at once, Alida's anxieties converged and crested. Three horrid, heterogeneous ideas broke over her.

One: Amelia, who had already been separated from her father, might be desolated by the loss of her nursemaid.

Two: What made a hair-set was the comb-out—an intricate process of brushing, patting, pushing, teasing, and blow-drying—a summit of skill beyond her ability to describe, let alone direct. She and May had spent an hour building a bird's nest on her head.

Three: Though her desperation about her hair was absurd, and she knew it was absurd, she could not control it. Symbol or symptom, if poor Eliot's invitation could do this to her, being a divorcée, which she would become whenever law caught up with fact, was going to be as wretched as being an adolescent. Those terrible years! Years when Alida feared that no boy (or the wrong boy) would ask her to dance, or that no boy (or the wrong boy) would talk to her and she would not know what to say. How much anguish a silent telephone could cause! How she had worried about sex! No authority told her whether everybody did, or nobody did, or when or if you should. Some fool had written that everything happens twice: the first time as tragedy, the second as farce. How stupid!

11

Nothing could be more tragic than to live over, for a second time, the worst years of one's life.

Alida stood up abruptly, waved May and Amelia away, and ran to find her mother, who managed everything—her gardens, the Garden Club, the Abraham Halsted Free Library, the Old Bridge Historical Society. No servant had ever left *her;* her life was routines, not surprises. Alida tore along the path that led through the oak grove around the guest cottage, circled the greenhouses, and ended at her mother's front door. A drowsy maid on duty in the cloakroom told her that her mother was on the back terrace, and Alida raced through the house, pushed open a French door, threw herself into a chair, blurted, "May can't fix my hair and she is going to leave me," and so provided exactly what her mother disliked—a surprise, and an unpleasant one.

Her mother had been seated on the cushions of a white painted-metal chair, contemplating her formal vista: brilliant green lawns divided by a white gravel path that led to a semicircular marble bench flanked by closely growing dark green yews. Nothing stirred under the sun; only the droning of insects testified that this green dream lived. Like the stitched canvas on her lap, the scene she was enjoying was all her own creation.

Alida's mother, Gertrude Waterman (née Clark), had begun to invent landscapes on the six-acre parcel that had been the Waterman family's wedding present in 1938, even before the house, the gift of the Clarks, had begun to go up. She had lost her husband, Alida's father, in the Battle of the Atlantic, in December, 1942, four and a half months before Alida's birth, and had never remarried, never moved away, but had gone on gardening with increasing devotion, as if to shape a world more to her liking than the one that had engulfed her beloved. As far back as Alida could remember, making land respond had been her mother's keenest pleasure. Alida herself preferred art to nature—painted and porcelain flowers to growing ones—and the dissimilarity of their tastes often confused them, the more so as their physical resemblance was striking. No one had ever taken Gertrude Waterman and Alida Kelly for anything but mother and daughter. They were both dark-haired and dark-eyed, with clear complexions, regular white teeth, and features that were symmetrical but well defined in a way some might consider too strong for women. They were not pretty but good-looking—handsome, well put together. They were slight. Alida was

12

very thin, and though Gertrude, nearing sixty, was thickening, she was far from stout. Her authority owed nothing to size, yet it was wonderful how she tamed her world. Everything about her—not only her land—obeyed her. Her white linen dress was naturally subdued, and the rakish scarlet ribbon on her straw gondolier's hat became sedate when Gertrude wore it.

Alida had no idea how she jarred on her mother's ambit of cultivated tranquility. Running and fretting had not improved Alida's appearance; her clothes were more rumpled than they had been when she had met Eliot, and her sudden irruption, with a headful of pink plastic rollers, emitting nervous babble about her nursemaid and her hair, shocked Gertrude. Alida did not look like a child of Gertrude's, but like an intruder—the demented wife of a tradesman, perhaps, driven to Mrs. Waterman's terrace on the afternoon of Labor Day by who knew what hallucination.

Gertrude's low voice was unmistakably irritated as she said, "You won't need May once Amelia starts school. I let the governess go when you were ten. Miss Flood. You remember Miss Flood. A watery woman—cried buckets when she went. Anyone from my house—Jenny, for instance, who is a very good worker—could help out. And what *about* your hair? You look horrible, like a grocer's wife."

At that unlooked-for rejection, Alida had wailed, "Ah, Mother, you never understand me," and her mother replied, "No dear, I suppose I don't."

Both women fell silent, fearing a quarrel. Insect buzz—fitful, disconnected, inarticulate, the sounds of life without reason—accompanied the notions that darted through the minds of mother and daughter as they struggled to bring themselves to a truce.

Alida could not stop thinking of Hugo. He was exactly like her mother. Neither accepted her as she was: both insisted upon their own editions—abridgments, selections—of Alida. Hugo never ceased complaining about what he called her reserve, her coldness; her mother refused to tolerate hair rollers, a moment's involuntary vulgarity. And both sought control, while Alida drifted. *She* was dreamy, but *they* were artists. Or, at any rate, professionals.

Her mother's professionalism was more recent than Hugo's. She had been taught a variety of genteel skills by an old-fashioned governess, and Alida could not remember her mother without a piece of needlepoint in hand. At first she worked ready-made floral patterns in every size from pin cushions to pillows and gave them away as presents. About the time Alida left for boarding school, Gertrude began to design her own canvases. Over the years, her work grew bolder and more inventive, and Alida, on a trip back east soon after she and Hugo had decided to buy a house in California, had greatly admired her mother's latest tapestry, a stylized garden that recalled a Persian rug. When Alida had described it to Mark, the decorator who was helping her with her California house, he had immediately understood Gertrude's artistry and agreed that Alida should have that piece for her dining-room wall. In his enthusiasm, he suggested he might be able to use some of her mother's work in other houses he was doing.

"Mother wouldn't *sell* her tapestries," Alida objected.

She did, however, write on her own behalf, and her mother wrote back that the piece she requested had been sold. Mrs. Waterman had contracted with a New York gallery for her more ambitious works, and gave her earnings to an inner-city mission founded by a tiny new order of Anglican nuns of whom Father Peele, the assistant at her church, had spoken highly. She had met the dealer, Morgan Davies, when he was a weekend guest of his cousins in Flat Rock, and she suggested that Alida write him at the McKinley Galleries, 747 Madison Avenue, New York 10021. Mr. Davies' note offered to put Alida on a waiting list. It must have been a very long one, for Alida's tapestry had arrived only a few months before she left Hugo. Mark was ecstatic: Alida suspected that he was about to create a chic little market in southern California for the work of that talented New England recluse Grandma Waterman, who at the moment was contemplating her daughter and solving her problem.

"If you need to do something about your hair," Gertrude said, "I've a couple of wigs and hairpieces I've never used. Mary Dickinson persuaded me that I needed them for a cruise, and I didn't. You're welcome to them. Now take those things off your head before anyone sees you."

Her mother went inside. Alida began to unpin the muddle that May had made, thinking how lucky she was to have such a resourceful mother and how unlucky to have such a cold one. Old Mrs. Babbage, Yvonne Taylor's mother, who was worse than a stage mother—practically a bawd—was constantly stroking her daughter's hair. You could see that Mrs. Babbage always felt, as Alida herself sometimes did, that birth had never occurred, that the flesh of mother and daughter remained one. But then Alida reminded herself that May usually combed Amelia's hair, and thought, too,

14

that she ought to tell her mother how this whole hullabaloo had started—with Eliot. When Gertrude returned, her response was gratifying.

"Eliot Jones?" Gertrude asked, and repeated with wonder, "Eliot Jones? An evening alone with Eliot will be terribly boring. You should have asked him here."

Alida, delighted by this insult to a man who had just insulted her, apologized. "I didn't think of it. He was suddenly there in the parking lot, and I didn't know what to say."

"Do you want to bring him up for a drink?"

"No point in wishing him on you. It's enough he's boring one of us."

"Then I'll send down some liquor and you can offer him something at the cottage."

Arrangements over, Alida changed the subject and told her mother how beautifully Amelia swam: "She can do a real racing turn in a pool. I can't imagine where she learned it."

"I once thought of putting in a pool," Gertrude said. "A long time ago, when your uncle Arthur was pestering me about the place."

Uncle Arthur was Gertrude's brother-in-law, the husband of her younger sister, Jane. He was an investment banker on a scale so grand one might think it fantasy, but it was not. He was also—Alida had lived with Arthur and Jane while studying art history—the most awesome human being she had ever known. She could not conceive the homely verb "pester" describing any of his doings.

"What did he want?"

"You know how he is," her mother said. "Always full of ideas. Right after the war, he wanted me to sell everything. He said there was going to be a terrible depression and I should 'unload' the place while I could. Later, he wanted me to take advantage of the real-estate boom around here, and he was all over me to sell off the guest cottage with two acres. That was when I told him the cottage might make a good pool house. I said it just to keep him quiet. Then I really thought about it. But I gave up the idea when I remembered how carefully we'd saved all those old trees. . . . I'd always dreamed of a cottage in a grove."

Reminiscence is a code. Gertrude's memory traveled back past the events she was narrating to recollect the thin, dark, timid girl she had been, how she had miraculously captivated the handsome, fair, spirited Josiah Waterman, and how she had bloomed in response to his love and appreciation. She remembered his enchanted laughter

15

when she said, "A cottage in a grove," and his asking, "The woodcutter's cottage or the gingerbread house? And do we have to employ the full chorus of angels?" Josiah read her mind—he traced her fantasy to *Hänsel and Gretel*—and found her whims adorable.

Gertrude was also recalling her doubts when Hugo and Alida wanted to marry. She had had her son, Josiah, make inquiries. Hugo's background was respectable enough. Though Gertrude never did know who Hugo was in quite the way she had expected to be able to place her son-in-law, she had overcome her misgivings when she saw in her daughter another dark, thin, shy girl flowering in the love of another sparkling man (though Hugo was nothing compared to Josiah). If today she offered to build a pool for her granddaughter, she would imply that she accepted the end of her daughter's marriage, and, though Gertrude was too shy to say so, she did not.

Alida had no way of deciphering her mother's meanings. She replied by reverting to little practicalities—what time May and Amelia should come up to the big house for dinner—until she left for the cottage, carrying her mother's satchel of hairpieces with her own rollers tucked in it.

Gertrude looked at her daughter's thin back and felt a failure. By the standards of Labor Day, 1975, in Flat Rock, Connecticut, or anywhere else in the United States, Gertrude was not "modern," but she had been born in the twentieth century and had absorbed some of its assumptions—among them, that parents are to blame for their children's unhappiness. Her own parents, born in the nineteenth century, had raised her on the assumption that children existed to make their parents proud and happy. Her character had been formed by this assumption, which had made her shy at the same time that it gave her what passed for authority. Her parents' rules constituted her sense of fitness or suitability, of how things were—or, if things were not, of how they had to be made to be. Living by inherited prescriptions (for example, being extremely frugal as a trustee of charitable endowments), Gertrude seemed filled with certainty, and nobody, including her daughter, suspected that Gertrude's assurance was not Gertrude's. Everything that *was* hers—the individuality that had come to be prized in children later in the century—had been discouraged in her upbringing. So she grew up, and remained, shy about everything that mattered to Gertrude *as Gertrude* rather than as a link in a chain of Clarks and Watermans. Except with her husband, and lately with Father Peele,

16

she had never discussed her feelings. Now it troubled her that all summer long she had not brought herself to be franker with Alida. Gertrude did not take Hugo's infidelity seriously. As a dutiful mother-in-law, she had watched *Galaxy Guards,* and knew that a man who had married Alida would have no more than a momentary interest in Yvonne. But Gertrude had been too timid to suggest that whatever Hugo had done, he could not be permanently enamored of a guttersnipe, however good-looking. Gertrude had merely listened to Alida and said little; she now realized that her unresponsiveness had deterred her daughter from confiding further. Gertrude had also worried about Alida's atypical carelessness about her looks, and tried to formulate a motherly warning. Then she reflected that she had used to think her daughter's dedication to her appearance excessive, and asked herself if she were the kind of mother who was never satisfied with her children. She had trusted to time. After Labor Day—everybody got down to business after Labor Day—Alida would fix up herself and her marriage. But time, it seemed, was not the answer. This afternoon her daughter was seriously upset. And what had Gertrude done? Spoken sharply and given her hairpieces. It was not enough; it was useless. Gertrude wished she could call Alida back; if words had not come, a kiss might have spoken.

When Alida returned to the cottage, May was sitting on the sofa in the living room. She had a pile of fan and gossip magazines beside her, and was reading one of them. She looked up, saw Alida's rollerless head, and asked with dismay, "Mrs. Kelly, what happened to our hair?"

Alida, sorry that the girl's labors had been wasted, said frankly, "My mother made me take them out. She gave me her hairpieces."

May only nodded. As a nursemaid, she expected grandmothers to be interfering. She told Alida that Amelia had become cranky after Alida's sudden departure; on May's suggestion the child had taken a cool bath and was now sleeping. Alida replied by informing May about their dinner time and her mother's liquor, wondering, as she spoke, if her mother would send ice as well. Alida put down her mother's satchel and looked into the dwarf refrigerator; it held two very small ice-cube trays. She opened the cabinets above it, searching for a large container in which to empty the trays so she could start a second generation of ice cubes, but the cabinets held only breakfast china. She distributed the cubes among several cereal

17

bowls, shut them in the refrigerator, and began to be amazed to discover that she had been living in a house so ill equipped to serve a guest a drink; during her marriage her principal work—her career, in fact—had been giving parties.

Stepping back to scan the minute kitchen, Alida began to think of all the things she should have thought of in June; she had not even noticed, until this morning, that there was no real kitchen in the cottage. Since a kitchen is the heart of an independent household, the cottage was a dependency, and as long as she lived there she would be so dependent upon her mother in so many practical ways that she could not be independent in any way. So far, her mother had not demanded anything repugnant. True, Gertrude had seemed high-handed turning up at the cottage every Sunday morning to drive her daughter and granddaughter to church. But perhaps that was understandable. When Alida was growing up in Flat Rock in the nineteen forties and fifties, children had to go to church and Sunday school until they were confirmed and/or left for boarding school. After these events, their attendance (and their parents') was apt to decline. At that time, Dr. Marshall, the minister, seemed to appreciate that the Episcopal church in Flat Rock was a community facility for the young and old—Alida's mother's churchgoing was also typical of Flat Rock, where piety (or anyhow, churchgoing) often returned with age. What troubled Alida now was her mother's intimacy with Father Peele, a newcomer since Alida's time, one of two assistants to the aging Dr. Marshall. Father Peele did not accept the civil-service, social-work role of Flat Rock Christianity; Alida had several times surprised him and her mother talking earnestly about the purposes of prayer and other theological balderdash. Alida regarded religion as interesting only when it was a subject of art. She had never hurt her mother's feelings by specifically telling her that the socially miscellaneous world in which Alida lived with Hugo set no great store by religious formalities, and that they themselves never went to church, although people they knew were forever discovering new religions and competing conversationally with people who had discovered new psychotherapies. Every Sunday all summer, Alida told herself that going to church was no worse than sitting through a boring movie, but because it was an involvement through her mother, she found it threatening. She could laugh at Tom Frank, the male lead of *Galaxy Guards,* who was a Vedanta nut, but her mother as a Christian maniac was too close for comedy.

18

Facing the kitchenette and these annoyances, Alida forgot that May was in the room. Suddenly the girl exclaimed, "Oh, Mrs. Kelly, Alfie Burrows has fired his manager!"

Alfie Burrows was a former rock singer, once the idol of the young. He and his audience had aged, and he was attempting to become an actor with—so far—minor success. Alida knew who he was, but she did not know him and had no interest in his career.

Brimming with excitement, May went on, "I once worked in relief, on the regular nurse's vacation, for Mrs. Burrows' best friend. I used to see them all the time."

That was all. To have seen the Alfie Burrowses at their friend's house was enough to give May a feeling of enduring connection with people who had probably forgotten her name. May's thrill was timely. It proved to Alida, all rue and regret as she was now, that she had been right on one point last June—she was right to have decided, when she learned of Hugo's infidelity, not to hang around in his world as his soon-to-be ex-wife. In Hugo's world, Alida had no face, as wretched Yvonne, silly Tom, or even has-been Alfie Burrows had faces; Alida had no name, as Hugo had a name. She belonged to an underclass of wives outside the entertainment industry, and such women received far less consideration than wives in Flat Rock. Alida had made a mark by the assurance of her style and the perfection of her parties, but these assets were hers only as Hugo Kelly's wife.

On the other hand, she had not returned to Flat Rock intending to become, once more, Gertrude Waterman's daughter. What had been uppermost in Alida's mind was her own responsibility as a parent; she was thinking of the school year that would start in September. For herself, Alida would have preferred New York City, where she still owned an apartment. She had rented it when she and Hugo had moved to California. But Alida, having been a child in Flat Rock, was uncertain about raising a child in New York City. Flat Rock Country Day was an excellent school; she and her brother had both gone there; her mother was on its board; and Alida, certain it would be right for her child, had telephoned Miss Blossom to find out if there was a place for Amelia even before she had called her mother and asked for the cottage.

Now Alida inspected the sitting room. Everything she saw was wrong. May, for instance, did not belong there. Yet the girl's own room was very small—the cottage not only lacked a kitchen; it lacked space for a servant. And then there was the furniture. It was in excellent condition, but looked as if it had come straight from a theatrical warehouse, the stage set for an old-fashioned English play, a time-tested combination of chintz and dark wood that Alida associated with inept semiprofessional theatrical groups Hugo was always dragging her to inspect. What was she, Alida, doing in a phony interior? She was possessed by titanic fantasies of totally reconstructing the cottage and immediately thereafter by an urge to burst into tears. Only the presence of May restrained her. May herself radiated uneasiness. She was sitting, while her employer stood, and it seemed disrespectful to go on reading, though she was entitled to the time off and desperately looking forward to an article of professional interest, the work of an unwed female star: "I Raise My Child Alone." She broke into Alida's thoughts, asking, "Is there anything I can do?"

"No, thank you, May," Alida said, and, gesturing toward her mother's satchel, "I must take this upstairs."

May followed her, went to her own room, and closed the door. Alida, sorting through her mother's donation of false hair, began to wonder what, exactly, Gertrude would send down for cocktails. She had said "liquor." They had not mentioned bar equipment. In her mother's house, a servant mixed drinks in the pantry and handed them around on a tray; it was possible that her mother's drinkmaking tools were too utilitarian for the kind of living-room service Alida would have to offer Eliot. Since the stores were closed, she could not buy what she needed, but she resisted telephoning the big house and bringing her mother in from her terrace to discuss ice buckets. There ought to be *something* Alida could do for herself. Then she recollected the cottage attic, a small space under the roof intended primarily for insulation, accessible by a permanent ladder at the end of the upstairs hall. Alida could not imagine why she supposed some things were stored there, yet the impression was very strong. Again she found that her multiple misjudgments of the past months hampered her at every turn: clambering into the attic entailed the risk of waking Amelia, who slept with her door open. The child had never admitted she was afraid of the dark or of sleeping alone, but her insistence on this point was unconquerable. Alida had once asked her California pediatrician whether it showed the need for psychiatric advice. The doctor had laughed and asked, "What difference does it make?"

The house in California was large. Little habits make big differences in little houses. Alida decided to be a thoughtless mother instead of a dependent daughter, and inject a little derring-do into her failed domesticity. She would pretend to be a cat burglar. She was wearing sneakers, which could be considered costume for the part, and after a summer of swimming and tennis she felt fit and limber. She tiptoed into the hall and started. The ladder rungs were steeper than they looked, and her palms sweated as she held onto the uprights. Scaling the ladder and then holding on with one hand while she pushed back the trapdoor required not only effort but concentrated coordination. So did scrambling into the dim attic, where she could stand only in the very center, her head touching the roof beam. Yet the venture paid off, for after her eyes adjusted to the dark, she saw, along one wall, a long, low shelf stacked with china. She bent over and discovered a large bowl that would do for an ice bucket, and beside the shelf, leaning against the wall, a tôle tray, almost the size of a coffee-table top, on which she could set out the bowl and glasses. These would serve her purpose if she could get them down. She found she could. She had to make three trips backward, one for each object and the third to close the trapdoor, and when she had finished, she could guess how dirty she was: her trophies were furred with dust. Ideally she would have plunged them into her bathtub and followed them, but Alida's bathroom, which she entered through her bedroom, lay alongside the child's room, and every gush and gurgle was audible through the wall. The cottage's bedroom story imposed an impossible unanimity in sleeping, dressing, coming, and going on all its inhabitants.

Alida went downstairs to the kitchenette. The sink was too small for her to submerge either object. Slowly, carefully, awkwardly, and resentfully she began to sponge them off. As she worked, she began to think, not about herself, but about her mother. Gertrude's changelessness, which Alida had always accepted without reflection, now seemed eerie: animation suspended. The tôle tray was a reproduction of no importance, but the bowl was real Canton ware, not invaluable perhaps, but too good, Alida thought, to be stowed away and forgotten. Everything about her mother's life—her dinners, her manners, her silver, the furniture in the cottage sitting room, and the bowl in the cottage attic—betrayed decisions made and never reconsidered: a castle in cobwebs.

There is something inescapably shady about going through someone's possessions in his or her absence, even when one's mission—estate appraisal, say—is innocent, or even if, like Alida, one is a child of the house whose right no one would question. Mute belongings betray confidences, and one feels one has taken unfair advantage of the absent owner, who is vulnerable by the fact of absence, who cannot hear one's judgment and reply, explain, or extenuate. Alida, having explored her mother's cottage from top to bottom, felt she had learned too much about her mother. She felt guilty, as if she had been reading her mother's mail, and, precisely because guilt underlined her discoveries, she knew she could not forget them. The phrase flitted through her mind, "a widow in reduced circumstances." There were other kinds of reductions besides financial: her mother had been living in reduced emotional circumstances. And in returning to Flat Rock, to her mother's protection and domination, Alida had been arranging just such a reduction for herself. It would not do: she would have to find a better way of life, something more like living.

The sun shone on the bowl as she wiped it. Its white became whiter, its blue bluer. Alida was restoring it to life. She rejoiced in its gleam while she regretted her mother's dim existence, and stretched her arms, holding the bowl at a distance the better to admire the familiar pattern. Her left hand, which had grasped the ladder so firmly, slipped slightly on the damp porcelain, and she tightened her right-hand grip on the bowl, which immediately cracked where she held it. Then both halves slithered from her hands like a pair of fleeing snakes and shattered in the sink. Was it her nerves? Was it the unspeakably narrow space? Was it her punishment for judging her mother? Alida, a worshiper of art objects, had never broken one in her life. As she stared in bewilderment at the fragments of what had been, but seconds before, charm resurrected, her world converged upon her. The noise of breakage had traveled up the stairwell: alarmed May and drowsy Amelia were at the top of the stairs, and as they began to descend, a knock at the cottage door announced a two-maid-and-gardener's-boy-with-cart procession from her mother's, bearing what appeared to be every necessity for a vast cocktail party. Center stage, rumpled, filthy, sweating, staring at the remnants of the bowl, the young mistress, surrounded by her mother's servants, her own servant, and her child, thought she was the star of a dramatic genre yet to be invented—the drawing-room tragedy.

Long ago, delighted by Alida's expertise in the visual arts, Hugo had undertaken to teach her how words, like cubes, cones, curves, and colors, could be organized for artistic effect. When one loves, one listens. Reclining in a tub full of tepid water scented with bath oil, Alida recalled Hugo's lesson about the arrival of an X character who sets a static situation astir. Hugo said it was a standard technical device for beginning the action of a drama, and that audiences accepted it in spite of its familiarity because it was so common in real life. "You meet someone and nothing is the same again. Think about it," Hugo told her.

"As I met you."

Those were her doting days. Today, alas! poor Eliot was the X whose entry would bring activity to her undramatic existence. She wondered if anybody would have risked such irony on the stage: to invent a tragicomic underdog like Eliot, and make him the mover of the other characters. Yet Eliot's entry on her scene had already guaranteed that she would start dressing decently again, that henceforth her hair, her nails, and her face would receive due attention, and that she would redo the cottage to support some kind of hospitality. And her desire to subdue him, to make him recant the insult he had administered earlier, gave him, as X, another job: he was helping her practice. Like an assistant stage manager, he would cue her while she rehearsed the role of magnetic woman.

But surely, Alida thought, no actress preparing was ever so be-deviled! She was sitting before her dressing table considering her makeup, still in her robe, when May, unbidden, came into the bedroom, followed by Amelia, who, restless and whimsical after a too-long nap, decided to sit on the floor to observe her mother's coiffing and primping. Their presence disarranged Alida mentally and crowded her physically as she tried to plan her war game, her mock assault upon Eliot. On the other hand—for a parent there is always an other hand—Amelia should get used to Mom going out with men who were not Dad. It did a girl no harm to see the pains a woman took dressing for a date.

Amelia was agog. She gazed intently at her mother's face as her mother looked into her mirror. Then, to see better, the child leaned forward, slammed her forehead against the sharp edge of a leg of the dressing table, and screamed. May took her to their bathroom, between their two bedrooms, to bathe the sore place. Alida began tentatively to brush her hair. She wanted her hair to lie down; it wanted to stand up and out. Amelia bawled while Alida brushed and wondered whether to abandon her mirror for her child. Then the doorbell rang. Amelia switched herself off like a radio, and went downstairs with May to answer it. Eliot's voice came up the stairwell. He had arrived fully half an hour early.

His prematurity destroyed every possibility of doing anything

23

right and put pressure on Alida to hasten the process of creating a party self, over which she always lingered. She was out of practice and less deft than she had been, so that the effect she used to bring off with two shades of eye shadow looked merely smudged, not subtly blended. Alida did the best she could with her face while sounds of animated conversation and the tinkle of glasses rose from the sitting room. She wondered if Eliot had brought a party. She opened her closet, and saw an array of slacks and shorts and T-shirts and tennis dresses. The time she had spent exploring the attic and smashing her mother's china ought to have been devoted to examining her wardrobe. Most of her clothes were stored at the big house. The few summer party outfits she had taken to the cottage had been shoved into a corner. They were creased beyond wearing. The single exception was an efflorescent printed silk jersey pajama with a top whose modesty she doubted. She had not bought it; she had been sold it. She had objected to its narrow shoulder straps, its low-cut V's in front and back, and she had told the salesgirl that she did not see how she could wear it either with a brassiere or without one. It was not bralessness as manifesto to which she objected, but bralessness as exhibitionism. The shop had a young clientele, and the salesgirl, who looked barely out of her teens, had said, with every sign of sincerity, "Mrs. Kelly, *your* figure doesn't need help."

Vulnerable to the flattery of youth, Alida bought the garment, and now this nearly topless extravaganza was all she had to wear. When she put it on, she saw she was going to have to sit up very straight all evening. Then she finished with her recalcitrant hair, pulling it back from her face, and, with hairpins, nailing in a small topknot and two falls. She looked, she thought, like a barbaric Alice in Wonderland, totally unsuited to dine at the Flat Rock Club—she knew of no other place in the area—whose membership, by temperament and principle, opposed novelty or fantasy, let alone public nudity. With a brief return of the afternoon's panic, she saw herself failing her second adolescence: the first had been a perpetual getting-ready—hair, clothes, and morsels of conversation preformed for the beguilement of men she had not met or even heard of.

Alida was greatly in need of some of her mother's liquor when she came downstairs to find that the party she had heard was May, doing the honors as hostess, drinking and chatting with Eliot. She had never done anything of the sort in California, and her presumptuousness suggested that she had mentally given notice. Amelia, who had often stayed through cocktails in California to share and interrupt the adults' conversation, had retired in glum silence to a corner of a cavernous wing chair. Eliot rose to greet Alida and make her a drink. Though he had no rash or sniffle and was wearing a presentable seersucker suit and madras tie, his eyeglasses and more-than-incipient baldness made him "poor Eliot" still. He rattled the ice and nearly dropped the glass as if Alida made him nervous. She worried again about her pajamas.

"What were you talking about?" she asked.

Eliot and May answered at once. "Denmark," Eliot said. "Home," May replied.

"Milly and I keep thinking we want to travel," Eliot said, "and send the kids to camp."

"And I told him you could take them with you if you found the right girl." May went on, determined to hold the social terrain she had taken: "The first year I was in California, they took me to Mexico, the next year Hawaii. Now I would like Europe again."

Eliot evidently accepted May's travels as equal in interest to any other subject of conversation. He offered her another drink, and May accepted. She began a second monologue while Alida realized—so much for drama—that she had walked into the hoary situation-comedy set piece called "first date," in which the entire family occupies the caller's attention, while the ingénue, comically afluster, cannot command so much as a glance. But comedy happening to oneself is not funny.

Amelia's resentment of May was less inhibited than Alida's. She broke in: "You never used to drink with company in California, May."

"California was California and Flat Rock is Flat Rock."

Eliot refilled his glass and said, "Let's drink to Flat Rock. Welcome home, Alida." To Amelia he added, "Your mother lived here when she was a girl, and we knew each other when we were children."

Amelia now entered the conversation, asking questions and imparting information, opinions, and confidences—"I miss my own swimming pool"—and it was May's turn to become jealous. She began to talk about how late it was for little girls' dinners and how Grandma's cook would grow impatient.

Eliot said it was time they all went, and after farewells, admonitions, kisses, and agreements, the parties separated. As Eliot led Alida to his car, he remarked, "It's lucky we aren't going to the club—you in that getup."

Alida, still suffering from the vaudeville just past, remarked carelessly, "I didn't have a thing to wear."

"That fellow didn't get any of your money, did he?" He answered

25

his own question: "He couldn't have. Your family really tied it all up."

He contemplated the dashboard of his automobile as if it diagramed the complexities of Alida's family trusts, and then, assured by his recollection of her unimpaired solvency, advised, "You go buy yourself some clothes, Alida. You're a young woman. Your life isn't over yet."

He started the car too fast and swerved to avoid a rabbit, which transformed itself into a piece of paper and blew away. Alida wondered if Eliot's edginess was attributable to her unsuitable garment, but he had always been edgy. He took an unfamiliar turn. "Where are we going?" she asked.

"To the Flat Rock Inn," he answered. "Things are different at the club. Not what they used to be. The tournaments aren't as important. Everybody travels. Even with business slow, everybody goes to Europe."

The only change Alida had noticed at the club was women's tennis. While Eliot rambled on about how Flat Rock and Old Bridge had changed, Alida began to think about sameness and change, and how one confused the where and the when of change. Tennis was a good example. As a girl, she had been taught a ladylike ground-stroke game that did very well until she went to California, where playing tennis was as important as having teeth, but where the game was different. Out west, women as well as men were aggressive and forcing, trying for aces, going to net, and volleying. Alida had learned to play that game, secretly contrasting show-business pushiness and Flat Rock gentility. But this summer, back in Flat Rock, what Alida thought of as the "California" game was the game at the club. Everybody played it, girls and women along with boys and men. Eliot was concluding, "Besides, we couldn't talk much at the club. We would be interrupted. You probably don't know many people here anymore, but I do. And we have so much catching up."

Alida could not imagine what he meant. They had indeed known each other for as long as people are likely to know other people, but anything they had had to say to each other had always been interruptible. Alida was concerned for a moment, because when a man avoided taking a woman to a place where they were both known, it ordinarily signified dishonorable intentions. But with Eliot that idea had to be absurd. No one, including himself, could associate him with the daring and assurance seduction required. Hugo had

26

taught Alida too much: she was seeing every word, every gesture, and every event as a piece of hackneyed playmaking.

She remarked that it was a beautiful night. It was. Beginning twilight colored the sky blue-gray-pink. The trees were darkening from green to blue-black, and their silhouettes—fountain elms, lollipop maples, pyramid evergreens—reminded her that the northeastern landscape, her original notion of the out-of-doors, still seemed to her the most natural way for nature to look. She was home, where she belonged.

She knew where they were when they arrived. The Flat Rock Inn was an old farmhouse that, in her girlhood, had been a tavern for Flat Rock help and service people. Young Flat Rock Club rebels sometimes sneaked there from junior dances because it had the glamour of a naughty reputation: their adolescence reveled in rumors that the upstairs rooms were let to illicit couples from New York. Eliot recognized that taking Alida there needed explanation, and said, as they approached, "It's been done over. Completely. We backed it. I had to talk Father into it. I had to make him see that Flat Rock needs a nice place for people who aren't in the Club. He said, 'We don't want these people here,' and I said, 'Father, they're already here. Who are you doing business with these days?'"

Eliot's optimistic account of the Inn's guests was borne out by the parking lot, which had been greatly enlarged for an array of expensive new automobiles that shone in his headlights. The Inn was freshly painted, and the building, which even in adversity had been genuinely Colonial, looked yet more Colonial. Inside, waiters and busboys in Williamsburg-tavern costumes moved through a series of electric-candle-lit Sturbridge Village rooms. The manner of the maître d'hôtel (he wore a dinner jacket) was so deferential that Alida could see that this preposterous place was, in some sense, Eliot's doing and that he was showing it off to her. Her determination to charm him demanded that she praise. "Oh, Eliot, it's lovely," she said gaily. "How did you ever do it?"

They were led to a room with a bandstand and seated at a table beside the dance floor. Eliot ordered drinks and began to tell her how he had done it. His edginess disappeared as he expatiated on the part he had played in the development of Flat Rock and Old Bridge. He confided that for a while he feared he had made a mistake in staying on under his father, but that gradually he had come to understand the power of a banker to shape a community.

As the room filled up, Alida examined the community Eliot was shaping. The guests were old and young; there were families with children as well as couples out for the evening. Some were stodgy; some were sporty; none was elegant. Eliot had made his point: Flat Rock was now home to quantities of unfashionable but by no means raffish or penniless people who regarded coming to the Inn as a holiday treat. Alida asked who they were and where they came from. "Around," Eliot said. "Around here, in all the new houses. All sorts, Alida. But quite respectable."

And he began to talk again about the growth of the neighborhood, reminding Alida that, if she counted her years at boarding school, she had spent most of her life away from Flat Rock and thus could not appreciate what it had become. While, at Eliot's urging, they had another cocktail, the band appeared. It was a small group, led by the pianist, who was also the announcer and sometimes sang. They played old foxtrots, to which a few couples sedately navigated. Alida giggled and said, "Eliot, you've taken me to a Lawrence Welk party!"

"It *is* nice," he answered complacently. He did not ask her to dance, and she wondered again if her pajamas embarrassed him. But Eliot had always been an uneasy dancer, and besides, he evidently wanted to go on about his subject: banking and local development. A parody Rotary-luncheon address was his way of talking about himself. Alida let her mind wander in search of a subject to raise after he finished: she ought, for instance, to ask about his wife and children. His father was too depressing to mention. Poor Eliot was indeed poor Eliot, dominated by such a figure. So thinking, Alida sighed.

"What's got you down?" asked Eliot. "Let me cheer you up. That's the purpose of this excursion."

He patted her hand. She withdrew it. She could not say that she had been depressed by her would-be cheer-upper's own plight, so she started to share her idea—it really struck her as a discovery—that everything changed everywhere in the same way at the same time, and that one mistakenly attributed changes to the places instead of the times. She explained about the Flat Rock tennis game and the California tennis game, and her realization that the new game, the "big" game for women, must have come in all at once all over the country. She reminded him how exceptional Maureen Connolly's serve once seemed and how Chris Evert was evolving from precision to aggression, but Eliot seemed bewildered rather than enlightened. To clarify, she gave another example: "When we were

28

young, Eliot, we thought this was a naughty place, but the kids I knew in California wouldn't think it was especially naughty—I mean, the way it used to be. I suppose they didn't here, either, before you did it over. I mean, it isn't East Coast or West Coast, it's the times, and all kids' ideas about sex nowadays are so different from what ours were."

"Thinking much about sex these days, Alida?"

Task after task falls to the would-be enchantress: Alida was going to have to learn to express herself with an exactitude hitherto lacking in her conversation. Years of marriage had meant years of talking to a man who knew how her mind worked; Hugo would have understood her. Alida wanted to change the subject—especially if Eliot thought it was sex—but she did not have to, because a handsome man about their own age, dark, well knit, and well dressed, who radiated cheerfulness and vivacity, came up to their table and said hello to Eliot, who introduced them: "This is Fred Palmieri. Mrs. Kelly from California."

In so describing Alida at the Flat Rock Inn, Eliot declassed Alida on her own territory. He had taken Mrs. Waterman's daughter to dinner with onetime butchers who now owned supermarkets, with former gardeners who now owned nurseries—with the sons and daughters of the people who had drunk at the old tavern—and made her, as an unidentifiable "Mrs. Kelly from California," sound as if she belonged with the help. The price of separation from her husband increased every moment; Eliot had just tacked on social demotion. Since Mr. Palmieri was at the Inn himself, he could not be aware of Alida's feelings. He looked at her attentively—almost, she thought, admiringly—and he did not sound like a butcher when he said something about West Coast building, paying her a regional compliment to the effect that he envied the West Coast its domestic architects. "After all, Neutra *was* the best. Better than anyone we've ever had here."

Alida, vexed at Eliot, replied dismissively, "Out there, nobody cares about architects. When we say a house is so-and-so's, we name the biggest star who ever lived in it, though he might only have stayed there once on a three-month one-picture deal."

Alida's snub apparently struck Mr. Palmieri as wit. At any rate, he laughed and asked, "Will you be here long?"

"I'm staying with my mother."

That was the moment for Eliot to tell Mr. Palmieri who Alida was, but he did not. The band blared, and Mr. Palmieri said, "I hope we see you again. We need pretty new faces. I see Eliot all the time. I've grown accustomed to his ever-renewable notes."

And he left.

"Who was that?" Alida asked.

"Did he attract you?"

"May we have dinner?"

So they ordered and ate, and Eliot explained that Fred Palmieri was an architect, and that when his father, a small builder, had died suddenly, leaving a widow and daughters (Fred was the only son) and his business up in the air, Fred had, on Eliot's advice and with Eliot's financing, taken it over and gone into building. "When he finished his first development," Eliot said, "I suggested that he buy the Inn and do it Colonial. He did, and it's doing very well."

"You mean he owns it?"

"With us." Eliot laughed. "They say banks own everything. I suppose we do. Let me tell you about . . ."

And he was off again. Perhaps, Alida thought, Eliot's sense of inferiority had inspired him to do well as a way of "showing them." And possibly Eliot was tolerant of outsiders like Mr. Palmieri, because he felt himself an outsider in another sense. His attitude toward the newcomers was certainly more honorable than her snobbery. Eliot could never become attractive, but he might have grown up to be good. His moments of verbal sexual assault should be forgiven as awkwardness, and his intent should be assumed as kindly: what else had she been discovering all day long except that being husbandless had made her—temporarily, she hoped—a kind of outsider? In any case, Eliot's banking efforts may indeed have done much for the community. While Eliot talked, she worked herself into the part of charmer, which is incompatible with that of critic; her role was to elicit, not reprove. When he paused, she asked, "Have you thought of going into politics?"

Eliot beamed. He apparently thirsted for every kind of encouragement. "Will you dance?" he asked.

They did. Her question was so clearly the kind of reward Eliot had been seeking that Alida, merely looking at his smile as he risked a dance, shifted her feelings; in a trice she ceased to act and began to be genuine. Eliot did not want to be pitied but admired, and Alida could genuinely admire his getting on with his job despite his many deficiencies, just as she could admire herself for appreciating his steadfastness and for showing her respect appropriately.

Having sounded a C-major chord of friendship, Alida felt really friendly toward Eliot. He danced badly, as she expected, but his clutching and bumping no longer seemed so lamentable. They were sent back to their table to sit amid cacophony while adolescents displayed their energy in a "disco" number. When the band took a break, Eliot returned to her question about going into politics and imparted his thoughts on public service, briefing her on politics in the county, a Republican enclave in a normally Democratic state. No, he would not run for office, because the ceiling of his electoral future was probably the lower house of the state legislature. Besides, he had always felt that his personality was more suited to appointive than elective office, and he considered that his experience in the last few years would make him useful in foreign economic development. What he looked forward to was a post in the State Department. Alida had no idea whether he was confiding a daydream or an imminent reality, but she had always associated diplomacy with finesse, and even in her brand-new mood of appreciating Eliot, she could not see him as a diplomat. She must have looked surprised.

"What's the matter?" he asked.

Alida thought fast. "It's *such* an ambition, Eliot. I've been used to hearing people hope to have their own shows, or get a better contract."

"You've been living with very frivolous people." Eliot's self-esteem was pompous but well meaning. After a pause, with the merest hint of shyness, he added, "And it's lucky you've come back, Alida, where you can be appreciated. You've always been a very profound and understanding person."

He pressed her hand, and Alida did not withdraw it. With a thrill of delight, she recognized that "poor Alida" had just been buried, and that she had indeed bewitched poor Eliot, for no proof of social success can compare to a sincere and unmerited compliment. She smiled at him, wondering how she looked and whether modestly to deny her profundity. While she was making up her mind, Eliot, who lacked the art of transition, was looking at his watch. He announced it was time to go.

"You're right," Alida said. "I've got to start shopping for Amelia's school clothes tomorrow."

After paying the check, Eliot asked if she knew that Country Day had abandoned its dress code and that girls now wore jeans to school. They drove back, not talking much. Alida, relaxed by her victory, leaned languidly against the seat and let the night air caress her face. As the breeze cleared her brain, she saw that, of the two theories of acting—technical control or psychological willing oneself into a part—she had opted for the latter. She had exaggerated Eliot's mediocre virtues in the process of persuading herself in order to attract him, and she was amazed that she had not given herself away—that he had heard no falsity or hysteria in her performance. But of course he had done most of the talking, while she had merely signaled her approval. That was the traditional recipe for feminine charm, and it permitted generations of women to understand men while remaining enigmatic. Certainly she knew more about Eliot than he did about her: he did not know how his old schoolmate had changed, while she knew that he had become a nicer version of his father—stuffy and self-important, but more charitable. Her thoughts dissolved in fatigue. She glanced at Eliot. He seemed lost in concentration. More than concentration: he was rigid. His whole body was clenched, like a fist, as if he had determined upon a difficult or perilous course of action. Had her "profundity" inspired him to a new venture in financing eighteenth-century pastiche? A chain of Flat Rock Inns from China to Peru?

Alida was surprised that Eliot got out of the car—it was an unnecessary gallantry in an old schoolfellow—and more surprised when he followed her into the cottage. She was really too tired to continue playacting. May had cleared everything away, and it would be a job to give him a drink, yet he stood around as if expecting something—at least the offer. "Do you want *another* drink?" Alida asked, stressing "another" almost to rudeness. Eliot merely grinned what appeared an acceptance, and Alida said, "Just a minute, then. You get out the ice. I'll be right back down."

Upstairs, Alida looked in on sleeping Amelia and went to her own bathroom. When she came out, Eliot was there, in her bedroom, the door closed behind him. He grabbed at Alida, partly an embrace and partly an assault, for he was pushing her backward while he kissed her repeatedly, aiming for her mouth and occasionally hitting it. His onset was so forceful that she had trouble breathing. Because of her conception of him as "poor" Eliot, Alida had never noticed, even when they danced, that he was physically powerful, although he was taller and broader than most men. She had had no sense of his masculine body, and hence no notion that, despite her own fitness and agility, she could never push him away. While he kept kissing her, she could only get out a single, angry, hoarse

32

whisper—"Eliot, stop, stop, go away"—before he knocked her onto her bed. The way he kissed her reminded her of something horrible she could not remember. Then she could.

After Josiah had gone to boarding school, while Alida was still at Country Day, her governess, Miss Flood, trying to make something of a job that amounted to very little, kept thinking of "stimulating" projects. One of them was a tropical-fish aquarium. One rainy afternoon when Alida was watching the not very stimulating fish, she saw a zebra fish, a fast-moving fish-shaped fish, peck at a dreamy, sail-shaped angelfish. The stripes on an angelfish go up and down. The stripes on a zebra fish go lengthwise. Alida did not realize the zebra fish was biting. She thought the fish were playing a fish game, because they did it over and over. Guppies drifted past unconcerned while the zebra fish darted in to nip and the angelfish tried to flurry away. The angelfish could not escape. The zebra fish was too fast, the angelfish too slow, and Miss Flood's tank was too small. By the time Alida understood that the zebra fish was hurting the angelfish, and called Miss Flood, it was too late. The angelfish was dead.

Eliot did not want to murder Alida. He was drunk and thought he was making love to her. He mumbled, "Oh Alida," in a voice almost loving, expressing something like gratefulness. That was the time for Alida to scream. And bring May. Never mind May. A scream would bring Amelia. And her mother's scream, and the sight of her mother pinned beneath a man, both of them with their clothes torn (Alida had ripped Eliot's shirt and one of her shoulder straps had snapped), would terrify a little girl. Eliot kissed Alida's bare breast.

When the angelfish died, it did not immediately rise to the top, but listed in the water. A lot of dead fish list in aquaria, with one fin drooping, as Alida's left arm dangled beside the bed: their corpses zigzag in the water, as if moved by invisible currents. Once, though, some people in Beverly Hills built an ornamental garden pond that they stocked with goldfish. All the goldfish, all at once, were smitten by a blight. They all rose immediately, floating exactly as Alida lay, bellies up, just under the surface of the water. Leaves fell on them and insects drowned over their stomachs. They did not care. They did not know. Alida was a dead fish. Nothing affected her.

The death of the fish made matters difficult for Eliot. He scrabbled at it, persevering as his father had taught him to persevere, and at last put himself inside the fish and began to thrust and pant and grunt and gasp, gasp, gasp—what a silly way to treat a dead fish! He

33

said "Darling!" to the dead fish and kissed it. After a while, he put on his clothes and went away.

At some moment Alida stopped being a fish and turned into a woman who was crying. Pieces of false hair crouched beside her like nightmare animals. She sat on the edge of the bed. Tears trailed down her face. She could not stop them; they just ran. Later, she leaned over and picked up her torn pajamas, which lay in a bright huddle on the floor, and pulled off the one leg of her panty hose that was all she had on. She put on her robe, went to the dressing table, removed her makeup with cold cream and brushed her hair. The face in the mirror showed not a sign of what its possessor had just gone through. The reflected image showed Alida Waterman Kelly, the well-brought-up daughter, the foresighted mother—not the ninny who had allowed the least attractive boy in Flat Rock Country Day School the use of her body because in her passion to beguile she had forgotten the viciousness that rejection bred. Her face did not even seem to be asking what Alida was asking: What would become of Alida?

Thanksgiving

Nothing became of Alida—not overnight, anyhow. While she slept, the country picked up its toolboxes and lunchboxes and went back to work, and May and Amelia went to the Club, leaving coffee and a note. By the time they returned, Alida had risen and dressed and thrown out her torn garments; her mother's maid Jenny had come down from the big house and tidied the cottage, and Alida had finished checking Amelia's chest of drawers and was going through her closet, pad in hand, making lists of northeastern-autumn clothing a schoolgirl would need. Hours of domestic duties proved sedative. When, at dinner, Gertrude asked Alida about her evening, she was able to reply calmly, "Just as we expected. Boring. Eliot talked about real-estate development around here."

Gertrude agreed there had been plenty of it; Old Bridge had enlarged the Main Street parking lots three times. That remark led away from Eliot to the question of where to shop for Amelia: "Is Fairfield's still good?"

"I'm not sure, but it doesn't matter. There are the malls. Stamford. And White Plains. And you really ought to treat Amelia to a few days in New York before school starts. Your aunt Jane would love to see her."

As Alida had evaded discussing Eliot with her mother, she evaded the man himself. He did not call her and they did not meet. In the next few weeks, she glimpsed him several times in large, crowded spaces—the bank, the school auditorium, the club dining room— and after a few such sightings, she realized with relief that Eliot was avoiding her. This mutual shunning that nobody noticed except themselves was the only trace of the horrid event. Alida began to persuade herself that it had never happened.

Amelia presented no problems. She did not cry when May left just before school started, but expressed pride that she no longer needed a nursemaid. She made friends quickly, and Alida owed her own social life to her daughter's popularity. Alida's invitations to the Richardsons' cocktail party, to Sally Ward's luncheon, to dinner at the Warrens' with Father Peele as the extra man, and to a fistful of similar unpretentious festivities all came from parents of children in Amelia's classes at school and Sunday school. And when it appeared that Country Day still stressed, as it had in Alida's time, academic achievement, Amelia buckled down and did beautifully. Her first report card was better than any Alida had ever brought home. Gertrude took the edge off that triumph (for Alida, at least) with the comment "I suppose she gets her brains from Hugo."

Gertrude did not mean to be unkind, but the more she saw of her granddaughter, the more she delighted in her, and the less she wanted her to be the child of a broken marriage. What Gertrude had intended as a reminder of Hugo's value sounded to Alida like a little insult, not big enough to distract her from her devotion to herself. She had had her hair styled several times in several places before she found her M. Jean and established a routine of hair-sets and manicures, facials and massages that occupied her when she was not buying clothes. She bought with dedication and imagination week after week while the leaves turned fiery and died. She bought irrationally—no event in her life required the elegance she attained—and brilliantly. She was always the best-turned-out woman in any group. But she was unaware of that success; she was not competing but creating, and, absorbed in creation, she forgot about redoing the cottage or asking Miss Blossom how to tell Amelia that her parents were separated. Alida did not even notice time passing until denuded branches opened up vistas she could remember—a view at a turning on the road, say, or the sight of a house she had visited as a girl, now with a stranger's name on the mailbox. Then she felt a plaything of time, "it" in a game between then and now, as she did when Amelia began to meet time's regularities, the succession of autumn occasions, in the setting where Alida herself had been a child.

Amelia spent Halloween exactly as little Alida had done, in the school gymnasium at an uproarious party conceived by Miss Blossom as a substitute for trick-or-treating. Like a magician, out of nowhere, Gertrude produced a Gypsy costume that Alida had worn to one of these very parties years before, and Alida watched Amelia walk from the car to the school door with the eerie sense that she was watching herself as a child.

Thanksgiving was heralded by requests for donations for the poor at school and Sunday school. The holiday now required two costumes, because at Country Day the Thanksgiving curriculum, which used to honor Puritans, had been expanded to honor Indians as well. For a week Amelia was a Nipmuk. In the school pageant, though, she was a Pilgrim wife who accepted an ear of corn and said, "Thank thee, Squanto. What is this boon thou givest me?"

Amelia's earnestness, absurd and touching, elicited nostalgia in Alida for the Thanksgivings of her childhood—perfect celebrations, ceremonious and cheerful. Until Alida married and began her own entertaining, she had not appreciated her mother's talent for embellishing occasions. Gertrude used to adorn all the downstairs rooms with immense, beautiful, and original bouquets. Alida, as a child in a tiny family, also loved the fact that her mother's Thanksgiving dinners were large; to be seated at the dining table extended to its fullest was rare, exciting, and dramatic. There was always a core of family—Uncle Arthur and Aunt Jane and their two sons, Paul and Arthur, Jr., and a crew of Waterman cousins from Rhode Island—and multitudes of friends, including many grownups whose relation to her mother Alida did not perfectly understand because she saw them only at Thanksgivings. These older adults sometimes made stiff demands; Alida recalled feeling tested and then reassured when their responses showed she had succeeded. She particularly remembered an ancient woman named Miss Lucy Cameron—she must have died long ago—who lived somewhere beside the Hudson River, and who used to appear at Waterman Thanksgivings covered in what Alida now realized had been a fortune in antique jewelry. Her speech and manner were abrupt, yet when Alida, the year she was five, dropped a curtsy, Miss Cameron said, "Very pretty manners, my dear, and you are very pretty altogether," thus bestowing upon Alida the first formal compliment she remembered receiving.

Marriage, forming new families, broke up old ones. After Josiah had married and moved to Butterville, near San Francisco, and after Alida had moved to southern California, arranging who went where on what holiday resembled one of those puzzles children bring home from novelty counters, little square frames holding movable plastic tiles that require hours of shifting to form a pattern of colors, or numbers in sequence, or letters that spell something. Spouses, relatives, friends, in-laws, and children's sailing or skiing vacations could rarely be slid into slots to form a pattern that satisfied everybody. Josiah's in-laws, the Rushes, were possessive, and Hugo was an only child whose father's heart condition was a tacit appeal. Thanksgiving had become the one holiday on which Gertrude, Josiah, and Alida counted for being together. Hugo, Alida, and Amelia would drive north to Butterville, and Gertrude would fly out from the East. They would all stay at Josiah's, and after the holiday, the Kellys would drive Gertrude down to visit a pair of spinster aunts who lived in Santa Barbara, all that was left of her older generation. Alida remembered that the sight of these great-aunts, a pair of cracked women with plenty of diamonds, domestics, and dogs, but no family—no one closer than Gertrude—used to make her ever more thankful for Hugo and Amelia. Or, more accurately, for Hugo & Amelia, the corporate family. Now that it had evaporated, she would have preferred to spend Thanksgiving, 1975, anywhere but Butterville—in her childhood, in the past, most of all.

She was not to have her impossible wish; they were going to Josiah's in California, and soon after that had been arranged, she received a letter from Hugo asking to see Amelia on the holiday; the child had evidently communicated their plans to her father. His request drove Alida to telephone her lawyer, Andrew Cameron, to ask if she could refuse.

"I am not, as you know, a specialist in domestic relations," he said, "but as far as I can tell, the document governing your family obligations remains your marriage certificate."

He did not see how she could deny her husband access to their daughter—he was not (for example) a danger to the child, and if he had been, she should have told a court. There was a trace of impatience in Andrew's voice; he was too much a man of his profession to tolerate such legal slovenliness as the Kellys' living apart without a legal instrument. He said that he and Alida needed to talk face-to-face about practical matters.

"What practical matters?"

"Everything that goes into legal separation. Custody. Visiting rights. Child support. Life insurance. Your share of community property."

"I don't want any of it," Alida said. "I don't want anything from Hugo."

38

"Community property isn't *from* Hugo; it's yours, and the law requires fathers to support minor children."

After an aside to his secretary to search his dates, Andrew commanded Alida to lunch with him on the eighth of December.

"Will you write Hugo for me?" Alida asked.

"Not now," Andrew said. "A letter from a lawyer about Thanksgiving might seem unduly formal, even threatening. You write. You don't have to go out of your way to make it easy for him. Make him come north; Amelia is still very young."

Alida was experiencing, in a concrete way, an abstract fact: Law, a crude instrument, does not register or respond to the minute distinctions of life, to all the fine gradations of feeling that compose human relations; its function is to hew passions into manageable commercial settlements. Many women blame their lawyers when they receive sound but unpalatable advice. Alida could not do that. Andrew's family and her own had been socially and professionally intertwined for generations; she would not have been surprised to learn that he was related to Miss Lucy Cameron. He had known Alida's father and had always been somewhere in the background of her life, and she would obey him.

Yet after she hung up the telephone, Alida found herself physically unable to write: she could not persuade her hand, holding a pen above a sheet of paper, to inscribe, "Dear Hugo." She changed chairs; she changed postures; she walked around the cottage sitting room; the morning passed, and the paper remained blank. She would have to turn to her mother.

Ordinarily, they did not meet until evening, when Alida and Amelia came to the large house an hour or so before dinner. They sat in a small parlor where, in Alida's childhood, their first television set had been installed. Alida and Josiah had bounced on the chairs and kicked their legs, had hidden behind the sofas, and used the large round coffee table as a desk, a tent, or a seat. Now Gertrude and Alida would have cocktails before dinner and listen to Amelia; much of her blossoming was due to this hour in which she received the loving attention of two women she loved.

Gertrude did not know why Alida was presenting herself in the daytime in the front hall, brandishing a letter she had extracted from her handbag. She was not out of control, as she had been on Labor Day, but she was in the way, for Gertrude was getting ready to go to lunch with an English horticulturist and two members of the Garden Club board. She curbed her impatience, and heard Alida out. Gertrude was not only willing to write Hugo, she suggested they invite him to Josiah's.

Alida was shocked. "How could you think of such a thing?" she cried. "I can't even bear to write to him, and the thought of seeing him and talking to him is—is disgusting."

Her vehemence surprised Gertrude. "Don't you feel sorry for him? He's losing his daughter's childhood. And *such* a daughter, too!"

"Sorry for *him*? It's his own filthy fault. You ought to be sorry for me."

Gertrude, defeated, agreed to write Hugo after lunch.

So there they were, on the plane to San Francisco, on the afternoon of Wednesday, November twenty-sixth. Gertrude was reading, and Amelia, who responded to engines as if they were cradles, slept. Alida simmered with resentment at her mother, who had agreed that Hugo would drive north, pick up Amelia at her uncle's on Thanksgiving morning, and keep her, presumably at a motel or hotel, until early Saturday. This was no proper Thanksgiving for a child, and therefore Alida supposed Amelia would like it—so many children of divorce enjoy paternal extravagance. Recalling her conversation with Andrew, Alida suddenly thought of the word "insurance" and realized she wished Hugo dead. Dead men, unlike divorced ones, did not ruin their children's upbringing; the dead became memories, legacies, and collections—cuff links, photographs, yearbooks, medals—not unwholesome indulgences. But then she reflected that fatherlessness might not be a perfect blessing; her father would probably have driven a harder bargain than her mother with Hugo about Thanksgiving.

Her brother met their plane. Josiah was very tall and fair, as their father had been, and radiated ease, competence, and affection throughout all the annoyances of an airport on a holiday eve. He brought along his oldest son, another Josiah, called Josh, who at seventeen was equally warm and helpful. Amelia adored the men of her family. She came awake quickly, roused to vivacity and flirtation; Alida noticed with amusement how the little girl tipped her head to give her big cousin a sidelong glance. Margaret, Josiah's wife, large like him, light brown to his blond, friendly and droll, greeted them at the house with her two younger sons (fourteen and twelve) who seemed to have doubled in size since last Thanksgiving. Gertrude, Alida, and Amelia felt overwhelmed by helpful giants amid the fluster of getting to their rooms and beginning to unpack. The jolly disorder was marvelously therapeutic, and the uncomplicated pleasures of family companionship lasted through dinner. Amelia shone. Josiah, as an alumnus of Flat Rock Country Day, drew out his niece about their school. Her enthusiasm was charming. When the subject turned to Josh's college plans, and Gertrude asked if he were considering an eastern school, Amelia joined in, "Oh Josh, do come. Eastern schools are *excellent*, as I have reason to know. Flat Rock Country Day is simply superve."

Her doting uncle blew her a kiss, and said, "And your vocabulary is superve, too."

So Amelia received her Miss Cameron compliment this Thanksgiving, but there ended any resemblance to Thanksgivings past. Morning came, and with it, for Alida, pain and anger and anxiety as she faced a holiday without her child. Amelia romped with her cousins while Alida, in the child's bedroom, paced nervously, stopping to repack the suitcase that Jenny had packed back in Connecticut and to look out of the window and listen for the sound of a car. The first motor Alida heard, grumbling and crunching its way up the long gravel drive from the gate to the house, was a florist's delivery van. (Margaret was no hand with flowers.) The day was cloudy; mist was in the air; rain had fallen and was threatening. The scene was greener and less bare than the November Connecticut landscape, but Nature here wept all through the autumn.

Alida watched the truck depart, and resumed pacing and listening. When the next motor sounded, she looked down and recognized the car she used to drive, a small blue Jaguar Hugo had bought for her. His driving it today was heartless—unless it was an instance of that artistic indifference Alida sometimes thought he shared with her mother. Alida watched the car park, and got Amelia's coat from the closet. The child came in and slipped into it. Josiah followed, gave Alida a kiss on her cheek, reached forward to take Amelia's case, and said, "Come on, Amelia, I'll take you down to your daddy."

Alida moved back to the window to observe the meeting of father and daughter. The child came into sight, her little girl's back wonderfully straight, holding her uncle's arm, just as Hugo opened the car door. He faced Amelia, looking down, and Alida saw only the top of his head. Then the door on the far side opened. There was another passenger—Yvonne. Her hair was its usual implausible bleach, and, though the moist day was mild, she wore a leather-bound coat of pale mink that matched her fake-creamy hair. She

41

looked, thought Alida, like the tart she was, the cheap little nobody from nowhere, with no taste, no manners, no morals. Less than an adventuress. A bitch. A trollop. A chippy. A slut. Not even an actress, only a liar. A whore. A hooker. A pig. It was monstrous of Hugo to introduce this polluted woman to his innocent daughter. And to Josiah. Her brother's nod seemed to Alida equally monstrous. Why did he not turn away? Why were they all chatting?

A clock in the house struck eleven; the car drove off, and Alida, exhausted by her fury, sat down on a chair. Josiah came in. "He introduced her as his fiancée," Josiah said. His anger was evident. Alida felt sorry she had mistrusted him. "*Fiancée*," Josiah repeated. "How ridiculous! I suppose he said it for Amelia." And then: "She looks much cheaper in person than on TV."

His loyalty allowed Alida to cry. He patted her shoulder, and said earnestly, "You never should have married him, you know."

Josiah meant that Hugo was unworthy of his sister, a cad, not a gentleman—expressions that their generation no longer used. Yet feelings outlast changes in language just as they outlast innovations in styles of life. Josiah knew that men—and sometimes men he liked—behaved exactly like Hugo during those marital hiatuses in which law and intent get out of step, but worldliness, taking men as they are, is inadequate when your younger sister is weeping before your eyes.

"Josiah"—Alida spoke between sobs—"he was so bright!"

Josiah, thinking she meant "clever," made the sage observation that character was more important than intelligence, but Alida had meant "high-spirited"; "entertaining"; "inventive." She remembered Hugo always diverting her or lifting her spirits. She could not imagine where all his tender and joyful concern for her had gone. "And I thought he loved me," Alida added.

She was not so much justifying her marriage as reexamining it, while Josiah began talking about Margaret's younger sister and her husband. Alida did not hear a word her brother said. Hugo had loved her. How had she lost him to a woman who was her inferior in every respect? Intelligence. Character. Breeding. Education. Or nearly every respect. Age? Looks? Sexiness? From any point of view, the loss was all humiliation.

Josiah finished whatever he had been saying, and asked Alida a question. Indeed, she did want a tranquilizer, and she rested in a semiswoon until her mother knocked at her door. Alida rose, made herself up, and put on a simple plum-colored velvet dress with a high-necked, long-sleeved bodice and rounded skirt. She wore high-heeled satin sandals dyed to match. Her hair was now short and curly, and her small head and covered torso demanded sizable jewelry; she had gone to her mother's vault for an old pearl collar and a big old amethyst ring. She misted herself in perfume, and, secure in her physical being, went downstairs determined to extract all the enjoyment she could from the rest of this so-far-dismal day.

She could hear the party in the library, a large, light room, with one wall of glass and the others shelved or paneled in bleached oak. The other guests were clustered near the fireplace in which a roaring, snapping blaze provided warmth and drama. As Alida stepped across the threshold, the group in view seemed too small, and as she neared them, walking across the pale ivory-and-blue Chinese rug, she was astonished. Her inattention to her brother had left her unprepared for the extent of this Thanksgiving's truncation. It was missing not two—Hugo and Amelia—but four. Margaret's younger sister, Mary Anne Hardman, was there with her parents, but without her husband, David, and without her little girl, Teeny (Antonia), who was just Amelia's age.

David's absence was a disappointment to Alida. He taught art, and Alida had studied art history; in southern California she had done volunteer work for a museum and had served on the board of a small art school. She and David used to gossip about the West Coast art world, its threads to the East, and its relation to the shifting tastes of the globe. Mary Anne had little to contribute to their conversation, and Alida had always found her less interesting than her husband. She was a frail, pale, shy woman who gave an impression of girlishness that neither marriage nor motherhood had cured. Her perfect little candy-box features were delicate but insignificant. Alida gathered that she was living with her parents, and that she regarded the dissolution of her marriage as an achievement—something in the nature of a graduation—that entitled her to new boldness, for she kissed Alida as if welcoming her into a sorority, and chummily inquired, "Why did you leave California, Alida? I finished with David in six months. It may take you years to get rid of Hugo."

Alida was as curt as she could be in answer to that brutally tactless question: "It was school."

Maids appeared, serving drinks and canapés, and the Waterman boys, who in years past used to stay and tease their younger girl cousins throughout the cocktail hour before Thanksgiving dinner excused themselves to watch football on television. Alida regretted this new subtraction from their party; any diminution of the gathering underlined loss. She hoped, however, that the subject of her reasons for moving east would be mislaid among drinks and departures, or that Mr. Rush would accept paternal responsibility for restraining his younger daughter's impertinences. Instead, after the boys had left, he himself asked Alida, "What do you mean?" and his wife (an older version of Mary Anne, with fluffy, apricot-dyed hair, who looked like a prosperous Pekinese), echoed, "Yes, what *do* you mean?"

Alida did not want to confide and tried to compress. While the Rush trio looked at her expectantly, she said that when her marriage had exploded at the start of June, she was naturally concerned about Amelia's schooling. Mr. Rush—large, stout, florid, and given to wide, vague gestures—said that, last Thanksgiving, they had since learned, Mary Anne's air of happiness had been a brave but mistaken effort to conceal terrible suffering. Was that true of Alida?

"Not at all."

"I remember when my little girl came to me," Mr. Rush said— turning to Mary Anne, he put in a parenthesis—"Sweetheart, you should have told me sooner"—and continued, to Alida, "When did things begin to go wrong with you?"

He was assuming the rights of headmasters and doctors, men entitled to demand women's confidences. (He was, in fact, an investment counselor.) Neither Gertrude nor Josiah had asked such prying questions, but these tactful relatives did not intervene to silence Mr. Rush, and as he was the eldest male present, Alida did not dare defy him by refusing to answer. Instead she offered a terse reply. "The night he went home with his star."

Alida had not undergone a period of prolonged trial. Hugo had begun to be cross around January, carping over trivialities—for example, some changes she had made in the plantings around their pool—as if seeking quarrels. He was so unlike his normally jaunty self that she began to fear he was ill, and she tried to find time to talk to him quietly and privately, but then he started working late and she hardly ever saw him alone. She began going to parties by herself, expecting (sometimes) to meet him or (at other times) to make excuses for his absence. Her naive unsuspiciousness shortened but sharpened her pain. Enlightenment came on the first of June, when she had gone to a cocktail party where her host and hostess cut short her apology for Hugo. He had not telephoned Alida, but he had called them to ask if he might bring Yvonne. When Alida saw them enter, she thought they were an incongruous couple. Hugo was as real as—well—her husband, while Yvonne was fantastic. He had started with the idea of making her unlikely—an exaggeration of the traditional dumb-blonde sexpot who, because or in spite of that personality, was an effective space policewoman. She came to this party in a shiny figment papered to her body, her face refulgent with paint. Hugo's devotion to her, his insistence upon hovering, on introducing her, seemed inappropriate, since he was not a press agent escorting or presenting her to reporters. But perhaps the occasion was another kind of presentation or announcement, for Hugo, having brought Yvonne, took her to her home and did not return to his own that night.

There was a good deal of headshaking and oh-how-terrible babble, and Mrs. Rush said, "How you must have felt!"

Alida shrugged.

On the morning of June second, she had been decisive, self-possessed, and businesslike. She had made her calculations about the school year and remembered the time difference between the coasts when she telephoned Miss Blossom.

Recalling that other day at her brother's on Thanksgiving, Alida began to suspect that her obsession with the school year had been a diversion created by one part of her soul to distract her from what another part was suffering. She wanted to reflect—to assess the extent to which she had suppressed her feelings and to try to understand what those feelings had been—but reflection and reticence were impossible in the presence of the Rush family. Mr. Rush asked, "Did he come home?"

Alida said, "Of course."

"When?" asked Mrs. Rush.

"That evening," Alida answered.

"And what happened?" asked Mary Anne.

"We argued about furniture and he hit me," Alida replied.

What had happened was very strange, and Alida, in recollection, realized (a wholly new thought) that the bizarre events of the evening of the second of June were partly her fault.

Hugo's secretary had telephoned to say that he would be home for dinner early, but when he arrived, Alida was not there. She had gone to rescue Amelia and May, who were stranded at another child's house because of a

*car breakdown. Besides May, the Kellys employed a couple who were new
and unfamiliar with the Kellys' ways. The houseman had brought luggage to
be packed into Alida's and Amelia's rooms with no more surprise than the
cook had accepted the information that both Kellys were dining at home.
They may have wondered why Alida had spent several hours gathering
objects—a blue-and-white Meissen tureen; a silver-framed photograph of
her father in uniform, an exquisite collage Amelia had made in nursery
school, a small Henry Moore bronze—and depositing them on the dining-
room floor beneath her mother's tapestry. She was assembling them for
shipment east, and she was also making notes to herself of other objects—like
her desk, a French piece, not so rare, Charles X, but she loved it—too large
for her to move to the dining room, so that when men came to crate what she
wanted, she would not have forgotten anything. There were still other lists to
make—furs in storage—and she had not finished all her tasks when the
telephone summoned her to collect Amelia. In her absence, it seemed that
Hugo, having looked for her, had asked Guido and Elena what was
happening, but they did not know why Madame had done what she had
done, or where she had gone, but dinner was for seven.*

*When Alida returned, Hugo had accused her of planning to loot his
house. She had sent May and Amelia to eat before she replied that she did not
insist on any one thing. He was free to tell her which objects he wanted—
surely not her father's photograph.*

In November, in her brother's living room, Alida saw that her
preoccupation with moving and packing must have appeared insensitive to Hugo: a woman is expected to show emotion, not efficiency,
when her marriage breaks up. Perhaps she would have cried—that
was probably the right thing to have done—if Hugo had not attacked her so unjustly.

*During this exchange, they remained standing in the hall. Suddenly they
both realized they ought to be someplace else. Alida felt she had done enough
packing for the day. She was tired. She thought they should do something
before dinner, and suggested the first idea that came into her mind: "Would
you like to swim?"*

*She knew that she sounded ridiculous, but she did not know how to make a
scene when one was called for. In the drama of her life, she needed direction.
She spoke that thought aloud as "What this scene needs is a director."*

And Hugo, as he hit her, said, "This is no time for jokes."

Having been struck won Alida immense sympathy from the
Rushes, expressed in more babble and tut-tut noises, but it also

46

seemed to Alida that they enjoyed her tidbit of violence. Gertrude said nothing, but Alida, seeing the shock on her mother's face, wished she had concealed the fact that Hugo had hit her. He had indeed behaved outrageously, but he had not struck her hard; he had slapped out in frustration or exasperation as one might cuff a sassy child or an irritating dog. No matter. Her tale must stand as it was, but it was ended.

As drinks were refilled, Rush throat-clearings indicated that they wanted their turn. They had dispensed sympathy; now they wished to receive it. Mr. Rush told Alida that David Hardman had quit his university teaching job to paint full-time. Alida waited to hear the rest of his crimes. Too late, she realized she had missed her cue; she should have spoken. Mr. Rush went on: "The boy was impossible. Absolutely impossible. We couldn't talk to him."

Alida, attempting to look interested, shook her head.

Mary Anne said, "My father spent hours, literally hours, trying to make him see what he was doing to us."

Mrs. Rush said, "And *I* called his sister."

Josiah and Margaret were quiet. Alida guessed they had heard enough of the subject. They had liked David, and they still liked his paintings—they kept one on the stair landing, although she now recalled a larger one that they had removed from the living room.

Determined to display their grievances before a new audience— Gertrude and Alida—the Rushes and Mary Anne began to turn themselves into a grotesque skit.

Mr. Rush (*having surreptitiously commanded yet another drink from the maid*): "It is a great responsibility to be a father, but David cannot see it."

Mrs. Rush (*after swallowing more canapés*): "One could not have expected this."

Mary Anne (*shaking her head in rejection at the offer of refreshment to demonstrate her emotion*): "He's made me very bitter."

They might have been a trio of comic bell-ringers, for Mr. Rush had a deep, round, rich voice, a bong: "David has no sense of responsibility at all."

Mrs. Rush had a feeble voice, a tinkle: "It was all very sad."

And Mary Anne had a high, piping, little girl's voice, a ping: "He doesn't love his child."

Bong: "He wanted to sell stock."

Tinkle: "How wicked!"

Ping: "I wouldn't let him touch one penny of mine."

Bong: "Quite right. No telling what he would have done."

Tinkle: "No telling at all."

Ping: "Sold us right down the river."

Everything about them became more and more ugly and absurd. Mr. Rush became redder, Mrs. Rush fuzzier, and Mary Anne paler. Alida, who was not scornful by nature, heard their California accents with contempt, and with contempt regarded their provincial style of dress in which mistaken sportiness mingled with erroneous brightness. On they went, round after round of rancor:

"At a low in the market."

"Terrible times."

"Not that *he'd* care."

Dinner was announced, and Alida's nephews returned and trooped into the dining room with the rest of the party. Alida looked around with pleasure. Her brother's house was architecturally modern, with discreet references to the Spanish Colonial style native to the area. The rooms were all spacious, and Alida remembered Margaret's anxiety, when they bought it, that the roominess, wonderful for three active, hulking boys, would swallow up their old things and that she did not know how to fill the vast areas with good-looking, son-proof furnishings. Alida remembered, too, that Margaret had enlisted David and his sister as advisers—they had actually worked with Margaret's decorator, and supplied both the theme and the hints that had made everything both practical and handsome. They had suggested many specially executed pieces, like the immense dining-room sideboard, made of old wood in a simple design that might have been Spanish, Mission, Shaker, Asian, or modern. Everything enhanced every other thing. Today, for example, the table was set with a fine old lace cloth; heavy cut-glass water goblets; thin, chased wine glasses; and Japanese place plates adorned with chrysanthemums (there were chrysanthemums in the centerpiece). All this formality mated perfectly with the forthright sturdiness of the furniture. To cap Alida's pleasure in the room's festive dress, she was seated between Josh and her middle nephew, Harold, who gallantly held her chair for her.

Josiah remained standing, ready to begin what an aging family joke had entitled his "wine grace." Like Alida, Josiah and Margaret were interested in food and cooking, and Josiah, who thought of himself as a naturalized Californian (unlike Alida, who had always felt a sojourner in the West) loved to discover superior local wines and traditionally opened Thanksgiving dinner, as he opened the wine, with a little lecture on his find of the year.

48

"This white is so good," Josiah began, "I defy anybody to tell it from a Saint-Véran."

Alida, relieved that the party was back on its familiar track, asked, "What year?"

Josiah said, "Don't tease. You know what I mean. This is dry, but it has a Burgundy generosity. So many California Chablis don't speak to me of Burgundy. They're ungracious, sometimes even a little mean."

Here Bong said, "This is a son-in-law to be proud of."

Tinkle said, "Indeed."

And Ping looked soulfully at her brother-in-law.

"I may have a chance to buy into the vineyard," Josiah announced.

"Waterman's winery." Gertrude was trying the sound of it.

"Doesn't that sound a little dubious?" Margaret asked. "Watery wine? California's own Bordeaux scandal."

"What about 'Josh's juice'? " asked Josh.

"Or 'Harold's hooch'? "

"Or" (from the youngest boy) " 'Lewis's liquor'?"

Josiah smiled at his family's feeble jokes; they were all hoping they had turned a social corner, and that Thanksgiving would now unite in merriment. "I'm not fooling about buying in," Josiah said, "so I want all of you to taste very carefully and give me your considered and honest judgment."

Bong: "This man wants our advice."

Tinkle: "How sweet."

Ping: "David thinks he knows it all."

Josiah gave up.

The first course was a delicately flavored fish soup that Alida had no chance to praise—she would try to remember to ask Margaret for the recipe—because Mr. Rush, inhaling rather than savoring, never ceased talking. He began by blaming himself for giving his younger daughter, "sweetheart," to a brute.

"But how can one tell?" his wife asked.

"That's the trouble," he said mournfully. "If men were only common stocks."

He proceeded to lavish on Mary Anne and Alida the overripe compassion that nobody wants, making of their misfortune such a riot of misguidedness and misjudgment that their lives seemed irreparable. He suggested that both men—Hugo as well as David—had won their wives by masquerades. They were shams, frauds, confidence men. Though he was arguing their duplicity, he was also proving Alida's and Mary Anne's idiocy.

Josiah and Margaret kept their eyes on their plates. Gertrude's expression was startling, even frightening. She looked as Alida had never seen her—stony. There was a look of loathing and of withdrawal from the objects of her loathing: Gertrude did not look as if she wished to murder the Rushes and Mary Anne; she looked as if she had just done so and was contemplating the mess their hated corpses were making, bleeding on a fine Oriental rug.

Mr. Rush went on without pause during the carving and serving of the splendid turkey. Alida was thinking that a subtle taste in the wild-rice dressing was the effect of cooking it with a little of the dried-mushroom water, when Mr. Rush caught her attention by perplexing her. He started to attack David and Hugo for being "the wrong sort" or "not our sort" in a way that puzzled her.

David was the son of a famous professor of art history who had written textbooks Alida had been assigned. His sister, who was much older than he and with whom he now lived, was Rosa Hardman-Stein, a famous potter, married to a famous weaver named Stein. Long ago the Hardman-Steins had sought to guarantee their independence by austerities that had become habit when they no longer needed to practice them. They still lived up in the hills, raising much of their own food and designing and building the simple structures on their property. Their work, and that of their students, was superlative, and they did not notice that their way of life had made them idols of a cult. The elder Rushes used to boast of this connection; now Mr. Rush accused the Hardman-Steins of "Communism" and "setting a bad example," and Mrs. Rush accused Rosa of spoiling David.

Hugo's background boasted no university chair and no craftsmen. His paternal line got its name from a Celt who had fetched up in the Southwest when it was Mexico; there were a family crest and a tradition of exile in the wake of the Stuarts. More tangibly, there had once been a good bit of land around Los Angeles that Hugo's family had begun selling off when it was almost worthless. "We say my father is 'in real estate,' " Hugo had once told Alida, "but the pity is, he's practically out of it."

Alida wondered if she ought to defend Hugo's social position by saying those three little words, magical in California, "Spanish land grant," but then decided not to. Hugo was his mother's son, and his mother was a daughter of the Middle West, responsible both for his nominal Methodism and his interest in the theater. Hugo's father was reserved, courteous, and melancholy; Hugo's mother was talkative, ambitious, earnest, passionate, and given to fads. Hugo was really Victor Hugo, named for his mother's once favorite novelist; his father never admitted to favorite anythings.

Alida did not argue for another reason: she had the idea that, despite their tenacity in clinging to their ostensible subject—their misery—none of the Rushes cared much. Her ear did not pick up a tone of deep feeling in any of that trio. Their sole sincerity seemed rage at David's disobedience—there was a ring of truth in their anger whenever Mr. Rush called him "irresponsible," Mrs. Rush lamented that he had left the university, and Mary Anne thanked heaven for her parents, who had saved her from destitution.

Mr. Rush, who appreciated Josiah's wine, gradually yielded the floor to Mrs. Rush, who finally clarified the meaning of "not our sort." David was not solid; he did not do his duty; he was inconsiderate, self-centered, hard-hearted, and insensitive because he was an artist. With horror, Alida heard this Rush parody of her own secret disparagements of Hugo and her mother. Was human resentment all of a piece? Was all anger—to change metaphors—drawn from the same well? Were the Rushes a mirror of herself, or a fun-house distortion?

Alida sighed. She could not usefully examine her emotional seesaws about her mother in the midst of Rush piffle, and Mr. Rush alarmed Alida by getting drunk. His large gestures grew uncertain, and his speech became incomprehensible. He waved an arm and one of the wineglasses fell and emptied on the lace tablecloth. The waitress had no sooner mopped up than another wave sent his water glass over, slopping its contents onto his grandson Lewis's second helping. A few moments later, his lettuce slid off his salad fork, and, while Mary Anne was querulously relating some iniquity David had committed about their silver, Mr. Rush began to cry. Alida was embarrassed for her nephews, but the composure of the family suggested that this was not an unusual occurrence.

His head drooping, Mr. Rush began to sag, almost sliding out of his chair. His wife and daughter decided to take him home without waiting for dessert. A few moments after they left the house, Mary Anne reappeared and said, as if it were another grievance, "My God, I forgot. David is supposed to return Teeny here."

"Don't worry," Margaret said. "We'll take care of her."

* * *

51

The meal was finished quickly after they left. Margaret's pies were as sumptuous in their way as Gertrude's bouquets had been, but the tiny congenial group, the core of Thanksgiving, could not recover its spirits. The boys longed to forget their aunt and grandparents in football; Margaret's humiliation was more noticeable than the pale wine stain her father had left on the tablecloth, and Josiah, Gertrude, and Alida would not make matters worse by saying what they thought of her parents and sister.

After coffee, Margaret took Gertrude on a drive to see a nearby garden before dark, and Josiah joined his boys watching football. Alida moped from room to room, longing for Amelia, while the maids hurriedly straightened downstairs before leaving. Soon after five, the doorbell rang, and Alida answered it. David was returning Teeny. The little girl had been crying.

"Hello, Alida," David said. "She wants to go to the bathroom."

Teeny screamed, "I want my Mommy!"

"She went home, darling," Alida said, her voice all honey while she thought that this was a wretched child compared to Amelia.

Teeny started crying louder.

David said, "Jesus Christ Almighty."

Like Mary Anne, David was fair and looked younger than his age, but while her girlishness irritated Alida, his boyishness always seemed fresh and attractive. Just now, though, it appeared slightly pitiable, for the father looked like a teenage baby-sitter out of his depth.

"Come in," Alida said.

But Teeny shouted that she wanted her mother. Alida said that her father would take her. Teeny insisted that Alida come, too.

Alida said, "Wait a minute," and went to fetch Josiah.

The dutiful uncle, dutiful for the second time that day, came to his other niece at the door, but Teeny, in response to more attention, cried more.

"She's like this sometimes," Josiah said.

He did not seem to be blaming David; the former brothers-in-law were as cordial as if they were still related.

"Poor Josiah," Alida said. "You seem to be specializing in children of broken marriages this Thanksgiving."

"Nonsense. I'm specializing, as usual, in football. Would you like to watch?" he asked David.

"No, no, no," Teeny screamed. "I want to go home."

"You'd better go, then," Josiah said.

Teeny screamed for Alida.

"You, too," Josiah said to his sister. "David will see you back."

Alida started toward the stairs, gesturing toward her dress, and saying, "I'll only take a moment."

But Josiah reached into a hall closet and put one of Margaret's raincoats around his sister, saying, "Never mind. You won't be long."

The coat was far too large and bore no relation to the formality of Alida's dress. As she got into the elderly station wagon David was driving, she remembered, in spite of her wish to forget, getting into Eliot's car, his comment about her mistaken pajamas, and her own sense of their wrongness: and here she was, after months of effort, once more riding away dressed wrong. Ever since she had left Hugo, it seemed, nothing came out right. Though she was riding with the wrong child, she put her arm around Teeny, who asked, in her normal voice, "Where's Amelia?"

"She's with her daddy," Alida answered. "As you were."

"That takes the cake," Teeny said, mimicking some adult so successfully that Alida could not help laughing. Teeny began to laugh, too, and said, with perfect aplomb, "I know I'm witty. Everybody says so."

But when they got to the Rushes' she started screaming again. Mary Anne answered the door. "Come to Mommy, darling," she said. To Alida: "He's impossible, isn't he?"

"How is your father?" Alida asked, with the nastiest of intentions.

"Fine," said Mary Anne, "but all this is very upsetting to him." She knelt down, crooning, "There, there, baby," unbuttoning Teeny's coat, and dismissed Alida by thanking her.

Alida returned to David in the car.

"Thanks a lot," he said. "You made all the difference."

"What's the matter?" Alida asked.

"We don't know yet," David said. "Teeny's just starting therapy."

"I'm sorry," Alida said. "Children *are* puzzling, aren't they? Teeny cares so much and Amelia doesn't seem to care at all. She doesn't even ask questions."

David started the car and changed the subject: "I could use a drink, Alida. You know Rosa never has anything except that awful wine she makes. Would you join me?"

Alida paused before she agreed. There was a deposit of wariness from her experience with Eliot. Yet she felt, as David appeared to, the need for time out on this abominable Thanksgiving, an escape from the shipwreck of family on a family holiday.

They found a restaurant open, serving Thanksgiving dinner. All her life Alida had imagined dining at a restaurant on a holiday as the most depressing of circumstances, but when she scanned the room, she saw no one in the dressed-up, lively crowd who looked as unhappy as she felt. They sat at a table in the bar, where, accompanied by Muzak and the clatter of dishes and silver and the din of voices, David began to tell his side of the story the Rushes had told her earlier. He seemed eager to justify himself to Alida, explaining that he had some money from his grandmother, that they could have rented the house they owned near the university and moved to a cheaper one he had found in the country—one with a studio, in fact, so that even their living arrangements would have been profitable. He made no mention of Mary Anne's money, the money she would not let him touch. David had savings; he had sold some paintings. He wanted to give himself a chance to paint while he was still young enough to return to teaching if he failed as an artist. "It's the same in teaching as it is in painting," he commented. "You're either a child prodigy or a grand old man. Nothing is as boring as middle age, and middle age nowadays starts somewhere around twenty-eight."

Alida agreed that one's thirties were the worst age to be in the 1970s. She had not thought of her own aging when she was living happily with Hugo, but lately she would search the mirror for gray hairs and wrinkles. David explained, further, that he had quit the university because it had repeatedly rejected his requests for a leave of absence or even for a lightening of his teaching load. Older, senior members of the art faculty got preference for time off to see what they could do for a year. They were not doing much. David dreaded becoming like them. "Did you ever have a feeling, like a vision, about your entire future and think that if that was all, you might as well cut your throat right now?"

When David spoke of the present, Alida saw that Mary Anne might be said to be bleeding him. He was paying for Teeny's therapy and all her bills, even though Mary Anne and Teeny were living at the Rushes'. He had had to move in with his sister, and nonetheless he began to fear he would have to go back to teaching. For the first time Alida recognized the importance of a fact she supposed she had always known—David was less well-off than any of her other family connections. In Alida's girlhood, she had learned that her family was not rich, but "comfortable," and she had learned about the poor, who received the charity it was her duty to give, but otherwise she had been cautioned not to speak of money. An absolute ban was, of course, an impossibility—Andrew Cameron, for instance, talked to her about money—but her training was certainly a reason that she had never focused on the financial disparity between the Watermans and Hardmans. The bond (apart from family) between her and David and Rosa was a shared interest in art and craft, and that tie obscured differences. Alida wondered if the Rushes had always thought of David as poorer than he should have been, too poor for their daughter. Did Mary Anne feel that, compared to her sister, she had made an unprosperous marriage? Was that the reason that the Rushes all objected to David's giving up the security of a university job? Then why did they not know that their rapacity was vindictive?

Alida thought about herself. Andrew had talked of what Hugo must pay, and Hugo, when he hit her, might really have believed she was going to empty their house. The world assumed that an aggrieved woman extracted damages, and Hugo was defending himself from a Mary Anne, a woman it had never occurred to Alida to be. Other people's lives are the only laboratory in which we can study our own, for our sufferings and perplexities are mere bludgeonings and incoherences. In November, sitting in a bar with her brother's ex-brother-in-law, Alida at last understood her husband the previous June: Mary Anne's grasping explained Hugo's violence.

Alida wanted to ask David how he felt about Mary Anne now. Had he stopped loving her? When? Did he love someone else? But perhaps he could not think of love, paralyzed as he was by the financial burden divorce had thrust upon him. Indeed, his future might well be as hopeless as he had feared, and his career wiped out before it started. The injustice of David's situation appalled Alida. She pitied him and wanted to help; perhaps she could buy one of his paintings. "What a stupid discussion for Thanksgiving," she said. "Alimony and acrimony. Tell me about your work."

David was eager. "Good for you, Alida. You remind me who I really am. You'd be surprised by what I'm doing. Quite surprised, I think. It's landscape. Not quite landscape, not entirely figurative, but it starts with the hills. Or it comes from the hills. I've changed the scale, though. . . . It's all a matter of scale. It's an extremely important new direction, I think, and not just for me. You really should see it. Could you come up this weekend? You don't mind Rosa, do you?"

"*Mind* Rosa? I like her very much."

"Some people do, you know. She's gotten terribly high-priestess."

"She never used to be."

David shrugged. "Maybe she just gets on *my* nerves. But what I'm trying to do . . . You must see it."

Alida suggested they go back and ask Margaret and Josiah about their weekend plans, so that Alida could find out when she could borrow a car. "Unless, of course, they think I'm not supposed to visit you. Trading with the enemy."

"I don't think they'd feel that way," David said, and then, like a child plotting to circumvent or forestall adult disapproval, suggested, "I know—we'll invite your mother. We've all heard about her mysterious little tapestry business, and perhaps if she and Rosa wanted to get together . . ."

When they came out of the restaurant, it was drizzling, and they scampered across the parking lot. Alida fastened her seat belt while David began to start the car. He put the key in the ignition and turned it; there was a click, followed by a brief crunch, as if the automobile had bitten into something distasteful, and then there was no sound at all. David repeated his action with the same result, or lack of result. He withdrew the key completely, and with a flourish of carefulness, observing his hand and the key's movement, reinserted it; the engine would not engage. He said, "It ran all day. Why isn't it working now?"

Machines were arcane to Alida. She knew about the tools of art, and about potters' wheels and the power saws that had permitted the luxuriance or superfluity of Victorian wood carving, but everyday practical inventions—their doings, their moods, and their diseases—were mysterious. She understood that the car was not starting, but not why not. David now inserted the key, turned it, and held it, but instead of purring, the car howled. He tried that failure once more: the machine's ululation was despairing. David said, "I hope I haven't run the battery down"—his notions of mechanical physiology were more advanced than Alida's—and once more pressed the key forward intensely.

The car cried out, and he released the key. Then he pumped the accelerator and tried several short jolts to the ignition. The machine balked.

"I may have flooded the engine," he said. "We'll have to wait to try again."

David repeated that he did not understand what could have happened. The car was Rosa's—he had sold his own—and he did not know it intimately, but so far it had performed well. His apologies or explanations were for his own benefit. Alida did not think they were in any danger; he would either start the car (that was the kind of thing men could do) or they would telephone for help—they were not lost in Death Valley or Antarctica. She thought David disproportionately disturbed. After a while, dampness brought chill, and she asked timidly if he thought the heater would work. He tried. It did not. "That may mean the end of the battery," he said morosely. "Or it may not. Oh, Goddamn Rosa's Goddamn brand-new secondhand car!"

He looked at his watch. It was time to try again. He exaggerated the gesture of inserting the key; he was engaged in magical propitiation, a rite whose significance was a wager: If I do all this seriously and gravely, calling attention to my seriousness and gravity, the spirits will notice and reward my efforts. Alas! The spirits were implacable. He turned the key, and there was no sound, not even a death rattle. "I guess I'll have to go back and telephone for a tow," he said. "Do you want to come with me?"

Alida said no; she did not need to get wetter. David got out, kicked the car in passing, and ran across the parking lot. She wished she had asked him to phone Josiah, but perhaps David would think of it himself, and perhaps rescue would come quickly. It was strange that, that very afternoon, when the Rushes were making her recite all the details of the second of June, another family's car's refusal to start was part of her story. She wondered how many realistic American narratives would involve machines and their failures—blackouts, brownouts, blown fuses, or, more tragically, burst boilers or smashed automobiles. But humans sought romance or drama in conflict with each other, and believed that their destinies depended upon their characters, not their machinery. Still, it seemed to Alida, as she waited chilled and alone in the stalled car, that machinery had character, too, and that its character was typically skulking, cowardly, and vicious. When human life glided happily along, there were no serious breakdowns. The demises of toasters and washers and the disabilities of automobiles invariably occurred when their owners were already in difficulties. Then machines revealed their personalities and forced themselves into human beings' life stories, attempting to make their own malicious mechanical marks in a mournful human history.

David seemed gone a long time. Alida, who was not wearing a watch, told herself that waiting always seemed long, and began ruminating on David's unthinkable plight. Poor man! Not even a car he could call his own! He had not been merely stripped but flayed. Like most women, Alida had always assumed men were the more powerful sex and that, unlike women, they could do pretty much as they pleased, but David's situation was a distillation of male defenselessness. He returned, very wet, and apologized for keeping Alida waiting. He had had to phone and phone repeatedly to find a place with a tow truck that was open this late on Thanksgiving. "God knows what it will cost," he said, and then said nothing.

They waited in silence except for the sound of the rain, whose patter on the car roof changed to drumming. At last the tow truck came. Its driver descended in the downpour, and, workmanlike and uncommunicative, trussed the front of Rosa's station wagon with chains and attached it to the boom. Alida and David squeezed into the truck's cab beside him. At the service station, Alida excused herself to go to the ladies' room, where she discovered that Margaret's voluminous raincoat had not protected her velvet dress from water spots; she could feel that her satin sandals were waterlogged; and when she thought of combing her damp hair, she noticed that she had left Josiah's house without her handbag. She yearned for warmth and dryness as she stood for a moment under the dripping eaves of the service station. In its brilliant lights the road and traffic were almost invisible; only headlights moved in the dark. She could hear rain, and cars whooshing and splashing, some competing for precedence, others obediently chugging along like circus elephants. There was something unsettling about the mechanical symphony and the undiscernible landscape, and she had the momentary impression that she was involuntarily acting in an avant-garde movie that sought to impart dread: matter-of-fact American roadside surrealism. She walked around to the front of the station, hoping the car's crossed wires had been uncrossed or a stuck valve unstuck and that they could leave. Instead, she found David arguing with the mechanic, who was shaking his head and repeating, "I can't do it. I'm not the boss," and variant versions, such as "The boss isn't here. I have my orders."

The mechanic was empowered to accept either cash or the credit card of the chain of stations to which this one belonged, and nothing else. He wanted thirty dollars in cash for the tow before he would look at the motor. David had twenty-seven dollars and an assortment of cards, but not the right one. The mechanic did not want to examine the others. What good would it do? He was not allowed to take anybody's check. "How do I know you are who you say you are? Who is this Rosa Hardman-Stein who owns the car? Is that you, lady?"

Alida identified herself and Rosa, but family connections were not cash. It seemed to her that the sensible thing to do was to call Josiah, and she said so to David, who shook his head no. "I'll think of something."

The mechanic observed that the station wagon was "a fine model in its day." Perhaps he complimented Rosa's car to show that he bore her brother no personal ill will. The mechanic was a middle-aged man going bald and running to fat, yet Alida could see that he had once been handsome. She remembered an old magazine article claiming that California had pioneered a new way of life, out-of-doors and athletic, and that the state was attracting and breeding a new species of American whose physical perfection was the perfection of the human race. No one ever wrote articles to say what happened when age marred beauty and time subtracted strength. The mechanic, who had only his job and his orders, might once have been a magnificent young surfer. Alida was upset that David continued to argue with a man who was not allowed to change his mind, who was all-powerful because he was absolutely powerless. Now David was offering the mechanic twenty-five dollars and his wristwatch.

Alida felt sorry for everybody—for the mechanic, for David, for her wet, bedraggled, worried self. "Let's call Josiah," she said again.

"I don't want to call Josiah," David said angrily. "Everybody always calls Josiah."

"It's nine o'clock," Alida argued—there was a huge electric clock in the office—"I'm cold. He's my brother."

"He's everybody's big brother," David said, furiously. "Like my sister's everybody's big sister. Damn them both."

Alida felt in the pockets of Margaret's coat. Not a penny. "Lend me a dime," she begged David.

"No," he said, and senselessly, frantically, went on, "if I had a painting to give him . . . Show him your ring."

Alida turned to the mechanic. "Will you lend me a dime to phone my brother?"

"Sure, lady."

She knew David thought she was betraying him, and, worse,

59

making the mechanic her accomplice, but she felt she had no choice; David was acting like an obstinate child, heading for further rejection, and Alida was forced to act like a mother, and cut short the scene to spare him. Josiah was relieved by her call. They had been worrying. He came with cash, dealt with the mechanic, and agreed to return David to the station before midnight. Carless David was carried to Josiah's house in Josiah's car. Josiah did not suspect the bitterness his helpfulness was evoking; he commiserated with David on the unreliability of machines cared for by women, and tendered the football results. But David radiated sullen wrath. He was angry at Alida and at what life was forcing him to become: everybody's kid brother and perpetual passenger. Alida made a few remarks on the ride back and a few more after they arrived at the house, all aimed at allaying his distress. She said what she really thought: it was a trifling mishap that might happen to anyone. She struggled to make light what David was determined to make heavy, and she did succeed in convincing her mother, brother, and sister-in-law that she had come to no harm in David's hands. But she could not cheer him; he would not chat; he continued monosyllabic, if not entirely mute. He resented her having witnessed his demotion from painter to dependent, and she could not persuade him that what had happened to Rosa's car was not serious, not tragic, not important to her. Everything that had happened to him in the year since they had last met had been terribly serious, tragic, and important to him.

Margaret led them directly to the dining room. She had been waiting to feed them, having set out some cold roast beef as well as cold turkey. Almost all the traces of the festive Thanksgiving dinner had been removed. The extra leaves had been taken out of the table, and the lace cloth and china had been replaced by woven mats and earthenware; the chrysanthemum centerpiece now sat on the sideboard. They were to help themselves from platters on the table. It was no longer a holiday, only a cold supper, and not enticing to Alida, who, in her effort to disguise her discomfort, had not changed her wet shoes and stockings.

As they sat down, Margaret asked after Teeny. Since David continued silent, Alida took it on herself to answer: "She was very funny in the car."

She was about to add, "and very good, too," but David broke in: "Teeny's fine, really. She only cried a little." He paused, and then started off in a new voice, saying, with quiet, deliberate force, "When I think over what Alida told me, I realize Teeny isn't seriously troubled at all, not by comparison with Amelia. Denial is much sicker than acting out."

"What did I say about Amelia?"

Alida was puzzled. Whatever she had said, she had not meant, because she did not think, that Amelia was "sick."

"You told me yourself she was terribly withdrawn."

David's face had changed. His youthful features took on a tinge of meanness—a boy desperado, capable of infinite harm, an unpredictable adolescent killer. Alida stammered, "All I said was that Amelia was—was incurious. Quiet."

"That's a terribly dangerous sign, Alida, and you know it."

David went on to list innumerable psychic disorders, from anorexia to schizophrenia, that surfaced after years of apparent normality, and was unswerving in insisting that all or any of these awaited Amelia in view of her good behavior. Alida did not think ill of her own sex, yet there was something commonly and unkindly called "feminine" as well as criminous about this David, the psychiatric chatterbox. He was using vocabulary as a weapon, as Billy the Kid might brandish a new gun, but he was also using his sacrifices as some women use theirs, for moral advantage: he *cared* for his child (his bankrupting himself for her proved that) as Alida did not care for hers.

It was clear to Alida that the collapse of the car was a symbol to David of the collapse of his life, and she would have forgiven him anything except his attack on her child: his unhappiness had unhinged him to the point of promising Amelia a breakdown because Rosa's car had had one. Well then, if David wanted a squabble, Alida would give him one, and she said, "You're certainly getting your money's worth from Teeny's shrink. Brainwashing wholesale. I never heard of half the things you mentioned."

David returned to the attack, again feminine, demanding pity: "How cruel can you be, Alida! Teeny's my daughter! I was only saying . . ."

And he said it all over again.

Alida would not attack Teeny; Margaret, her sister-in-law, at whose table she sat, was the brat's aunt. David was forgetting that Josiah was Amelia's uncle. Or perhaps remembering. Perhaps he really hated Josiah.

Not Josiah, Amelia's uncle, but Gertrude, Amelia's grandmother, stopped David. Mrs. Waterman clearly assessed David differently from his ex-wife and her parents, and decided that the efforts she had not exerted earlier were now not only required, but appropriate. Her voice, ordinarily low and pearly, was also authoritative. She knew how to interrupt. She did not shout; she had a trick of projection, like an actor's, and perseverance, too. She remarked firmly that there was never any sense imagining problems. She said this three times in slightly different words before David's tirade petered out. Amelia was not, Mrs. Waterman went on, necessarily sounder than Teeny; perhaps (Gertrude, socially shrewd, knew how to bribe in conversation) Teeny was more sensitive. But it did happen, just out of luck, that one sometimes had a child who was no trouble at all. "Like you, Josiah," she said, turning to her son, and, by the merest shift of her body, switching a spotlight onto him. "You were never any trouble. I remember how I worried about bringing you up without a father—oh, the books I read! And then, in your last year at Country Day, Miss Blossom called me in ... She was a young woman then, full of ideas, without much experience. We took her during the war when we couldn't get a man. Country Day always had headmasters before the war, the Second World War. You couldn't get out of it by teaching, the way boys could get out of Vietnam. They took *all* our men. Nearly all. Anyhow, Miss Blossom said to me, 'Mrs. Waterman, looking over Josiah's records'—we were getting your boarding-school applications ready, Josiah—'looking over Josiah's records,' she said, 'I am concerned.' 'What is it, Miss Blossom?' I asked. I was terrified that she had found something that would keep you out of my father's school. *Your* father went to school in Switzerland, as you know, and we were just girls, Aunt Jane and I, and my father was dead, so it wasn't much of a connection, but somehow it mattered to me. 'The trouble is,' Miss Blossom said, 'Josiah is too good!' "

They all laughed, except David, who smiled. His face was itself again: pale, young, no longer vicious, merely tired. Alida forgave him; she hoped he had forgiven her. Margaret looked at her husband with fondness, his sons with awe and suspicion, and Lewis asked, "Wasn't he *ever* bad, Grandma?"

"Well, once, there was one time I remember ..."

Mrs. Waterman began telling family stories. She told of Alida as well as Josiah, of Margaret as a bride, of her grandsons' bright sayings, of Amelia and Teeny and Rosa and David and how courtly David's father had been. "I never could believe he wasn't southern, David. Those charming, charming manners."

Thus she began to weave these people—some bound by unbreakable ties of blood, others by marriages that could never wholly be severed because of the community of blood that ran in the children—into a family. Like an old woman retelling familiar legends to the remnants of a shattered tribe, she gave them confidence through narrative. Their remembered past—their history—redeemed their present and assured their future.

Christmas

Sunday, the seventh of December, was icy; there were frost flowers on the windows, rime on the ground, and glaze on the roads. Alida would have spent the morning in bed if Amelia, Gertrude's convert, had not insisted on going to church. After lunch, the child settled down to homework, and Alida drove to Kennedy to meet her mother returning from Santa Barbara. On the way back to Flat Rock, at the moment when their route pointed decisively northeast toward Connecticut, Alida longingly recalled the lax Manhattan Sundays she had spent with Hugo years ago. While the wind buffeted the car and whipped the bare branches of trees beside the highway, she imagined that, at this very moment, men and women not far away on Manhattan were still lounging and lolling or perhaps teasing and kissing as they buttoned and zipped, getting dressed to go out. Gertrude broke into Alida's reverie by asking about the morning's service. Her traveling schedule had not permitted church, and she had read her prayer book on the plane. She told Alida that she would have preferred a more formal recollection of the anniversary of Pearl Harbor, but what Gertrude, who had been no churchgoer before her son was old enough for Sunday school, did not say was that she had spent that Sunday exactly as Alida was remembering her newlywed Manhattan Sundays: Gertrude and her husband had gone back to bed after breakfast and made love. The radio, bringing news of the Japanese attack early that afternoon, had shattered their mood of relaxed sweetness, and Pearl Harbor Day remained in Gertrude's memory ever after as a tangle of pleasure, love, anger, and fear—for Josiah had been in the naval reserve.

64

To Alida "Pearl Harbor" denoted a mythic event like "Gettysburg," and her mother's piety was a continuing irritant, particularly as it included her disbelieving self. Besides, like all children, she could not imagine a parent's life as having been lived with a density of event and feeling comparable to her own. Gertrude, silenced by Alida's terse account of the sermon, listened to her daughter's outpouring on the subject of Christmas cards. Alida complained that she had forgotten her large address book in California, and that she feared that cards signed "Alida and Amelia" would be read as bids for invitations and attentions—as pleas, not greetings—but that sending no cards was tantamount to announcing her own extinction.

"You forgot your prayer book, too," her mother reminded her. "You must ask Hugo to send them on," she continued, "but for Christmas you mustn't hurt people because you're shy. Send out as many cards as you can. You've plenty of addresses in your handbag address book, and I'm sure we can find more in the house. Buy UNICEF; they're best when you don't know what note to strike."

Alida listlessly assented. Gertrude was thoughtful, sensible, supportive, and loving. She had invited her sister's family for Christmas to cheer Alida and had postponed her cruise to give Alida a New Year's Eve party, yet nothing she did rejoiced her daughter, who was sour and guilty and, for the first time in her life, apprehensive about Christmas, a holiday for the happy children of happy, intact families. Alida was aware of how unwelcoming she seemed, but could not overcome her crankiness. Happily, there was Amelia at the conclusion of this glum drive. When the car turned in at the gate in Flat Rock, she darted out into the cold; her eagerness to greet her grandmother was almost explosive. They were inseparable for the rest of the afternoon, and when, after Hugo's Sunday-night call, the three dined, as they always did on Sundays, at the Club, Gertrude and Amelia chattered unceasingly, while Alida, fearful and morose, remembered that tomorrow sybaritic Sunday Manhattan would become workaday Monday Manhattan, where she would have to justify herself to Andrew Cameron.

When Andrew rose to greet her in his office, however, he did not look nearly as impatient and unsympathetic as Alida had expected from their telephone conversation before Thanksgiving. He looked attractive. There was no great change since she had last seen him: he was, as he had always been, tall—more than six feet—and had, as he had always had, a big-boned frame without much flesh on it.

The change was that Alida, older herself, no longer saw him as an older man, but as a handsome one. Andrew moved quickly as he arranged papers on his desk, and when he looked directly at Alida, she decided that the alertness in his gray eyes was more than lawyerly briskness—the liveliness belonged to the man as well as the profession. He seemed young for his age (he was perhaps half a generation older than herself, which would put him somewhere in his upper forties), and though he had always played an authoritative if remote role in Alida's life, she began to hope that she could talk to him frankly about herself and her perplexities as well as about her business affairs. His comparative youth suggested him as a confidant, and his good looks—how odd, how very odd, that she had never before perceived them!—hinted that he might understand her yearning for a fuller existence. "I will call you just 'Andrew,' if I may," Alida said.

"Why 'just Andrew'? I want to be 'wonderful Andrew,' 'unique Andrew,' 'merry Andrew,' or, from a truly satisfied client, 'Saint Andrew.' "

"I used to call you 'Uncle Andrew.' "

"Well, I may have to talk to you like a Dutch uncle." After a final glance at his desk, he said, "Come on. I've made a reservation upstairs."

From their table in the building's top-floor luncheon club they had a magnificent view of New York Harbor, embracing the Narrows Bridge and the Statue of Liberty under the blue sky of a clear winter day. The sun beamed benevolently on every morsel of glass and metal and on all the waters in the metropolitan area, and in response they glittered like prisms. The scene resembled a postcard, and offered the reassurances that art imitates nature and that famous beauties are not overrated—that life, in short, is not a string of disappointments. But Alida, fearing she would lose heart if she delayed, did not comment on the vista before them, and, the moment the hostess left, blurted, "Andrew, I feel I made a terrible mistake moving to my mother's. I'm turning into a middle-aged brat. I depend on her for everything, she's always right and always helpful, and yet I'm irritated by her all the time. I think she knows it. I'm very unfair. I hate going to church and I don't do anything."

Andrew smiled and said, "That's quite an indictment, Alida. Let's have a drink"—a waitress had appeared—"and consider the particulars one by one." After they ordered, he went on, "You probably did make a mistake moving back to your mother's, but you'd had a severe emotional shock. And I daresay you resent your mother because you depend on her. But she's a good woman, a very good woman, and you know it."

"Of course I know it. That's why I'm so angry at myself."

"You don't have to stay with her forever, you know. You could move back to the city. Have you thought of working?"

"I don't know what I could do. I never got a degree."

"You studied art history, I remember. If you went back to school and graduated, what could you do? Teach? Work in a museum?"

Drinks came; two young lawyers from Andrew's firm stopped at the table to say hello, and then Alida replied, "I'd hate teaching. And museums are full of dead-end jobs. They're hard to get but they don't lead anywhere. And I've always been more interested in furniture and objects than in pictures or sculpture"—Alida was thinking aloud—"and there aren't that many good furniture collections. They're scattered around the country. And I'm probably scared, when I think of my age, and the age I'd be when I finished school, let alone graduate school . . . All those bright young people are out there ahead of me right now."

"What about decorating?"

"My God, Andrew, that's what half the divorced women in the world do—shop for their married friends and fight with queers!"

Andrew persisted. "There's more to it, Alida. Decorating doesn't have to be pretentious or frivolous. One of Janet's boards hired a decorator—a designer, if you like; his name is Guthrie—for a child-care center. He did a marvelous job—artful work. I never saw anything like it. I was there at the opening. And Janet says it works perfectly. You could do something like that, something useful. Like legal aid—decorating aid or design aid."

"I see what you mean," Alida said. "Every place has to look like something."

While she was contemplating the demure steel-and-glass and brown-and-beige looks of the sky-high dining room, a handsome woman about her own age stopped at their table and said something to Andrew about seeing him at a meeting. Her straightforward assurance awed Alida, and, as if responding to the stranger's effect, Andrew said, after she left them, "An economist in the building. Nice woman. No nonsense, though. This club used to be men-only until she organized the women and demanded the right to join. So a job isn't Tillie the Toiler or pity-the-poor-working-girl anymore. And you shouldn't undervalue yourself, Alida. It's always struck me that you sell your talents short. A sense of style is something, and you've always had it—even as a child . . . A lot of people don't have it. Good people, smart people, some very brilliant, worthy people just don't have it. It's worth something. I mean, apart from money, and it *is* worth money. Design. Taste. You know, putting things together right—just the way you've put your outfit together so well today."

Andrew gestured toward her clothing—Alida was wearing a brown tweed coat lined with otter, a brown dress, and an otter hat— but she had no chance to protest her ordinariness, for Andrew went on praising her and demonstrating his esteem for her abilities, which surprised her, and his long, quasi-paternal attention to her doings, which touched her. Over their omelets, he suggested she study, for he did not imagine she was ready to work as a decorator immediately—"I'll bet you could start a course at a community college next semester, right up near your mother's"—and he mentioned that study might also be a better idea than full-time work until Amelia was older. "Janet thinks it's probably better for mothers of young children not to work—unless, of course, they must. You know, she studied child psychology, though she never worked professionally, on account of the children. She's very active as a volunteer. And that reminds me, whenever you do move back to the city, Janet knows all about day schools for Amelia."

It was certainly more than a decade since Alida had last seen Janet Cameron, and she had no clear memory of her; Janet must be remarkable, Alida thought, to have created so much pride and respect that her husband repeatedly cited her at a business luncheon. Salads came, and a stockbroker from the building said hello, and then Andrew asked Alida, "Do you want a divorce?"

"Yes, of course," Alida said.

"But Hugo doesn't."

"He introduced Yvonne as his fiancée."

Alida told Andrew about Thanksgiving morning. Andrew was skeptical. He said that people could be trapped in affairs just as they were in marriages, and he suspected that Yvonne had trapped Hugo. "If he loved her and wanted to marry her, he'd be pestering you for a divorce. I gather he's done nothing of the kind. I'll bet he's been stalling her, telling her you're making difficulties."

"I don't know *what* Hugo's told Yvonne. I can't think of him. I just can't. You'll have to do it all."

"You're talking like a child."

Andrew said patiently that he knew several able divorce lawyers.

He would work with one of them on her behalf. They, the professionals, would negotiate for her, but she had to tell them what she wanted them to do. There were no more interruptions after coffee arrived; now that they had come to what Alida thought of as the rough part, no one came near them, and Andrew could drive her into corners, asking hard questions, giving hard advice, and making her think hard thoughts.

"How much money does Hugo make?"

"I've no idea. The accountant took care of everything."

"Do you know his name?"

It was in the address book in her handbag.

"Good. Do you know the name of Hugo's lawyer?"

"He's really the lawyer for the company," Alida said. "Hugo's partly a corporation, I think."

But then she said that if she could say what she wanted, she wanted nothing from Hugo, not a penny. She told him about David and the Rushes, but Andrew was not touched.

"Naturally a father pays school fees and medical bills. Hugo will pay Amelia's."

"But I don't want him to."

"Why not?"

"Because then he would have some say about her education."

"You are not going to be able to separate Hugo from Amelia," Andrew said. "You know that. And you know, too, that everybody's life is one unexpected event after another, and you, like everybody else, have to be protected against circumstances you can't imagine. I have to protect you. I'm *paid* to protect you. Suppose Hugo marries somebody else—my guess is, not Yvonne—and has six more children."

"You know I can take care of Amelia."

"*Now* you can. Now you certainly can. But Hugo is not poor and we must establish her claims on him. And yours, too. Suppose *you* married again—someone like this David you feel so sorry for, a nice fellow without a penny. Suppose *you* had six more children. And suppose"—Andrew, seeing her unresponsive expression, became exasperated—"suppose one boy was an idiot, the other an embezzler, and the girls never married."

"Lucky girls," said Alida.

"Don't *you* hope to marry again?"

"Oh Andrew, I don't know about marriage. I wish—I only wish—somebody would love me."

"Holy jumping Jesus Christ! First you're smart, then you are

69

dumb, and now you are pathetic. How your father would have adored you! He was supposed to be—he was—a terrible flirt. He was enough older than me so I never really understood everything he was up to, but as I look back on weekends in the country when I'd be in a corner of the room hero-worshiping what I thought of as 'men,' and watching them and their 'women,' I remember how your father went for the girls who flirted, little actresses who'd turn it on, turn it off—you know, play up. He played right back. Your mother is very good, and so is Josiah, but you, Alida, are just like your father; you are the naughty one."

"I am not," Alida said, and indeed she had never thought of herself as naughty, but rather as plodding and dutiful.

"You are now. You're just as bright as the rest of us. I shouldn't have to tell you that marriage is, first of all, a contract, and that contracts are enforceable and contracts are breakable, all according to law, and law is reasonable. That's what law is, reason applied to human affairs. As far as it can be. So your nonsense is just a girlish racket. It's trying to get out of going to the dentist. Or not taking your medicine. Or pretending to get sick so you don't have to take an exam. 'Naughty' is the word. You're charming, but you're faking, and I can't let you get away with it."

Andrew had turned his disapprobation into a compliment as handsome as any Alida had received: he had told her she was intelligent and wayward, stylish and winning, all at once. "Do you mean it, Andrew?"

"Of course I do. I always mean what I say. My complaint is, you don't. Now, listen. We—Janet and I, little Janet, and Andy, if we can find him—are going away next week for a month. When I come back, I expect to find a letter from you, telling me, in a general way, what you think you're going to do—stay in Flat Rock, move back to the city, go to school, whatever. I'll have to review your affairs with Charlie Saunders at the bank. I'm not your only trustee. All of us together can figure out what we're going to ask for. Child support, of course. But more. We're going to make this man pay. I don't like the way he's treated you." As they stood up, he said, "I'm troubled, Alida. I should have called you in last summer, when you first came east. I'm afraid I've let you wheedle me today. Everything slows down for Christmas and New Year's. We're going away, and so are half the people we want to talk to—December is no month for getting things done—but even so I wish we had begun our business sooner."

70

"Don't worry, Andrew. I won't do anything naughty."

"Of course you won't. You *are* your mother's daughter."

They "Merry Christmased" each other and sent regards to the families, and Alida thought Andrew looked at her with a father's tenderness as he stepped off at his floor. She went down to the street, found a taxi, shopped uptown, and then boarded a late-afternoon local out of Grand Central. Early for the train, she found a seat by a window while the car filled up with shoppers and commuters. When they surfaced at 125th Street, the evening had begun to extinguish everything outside; twilight seemed to be killing the world, until, in a little while, almost as if on command, lights came on everywhere when the sky went black. The countryside was dotted with electric clusters that ringed New York; Alida rode past suburbs that looked like armies encamped, preparing to assault the city. In Old Bridge and Flat Rock, Alida knew, the image was reversed: there the unceasing anxiety was that the city was marching out to ravage their idyll, and that a hostile "they" would find a way to break Flat Rock's complex of defenses, which, though constructed largely of paper, had so far been as resistant as stone. Did she, Alida, want to go on living in a fortress? Was she protected or imprisoned? Andrew, it was clear, thought she should move to the city, and perhaps she should. But she was not ready to decide anything. She reminded herself, instead, of Andrew's compliments. At this moment in her life, an ounce of praise was worth more than a ton of advice.

The train stopped, the woman sitting beside Alida got off, and a man who had been standing, awkwardly holding a flat parcel, like a framed picture, sat down beside Alida. He put the package on the floor, propped up against his legs, before turning to apologize for jostling her. It was Fred Palmieri. He greeted her warmly, and said, "Eliot should have mentioned you were Mrs. Waterman's daughter."

"How do you know my mother?"

"She picked my design for the new wing on Country Day."

"I didn't know you did it. It's lovely."

"It's the only good thing I ever did. It started as a student competition: design a wing, an addition. It won the prize. My proud parents saw to it that the story was all over the Old Bridge *Chronicle*, and then your mother called up and said that the school trustees had decided they needed a new wing, that she was the head of what I guess you'd call the design committee, and could they see my plan. It was gone over and built by a graduate architect, but it's mine, all right."

"How wonderful!" Alida said. She meant it. The wing was a simple, charming building that looked new without challenging the older structure to which it was attached. "What are you doing now?" she asked.

"You saw what I'm doing. Parody. I'm an entrepreneur. The Inn was genuine, and we took it over and made it look fake. You heard the 'we.' I don't design anymore. I'm beyond that." He repeated, "I'm an entrepreneur, a developer," in a tone so self-mocking that Alida was not sure how to reply. Fred spoke instead. "I got myself a Piranesi, the architectural orders, today to cheer myself up. Funny, though. Nothing cheers me. Why should it? When I was a kid I was so impressed with Ruskin. Now I'm doing just what he preached against. Remember those terrible row houses he hated?" Fred paused, and added, "It's in *Fors Clavigera*."

"I never got very far with Ruskin," Alida said. "Like Herbert Read. Absolutely great criticism up to a point, and then suddenly sermons."

"But don't you see—don't you want to make—a connection between art and morality?"

"I don't think much about morals," Alida said. "I suppose, really, I count on getting by with manners."

Fred started to laugh. "You say funny things. And original ones. Everybody talks morality nowadays."

"Who?"

"To begin with, my wife and my sister, my older sister. She started to be a nun. Now she's a social worker. They've been into every-thing—Montessori against the open classroom, the new liturgy, church reform, the Berrigans. It's all morality to them. Or immoral-ity. They've talked about 'the Pentagon' for hours, and it never occurs to them that a hundred years from now, when schoolchildren won't know the difference between Vietnam and Venezuela, that hideous piece of—you can't call it architecture—will be stinking up the landscape. Or 'Watergate.' They were never talking about urban scale. Yet that's our real iniquity. No urban scale. No modern vernacular."

"*You* say funny things," Alida said.

"Only when it hurts. Bad building hurts me, and it's what I'm doing."

When they arrived at Old Bridge, Fred helped Alida alight, and asked her to have a drink with him: "I'm dying for somebody to talk to."

72

As they crossed the station parking lot, a cold December country wind rose in the dark and slapped Alida's face and chilled her legs, while voices greeting other voices sprinkled the sound of car doors slamming; the combination of natural chill and human warmth made Alida grateful for Fred. She, too, was dying for someone to talk to—a peer, a stranger yet a friend. They went to Ye Towne Taverne, a sometime hotel on Main Street near the station. What was upstairs Alida did not know, but downstairs was a business-man's-lunch restaurant that turned into a steak house at night, and the bar was Olde Englysshe. Half to herself, Alida repeated her remark to Andrew, "Every place has to look like something."

Fred asked her what she had said. She told him, and went on to sum up that part of her conversation with Andrew. Fred said that Andrew sounded unusually perceptive, for, in his experience, not many lawyers appreciated the importance of design. "Barlow has a course," Fred said. "Very elementary, just what you'd expect—community college, uninspired commercial art. You'd probably find it disappointing. I've hired people from the place to do renderings. They turn out docile draftsmen. I don't know what you'd get out of what they teach, except they *do* teach design-office routine."

The waiter came.

"Campari and soda," said Alida. Fred opened his eyes. "I worry about driving at night," she admitted.

"I don't."

He proved it by ordering vodka. He did not wait for drink to unlock his tongue, but began to talk as if their being together in a bar were a recognized confidential situation. Perhaps it was, Alida thought; perhaps the reason that bars flourished was not that they offered alcohol but a different context, more intimate than a club and freer than anyone's household, something like a confessional without penances. Fred began by saying that he hated Christmas because it brought together families that were already too much together, such as his own. His story recalled what Eliot had told her: Fred's father, who had started as a contractor, had become a small developer; in the middle of his most ambitious project, shortly after Fred's graduation from architecture school and his marriage, the elder Palmieri had died of a heart attack. Fred's sister had just left her novitiate and was living with her parents. Everything was in jeopardy—or so they were told by Eliot, representing the bank—and Eliot had persuaded Fred to take on his father's obligations to save the whole family from pauperism. The development was a success, and Fred went on with the business. "Somewhere in there Molly got pregnant with my son, who doesn't care about anything except space travel and football, and then my other sister's husband started drinking, and I have been making pots of money for all of them by building God knows what kinds of abortions—and *they* talk about morality!"

Alida was attracted to Fred; like Andrew—like Hugo, for that matter—he had a crackling quality she liked in men. At the same time, she could not help feeling for the absent Molly, who had a claim on her husband's loyalty no matter how she moralized. For the second time, Alida found herself snubbing this man she liked. She said, "You know, there must be something I can do besides sitting around in bars listening to the complaints of unhappy, artistic men."

"What a terrible thing to say," Fred replied. "*Men.* I don't talk to any old body. Maybe I am a bore, but talking it out helps, and you can't imagine how I wanted to talk to somebody who had an opinion on Ruskin. Or Read."

"I'm sorry"—Alida decided to be as honest with him as he was with her—"but you probably wouldn't be telling me all this if you weren't drinking so much."

"Goddamn," he said. "Women are all alike."

"And so," said Alida, "are men. You're turning nasty." She told him how David had quarreled with her because of his family problems, adding, "And I'm sure he's read Ruskin and Read and Berenson and Venturi and that fellow who wrote about the hand—I never can remember his name . . ."

"Focillon, I think."

"And his sister's probably another William Morris."

Fred was impressed by Rosa Hardman-Stein's name but unpersuaded by Alida's story. "You've proved my point. David's a relative of yours. An ex-relative. You know him as family. Relatives never say anything funny or interesting. In fact, most of the time they're cruel. Or distracted. Or demanding. That's why you need friends. Families are something else. I don't know what they are."

Fred seemed as impervious to alcohol as he claimed; he walked back to the parking lot as steadily as he had walked from it, and Alida, halfway apologizing for her sobriety, said, "I really hate to drive in the dark. And there's that horrible double turn on the road to my mother's."

Fred's reply showed that, though he had talked of himself, he had also thought of her, for he answered sympathetically, "I know that turn. It's a disgrace. And I think that a woman alone—I mean, left alone after having been married—is apt to be frightened or uncertain. For a time, at least. My mother was a very forceful woman until my father died. Then she crumbled. I don't know about your mother. She struck me as very sure of herself, but I was very young then." He stood at her car door, and suddenly said, "I forgot to show you my picture. You must come and see it."

He waved and walked away. Alida switched on her ignition and began to drive. As she moved off, she could get no more than an impression that Fred's car was something spectacular—an imported sports car, she thought. A Ferrari? She drove toward her mother's and conquered the fearsome bend where the narrow blacktop road looped twice like a letter *m*, whose downstrokes were filled with stands of enormous old trees that, even leafless, obscured a driver's view. Elated by Andrew's compliments and Fred's companionship, she was in better spirits than she had been for months. It occurred to her that, since she was using her mother's New Year's Eve party to pay off some of her own social debts, she might also use it to open a new account in friendship, and she resolved to ask her mother to invite the Palmieris. Alida entered the television room, her mind all party and gaiety, to find Amelia deep in *Galaxy Guards*. Gertrude, who had been sitting beneath a lamp, working needlepoint, rose, led Alida out of the room, and, standing in the hall, whispered that Alida had just missed a call from Hugo. He had first asked to speak to Alida, and instead had talked to Amelia and invited her to spend Christmas with him in New York City. Alida completely forgot Fred in her fury at Hugo. "He could have called again and talked to me," she muttered angrily. "Why does he have to get Amelia involved?"

Gertrude's reply sounded as if she had been consulting Andrew. "He didn't *get* her involved. She *is* involved. She's his child."

"But why Christmas?" Alida wailed. "Our Christmases were always so wonderful. I wanted Amelia to know what they were like."

"Thank you," her mother said. "That's the first kind word you've said to me in weeks."

"Oh my God," said Alida. "Have I been hurting your feelings?"
"Not really."

Gertrude's voice suggested she was aching all over. How right Fred was about family and friends! Alida could do nothing but join Amelia and silently stare at the hated Yvonne until dinner.

At the table, Alida asked, "Haven't you something to tell me?"

Amelia looked blank.

"About Daddy?"

"Oh yes, Daddy called."

"Don't talk with something in your mouth."

"You asked me a question."

"You could wait to answer until you swallowed. You don't sound excited." Amelia, chewing, did not answer. "What did Daddy say?"

"He's coming to New York and wants me to spend Christmas with him."

Alida tried to keep her voice neutral. "Would you like that?"

"Yes," Amelia said.

"Rather than stay here with me and Grandma?"

"Well, you see, Mommy"—Amelia was placing her voice carefully, too—"since I started school in Flat Rock, I hardly ever see Daddy anymore."

That truth could not be argued away, but Alida was stupefied by disappointment. Her mother's dinners were gustatorially sober affairs; Gertrude had never exercised her imagination on food. Alida was served as an adult the menus she had been offered as a child. Tonight there were lamb chops and green peas. She felt she had been eating the same meal her whole life long, and that it had never been worth the effort of eating. Alida stared at her mother and child, and then an idea came to her. "Amelia," she asked, "did Daddy want me to call him back?"

"I don't know. He didn't say."

Amelia's uncertainty made her seem very young and helpless. Ah, families! Alida could recognize that she treated Amelia exactly as Gertrude treated Alida, never presuming, never pushing, never questioning. Alida had never asked about Amelia's Thanksgiving partly because she did not want to pry and partly because she was not sure she could conceal her rage at Hugo. His Christmas invitation gave Alida a pretext for satisfying her curiosity: "Did you have a good time with Daddy on Thanksgiving?"

But before Amelia answered, the telephone rang, and Sally, the waitress, came in and asked Mrs. Kelly if she wanted to talk to Mr. Kelly.

Alida was still angry at Hugo, but all she said was "Oh Hugo, I hear you're taking Amelia for Christmas."

"That's right," Hugo said. "I'm coming in next week on business, so I thought I'd stay over and see her on the holiday."

Alida did not know how to ask if he was bringing Yvonne, and asked instead where he was staying. He told her the name of his hotel, and asked her to bring or send Amelia down on the twenty-fourth unless she preferred him to call for their child at Flat Rock. Alida chose New York, and added, "By the way, Hugo, could you do me a favor and ask Mrs. Norris to mail me my address book? And Mother has been wondering what happened to my prayer book."

"I'll bring them both myself," Hugo said. "The show is finished. Mrs. Norris is gone. The office closed as of today. That's why I'm coming to New York."

"Oh dear," Alida said. "When did all this happen?"

"It was happening all last year. Didn't you notice? Can't you remember how worried I was?" Hugo sounded aggrieved. "They had nothing to put in its place this fall, so they let us start another season and gave us the ax this morning, as a Christmas present."

"How terrible!" Alida said. "Will you let me know what time you want Amelia?"

"Of course. I'll call."

After they hung up, Alida thought she should have mentioned her visit to Andrew. Then she shrugged. Business could wait while she enjoyed Hugo's bad news. It would have been still more delightful if she could believe that this was the beginning of Hugo's end, and that he would shortly become a boring has-been, shunned everywhere he had been sought, but reason told her that he was so resourceful he would think up something new. Still, the failure of this show, Yvonne's show, rejoiced Alida. Serve him right. Serve them both right. She sat at the telephone for a moment smiling to herself before she returned to the table, hungry for her baked apple.

Mrs. Waterman had planned the following Saturday as a shop-and-see-the-decorations holiday in New York City for herself and Amelia. James, the gardener, would drive them, so that they could go where they liked without worrying about parking. Alida spoke cheery farewells and waved as the car pulled away, and then, turning back into the cottage alone, was seized by a spasm of jealousy and self-pity. She knew she was unreasonable—they were chiefly shopping for presents to surprise her—but even so, she felt excluded. The walls of the sitting room vanished and, as in a theatrical transformation, Alida was back at boarding school, in the lounge of the main building on the first Friday afternoon of her junior year.

The headmistress, experimenting with an advanced policy, allowed ju-niors and seniors who had parental permission to take weekends off; the young women were supposed to learn maturity by deciding for themselves if their schoolwork was up to date. Alida had never been entirely at ease with her classmates at boarding school—they were bolder and gayer, more daring and more giggly. She had spoken to a few girls about plans for the weekend, but perhaps she had been shy or vague. No one said anything definite to her, and she had assumed that nobody was leaving the campus. But on Friday afternoon, as she went to the main building to buy stamps, she saw groups of girls waiting on the steps and in the hall. Just as she recognized that practically every upperclasswoman was leaving without her, taxis appeared, and they all vanished. Alida went into the lounge, a long room with chintz-covered furniture and an Oriental rug, to see if anyone else remained behind, and, while astonishment was still competing with humiliation, she heard a hideous sound, a choking sob with bizarre, gulping interruptions, and saw, half-hidden behind a tree-of-life-printed chintz curtain, a monumentally fat Iranian, the least popular girl at school, weeping and eating a candy bar. The girl made everyone feel guilty because she was so ugly, so far from home, and so sorry for herself. Alida looked at her with disgust, asking herself, "Am I like that?" and, suspecting that she was, turned from the mountainous image of her own rejection and fled to her dormitory without a word of friendship or compassion.

The boarding school set rose to the flies, revealing once more the cottage sitting room, a dwarf of the lounge—chintz and rugs, by now familiar and accepted in their mediocrity and inconvenience—with Alida standing, struggling to quell the adolescent passion that her mother's and child's departure had resurrected in her. How was it possible that she was still the same—the same mass of misdirected feeling she had been in her teens? She noticed a defect in the room's decor that had escaped her attention—the writing desk, standing catercornered beneath the staircase, was too small and badly out of scale—and she recalled that, on Labor Day, preparing for Eliot, she had planned to reconstruct and redecorate the entire ground floor as a prelude to inaugurating a new social life. Alas! Without a husband, her life resembled an ill-made play—a series of false starts and dead ends with no discernible theme. If she understood Andrew, it was her business to supply her existence with a plot. She flung herself into the great wing chair, thinking helplessly that that was precisely what she had not been trained to do: she had been raised to be a daughter, a wife, a mother. Andrew had talked of work, of a job or a career—in effect, of ambition—as the organizing principle of one's life, but to imagine herself working and having pecuniary value to strangers, she would have to start afresh, to invent a new childhood. Her training and education had left her unprepared for any roles but those defined by others and biology. Now she faced the task of making herself over, of being her own parent and teacher as she was born again as another kind of person.

But how? She almost spoke the words aloud, and the too-small desk replied, Write, and write *now* for a Barlow catalogue. No matter that the Christmas season slowed activity to the point where she would probably not receive it until after the new year; no matter that Fred described the place as uninspiring: it was a beginning. Alida spent a long time over the letter: the act of writing, so full of significances, increased her self-doubt. To whom should she address it? A registrar? An admissions officer? Was her handwriting legible? Should such a letter be typewritten? (Apart from having no typewriter, she did not know how to type.)

When she had satisfied herself and folded and stamped a simple note, she thought it time to spend a few hours Christmas shopping, and went upstairs to make herself up for going out. As she sat at her dressing table, idly looking over its array of objects, the lipsticks recalled penises. Then it seemed to her that eyebrow pencils, eyeshadow sticks, tubes of mascara—all cylinders that moved, elongated, increased or decreased in size—were unmistakably phallic. Who had invented them? Men? Women? Was some collective unconscious responsible for shaping cosmetics as emblems of the sex for which the female painted? Panted. Alas—now she saw how the damage had been done! All summer she had nursed her rage at Hugo and lived like a prepubertal child. Eliot had killed desire before it could assert itself, and David's fit of childishness had done nothing to revive it; but Andrew and Fred, handsome men, quick men, bright men, had revived the whole complicated, enticing, miserable business of sex, or love, or both. She had meant what she had said to Andrew—"I want somebody to love me"—but for a woman, not a child, that meant "somebody to *make* love to me." Was she thinking of Fred? Could she imagine them as lovers? To imagine his disrobing, she tried to recall how he had been dressed, but the train had been dim, the bar dimmer, and all she remembered was his face, especially his lively eyes; she could not even mentally take off his necktie, since she had no recollection of it. She had to laugh at herself, or at the world, or where it or she had arrived, for, after all, which sex was by tradition supposed mentally to undress the other? Was it only a new freedom that allowed her these thoughts? Or had her widowed mother, too . . . ?

All the following week, Alida was assailed by disconnected sexual intimations. One day, for instance, when she was shopping for presents for her mother's maids and trying to think of Jenny, out of uniform, as a person, Alida suddenly noticed the cupped hands of a man on the street lighting a cigarette, and imagined those hands touching her. Or the back of the boy who helped James. There was some end-of-the-year digging and fiddling in her mother's gardens, and James's boy, the youngster whom Alida had hardly noticed since Labor Day, when he had arrived in the drinks procession the moment after she had smashed her mother's bowl, was working in a sweater that followed the curve of his back and outlined his shoulders and arms. Those shapes reminded Alida how the bones and muscles of a man's back felt to the touch. All week, pieces of men kept detaching themselves everywhere she looked, like fragments of gods at an archeology dig, and, like gods, they had power. For however backward Alida had been as a girl, she was now a woman who did not want to work, to be a man and play a man's part; she was a woman who wanted to have a man and be a woman for him.

And then God, or Santa Claus, or Whoever her mother was so keen on, put in Alida's way a man who, at their very first meeting, appeared to have been created especially for her.

This is what happened: One evening Gertrude mentioned the Davieses, whom, by chance, Alida had not yet met. They were a childless couple who wrote and illustrated children's books; they traveled a lot, but they had a small house in Flat Rock where they had been for several weeks; they were coming to the New Year's Eve party; and, more to Alida's immediate point, they had originally introduced Gertrude to their cousin Morgan Davies, the New York City dealer who sold Gertrude's tapestries. Alida had not yet found a present for her mother—nothing as useless, beautiful, and astonishing as the proof of love and sign of atonement Alida had been seeking—so that when her mother said, "Davies," Alida recalled the name of Morgan Davies and decided that he probably knew Gertrude's taste better than anyone, and determined to visit the McKinley Galleries the next morning.

The Galleries was a ground-floor shop on Madison Avenue. The moment Alida entered, she began to feel the peculiar happiness that objects had always brought her, for, ranged on shelves and in showcases, there was an immense, variegated assortment of objects of every description and all periods, some new, some old, of all values and provenances. Some were treasures, some mere curios, but as an assemblage it was—to Alida—a delight and a challenge. The gallery was an eye test, a taste test, a knowledge test. For example, scanning a shelf that held glass, Alida could distinguish a German seventeenth-century pokal set next to a large contemporary Scandinavian crystal vase beside a late-nineteenth-century English?—American, more likely—cut-glass bowl beside a very small, very plain pitcher—early American blown glass—and then along to the familiar nineteenth-century ruby-glass three-piece mantel garniture, and a few pieces of Tiffany.

As Alida's eyes roved, she began to feel rejuvenated. Her passion for objects went back to her teens, when her mother, absorbed in her garden, had sent Alida to Europe for some part of each summer vacation, once with a friend and her family, and after that with groups of girls led by teachers who chivied them through museums, cathedrals, castles, great houses, and monuments of every description. While the guide lectured about a painting on the wall, Alida's eyes would drift to a snuffbox on the table. She had no professional ambition, and college seemed another four years of communal female living, no more entertaining than boarding school and devoted to such pleasureless exercises as calculus, so she persuaded her mother to let her live in New York City with her aunt Jane and uncle Arthur and take courses in art history. Her mother needed little persuasion, because she herself had not gone to college and had not realized that the coming-out part of a coming-out year was less absorbing than it had been in her own girlhood.

But Alida was lonely in the city. She discovered, in the weeks between dances, that not going to college left her out of things. Her fellow art-history students were intelligent, but few were available as friends—most of the younger people worked part-time, and the married women's domestic lives claimed their out-of-class attention. Her cousins were away at school, and her uncle Arthur, though polite and beautifully mannered—he gave the impression of deferring even to maids—was a tyrant. Everyone did as he wished. He loved precision, and family dinners were intimidatingly formal. The conversation consisted of whatever Arthur chose, and no one dared speak if he did not. During her first year at her aunt and uncle's she had made the mistake of asking one of her teachers to dinner. He was a man famous in his field, an elderly German who at some point had said innocently that he supposed everybody was a socialist nowadays. No one had noticed that remark except Arthur, who from that moment retreated into silent sorrow. That was one of Arthur's techniques of tyranny: he did not express anger, he exuded unhappiness. Immediately after dinner he retired to the library—another resource was the creation of guilt, Arthur working while everybody else was having a good time—leaving stricken Jane and panicky Alida to make conversation with Professor Hoffheinz, who knew everything about North European art from the Middle Ages through the seventeenth century, and not much else. He, poor man, was too unsettled by the nervousness of his hostesses even to say, "Rembrandt," and left early.

The next day Alida learned from her aunt, who always transmitted her husband's feelings, what had gone wrong. Alida wanted to apologize to her uncle for her socialist teacher, but Jane stopped her. "It would only upset him again," she said. "He worries terribly about these things. I'm too stupid to care, but I remember the last time we were in England, we heard perfectly terrible things about the Labour government. You wouldn't believe them. They were taxing deer."

That was the last time Alida attempted to entertain at her aunt's house. In those years, objects provided Alida's companionship. Sometimes she thought her taste arose from resentment or, more accurately, fear of the domination that art exercised. Craft was less demanding, more pleasing, in a word, feminine, while art was masculine in its intent to overwhelm, to ravish; when it succeeded, for the most part, it was terrible, it hurt; she had an instinct to flee its effect. She was undoubtedly a coward to prefer a teapot to a Crucifixion, but she did. For almost three years her vision was fixed on netsukes and scrimshaw, her heart given to the purity of blanc de chine when it was not seduced by the sturdy forthrightness of Bennington ware, and no one, least of all herself, suspected that this was an odd life for a young woman. She did begin to feel she wanted not to live with Uncle Arthur and Aunt Jane, less because she had a dream of independence than because she had no real place to display the few treasures she had acquired. For the first time in her life she began to think about working, and realized that she would have to focus, to specialize—to find a class of objects or a period to be expert in. She could not decide. And then Betsy Weinstein, one of the older married women in her classes, who had taken a liking to Alida, asked her to a cocktail party where there were some people Betsy's husband knew from backing plays. Hugo was among them, and in a little more than two years Alida married him. She decorated the apartment her mother gave them. She took courses in cooking. She gave parties. She had Amelia. She moved to California and decorated another house and gave more parties.

She felt now, at this moment on the morning of the eighteenth of December, 1975, as if her married years had never been: she was again the teenager exhilarated by enamel, the twenty-year-old elated by pottery; she was, if not born again, fresh and new, exulting in the work of human hands. And a man in the shop, who had been watching her, stepped forward and said, "You are touching every-thing with your eyeballs."

He, rather than Josiah, could have been her brother. He looked like her, being dark and having strong, squared-off features. Alida was sometimes called pretty, but she knew that what pleased people about her face was what pleased her about Morgan Davies' face (she was sure the stranger was Morgan Davies): namely, that the features went together. Morgan Davies looked at her out of eyes that matched her own, and, though Alida could not be certain that she smiled at people the way she smiled in a mirror, she imagined that she smiled, at least sometimes, the way Mr. Davies smiled at her—broadly, frankly, openly. They were connected already, though he did not know it, and she announced immediately that she was Mrs. Waterman's daughter, and that she hoped he would help her choose a present for her mother.

"I might have guessed," he said. "You look like her. I'm Morgan Davies."

Morgan and Alida began to talk about the objects in the shop; they were describing themselves to each other. It was evident that Morgan loved objects with a taste as catholic as Alida's. He admitted that he loved them for themselves, while Guthrie, he said, liked to *place* them. That name sounded familiar, but she could not identify it, nor, enthralled by the conversation, did she attempt to.

"Would you like to see where we hang your mother's work?" Morgan asked.

Alida was happy to see anything Morgan cared to show. She followed him along a narrow Persian runner on the tiled floor to a staircase at the rear that took them up to a large room with windows on the side street. A young woman was sitting at a desk, typing, and Morgan asked her to take over the shop. She rose, nodded, smiled, and left. She was wearing tinted goggles, and her long blonde hair and bangs obscured her face; she might be plain as a post, but Alida envied her youth. Morgan, however, reserved his attention for Alida. "We show paintings here," he said, "or, anyhow, things in frames. There isn't much to see now. Everyone shopped early this Christmas, and your mother, of course, sold out months ago."

Among the miscellany on the walls there was a primitive painting of a kitten and a ball of yarn, and Alida remarked, "You know, that would be cloying if it weren't somehow monumental."

"Sheer awkwardness," Morgan replied. "I enjoy primitives, but I doubt they plan their effects."

Where had he come from? How could such a man exist? Who had made him? He was beyond Alida's fantasy, for Morgan was not only knowing but presentable, unlike most of the men whose taste in art she had admired. Most of the esthetes, scholars, artists, and craftsmen she had known were savage or overrefined or childish or self-centered or pedantic or gnomic or badly dressed. Morgan wore a fine dark suit, his speech and manner were charming, and he seemed to want to tell Alida all about his plans. Or, as it seemed, *their* plans, for the name "Guthrie" came up again. Guthrie, Morgan said, was out to conquer the world and he, Morgan, would have to tag along. They were going to run this floor as a real art gallery, with shows, and since Morgan had started out to be a painter, Guthrie had decided Morgan should find their artists. Did Alida have anyone to suggest?

Alida liked Morgan's assumption that she belonged to his world, the world of art, and mentioned David, whose name was familiar—as was usually the case with David—because of his father's textbooks and his sister's fame. Morgan made a note and resumed chatting. His tastes were so like Alida's that, though they touched on no personal matter, their conversation seemed to her intimacy itself. She could not believe he treated every customer with such time-consuming consideration, and, indeed, he hinted as much, exclaiming, "What a delightful interval in a dull day! Don't you find it wonderful to be understood?" He paused for a moment, and then said, "While you're here, I might as well show you the studio."

They went up another flight of stairs to a room identical in size to the gallery. It was chaos. One wall, covered with cork, served as a giant bulletin board, with scribbled memoranda, swatches of fabric, and renderings pinned all over it. A woman sat near the window, working at a drawing board, transforming a sketch into a rendering, and a young man was straightening a large and amazingly cluttered desk. "Hello, Johnny," Morgan said, and introduced the boy to Alida.

Johnny was extraordinarily handsome. His hair was blonder than that of the girl downstairs, and beautifully cut so that he looked like a medieval page, and his exquisite youthful slenderness was revealed by a navy blue jersey shirt and slacks. The girl doing the rendering, who did not look up, was drab—Fred's description of Barlow's graduates summed her up—but she, too, was young. Morgan asked Johnny when Guthrie would be in, the youngster told him, and then Morgan led Alida downstairs, and started confiding more plans. They owned the building, and the top-floor tenant was moving, so that they hoped, besides the art gallery, to add another floor, either showing furniture or expanding the studio—they had not decided which—but, at all events, they had some furniture in the basement he would like her to see. Then he stopped himself, and said, "But you're not giving your mother a sofa," and they walked on down.

As they crossed the gallery, the sunlight picked out some gray in Morgan's hair, which, proving him senior to her, reassured Alida; though he was surrounded by infants in their twenties, she might appear reasonably young to him. His unhurried attentiveness continued when they reached the shop, although there was another customer waiting. Hearing their voices, the stranger looked up and greeted them. It was Alida's aunt Jane. Alida was surprised. Aunt Jane was not: "We all wind up here sooner or later," she explained, or thought she explained.

Aunt Jane asked Morgan if he planned to be in Flat Rock for Christmas, and he replied no, but that he was coming for New Year's. Alida understood, with a joy near giddiness, that his cousins were bringing him to her mother's New Year's Eve party. Better yet, Morgan was not married, for he had said, "Harry and Robin are bringing me," not "us." Alida could not believe her luck, and stood, wordless and infatuated, forgetting even why she was in the shop until two more customers, bulky in voluminous minks, entered, and their flurry recalled her to everyday. "Kate took care of me," Jane told Morgan. "I was just waiting to say hello. What about you, Alida?"

"I haven't found anything yet," Alida said. "Or, rather, I've found too much. I want something for Mother."

Morgan reached into a drawer. "Take this," he said, and put into Alida's hand a small ivory ball intricately carved with stems and leaves that opened to display a delicately carved flower inside it.

Jane took charge before Alida could say a word. "It's perfect for my sister," she said to Morgan. "Isn't it, Alida?"

Jane, ordinarily the mildest of women, was high-handed, domineering, and interventionist in stores, for shopping was her vocation. Alida realized that Morgan, a miraculous man, had found a miraculous gift for her mother, but she also realized that the moment she bought it she would have to leave him. How to delay?

"It's Chinese, isn't it?" she asked.

"Early nineteenth century," Morgan said.

85

He was evidently reassuring her about price. She was transmitting the wrong message, and indeed she did not sound nearly as enthusiastic as she felt.

How do you flirt when you are out of practice? "You must have saved that for my mother," she said. "What would you have done with it if I hadn't come in?"

Now Morgan understood her. One might even suspect that *he* was flirting. "I would have found you sooner or later," he said.

But Jane, beloved and insensible Jane, went on commanding. She said to Alida, "You're coming to lunch with me," and, as Alida opened her handbag and took out her checkbook, said, "Don't bother, Alida. Morgan will put it on my account and you and I can settle later. And Morgan will wrap it up and mark it so we know it's yours, Alida, and send it to my house. We're driving up Christmas Eve, and this way we know it'll be on time."

Jane's disastrous efficiency was abbreviating Alida's moment. Kate, who was engaged with the minks, asked Morgan a question. He turned to her and her customers and Jane turned to the door. No farewells? Were they to part without another word? Alida reached into her bag and took out her pen and deliberately, and, as she thought, surreptitiously, dropped it. It fell soundlessly onto the Persian runner and rolled toward Morgan. "I've dropped my pen," she said.

One mink was helpful: "It's right there. You could pick it up."

Morgan bent down. "Very pretty," he said, as he returned it. She felt his fingers with a thrill. "Cartier of the twenties," he added, and winked at her.

Alida allowed her aunt to lead her out of the shop and down the avenue toward her club. Their progress was slow, partly because the streets were crowded, and partly because the crowds were largely composed of Jane's acquaintances. She stopped to greet, to chat, to introduce Alida, to look in windows and nod to shopkeepers, flicking her fillips of phrases and chirps of pleasure into Alida's love trance, like a hypnotist snapping his fingers. Alida, musing on the likenesses between herself and Morgan, wondered at the temperamental disparity between good-natured Aunt Jane and fearsome Uncle Arthur.

In the club dining room, Jane began prattling. There was a physical family resemblance between Jane and Gertrude, but Jane's personality was less imposing than her sister's, and Gertrude was soberer, rarely as overflowingly cheerful as Jane was.

Alida, pursuing her thoughts, asked, "Aunt Jane, what was Uncle Arthur like when he was young?"

Jane, though surprised at the question, was cheerful talking about her husband. Her pride in him was enormous. "Just the same. Brilliant and ambitious. He used to talk to me about what he wanted to do, and of course I couldn't understand any of it. You know how brainy he is. I thought he had plenty of money when he came courting—did you know that the lumber was more than the mills?—and could never see why he wanted more. But he used to say that that was just a local kind of money and he wanted international money."

"But you didn't marry him for money."

"Of course not. Somebody brought him to a small show I was riding in—they don't hold it anymore—and I won two events, and afterward, he just *looked* at me when we were introduced and that was it! I didn't know who he was, but I was in love! Later, he told me that, growing up in the West, he thought sport was crude—men in hunting cabins getting drunk—but that when he saw me ride he realized sport could be elegant."

The notion that her aunt Jane had fallen in love at first sight pleased Alida enormously, although her uncle's peculiar looks (he was immensely tall and almost frighteningly bony, and the pallor of his skin emphasized his resemblance to a skeleton) made her passion difficult to understand. Yet it was reassuring to have her aunt confirm the reality of the bolt of lightning. It was not all dreams, all poetry and song, this sudden convulsion of discovery and desire Alida felt for Morgan: still more comforting, Jane, prattling away about Arthur after thirty-five years or so, sounded like an adoring bride. Encouraged by her aunt's revelation, Alida shyly asked about Morgan. Jane could not tell her much. The Galleries, of course, were an established old firm, and the new partners had started there under the supervision of the late Mrs. McKinley. All Jane knew was that the young men, as she thought of them, were very talented, and that Morgan was exceptionally kind as well as charming, and was "asked everywhere." Then, pursuing a mission of her own, Aunt Jane said, "Alida, before we go"—they were by now sitting over empty coffee cups—"there is something Arthur has wanted me to tell you. It's lucky we ran into each other like this, I never see you alone anymore, it's really your fault, but I know, young people are always busy. Arthur has been after me to tell you that you must come to us if you need anything."

"Need anything?"

Alida merely echoed a phrase that made no sense to her. Aunt Jane went on, saying that *she* was sure Alida had everything she needed, but that Arthur worried about her—"your uncle loves you very much, you know"—and had asked Jane to make certain that Alida was all right. Jane put it very delicately, wrapped up in a veil of babble, but she told Alida that Arthur had always disapproved of Gertrude as a mother, had thought she had failed Alida in some way or to some degree; she was not unprotective but, as Alida grasped her aunt's meaning, insufficiently ambitious. "He feels everything so deeply, you know. He thought you should have had a ball of your own the year you came out. He told your mother to take you away when you started seeing that playwright, and he's so upset you are where you are now. We both love you, Alida, you're like a daughter. And it *is* a pity she let you marry him, but I tell Arthur not to worry so, you're well out of it. I suppose that's why we're so happy to-gether—he's so serious and I'm so happy-go-lucky."

Alida was uncomfortable at the thought that her aunt and uncle were discussing her affairs, since she felt she had not managed them very well, but she parted from her aunt affectionately on the street with kisses and smiles and general promises of future confidence and communication. It was only while Alida was making her way down to Grand Central Station that she was aware of her anger at the traditional pattern of deciding for daughters. Still, resentment would not linger on a day of romance, and Alida, thinking of Jane's endearingly unself-conscious confession of how she had been trans-fixed by the same arrow that had just struck Alida, forgave her aunt. Musing on Morgan, and looking forward to New Year's Eve—how could she wait?—Alida remembered that she had meant to speak to her mother about inviting the Palmieris. She thought Morgan and Fred would enjoy each other. But then, a second time, she forgot Fred because she and her mother quarreled.

Gertrude was stitching alone in the television-sitting room. Amelia was at a Christmas-pageant rehearsal at church; Father Peele would drive her home and stay to dinner. In Alida's and Amelia's absence, another invitation had come for the child, and Gertrude was concerned about overdoing, overtaxing, overtiring. She did not order Alida to make excuses for Amelia, but began enumerating her popular granddaughter's engagements. At first Alida was disturbed by an echo—Arthur and Jane discussing her—but then, as the list lengthened, she grew alarmed and broke in, "And we have to fix a date for our Christmas, too."

Gertrude did not understand. Alida explained that she wanted to have a Christmas before Christmas, when Amelia, Gertrude, and Alida would open all their presents together under the tree in Flat Rock. To her amazement, she heard her mother disapprove, arguing that there could be but one present-opening, one great jamboree of unwrapping, and that perforce it had to take place on Christmas morning at Hugo's hotel.

Alida, aghast, cried, "Hugo! Hugo! You're always taking Hugo's side!"

"Think of Amelia," her mother said. "Remember how important quantity, sheer quantity, is to a child. We don't know what Hugo will have for her, and if it isn't much, Amelia will feel—no matter what we do earlier—that her Christmas is a failure."

"But I wanted to *see* her open her presents," Alida said. "You know what she's like—so quiet and good. She always unwraps them carefully, and she doesn't whoop or holler, but her face begins to shine, and every Christmas, *every* Christmas, I've seen it. Remember the pink plush robe you sent her three years ago? She kept stroking it like a puppy and asking, 'Is it really for me?' And you know, that's all I really care about at Christmas—Amelia's face."

Gertrude let pass this indirect avowal of her daughter's irreligion. She understood Alida's unhappiness. They were part of a chain of mothers, responsive to unhappiness, if often only to unhappiness. Gertrude, feeling her daughter's feelings, rose (they had been facing each other across the old coffee table) and walked around to Alida and leaned down and raised her daughter's face by the chin, and kissed her brow, saying, "Oh my dear," and nothing else.

Alida started to cry. Of course her mother was right: competing Christmases would destroy each other. Gertrude, watching her daughter cry, said, "I shouldn't be so happy to have you with me for Christmas, but I am, though it's wrong." And then, as if she did not want Alida to dwell on regret and repentance for the Christmases they had spent apart, Mrs. Waterman reverted to management: "You know, I'm going to have James make a crate. He and his boy will take you in with all the presents."

The Flat Rock presents filled two crates. They were packed and stowed in the back of the station wagon when James and the boy came around early on the afternoon of the twenty-fourth. Alida and Amelia got in behind the men, and after a brief interchange in which James worried about traffic and Amelia complained that the snow that had fallen on the previous weekend had vanished, they drove toward New York City in silence. Amelia had been subdued all day. Even a Christmas card from May that arrived that morning with an affectionate message enclosing snapshots of May with the little boy she now cared for did not bring any marked response, although Amelia might have been happy May remembered her, homesick for the patch of California in the background, or jealous of the new child in May's life. Alida had been feeling slow and stupid. As she sat in the car, she began to feel odd. A trace of a headache, a pain in the sinuses, a twinge in the neck would come and go. She felt hot, then cold, but always, and most of all, sad. Alida often felt ill when she was unhappy, and when, as a child, she had said, "I'm sick," instead of "I can't understand fractions," she was not (whatever Andrew might maintain) being naughty. Today, however, she did not want to worry Amelia with the notion that her mother was ailing and miserable, and so Alida sat stiffly, staring at the roads unreeling between the heads of James and the boy. After a while, she began to imagine a scene in the future: grown Amelia, angry or resentful at her mother, would recall this drive and reproach her for showing so little feeling. She would say, "Mother, you never really cared for me. I remember the first time you took me to spend Christmas with Father, you were cool—cold." So Alida took Amelia's hand in her own; protected by gloves, their skins did not touch, but the *form* of hand-holding was there: at least, Alida hoped, it shows her that I love her.

Alida had planned that James and the boy would take Amelia and the crates up and bring down her prayer book and address book while she would remain in the car. Thus Alida could avoid meeting Hugo. But when they drew up before the hotel, the doormen had been alerted; bellboys and porters came running, while Amelia, amid this unexpected commotion, clung to her mother's hand. The crates were taken off to a service car on a hand truck; James and the boy asked for instructions; and Amelia looked up as if pleading. It would have been brutal to leave her. Since Alida could return to Flat Rock with her aunt and uncle, and James had a series of errands for his employer, Alida sent him away and went into the hotel with Amelia.

When Hugo opened his door, Alida realized that she had been imagining him a total villain instead of the partial villain he was. She had been halfway expecting him to cheat Amelia—for instance, to have no tree. But the first thing Alida saw, past Hugo, who was in his shirt-sleeves, was a big tree, not a hotel child's table tree and not a fake. Boxes of ornaments were piled on the floor around it and on the table, and Hugo had begun putting on the strings of lights. "You're just in time," he said to Amelia. "I was starting without you. We have to trim this whole tree all by ourselves."

Amelia darted into the sitting room of Hugo's suite, looked at the tree, and then looked out of the window. "It's funny," she said, "to have a tree way up in the air like this."

Amelia could not remember having lived in the New York City apartment, and Hugo and Alida, without thinking, began speaking at once:

"In New York . . ."

"We used to . . ."

Then they became aware that they were talking about their joint past and stopped in embarrassment. Alida said, "It's a grand tree, Hugo," and, after a moment, asked, "Do you have my prayer book? I mustn't forget it."

Hugo smiled the smile of an accomplice, or a husband, and made a remark about her mother's piety that Alida did not hear because she was feeling dizzy. She sat down. She felt better again, but sadder, and especially sad at Hugo's and Amelia's hotel Christmas. Hugo, however, was brisk and bright. These were his native characteristics, and they did not appear forced or assumed. Faces were worse than masks, Alida thought, for one expected flesh to reflect changes and betray sentiments, and it did not: whatever Hugo felt—about Christmas, about Amelia, about meeting Alida—he looked as he had always looked. He came back from the other room with the prayer book and address book and behaved as if Alida's sitting down meant that she intended to stay and as if her staying were perfectly natural, reasonable, ordinary. He asked if she wanted a drink. She wanted a glass of water, for her mouth was very dry, but she was loath to ask for it; she did not want to enter a social relationship. She wanted to leave, but the depression that had been affecting her all day made many things—just now it was getting up—difficult. Amelia was looking out of the high window, but there was an alertness in her posture that suggested to Alida that the child was attending closely to her parents' conversation. Alida warned herself to be careful and polite. There was a noise in the hall, a knock on the door: the crates were arriving.

"What's all this?" Hugo asked. Amelia and Alida began to tell him. He was irritated. "How do I get the damn things open?"

91

The porter had brought a screwdriver and hammer; he pried the boxes apart and took away the wood on the hand truck, leaving the presents in heaps on the floor. Alida could see that Hugo was angry and trying to restrain himself in his daughter's presence. He said, in a transparently false voice, "Santa Claus has been exceptionally busy this year."

Amelia turned into the room and corrected him. "Grandma says, and so does Father Peele, that we shouldn't fuss so much about Santa Claus when we're my age. We must think about the infant Jesus."

"Father Peele is the assistant at Mother's—our—church," Alida explained. "Amelia has been going to Sunday school, and she was an angel in the Christmas pag—" Alida stopped, because she sounded as if she were rendering an account of herself-as-mother to Hugo-as-father. But everything she said to Hugo sounded wrong. She felt strong enough to get up, and abruptly said, "I must go. When shall I call for Amelia?"

"Let me call you," Hugo said. "Probably Monday, but I'm not sure."

"Merry Christmas," Alida said. Amelia remained at the window. "Kiss me," Alida commanded.

Amelia came to her, kissed her, and said, "Merry Christmas," and then, in a level voice, perhaps to reassure herself, "You are going to have your Christmas with Grandma."

"Yes, I am," Alida answered, and then, defying everybody, including herself, added, "We will miss you very much."

And rushed out into the hall before Amelia could see her tears.

Alida sat back in her uncle's car as the chauffeur started for Flat Rock. Though the worst (seeing Hugo and leaving Amelia) was over, she felt even sadder and stranger than she had all day. The headache that had come and gone returned to stay; her shivering had stopped, but she felt sweaty. Aunt Jane settled in, repeated how pleased she was to have Alida's company on the drive, and asked after Amelia. Alida assured her that Hugo was doing his best.

"You saw him?"

"Only for a moment."

As her only reply, Aunt Jane took Alida's hand and held it exactly as Alida had held Amelia's. Uncle Arthur heard this interchange, shook his head, and went back to studying business documents. Alida stared at the same roads she had observed earlier; the darkening landscape illuminated by Christmas lights on trees and in doorways seemed infinitely melancholy, and she felt too depressed even to daydream about Morgan. In the winter twilight, they passed through a hamlet whose single shop, now closed, still shone forth a red neon sign that Alida, in her hazy gloom, wonderingly misread as "Joey." Puzzling her way to "Joy," she was aware that her uncle had switched off the dome light, put away his papers, and was saying firmly, "Now I will be merry." Very much unlike himself, he asked teasingly, "What did you get me for Christmas, Alida?"

Responding to his effort, Alida tried to be merry, too, and said, "Oh, Uncle Arthur, something hideous in plastic they told me was for uncles who have everything."

"Your voice sounds hoarse," he said.

Alida thought he was criticizing her; despite her aunt's assurances, it was hard to believe that this distant, difficult nabob cared for his niece. "Does it?" she asked.

And he asked, "Is your throat sore?"

"I don't know."

The car arrived at the house soon after, and Arthur would not let Alida leave for the cottage. While the chauffeur carried the bags in, her uncle took Alida's arm and steered her into her mother's front hall. Gertrude entered and, seeing Alida beneath the hall chandelier, asked, "Alida, what happened to you?"

Alida was perplexed: *two* grown-ups were picking on her. "Nothing," she said. And then, "I feel tired."

Aunt Jane said, "We think you're sick."

"Jenny," Gertrude said, speaking to the sometime chambermaid and children's nurse who was helping with the bags, "will you please bring my thermometer?" And, to Alida and Arthur and Jane, "Come in and sit for a moment."

They waited in the television room chatting disconnectedly about the drive until Jenny appeared; soon after the family learned that Alida's temperature was just above 103. Mrs. Waterman called the doctor, and with Jenny's help, put Alida to bed in her old room, her girlhood room. While they undressed her and put her into her mother's nightgown and wrapped her in her mother's robe, Alida remembered how, years ago, when this room had been hers, she and Josiah and her mother used to trim the tree together on the twenty-fourth. They would dine early so that the cook and the maids could go to church. The three Watermans went to midnight mass together. It seemed to Alida, as she lay on the bed, swathed and

93

swaddled in blankets and quilts, that the best Christmases she ever knew were those in the years when she and Josiah came home from school. They had such fun, just the three of them, on Christmas Eve! Josiah loved to be the man of the house on the stepladder (this year James had trimmed the tree), and her brother's youthful masculinity showed itself in jokes that helped them all express their love for each other. This good memory of childhood, of home, recollected in her childhood home, was made more vivid by Jenny's suggesting to Mrs. Waterman that she bring "Miss Alida" a cup of tea.

Dr. Dunne, who came in then, approved and suggested soup as well. Jenny left, and Dr. Dunne examined Alida and concluded that she had an infection, probably viral: bed, aspirin, liquids. Should her temperature rise, Alida was to have an alcohol rub and they were to phone his service; he would call in after church. But he stressed that there was nothing to worry about. Gertrude plumped up pillows, Jenny brought soup, and Alida began to drowse. She opened her eyes and told her mother she felt fine, and closed them. When she opened them again, Arthur and Jane and her mother were coming in. The three stood around her bed. She smiled at them as she gathered they had been having an argument.

"So you see," Uncle Arthur was saying, "it is all settled. Church doesn't mean as much to me as it does to you and Jane," he said, "but it's more than that. I don't suppose anybody except Jane knows how much I love Alida."

"I've always suspected you had a soft spot for her," Gertrude said, "but it's only a bad cold or a flu."

"Naturally. You wouldn't leave her if it were anything serious. So I'll just stay in her room till you return."

Alida heard his avowal through a fog of fever. Uncle Arthur loved her, just as Aunt Jane (who also loved her) had said. In her own bed in her own room, Alida was the beloved daughter in whom everyone was pleased. This Christmas the child they adored was herself.

New Year's Eve

To whatever degree illness resembles infancy, to that degree getting better is growing up. On Christmas Day, when Alida's fever was still high, she dozed between servings of soup and tea, sessions of pillow-patting and sheet-smoothing, no more aware than a newborn of who came or went. Her cousins, Arthur's and Jane's sons, and their wives and children stood at her bedroom door and wished her Merry Christmas. She wished back and then fell asleep and forgot that they had been there, until the following day, when her mother, telling her about Christmas, mentioned that they had missed her at dinner. Alida was more alert on the twenty-sixth, and began to look at her surroundings, her girlhood room, unchanged from the time she had chosen its fabric and wallpaper, her youthful taste calling for a riot of ruffles and tiny buds. The alterations were all ad hoc: her bedside table was decorated with an aspirin bottle, a tissue box, cough medicine, and a water pitcher; a vaporizer steamed away on a stand, and toward the end of the day, her mother directed the placing of a television set at the foot of her bed. Observing her mother and her aunt Jane together, Alida saw that life itself had cast Gertrude, the firstborn daughter of late-married parents, as the serious one, and that Jane had also been given *her* role—the baby sister. They sat in the room after Gertrude's rearrangements, and Jane's prattle, designed to entertain Alida, diverted Gertrude, who laughed at her sister's recollections of the mild merriments and mischiefs of their girlhood. They were both good women. Jane's goodness was cheerfulness and generosity; Gertrude's, care and thoughtful management. And Uncle Arthur: Alida, having lost her

95

fear of him, appreciated that his personality, so difficult for others, might equally be difficult for himself. But he, too, was good. He sat with Alida in the evening and offered her, as tokens of his affection, news items from the world of finance, still atwitter from the terrorist invasion of OPEC headquarters.

On the morning of the twenty-seventh, Alida, yet another step toward recovery, began to feel, as do growing children, the limits of what one's family, however good or loving, can do. Children want to be popular beyond birthday-party invitations their mothers arrange; they want to be chosen for sides and teams when no adult is around, to be told secrets, and then, by adolescence if not earlier, they want a stranger's love.

Morgan Davies. He settled into Alida's head, took command of her heart, and ruled her imagination. When Dr. Dunne came, late on the morning of the twenty-seventh, Alida wanted to know if she were well enough to go to her mother's New Year's Eve party. The doctor, a stout, dapper, handsome, self-important young man, heard her, gagged her with a thermometer, and, like many another oracle, began answering a question she had not asked. While he took her pulse, he embarked on a lecture about flus and viruses with the possessive knowingness of a man who keeps a snake farm. He used "we," as in "We have found streptococci that blah-blah-blah," presenting himself not merely as the family physician, but as the spokesman for universal, historical medical science. His point, as far as Alida could relate it to herself, was that the bugs now varied from year to year, and that extreme caution was required, for this year's, deceptively brief, had proved, in many cases, relapsing. But how the man strung it out! Alida was certain that Morgan, say, when buying from someone who needed to sell, would never dawdle and parade his power like Dr. Dunne: delay, producing uncertainty, is a coward's cruelty. The doctor scrutinized the thermometer with particular deliberation, as if uncertain whether he dared share its report, before he announced, "A little low. That's only to be expected."

He proceeded to a prolonged nose, throat, and chest examination, and told Alida to keep to her bed until he looked in again on Monday the twenty-ninth. Mrs. Waterman asked if the doctor had time for a cup of "the Ceylon tea you like so much," and the doctor had; while she rang for Jenny and gave her the order, he telephoned his office and received a message that made him shake his head and comment irritably on someone's folly. Alida realized that, like Father

96

Peele, who always came when invited, and frequently dropped in when he was not, Dr. Dunne enjoyed stopping at her mother's house. Their professions undoubtedly engaged them with more hysterical women than they wished, and Mrs. Waterman's decorum might be an attraction. Father Peele, who visited late that afternoon to ask after Alida, was given sherry and taken up to the invalid. He looked earnest and mystical; his face was large and flat and lumpy, like batter not thoroughly mixed; he seemed youthful in his sincerity and old in his intensity. (Mrs. Waterman had told Alida he was forty-five.) He brought unction to everything: he was genuinely concerned about Alida's health and genuinely interested in Mrs. Waterman's doings in the greenhouse. His sweetness made Alida feel guilty and hypocritical, which was all the more exasperating because he did not know what he was doing. He did not guess that while he, so to speak, adored the relic, she admired the reliquary. As, she guessed, did Morgan.

Morgan, Morgan, Morgan. Books, television, puzzles—these seemed sham or tiresome compared to Alida's dreams of Morgan. Like all lovers, she resembled an unsuccessful actor who fantasizes his own play or film. In her drama she saw herself and Morgan dating, making love, and marrying. She was scriptwriter, set decorator, and director as well as leading lady; she composed their costumes, invented rendezvous and dialogue, and took them to bed in his apartment, where she would have gone in response to an invitation to examine or admire some possession, some object, he particularly cherished. Her mind roved this way—one moment, she remembered Fred Palmieri and regretted that it was now so close to New Year's Eve that an invitation to her mother's party would be an insult—and that way: she promised herself that as soon as she could, in the New Year, she would bring Fred to Morgan's store—she was sure they would enjoy each other. And this way again: if her aunt and uncle had disapproved of her marriage to the playwright Hugo, what would they think, what would they say, of her marriage to the dealer Morgan?

On the morning of the twenty-ninth, Alida was momentarily distracted from the superreality of her visions of Morgan by Jenny, who was tidying the room. Did brisk Jenny, Jenny with the short, straight, iron gray hair, have any daydreams? Any secrets? Any loves? Jenny was perfection. She left nothing to be desired, ordered, or criticized, whether she was maiding, nursemaiding, or nursing. "Well done, thou good and faithful servant." Was that the sum of

Jenny's life? Just then, Father Peele came in. He sat in a chair beside Alida's bed, and before a word was spoken, Jenny pulled the blind to keep the sun out of his eyes. He was so grateful for her service, and she was so delighted at his thanks, that Alida was awed at their simplicities. They belonged to another species of humankind with no need for dissimulation or even reticence: their innocence could never be embarrassed.

Dr. Dunne came in the afternoon. He proceeded with his meticulous routine: questions (how did she feel? eat? sleep?) and temperature- and pulse-taking, and placing his icy stethoscope all around her bare torso while ordering her to cough and breathe until he had satisfied his notion of the medical proprieties. Then, almost reluctantly, he agreed to let her attend her mother's party. He would be there as a guest and would keep an eye on her. In the meantime, she should begin to move around but avoid fatigue. Alida did not listen past the good news; she cried, "Mother, I must have M. Jean here!"

Dr. Dunne was doubtful. Mrs. Waterman overcame his doubts on Alida's plea: "I can't go to a party looking like this!"

The doctor then gave Jenny precise, long-winded instructions about the care of a wet head before she went for tea. Gertrude filled in the wait by negotiating on the telephone for the services of the hairdresser. The next moment Amelia bounced into the room, retrieved from New York, Alida learned, by James, the gardener. Amelia entered like a child whirlwind, spinning with the twin excitements of having been away and of having come home: "Oh, Mother, James is bringing up the presents Daddy gave me . . ."

She stumbled over the electric cord to the vaporizer, which was jarred but did not fall off its stand. She started to apologize. Dr. Dunne interposed his authority, not unkindly, but slightly pompously: "Amelia, dear, your mother has been a very sick young woman. Perhaps you should stay away from her just now. She shouldn't be fussed at, especially if she's to go to your grandmother's party."

"I *am* sorry," Amelia said.

"Don't worry, darling," Alida answered.

"Aunt Jane must be lonely," Gertrude hinted.

Amelia left the room, taking with her the story of her Christmas with Hugo. Its evident triumph disappointed Alida, who cheered herself with tea and thoughts of Morgan.

On the morning of the thirty-first, Jenny washed Alida's hair in expectation of M. Jean. Jenny was forceful and rhythmic; as her fingers scrubbed Alida's scalp, Alida leaned back, her head in the washbasin, staring at the ceiling and beginning to take in the imminence of Morgan in the flesh. What luck that New Year's Eve was a night of gaiety and abandon, when partygoers were expected to kiss! Morgan's kiss. What would his lips feel like? Wet or dry? Hard or soft? His tongue? Even a single kiss, a kiss in public, could speak unmistakably. But why only one? They would find the first shy meeting of their lips inadequate. They would kiss again. They would open their mouths. He would embrace her. She remembered Morgan's smile as she thought of his kiss to come. While Jenny rubbed and rinsed and rubbed and rinsed, and while, later, M. Jean, dryer in hand, combed and brushed and shaped, Alida picked up their meter, their tempo, and, to the best of their labors, sang an inner tune: kisses, kisses, kisses. Ah, Morgan's kisses.

Jenny helped Alida dress for the evening in a splendid caftan, more gold than anything else, that Arthur and Jane had given her for Christmas. When they were finished, Jenny said, "Oh, Miss Alida, how beautiful you look!" with admiration so wholehearted that Alida was momentarily saddened: Jenny's romance was all vicarious; her triumph was arraying the young mistress. They were adjusting the hang of the skirt after the robe was belted when Amelia came in, dressed (by whom, Alida did not know) in a lace-collared brown velvet dress Aunt Jane had given her, carrying a doll in a matching dress, also Jane's gift. Amelia and her doll were to be guests at the party for as long as they could stay awake. Mother and daughter went downstairs hand in hand, in this house both children.

Mrs. Waterman had spoken of the party in diminutives—"small" and "little," by which she meant no more than twenty to dinner and about fifty or sixty, "just from the neighborhood," afterward. Gertrude's language had left Alida and Amelia unprepared for the splendor they found downstairs. Since they had come to Flat Rock, they had visited on the margins of the ground floor, sitting in the television room and dining in the breakfast parlor, and they were surprised at the spectacle of the larger reception rooms all alight, and fires going in the fireplaces. Alida had forgotten how handsome her mother's rooms were, how well proportioned, how intelligently underfurnished with (mostly) old pieces and inherited pictures on the paneled walls. The television room and the library might be called cozy: but the other rooms were grand. And Gertrude's flowers! To the traditional reds and whites of the winter holiday season, she had added blues—iris and statice, hyacinth and cineraria, and several other flowers Alida could not identify—as a reminder that they were ushering in the Bicentennial Year. Elated Alida felt like one of those happy heroines who, in novels, are said to float rather than walk. She found her mother and aunt waiting in a sitting room off the entrance hall. Her aunt was wearing gray and diamonds and her mother black and pearls; they shared a look of rightness that made Alida proud. As for her uncle, Alida found that his physical strangeness—his immense height and his frailty (he looked like a carpenter's rule unfolding when he rose to welcome her)—had acquired a kind of rightness, too, and she impulsively kissed his cheek, saying, "How handsome you look!"

"Nonsense, Alida," he said, and blushed.

She insisted, "Yes, really," and they all went on talking fond, reassuring nothings until they heard a car outside bringing the first of the dinner guests.

They were Morgan Davies, a man Alida assumed was his cousin Harry, and, to her horror, *two* women. One would be Harry's wife, Robin. Was the other someone special to Morgan, someone he had chosen for his date on New Year's Eve? What a desolating possibility! Morgan's square dark looks were more attractive than Alida remembered. His graceful movements recalled his deftness with delicate objects, and his dinner jacket became him so! His cousin Harry, who resembled him, was a Davies in another key: fine-drawn and worried-looking. But the women: who or which? One had short, straight hair with bangs; her makeup was a dab of powder and a touch of lipstick, her dress a floor-length dirndl skirt of dark-green jersey topped by a handsome embroidered peasant blouse. With this unimposing outfit she wore a little string of pearls and a modest engagement-wedding-ring set. The other woman's hands were so bejeweled that it was impossible to decide which, if any, of her rings was maritally significant. Her dress was a beautifully cut white jersey draped over a gymnast's figure. Her hair was bleached white, her eyes were rimmed and shadowed with black, her lips painted blood red. Her earrings and necklaces and bracelets, as profuse as her rings, competed with the drama of her face. Alida stared at the gems—there was a theme, not mere profusion: diamonds and emeralds and sapphires—and the lady looked steadily across the room at Alida while muttering greetings to Mrs. Waterman. Could Morgan be the lover of the Mad Millionairess?

After how-do-you-do's that seemed to last an eternity, Morgan moved decisively toward Alida and her aunt Jane, and Alida's anxiety was partially dispelled when introduction led the showy un-known into autobiography. The plain woman was Robin Davies; the flashing one objected to Morgan's identification, "Mary Smith."

"Lady Mary," she corrected. Her voice was hoarse, her manner domineering, and her accent Chicago with an overlay of cosmopoli-tan, perhaps affected. "None of the bastards I married gave me anything but trouble, but Smith fell off his horse and broke his neck." Aunt Jane, a onetime rider, was touched, and tried to say something condoling. Lady Mary paid her no attention. "He left me that half-assed title. It sounds like something when you're intro-duced, at least compared to the year I came out, when I was 'Mary Powers, pork.' " She suddenly demanded of Alida, "How do you like living with your mother?" and before Alida could think of a re-sponse, returned to autobiography: "I went home after my annul-ment, but Mother didn't want me. She had plans of her own."

As the group stood, Morgan was closest to Alida, and Lady Mary attached herself to him, or to them. Immovable as lead, she talked to Alida about herself with asides to Morgan—"you remember that crooked little faggot, Morgan, who used to steal rugs." Many of her stories cast her as the shrewd foiler of assaults, sometimes upon her person or possessions, more frequently upon her capital, by men of all professions and nationalities. Alida could not guess whether she was trying to show off or to shock, but all she achieved was the slaughter of any conversation but her own. Alida was rescued by her uncle Arthur, who came up and attracted Lady Mary's attention with a—to Lady Mary—electrifying statement: "So you're a Powers. You people did very well selling out. I never knew a family to do better."

"Balls," said Lady Mary. "What are you, anyhow, a lawyer?"

Uncle Arthur identified himself. It was the second time they had been introduced but the first time Lady Mary realized who he was. He took her arm with a grip that combined father, banker, and bouncer; she, one huge fortune recognizing another, did not resist. After she left, Robin and Harry came up, and Robin said, "She *can* be charming."

Harry qualified: "When she wants to, which isn't often."

And Morgan explained, "She's a thirty-second cousin of Robin's. They're trying to make me marry her."

"No, no, no, Morgan"—Robin was earnest—"don't joke about it. The poor girl has had no luck at all with men."

"Rich girl, you mean," Morgan said.

"Rich girl, then," Robin answered. "But she and her mother were awfully good to me when I was their poor relation, and even though"—Robin was apologizing to Alida—"she likes pretending to be difficult, she's really very good at heart. She's suffered terribly, I think, and she's very lonely. She's always been married for money." The room was filling up, and Robin, looking around, said, "Excuse me, there are the Wards, I must speak to the Wards about . . . Come, Harry, we were going to get them those books . . ."

"What is her title?" Alida asked Morgan.

"I've no idea," he said. "She's Robin's family, not mine. But I'm pretty sure she has it wrong. I think she would have to be 'Lady John,' or 'Lady William,' the way Jenny Jerome was 'Lady Randolph.' " But he did not go on about Lady Whatever; he turned the conversation to themselves: "I hope your mother liked her present."

"She adored it," Alida said, "though I didn't know that for a day or so—I was down with flu on Christmas."

Morgan sympathized with her, told her that she looked smashing, flu or no flu, and added that he looked forward to seeing her in the shop soon, because he had had some wonderful luck buying right after Christmas, and early in January would be unpacking his treasures. Morgan was following Alida's fantasy script—the invitation to the Galleries that preceded the invitation to his house.

"I'd love to see what you've found," Alida said. "You've no idea how much I enjoyed my visit."

She attempted to convey how happy she had been at the Galleries and to impart some of her own intense feeling for objects. She was not flirting or feigning, and Morgan enjoyed the sincerity of her pleasure. His response led her further. She found herself tentatively describing her half-formed plans: the conceivable course at Barlow, the possible move to the city, the ultimate search for a job. She also quoted Fred's cautions about Barlow.

"Don't disdain schools," Morgan said. "Even dull ones. Especially dull ones. All anyone can teach is routine, shortcuts, and tricks of the trade, but everybody needs them. Unschooled geniuses have a hard time. *Schooled* geniuses are another story. Like Guthrie. He appreciates what I buy—he's got an eye!—but he hates to think of decorating as scavenging. He's doing more and more modern work, designing everything—insides, furniture, fabrics. . . . He even did a charity job, a day-care center . . ."

"Oh my goodness!"

At last Alida recognized Morgan's Guthrie as Andrew's Janet's

Guthrie. She mentioned the connection. Morgan remarked that Guthrie's achievement was astonishing—"He knows how to get the most out of very sparse line and plain material"—and then asked how well Alida knew Janet.

"Hardly at all."

"She's very worthy," Morgan told her. "Without a trace of style, though. She probably hasn't a clue to what Guthrie brought off."

"I understood she was brilliant."

"Perhaps, but not in any way that I can recognize."

They looked around the room at the groups forming and ebbing: Amelia had taken the Harry Davieses away from the Wards, and Morgan, following Alida's glance, exclaimed, "How lucky you are to have such a lovely girl!"

At that moment dinner was announced, and the party filed into the dining room, where Mrs. Waterman's handsomely set table reminded Alida of festivals in years gone by, and where maternal instinct had seated her between Morgan and Harry Davies. Lady Mary was across the table, some way down. Her harsh voice blended with those of the men, all a little loud, perhaps the effect of cocktails. They were talking investments, a subject that interested them keenly and elicited a variety of opinions.

Alida had other interests: the white-wine glasses were immemorial in the family, and she thought how all art moved from hand to hand over years—indeed over centuries—oblivious of the identity or the fates of their temporary possessors. "Objects *are* faithless, aren't they?" she said to Morgan, "and provenances are really just lists of rejections and desertions, like Henry VIII and his wives. But once they're made, that can't be helped. No matter what Guthrie thinks, his furniture will be somebody's loot some day."

"To be sure," Morgan said, "but artists always learn too late that the little bits of themselves they put into the world don't belong to them anymore. Or to anyone. For me, as an impecunious trader, I've all too often had to say, 'Farewell, thou art too dear for my possessing,' and now I've come to feel that not owning—the impossibility of owning—is an attraction, because it's truth. Reality. Nothing—nobody—is ever owned; everything is borrowed. Just as you said—separability is the fact; life is all desertions, all divorces. One's safer keeping one's distance."

Morgan's philosophy was more than Alida could assimilate between courses. She would have liked to think about it, since she was by nature a keeper, a treasurer of her treasures, but then, as she

103

looked along the table, alerted for the third or fourth time by Lady Mary's voice (she seemed to have firm and controversial ideas about money management, and was arguing with Jack Ward, who did something in Wall Street), Alida thought that again, as every time her own eye drifted in that direction, Lady Mary was either looking toward Morgan or had just looked away. Morgan's joke about marrying Lady Mary evidently had this much foundation: Lady Mary was interested in him. Only love and its bastard brat, jealousy, could account for that pattern of covert watching. Alida did not want to provoke Lady Mary, and knew it was time to turn, anyhow. From Harry Davies she learned that his and Morgan's grandfather had claimed a connection with the American painter Arthur Davies, though as far as Harry knew, the painter never heard of any of them, but Harry did believe there was an artistic streak in the family that had made Harry an illustrator and Morgan a painter before he became a connoisseur and dealer. "And we've another cousin who became an art director. Very good, too. But he turned into a noisy advertising type. We don't see him. Morgan's always teasing that Robin and I collect lame ducks, including himself, but the truth is that when Robin and I finally settled down—we lived here, there, abroad mostly, for years—I was very cautious about renewing old ties. Unfortunately, Robin's kindhearted, and I have to put up with it. But good nature is really acceptance of failure, isn't it? Great people are never 'nice.' "

The courses sped. Alida talked to Morgan about pottery and to Harry about watercolor technique, and then it was time to leave the table. Having long lacked a host, Mrs. Waterman did not plan protracted English separations of the sexes after dinner. She sent the men ahead to a drawing room to wait for coffee, and led the women away to fix their makeup. There was a powder room off the coatroom just inside the front door, but this evening, with ten women on hand, Gertrude took them to the bedrooms and baths upstairs. Alida watched the ladies raise their long skirts to climb the staircase, and then, in profile, like a frieze, follow each other along the upstairs hall. She saw them, not as individuals, but as a decorative combination of shapes and colors, and she was taken off guard when she herself reached the top of the stairs to find Lady Mary, who had evidently been waiting for her, and who, with aggressive familiarity, put her arm through Alida's as they walked to Alida's room. Lady Mary waved Alida ahead, and, as Alida sat at the dressing table, began ferociously warning: "Watch out for Morgan," she said. "You mustn't let him take you in. He's a professional seducer. You think he likes you, and then you find you're stuck with a piece of junk he calls a 'collectible.' "

Alida could not help smiling at Lady Mary's appraisal of Morgan's stock, while thinking that her contempt was not the language of love. Love usually casts a halo around all a man's doings: today Alida would not have objected if someone called Hugo a hack; this time last year, she had believed him a considerable creative talent. Lady Mary's forcefulness was puzzling; it was also disturbing; it seemed to have in it the seeds of a quarrel or, worse, of an approach to intimacy. "I don't think he expects me to be much of a customer," Alida said, "though I do like his things more than you do. Actually, we've probably sold him more than we've bought."

Lady Mary's eyes, clear bits of alert gray amid the puddles of black paint, opened wide to express concern. She associated sales with distress. "Oh my dear, have you come to that? I had no idea. So many, many people I've known have had to be brave. Like poor little Robin. It's horrible, and horrible to be too proud. False pride, I think. You must let me help you."

Lady Mary moved toward Alida as if about to touch her. Alida drew back and started explaining about her mother's needlepoint. "I was afraid you were breaking up," Lady Mary said. She went on reflectively, her voice suddenly surprisingly soft, her speech melancholy and sensitive: "So much depends on who women marry. Robin's mother, poor thing! What mistakes she made! That side of the family, those girls . . . What lives they all had! There was plenty there once, but their husbands got it away. So Robin had to take a scruffy secretarial course. . . . And she always had to be good and polite and thankful. . . . Men shouldn't be so important." She sighed and shrugged: "But here she is now, happy enough in her scruffy suburb."

When Alida had freshened her makeup and hair and sprayed on perfume, she rose, and Lady Mary took her place. Before she began making up, she repeated, with intensity and anger: "Believe me about Morgan. Don't waste your time on him."

As Lady Mary worked at her face, Alida saw that she was not as old as her cosmetics made her look. She might still be in her thirties. What a life *she* must have had! Such oddity! Such rudeness! Such incoherence! Nothing she said made any sense. Though she appeared fully occupied in relacquering her features, Alida felt the woman wanted to say more; she gave an impression of pause, not conclusion. Something else—confidence, probe, attack, advice—impended. Whatever it was, Alida did not want to hear it. The sounds of cars stopping and the front door opening provided an excuse to escape from this troublesome or troubled stranger. Alleging her need to help welcome after-dinner company, Alida left Lady Mary and went downstairs.

Like migratory birds, guests come in flocks. Alida found herself in the midst of coveys alighting on the doorstep, wriggling out of their coats with Jenny's aid, preening in the cloakroom, and chirping greetings. Alida recognized men and women she had glimpsed coming to or going from her mother's committee lunches or teas, and they in turn recognized Mrs. Waterman's daughter, and nodded or smiled or said polite hellos before they became absorbed in their own small talk as they left the front hall to drift toward the sounds of the party. Alida lingered irresolutely in the hall, smiling at no one in particular, signaling a welcome to all the friendly strangers. She had invited three couples to the party, parents of Amelia's playmates who had offered Alida hospitality. The Wards had come to dinner; the Warrens and the Richardsons had promised to come afterward. Alida wondered whether to wait to greet them; wondered whether they had come while she was upstairs with Lady Mary; and wondered if her impersonal smile had become set and if she looked odd. All she really wanted to do was to find Morgan. She moved tentatively with the guests, who were using the first room off the hall as a kind of passage. A waitress hired for the evening appeared at its far door with a tray of champagne glasses, and Alida's little cohort stepped eagerly ahead, leaving behind only an elderly gentleman studying an enormous bouquet arranged in a white vase on a Federal console. His sham attention suggested he was lonely and shy; the convex period mirror above the console magnified as it reflected Alida, the man, and the bouquet in a visual pun: wallflowers. Alida was about to introduce herself when the Richardsons and the Warrens entered on the next wave of guests, and Mrs. Warren walked up to Alida's solitary gentleman and said, "Why, Pop, what are you doing alone? You should have come out to dinner with us." To Alida, she said, "Alida, do you know my father?" and turned to greet another friend, someone else unknown to Alida, asking expectantly, "I wonder who else is here."

Taking her father's arm, she led her group out of the room. As they left, Tom Richardson mumbled something to his wife in which Alida thought she made out the words "very grand," in no friendly tone, while his wife's higher and sharper voice carried a reply that might be reconstructed as "They're supposed to be very rich."

Alida wondered what Ethel Richardson would say when she saw Lady Mary's jewelry. Alida began to walk through the rooms, looking for Morgan. Colorful and dressy, coiffed and barbered and glinting with jewels, her mother's guests were as persuasive as a crew of film extras recruited to make believe they were enjoying themselves. Yet it seemed to Alida that she was overhearing a lot of conversation about money. Was this Flat Rock? Not as she remembered it from her girlhood. While the maids moved through the crowds, assiduously serving champagne, the guests seemed to be talking of falling stocks and tax shelters, and it also seemed to Alida that they were looking around with an element of estimating curiosity at Mrs. Waterman's hospitality. Mrs. Waterman had summoned the countryside like a medieval chatelaine, but among her loyal allies she had brought forth many calculating tourists. Alida was hurt on her mother's behalf as she sensed some malice alloyed with the ostensible sterling of friendship. Just inside the library, a young man was trying to impress old Mr. Jones, Eliot's father, and another old man. (Eliot and his wife, to Alida's relief, had sent regrets; they were visiting her family.) The men were talking about the uncertain national economy as it affected businesses they knew.

"Divco has been destroyed, you know," said the older man.

The young man objected: "It was terribly managed all along."

Both men turned to Mr. Jones, who announced that management was a lost art and prudence a forgotten virtue. "Nobody nowadays knows what 'overextended' means," he said, and went on to repeat negative advice he had given someone, perhaps a decade earlier, who had been thinking of joining or buying into Divco (whatever it was), to such effect that neither of his companions could reply.

But the younger man, who still wanted to make an effect on old Mr. Jones, went on to talk about members of the administration he had seen on a recent visit to Washington. "They don't get credit for their ability," he said. "They're really taking hold."

Mr. Jones shook his head. "I can't believe it. I don't believe it. There's been nobody since Taft. The worst thing that ever happened to this country," he concluded, "was the 1952 Republican convention."

A regret so bizarre cured Alida of her own. She nodded to the morose trio and left the library in search of Morgan, passing a group around Robin, who had succeeded in reconstructing a Country

107

Day parents' meeting. Tom Richardson, a pink-faced blond—pig-faced, thought Alida—caught sight of her and called out to ask if there was music. She told him that there was a phonograph in the music room as well as a piano, but that she had no idea what records her mother had.

"Some funny old ones," put in Harry Davies. "Dwight Fiske, for heaven's sake!"

"Nothing to dance to?"

Tom Richardson sounded aggrieved. Alida grasped that that was what happened when you called out your vassals: they sneered at your mead while they drank it and complained that your jester wasn't funny.

She turned away with a mental shrug. A corridor parallel to the front hall separated the rooms through which she passed from the grandest of her mother's salons. One end of this corridor opened onto the terrace, and beside it there was a little nook, a semi-cloakroom, where Alida found Amelia sitting in a corner of a loveseat struggling to keep awake. She was too sleepy even to speak, and only shook her head "no" when Alida asked if she wanted to go to bed. Just then someone tapped Alida's shoulder. It was Morgan, holding out a string of worry beads.

"I got this for Amelia," he said. "I usually bring them for children. I left them in my coat. Here—"

He gave them to Amelia, whose hand clutched them reflexively. Morgan and Alida, secluded from the party, stood over the dozing child and began talking about everything and nothing. She mentioned Mr. Jones's regretting Senator Taft.

"Some of my best customers regret Senator Taft," Morgan said. "For some people 1952 is as bad a memory as 1929. Worse. Nineteen fifty-two meant the New Deal was here to stay."

Alida asked him to explain, and he did this concisely, adding that he had no interest in politics but that when he began to deal, he found he had to take an interest in whatever interested his customers. "It was hard at first. I thought that beautiful things sold themselves. But there are very few disinterested esthetes like you and me, Alida, and so I learned selling, which is an art in itself, a performing art."

At Morgan's recognition of their likeness, Alida thought, "He loves me. He knows I love him," and waited for a more personal, more intimate turn to their talk. He began questioning her about herself—her training, her taste, her work for her California art boards—as if he wanted to learn everything about her. He seemed to find her intellectually engrossing, while she found him physically enticing. She was ready to cease conversation; she wanted to touch Morgan, to stroke his cheek, to feel—to hold—his hand. Rapt as she was, she could hear the noise of the party growing; she turned her head and looked down the hall and saw a stirring: maids were combing the rooms for guests without champagne, and she could hear television sets being turned on in the television room and the library. With joy she recognized the approach of the moment when the year ended, the borderline whose celebration was the high point and purpose of the party. Morgan picked up Amelia, and carried her into the television room, where they joined guests waiting to watch the ball descend from the top of the tower in Times Square. Lady Mary, who had been talking to Dr. Dunne, pushed her way to Alida's side, and said, "I hear you've been very sick."

Morgan put down his glass and held Amelia high over the adults' heads so she could see the screen, and the child, coming awake, began to count, and then cried out, "There it goes!"

The company began to cry out, too, calling, "Happy New Year!" Many of the older people linked hands to sing "Auld Lang Syne," while the rest began kissing, some of them—Alida could see Tom Richardson and Maria Ward at it—embracing with an enthusiasm that belonged in bedrooms rather than drawing rooms. Morgan put Amelia down and gave her a peck on the cheek. He turned to Alida and touched her forehead gently with his lips. They were soft and dry, like chamois, and their grazing, skimming application to her skin suggested Morgan was caressing crystal or old ivory.

Alida stared at him. Was that all? Was that the kiss she had been awaiting since morning? Was it deliberate insult? Calculated rejection? Did he see her as an object, not a person? A collector's item? While she stood there, trying to assess—and, more important, conceal—her disappointment, Harry Davies, grinning, came up, and drunkenly, insinuatingly, said, "For a girl raised on your mother's naughty records, you're not doing very well, Alida."

He maneuvered to try to kiss her, and stepped on her dress. She heard a slight tearing sound, and exclaimed, "Oh, my dress!"

She pushed Harry away with difficulty and bent to examine her hem.

Harry giggled. "That's a stiff dress you're wearing, Alida. You're a *hard* woman. Isn't she, Morgan?"

Morgan said mildly, "It's an expensive dress, Harry."

Observant Lady Mary closed the brief scene by ordering Alida to put Amelia to bed. "Late hours are bad for children. They spoiled me."

"Oh Mary," Harry said, "I wouldn't call you spoiled, just a bit high."

Alida put Amelia to sleep and sat in the dark listening to her regular breathing. At some moment in the struggle to undress the limp child, Alida's infatuation for Morgan had evaporated. The product of loneliness, despair, and hope, it had left but one trace: a small speck of shame that Lady Mary had evidently guessed Alida's foolishness. Had Morgan? Or did he believe that Alida dedicated her senses only to art? He *was* a puzzle. Alida recalled her aunt's characterization—"very kind"—and Lady Mary's—"a professional seducer." Did he confuse the arts of seduction and of salesmanship? Lady Mary had suggested that Morgan was always and only selling, but his attentions felt different to Alida from those paid to prospective customers, and there were others at the party to whom attentiveness would have been profitable. Alida sat in the dark, desperately trying to assign a motive, a reasonable reason, for Morgan's behavior—had she, unawares, led him on by *her* attentiveness?—shirking the party her mother was giving for her. Supper was doubtless occupying the company, but Alida was not hungry. Presently the sound of music drifted up the stairs; Tom Richardson must have found some records. Recollecting his embrace of Maria Ward, Alida realized that she had invited some rackety people to her mother's house, and decided it was her duty to reappear and offer help, if necessary, in repressing some of the wilder guests.

She checked her makeup again. Freshened in looks, if not in spirit, she went downstairs. When she reached the front hall, Alida noticed that Jenny had left the coatroom unattended, and that there was no one to help guests leaving or, possibly, still arriving. Alida tried the front door—it was open, so that a latecomer could make his way in—but surely someone ought to be on duty to receive and direct future guests: there was Father Peele, who might have come by this time or might not; he was taking a New Year's Eve service jointly sponsored by several local churches. She heard the lavatory flush and waited for Jenny to emerge and take up her station, but it was Lady Mary who came out, saying, in her subdued voice, "I'm so sorry, Alida, I can't tell you. Those Davieses are impossible! Poor Robin! She could have done better for herself. Harry is dull, but he's not so bad except when

110

he's drunk. I hope he didn't ruin your dress. No, I see he didn't. That was luck. But Morgan is a terrible fraud. He can't stop flirting, and he can't do anything. What I mean is, *nothing*. Not with boys, not with girls, and probably not with animals. He just likes to bring people to their knees."

Lady Mary's little speech was the reverse side of the Davieses' earlier apologies for her. Both times, Alida thought, everyone was right. Behind these verbal amends, she assumed, lay family relationships an outsider would never disentangle: the weekend might have originated with Harry and Robin trading off one cousin for another; the Davies' house party might involve all sorts of emotions—hurt feelings, snobberies, affections—going back to four separate childhoods. No matter. Alida did not want to discuss anything with Lady Mary, and remarked vaguely that there was something appealing and hence forgivable about the "artistic temperament." Then she added, "You go on in. I'll keep the door till Jenny comes back."

But Lady Mary answered, "I'd rather stay with you. Though we've scarcely spoken this evening, I feel very close to you. I felt that way from the moment I saw you. And I know how you feel after Morgan's given you the treatment. Women are so vulnerable. They fall for pansies and are jumped at by drunks and they always think it's their own fault. The trouble is, we were taught to depend on men, and we can't."

Alida started a gesture with her arm to wave away the idea that she had been disturbed by any of the evening's events. As she began to speak her denial, Lady Mary caught up Alida's moving hand and kissed it. She followed up this unexpected demonstration by stepping into Alida, kissing her face, blowing in her ear, sighing and crooning. She stopped for breath and asked, "Haven't you been thinking we need each other?"

Amid her rage and revulsion, Alida recognized Lady Mary's perfume, a scent that was everything Lady Mary was not: tender, alluring, delicate. Alida realized she was expected to reply and, had she spoken frankly, would have used some of the inelegancies with which Lady Mary speckled her conversation, or something equally coarse of her own, such as "Drop dead, you dyke." Instead, improvising, and pulling together her muscles as she prepared to fall, she said, "I think I am going to faint."

She took a breath and let herself go, backward, backward, backward, backward . . . She felt herself supported; arms were around her—masculine arms, by the coat sleeve. Father Peele.

111

"I think I am fainting," Alida said, hoping that Father Peele had not been standing long in the hall.

"Of course; you have not been well," he said solicitously. "Perhaps you had better sit down."

He helped her onto a little gilt chair and asked Lady Mary to bring Alida a glass of water, but Lady Mary merely walked out and, reverting to her earlier role, the noisy shocker, commented, "Jeezus H. Christ, a priest. That's all we need."

Jenny, returning that moment, got Alida's water, hung up Father Peele's coat, and before Alida could ask where she had been, volunteered, "Oh Miss Alida, there was such a mess in the music room. We all had to clean it up."

"Dear me," Father Peele said. "Let me see what I can do. You stay here and rest," he said to Alida, who thought she might as well maintain the camouflage of invalidism.

But a burst of voices coming toward her made the coatroom an unsafe refuge. She rose and followed Father Peele, while the Richardsons passed, too absorbed in their quarrel to notice her. When she got to the music room, her mother told her that Tom Richardson and Harry Davies had been throwing glasses at each other, but her tone was polite deprecation: men would be boys, on New Year's Eve at least. Alida, looking around, saw no traces of disorder except a few wet spots on the rug. Her mother reduced the incident's importance as she described it to Father Peele; he accepted that diminution, and told Mrs. Waterman that Alida had not been feeling well. Gertrude asked if she wanted to go to bed. Alida said she was feeling better. The party was dwindling; maids were clearing coffee cups and plates; some guests were thanking Mrs. Waterman as they left, while the group that remained seated in the music room was sharing a conversation, some over coffee cups, some over brandy, some over champagne. It had come out that Mrs. Warren's father (Alida had never got his name) was an expert on bulbs, and that had started Uncle Arthur discussing the seventeenth-century Dutch tulip mania as an instance of financial boom and bust. Morgan was contributing bits of expertise about glass and porcelain flowers. Lady Mary was listening, or perhaps thinking of something else, and Harry, too, was subdued. Presently Mrs. Warren drew him and Robin into the conversation by mentioning a book they had written for children beginning to garden; and then the talk moved on to styles of gardening, and from there to travel, and Lady Mary, who had traveled widely, offered a few sensible remarks. It was just the kind of conversation Alida expected at her mother's—intelligent, impersonal, and cultivated, engaging everybody but offending no one, yet it had nothing whatever to do with these people's real selves. Or did it? Was the reality of Morgan and Lady Mary and Harry only their deviances or misbehavior? Or was it their intelligence and their gifts? Worrying the ancient philosophical question—which is appearance, which reality?—Alida found that her anger had dissolved like her love for Morgan. She forgave everyone, even herself, and joined the conversation with a comment on the pineapple motif. The guests all knew that the pineapple was a symbol of hospitality, but none knew how that had come to be. Father Peele began to talk about those old-time punches for which pineapples had been in demand—years ago he had been offered one, made from an eighteenth-century recipe, and it was much more potent than a martini.

So they were off again, chatting about the strength of the potations ingested by the Founding Fathers, and wondering how those august men, who had floated our independence on oceans of alcohol, would regard the comparative sobriety of twentieth-century America. The Warrens went, taking her father. The Davies party now rose, and Morgan said, "Alida, phone before you come in January, because I want you to meet Guthrie. I'm going to need an assistant, and I'd like it to be you. It'd only be a beginning job, but who knows? So start that course you told me about, and then we'll see how we can work it all out."

Lady Mary looked on, amazed, as Morgan explained to Mrs. Waterman: "I've been thinking I want Alida to work for us, and the more I think about it, the better the idea looks. It's been lurking in my mind all evening, and it doesn't make sense for me to keep it to myself. Alida's a qualified, sensitive person, and I'm sure she can learn."

Alida agreed in a not very coherent or fluent babble in which her surprise and joy were evident.

After they left, Father Peele stayed, at Mrs. Waterman's request, to tell them how his service had gone, but instead he asked Alida about Morgan's invitation. The little group was very proud of her, although even before she was able to explain how unexpected the offer was, her uncle Arthur had begun huffing at the notion of his niece as a student or semiapprentice. He was well on his way to setting her up in her own business, and Father Peele was regretting she might leave Flat Rock before Alida was able to tell them that she had no idea what, exactly, Morgan meant. She could tell them about the course at Barlow's, she could tell them about how she and Morgan had chatted and how he had questioned her after dinner; but the nature of the job was something to explore in the new year that had just started. The men checked their watches. Father Peele rose, complimenting Mrs. Waterman on the champagne, a compliment that gave double pleasure, since it had been Arthur's choice.

Alida remained alone by the fire after the others had gone. She wanted to sum up, recollect, and resolve. It was impossible not to contrast last New Year's Eve, when she was almost smug in her security as Hugo's wife, with this one, in which she threaded her lonely way through a farce, looking for love, finding it in the wrong person, and ending up with the offer of a job that sounded very much the sort of work Andrew had recommended. She told herself that last year's security had been false, and that though she had failed and sulked and wasted time since she had left Hugo, she was starting 1976 with friends, with opportunities, and yet, and yet . . .

She sighed. She could not help wishing for love, romantic love. All the world loved love, loved love stories. Hugo—damn Hugo, would she never forget him?—was very firm on that—no plot without love. No adventure, no quest, no battle without the reward of love. But that was art, or craft—deception. It told people what they wanted to hear. Many lives, real lives, were not love stories, just lives lived along. Lived in work. Lived alone. Lived vicariously. Jenny. Alida?

Fatigue emptied her mind, and the flames in the fireplace drew her eyes. She stared entranced, watching the last blaze before extinction. The fire gasped, and its death rattle filled the room, so silent was the night, silent across miles of bald fields and bare trees. From time to time Alida heard a car, and once she heard brakes screaming through the silence, and, later, it seemed to her that she heard a crash.

She was asleep and did not hear the crash in which, still later, on the bend in the road she feared for herself, Fred Palmieri was killed or killed himself. He was driving alone. The Old Bridge *Chronicle*, which reported the story on January second, did not explain why. Could she, Alida, have saved him? If she had remembered to ask her mother to invite him and his wife, might Fred have been alive? The question tormented her. There was no one to reassure her, no one to tell her that she was tough—tougher than she knew—but that Fred had been one of those people for whom loneliness, sooner or later, one way or another, proves fatal.

II

THE ADULTERESS

Intersession

Partly because of the extreme cold and Gertrude's distrust of the cottage's insulation, partly because Amelia's and Alida's belongings had been moved during Alida's brief illness, and partly because Mrs. Waterman was about to leave on her two-month cruise, Alida and Amelia were settled at the big house. On Saturday morning, January 3, an icy rain attacked Flat Rock, and the water's drumming gave Alida a sense of the solidity of her mother's roof. In the early afternoon the mail truck sloshed belatedly up the road, bringing the Barlow catalogue. Alida settled down to study it, and eventually found that the Department of Applied Arts offered "Interior Decoration One" in the fall term, and that it was a prerequisite for "Interior Decoration Two," given in the spring. However, a footnote informed readers, previous experience or studies, if supported by documentary evidence, such as a transcript of record, might permit advanced placement. On the frozen Monday, beneath low gray skies that, like mourners on the brink of tears, struggled to hold back rain or snow, Alida, unable to understand the meaning of Fred Palmieri's death, and still guilt-ridden about the forgotten invitation, drove over to Barlow to seek the individual she must persuade that the art-history courses she had taken were equivalent to "Interior Decoration One."

When people die who are older than ourselves, we can usually accept their deaths—older people always seem old enough to die— but the death of an age-mate is an attack by destiny upon oneself, and raises questions, not only about the dead person's life, but about one's own. As Alida drove over the network of blacktop lanes

117

between her mother's house and the highway, she remembered Fred's confession of thwarted ambition, and felt the irony that, her own ambition to live out her days as Hugo's wife having been thwarted, her new ambition was Fred's frustration: art debased, art debauched, art sacrificed to the market. She was uneasy about Barlow, not because Fred had said it was mediocre, but because the catalogue revealed that it was unlike any school she had ever attended. There were black faces in the photographs and a United Nations galaxy of ethnic names on the faculty; and then there were Barlow's cheapness, its manifest efforts to include rather than exclude, and its emphasis on training for specific, limited jobs. Marriage to Hugo and her own forays into the world of art had introduced Alida to social universes whose existence she had not suspected in her girlhood, but the new kinds of people she had met had this in common: no matter where they had come from, they had already arrived. Barlow might be akin to their beginnings, but it was alien to her. Taking a course meant traveling farther from her mother's than the mere mileage, and Alida's shyness would have deterred her if she had not felt pledged to Fred, to Andrew, and to Morgan.

After some twenty miles on the highway, the route demanded Alida's concentration. Barlow was located in the renewed downtown of a small industrial city she had never visited. Cars approached its shining hub over a spaghetti of elevated roads high above unrenewed neighborhoods; each tangled intersection bore a sign directing motorists to exits, now on the left, now on the right. The signs, however, were only locally explicit—"Harvest Street First Left," or "Market Street ¼ Mile"—so that no one but a driver who already knew where he was could find his way. In the streaming traffic, Alida glimpsed "Mill Road," her exit, came down the ramp, and found herself on a one-way street, bisected by the highway, lined with sagging wooden tenements and deserted red-brick factory buildings. Poverty and time had leached almost every bit of color from the scene: the unpainted houses were gray, and grime had dulled the brick to a sad brown, the color of dried blood. Alida drove past small groceries and bars, bargain dry-goods shops and auto-body repair shops, vacant lots, and occasional storefront agencies dispensing religion or charity. There were few people out in the cold. Mill Road was supposed to run into Hale Plaza, but Alida went up and over a hill, and there was no plaza in sight. She pulled over to the curb in front of an empty lot, and consulted the map; she had made a mistake and gotten off at Mill Road East instead of Mill

118

Road West. She turned right, hoping to make her way back to the highway, and became trapped, circling the same forlorn area on a slow merry-go-round of one-way streets and stop signs. What was the use of good design? What could poor Fred have hoped from urban scale? Alida stopped at an intersection at right angles to wrong-way Mill Road, and saw, in the distance, the concrete-and-glass towers of renewed downtown. *They* were the product of somebody's notion of urban scale, and they were an embittering mirage from Mill Road East.

Thereafter everything Alida encountered argued that, whatever good design could not do, bad design was a plague. Downtown had become a checkerboard of majestic squares and plazas whose heroic spaces allowed winter winds to rampage. Alida's long walk from the visitors' parking lot to Barlow's administrative offices was an arctic struggle. She entered a small gray-stone Gothic building (attached to, and dwarfed by, a glass tower), perhaps an older academic institution engulfed by Barlow. Its interior had been chopped up here, extended there, and theoretically unified by an overlay of "modern"—fluorescent lights and signs in large sans-serif type. The last led Alida to the admissions office, a long room with high ogival windows, suggesting a chapel. The room was divided by a chest-high plastic barrier, desks on one side, visitors on the other. A young woman with dark hair, a large nose and bosom, and a name badge reading "Miss Kurtz" rose from her desk, came to the counter, and heard Alida out. Miss Kurtz seemed torn between exerting her bureaucratic power to impede and obeying the catalogue's mandate to assist. Her speech was nasal and local. She seized on the fact that Alida asked to enroll in only one course, and suggested that extension school—nighttime courses—would be more appropriate. Alida, thinking of her mother's imminent departure for her cruise and the long winter evenings when Amelia would miss her, exclaimed, "But I couldn't leave my child!"

The existence of a child softened Miss Kurtz, and together they filled out Alida's application. Miss Kurtz told her that her transcript should be addressed "Attention Dean Talbot"—he was the assistant dean of admissions who would consider her records and decide if she could take the course and whether tests or an interview would be required. Alida asked how long the process would take.

"You're a little late," Miss Kurtz said, "and they're a little behind because the computers went down for a few days during Christmas. But they'll get to you in time if you can get your transcript up fast."

119

Alida went home and telephoned her old school. They promised to have her papers in the mail no later than the next morning. There was a message to telephone Betsy Weinstein in New York, but Alida put off calling because she had to dress for dinner; she was to ignore several messages from Betsy in the days ahead. Mrs. Waterman was leaving the next day, flying to rendezvous with the ship that had sailed on the last day of the old year on a botanical study cruise of Central America and the Caribbean coast of South America, and she had asked Father Peele to dinner. The adults sat in the library while Amelia watched *Galaxy Guards* (Hugo had told Amelia, and Amelia had told Alida that it would run through June, was scheduled for reruns, and so far had three foreign sales) and Alida described her pilgrimage to Barlow. Her mother, hearing a note of anxiety, asked if Alida was fearful for her physical safety.

"It's nothing like that at all," Alida said. "It's only the contrast with Flat Rock, the realization that places like that exist . . ."

"Do you mean Barlow?"

"No, Barlow is strange, but . . . No, I mean where I was lost."

"But surely you've seen poor neighborhoods before."

"Yes, but I never looked at them. Now it seems more horrible than I ever thought. And when I'm doing what everybody thinks I ought to do—taking a course in interior decoration—it doesn't seem important, somehow."

Gertrude said, "I didn't realize until late in my life how limited my experience had been. I've imposed the same limitations on you. We used to think we had to protect, to shield, our daughters. But I hope I haven't shielded you to the point that you'd give up a course you probably want to take because you drove through a slum or because the school building is ugly."

Father Peele said quietly, "I think Alida wants a promise, a guarantee that whatever she does will be important, will count."

"I suppose that's true," Alida said, remembering her adolescent yearnings for certainty about her future.

"But we can't *will* ourselves to be important. Everybody wants to matter," said Father Peele, "but the best you can do, as I often tell my confirmation classes, is the best you can do with the gifts you've been given. If your gifts are for the visual, enjoy them."

The next day Alida telephoned the McKinley Galleries. Morgan said, "Alida, I'm so glad you called; I was going to call you. I've told Guthrie all about you. Can you come in next Tuesday, the thirteenth, around four-thirty?"

120

Business was winding down when she arrived, and Kate, who was tidying the shop, looked up in annoyance at what she took to be a late customer. In a moment she asked, "Mrs. Kelly?" At Alida's nod, she said, "Go right up to the studio."

Morgan heard Alida on the staircase, greeted her at the door, and introduced her to Guthrie, who rose from his seat behind the large desk to offer a perfunctory handshake. He might be five years older than Morgan. Guthrie's face was white and sharp, the features marked and pinched in a way that Alida mentally catalogued as poor and rural, and he was going bald. Unlike Morgan, who dressed in formal city clothes, Guthrie wore a gray wool turtleneck sweater under a brown corduroy Norfolk jacket whose pockets were crammed. He was tall, and his hands were large—their bony knuckles and square fingers suggested strength rather than Morgan's delicacy, as did his brief grasp of Alida's hand. His voice, in the middle range, was edged, and the placement of the r's and flattening of some vowels suggested the small-town Middle West. Alida recognized that she was meeting exactly whom she had imagined last week: Guthrie was the successful alumnus of a Barlow. Morgan drew up the draftsman's stool and perched on it, and motioned Alida to an office chair beside Guthrie's desk. Guthrie said, abruptly, "I hear you're consigning all my work to auction." Alida had no idea what he was talking about, and looked surprised. " 'Guthrie's furniture will be somebody's loot some day,' " he quoted.

Alida met his challenge: "Hepplewhite," she said. "Charles Rennie Mackintosh."

Guthrie twitched his lips in a semismile, and said, "All right, Morgan, tell her about the warehouse."

"Just like that?" Morgan asked. "Shouldn't we explain?"

"Make it short," Guthrie said. "I don't want to be here all night."

"It's a long story, Alida," Morgan began. "It goes back to when we were working for Mrs. McKinley and began buying her out. She had a terrible old age, half-retired, going out of style—not artistically (she could do anything she wanted) but socially (she had some mythical concept of the 'right people' and began insulting customers). And she also began to drink. She lived too long for her impatient heirs. They were more impatient after she died. I suppose we got a bargain—this building and its contents and the goodwill, which wasn't much; we kept the name because, for all her faults, she was a great woman and a major artist and she gave us both our chances. But we had to borrow. And work! We're just about paid off now, and Guthrie and I have plans for expansion. I've mentioned them to you."

"Morgan, get on with it," Guthrie interjected.

"I am," Morgan said, without resentment. He turned back to Alida. "It seems we also bought a small warehouse downtown. It was nowhere then. Now it's SoHo. You see what I mean about a bargain. We just bought it as part of the business with everything in it. Her heirs were in such a hurry that they just trusted the old inventory, which we think was marked way down. The place is stuffed with I don't know what—furniture, lamps, tapestries. We always meant to go and check it over, but we never had time. Now our accountant and our lawyer want us to do something about the warehouse. I don't need to tell you how everything's gone up. And being redis-covered—late nineteenth century, that I was taught to despise. We need somebody to look over Mrs. McKinley's goodies and tell us what they are. Will you do it?"

Both men looked at Alida earnestly, expectantly. Their half-doubting eagerness—they leaned forward as if they were asking her a favor instead of offering her a job—perplexed Alida. "I'm not an appraiser," she said.

"No, of course you're not," Morgan answered. "You're somebody harder to find, a connoisseur. I'm an appraiser—at least in certain fields, and I know what I get paid for my expertise. We don't even know whether the stuff is worth an appraiser." He paused and sighed. "Alcoholics, you know. They become unreliable. In her latter days, Ruby—Mrs. McKinley—was sometimes a little shifty, some-times a little grandiose. She might have left us three stories of utter junk. Or a mixture." Morgan's tone became caressing in its efforts at persuasion. "I think you could make a very rough estimate—don't think about prices, not for a moment, of what's good, what's genu-ine, of what things are—that'd give us something to go on. Just what your eye sees. And I also think you're honest enough to come back and tell us when something has you stumped."

Alida needed not even a moment to realize that Morgan had placed her perfectly. She remembered his asking, "Isn't it wonderful to be understood?" and marveled how he understood her, for if there was anything at all, one single thing, she had been able to do from her teens on, it was to recognize what an object was. "You're right," Alida said. "I could do that, and I think I'd like it."

"There's a physical side," Morgan said. "You'll need a man—maybe two on some days—to open packing crates and move things. We can take care of that. How much time can you give?"

Guthrie said, "It's a dirty job, physically. You won't be able to dress like that"—Alida was wearing the tweed-and-fur costume she had worn to lunch with Andrew in December—"and you won't have time to shop the trendy boutiques."

Alida understood Guthrie's warning and its implied assessment of herself. She decided to ignore it, and answered Morgan's question instead. "If I get into the course—you know, at Barlow; we've talked about it—I'll have classes on Tuesday and Thursday afternoons up in Connecticut. Would Monday and Wednesday be enough for you?"

"*All day* Monday and Wednesday?" Guthrie asked.

"If you like."

"Two days at the beginning," Morgan agreed, "and perhaps more when school's out. When can you start?"

"Amelia—my daughter—" she explained to Guthrie, "has inter-session the last week in January and the first week of February, and my mother's away. After Amelia goes back to school, I'll be free."

Guthrie began searching his big, messy desk; Morgan got up and went to a smaller one, in the rear of the room, on which he found a calendar. "Monday, February nine," he said. "Could you be in by ten? I'll be here—I'm going to California but I'll be back then, and we can discuss that day's work. We'll need your Social Security number, but nothing else. We're hiring you as a consultant, on a daily-fee basis. That means you can put in more days or fewer, and we won't take out withholding." Alida realized that they were taking no great risks with her; Morgan read her mind, and said, almost pleadingly, "For a start."

Guthrie's restlessness took over. "Settle the details," he said, "settle the details. We think a hundred dollars is fair."

"A day," Morgan added.

Guthrie stood up and held out his hand, saying, "Pleased to have met you."

"Guthrie," Morgan asked, "aren't you coming out with us for a drink? To celebrate?"

"Ah, the social side," Guthrie said, with a grimace. "All right. I'll practice my company manners on Mrs. Kelly."

"Alida," said Alida.

They crossed the street to a hotel bar, a discreet, dim, spacious room with a vaguely horsy motif. As they sat in their booth waiting to order, Guthrie asked, "Morgan, why do we always come here? It's the ungainliest bar on Madison Avenue."

"It's near," Morgan said, "and the night is cold."

It was: the freeze that opened 1976 was setting records, and

Alida, who had forgotten how brutal northeastern winters could be, was surprised by her own discomfort and by Amelia's enthusiasm: the child was ice-skating and yearning for snow.

Guthrie said, "Though we're celebrating, you know you're on trial, Alida. I respect Morgan's judgment, but we must all be prepared for it not working out."

Alida knew he was right, but she also knew how she felt about the task they had given her, and replied, with calm confidence, "I can do the warehouse for you. And I'm looking forward to it."

Her reply seemed to relieve both men. Morgan said, "Guthrie's a little harsh, but he's a genius. He's a great appreciator, too. If you're half the girl—no, woman—I think you are, he'll know that, he'll appreciate it. And since we aren't organized like the army or General Motors, you may wind up doing anything. Or everything."

Guthrie interrupted. "Morgan's a genius," he said. "Ever since I've been in design, the style has been for what I think of as incongruities. Nobody wants purity. There are no period rooms except in museums, where they mostly get it all wrong. And *everybody* insists on intruding on the modern. I call on Morgan for these punctuations or interruptions or whatever, and he always knows what I mean, what I need, he always knows the scale and the placement—it doesn't matter if it's a sofa or a screen. Besides, his dealing is very profitable and he's wonderful with people."

The partners' mutual admiration was attractive. As they went on talking, accepting Alida as a member of the family, it was evident that Morgan, who idolized Guthrie, did not mind smoothing the ruffles he created or serving as his interpreter. Her employers reminded Alida of a married couple—specifically, of her aunt Jane and uncle Arthur—and the resemblance was very comforting.

Although Alida had not done as Andrew Cameron had asked and made up a financial schedule to send to Hugo, she went into the city to lunch as they had agreed, on Thursday, January fifteenth. Andrew had a light tan, and when they were settled at their lunch-club table, told her in reply to her question that the family had skied in Colorado, but an odd look—pain, fatigue—and a quick change of subject gave Alida an impression that his vacation had displeased him. "What have you been doing?" he asked.

Alida, for a change, had something to report—Barlow and the job. "They really must have thought it was a terrible job," she said. "Morgan was rather apologetic and Guthrie was, well, taunting, and they seemed so relieved when I took it. They couldn't know what fun it'll be for me."

Andrew smiled. "I'm very pleased with you, Alida. Impressed. Proud. Frankly, I wasn't sure you could pull yourself together so fast. When I saw you in December, you seemed to me very angry and depressed—almost sullen, and I . . ."

"That's the trouble with nowadays!" Alida exclaimed. "Nobody's allowed to be sad. I *was* angry, I *was* depressed, and if I'd done what was in my heart, I think I would have cried, just cried, for months on end. I didn't let myself cry. Why isn't crying allowed anymore? Is heartbreak illegal?"

They were both surprised at Alida's outburst. Something about Andrew freed her—she spoke to him as if he were a father or a brother. He said quietly, "You may be right. But we're living now, and—yes, you *are* right—heartbreak is illegal. Mourning's forbidden. Tragedy is not allowed. Nowadays the law is, keep smiling and keep moving. Have you made up your mind about moving back to the city?"

"I wish I were surer about everything," Alida said. "Suppose I finish the warehouse job and they let me go. I'd be in the city without . . ."

"You'll find something else."

"And I'm scared."

"Of what?"

"I don't know. Loneliness."

"Do you find your mother's company suffices?"

Alida looked out of the dining-room windows, which were wrapped in clouds of fog. Within all was clatter and chatter—men and women, under bright electric light, filled with themselves and their purposes—outside all was veiled and indecipherable, like the future. "It's the unknown. That's all," Alida said at last.

Andrew was sympathetic. "Fear of the dark. Of dying," he said. "We think of those often enough. But we don't always appreciate that we also fear living. Something new, no matter how exciting or enticing, is frightening. Changes, even happy changes, are scary. Not that moving to the city is necessarily happy. It might make you happier, but I don't know, and you don't either. But you should decide soon."

"Why?"

"For several reasons. The main one is consideration. Your mother: give her time to get used to the idea. Then, your tenants—what's their name?"

"Gibson."

"The Gibsons. They've rented your apartment for years. You

should let them know if you don't intend to renew their lease. And schools. Janet tells me there isn't the pressure on city day schools that there used to be, but you make it harder for everybody by turning up late. And Flat Rock Country Day will probably be sending you next year's contract in March."

"Then March is my deadline."

"Let's be honest. You *have* no deadline. You can spend the next twenty-five years in Flat Rock making up your mind if you like it well enough to stay there. But once you decide, you must act with consideration for other people, and keep in mind how the machinery works."

"I think," Alida said, "that you want me to go home today and write the Gibsons about my apartment, and tell Miss Blossom that Amelia will not be coming back—"

"And you really should speak to Janet about day schools," Andrew interrupted. "Yes. I think it's better to do, to take our lives in our hands—taking chances, maybe, being frightened, maybe, and getting over being frightened. That's how I feel. It's not legal advice. It's a value judgment." Andrew stopped for a moment, and then added, "My values. What are yours?"

"Probably the same, but it's not how I've lived."

"You married—that's a chance you took. You had a child. You left your husband."

"Those were passionate decisions, not deciding decisions."

Andrew pointed out that all decisions were products of feeling as well as judgment, and asked, "Now, then, what do I write your husband about money?"

Alida had to confess that she was unprepared.

"Then I will make an estimate," Andrew said, firmly and conclusively, "on the assumption that you will return to your apartment in the fall, hire a nursemaid and a housekeeper, send Amelia to school, have her take lessons—dancing, music, riding, whatever— see a doctor and dentist, and so on." They stood up, and Andrew said, "I congratulate you on your decisions."

"You're a bully," Alida said, thinking to herself how attractive he was, and how reassuring she found it to have someone attractive as well as intelligent to make up her mind for her.

Andrew telephoned Alida a week later, when he got an answer from Hugo's lawyer. Andrew read the letter on the telephone. It said that Mr. Kelly did not wish to make a permanent financial arrangement at present because he was uncertain what his future earnings

126

would be, but that he was prepared to pay all his daughter's expenses from the previous June. Would Mrs. Kelly or Mr. Cameron forward a list? However, Mr. Kelly hoped that he could see and speak to Mrs. Kelly before they went any further in negotiation. He expected to come to New York at the end of June, but would fly in sooner if Mrs. Kelly wished.

"It's as I thought," Andrew said. "He doesn't want a divorce. He's probably gotten rid of that girl already." Alida could hear Andrew clear his throat before he asked, "How do you feel about a possible reconciliation?"

Alida visualized her return, resuming the status of wife in exchange for an independence she did not really want, but the thought of trying to reassemble what Hugo had splintered filled her with nausea. She said quickly, "I wouldn't consider it."

"All right, then." Andrew was back to business. "Then send me a list of your out-of-pocket expenses for Amelia, and I'll tell his lawyer you'll see Hugo in June—if you will—and you can tell him no yourself, face-to-face, and then we'll really get down to work on the settlement."

"Except one thing," Alida said. "I still don't want Hugo's money. Not even for Amelia. I feel sick, revolted . . ."

"We've had this out before. You should talk to your uncle. Or your mother."

"I don't want to talk to my uncle, and my mother isn't here. Besides, I suspect she wants me to go back to Hugo."

Andrew said, "I don't understand you. You're making a lot of trouble, and you must know you're wrong."

"Maybe."

"You let me send that letter asking for money. What made you change your mind?"

"I don't know. It seems to make sense when I'm with you, and then it seems different when I'm by myself."

"You're terribly alone," Andrew said. "Without a father. Your mother away. Your brother in California. Are you sure you don't want to consult your uncle?"

"I'm sure."

"Then let me persuade you. Permanently, I hope. You make up that list and bring it in, and we won't send it unless I can change your mind."

Alida agreed. Her rational self admitted Hugo's responsibility, and she did not know why she resisted it. Andrew asked her to hang

127

on while he checked his schedule, and came back to regret that he seemed to be in a crush. Would she be willing to come all the way into the city in this terrible weather today just for the time he could give her over a drink?

Alida made the date and hung up. The phone rang again, and a woman whose name Alida did not get asked if she would see Dr. Talbot the following afternoon. The phone rang again, and Mrs. Southern, Mr. Cameron's secretary, apologized for a change in schedule, and asked if Mrs. Kelly could meet Mr. Cameron for a very early dinner. She named the hour—6:45—and the restaurant.

That left Alida a morsel of afternoon to reflect on her reasons for rejecting Hugo's money. As far as principles were concerned, the paternal responsibility that Andrew was upholding was undoubtedly just. Why her passion to oppose the way the rest of the world defined justice? Alida walked up and down her room. From her windows, the yew trees at the end of her mother's vista looked funereal without the contrast of the brilliant green lawn; Alida remembered wishing Hugo dead. And then it came to her that taking, as much as giving, is a sign of love. Taking acknowledges a relation and accepts the donor. Taking from Hugo, in any amount, for Amelia or for herself, implied acceptance of what he had done to her—shattered her life.

Alida heard the school bus just then, and the front door opening and shutting. Amelia came upstairs, her cheeks red from the cold, all agog to report the day's events at school. Alida listened, and commented, and at the close of that conversation told Amelia that she was going to the city for dinner.

"Not again!" Amelia cried. (Alida had not returned from her job interview the past week in time to dine with Amelia.)

"I'm sorry," Alida said. "This came up just now. It's business. We'll have to plan for when I can't be here. You could ask a friend to sleep over."

"Helen Richardson," Amelia answered promptly.

Alida would have preferred the child of other parents, but that was a detail. When she looked ahead to spring, she could see that school and work would take her away from Flat Rock and Amelia, and when she looked further ahead, she could see that the choice she had made when she told Andrew she would not consider a reconciliation was going to entail more serious deprivation for her child. Enough was enough. Alida decided she could not, would not, take away Hugo. Not his money, not himself as father. Andrew had won the argument before they argued.

Alida went over her checkbook and compiled her accounts, and then looked over her wardrobe. Amelia's bills were no problem, compared to the question of how to dress for dinner with her lawyer in a French restaurant. Up to the restaurant or down to the business occasion? She was truly perplexed. She settled on a black suit and then puzzled over its hat—a black-satin pillbox—not wanting to let Andrew down by looking too daytime-drab or by looking too evening-giddy. Just as Alida was deciding for the hat, Amelia came in to tell her Clara's grandmother loved Heidi, and exclaimed, "You're going to a party!"

"No, it's really just business," Alida said, "but it's important to look one's best all the time."

"I see," said Amelia, sat down at her mother's dressing table, picked up the powder puff, and asked, "May I?"

"Of course," Alida laughed, and kissed her. "Only not to school."

Yet it was a party, Alida thought on the train. Andrew had resolved a question for her, as he had been resolving innumerable questions, and she felt more than relief—active pleasure—in finding solutions. She supposed she was still unhappy, but she was also cheerful, and she owed her cheerfulness to Andrew, who was doing far more for her than his profession required. Perhaps he felt attached to her family, or to the memory of her father. He certainly pitied her solitude, but she did not resent his pity. She was grateful, and decided to show her gratitude by announcing that dinner was her treat and ordering champagne.

The train schedule brought her to the restaurant early. When she stepped inside the door, she was glad she had worn the giddy hat. It was a stylish place, with crisp, witty murals of Paris in the entryway and bar, and with fresh flowers and shaded lamps on the tables. As she walked past the bar, Alida saw a familiar face reflected in its mirror, and Tom Frank, the leading man of *Galaxy Guards,* called out, "Alida, what a coincidence!"

Alida was taken aback to meet someone from her old world—Hugo's world—a West Coast face—in New York City. Though she had persuaded herself that she could not pretend she had never been married to Hugo, that recognition was new and theoretical—no older than this afternoon—and she was almost afraid of Tom, of what he might say, or how he might judge her—what meanings he would read into her hat when he gossiped. But Tom was easy, unconstrained, and openly delighted to see her. "I just got off the plane," he said, "and the first person I meet in this cold city—brr—is you, dear. It's a good-luck sign. Have a drink?"

Alida sat beside him. He looked at her approvingly, and said, "You look very New York, especially the hat."

Alida smiled and asked him what he was doing in the city.

"Looking for work. You know the show folded?" Alida nodded. "What'll you have?" Alida chose sherry, and Tom continued. "It's true you get spoiled in long runs. Everybody knew it, back when the theater was all there was. Oh me, oh my, it's hard to be pounding the pavements again."

Her years with Hugo had taught Alida to spot actors' self-dramatization. "You're not pounding anything, Tom. You're probably up for a Broadway lead."

Tom acknowledged the accuracy of her guess. "My agents think a play will do me good. I don't know. Do you think there's anything left of the theater? What good *can* it do you? I mean, nobody sees you, not like television. It's a showcase, maybe, but Rachel says it's out of date, elitist."

Rachel, Tom's wife, employed a radical vocabulary that Alida could never understand. She asked, "Is Rachel with you?"

"No," he said. "She stayed home with the kids, waiting to find out what happens. We don't think we should change schools in the middle of the term. If we have a long run, that's another story. But I can't *tell* about plays anymore."

People passing glanced at Tom. He was handsome, with rugged features whose impression of virility and power belied his somewhat uncertain, wishing-to-please personality. The strangers' eyes, first attracted to Tom's good looks, would typically linger in recognition. Tom noticed his effect, and pretended not to notice it. "What do you make of this weather?" he asked. "I wouldn't have believed it if I hadn't walked into it."

Just then the headwaiter interrupted and told Tom there was a phone call for him. He excused himself. Alida sipped sherry and briefly meditated on the tyranny of the school year. The restaurant door opened, and a tall, handsome man stood for a moment framed in the vestibule, pulling off his gloves while his eyes ranged the room, looking for someone. He lacked Tom's public face, but a cold-weather ruddiness overlay a light tan, and his decisiveness in movement contributed to an impression of forceful, prime-of-life masculine attractiveness. In a split second, Alida recognized the stranger was Andrew. She was embarrassed: Tom would never believe this good-looking dinner partner was her lawyer. When Tom returned, she made extensive introductions—capsule biographies—to blight Tom's suspicions before they bloomed. Andrew stared. He said, "I know you. Not from *Galaxy Guards*, but from a long way back. The only time I ever saw *Titus Andronicus*, you were Marcus."

"My salad days," Tom said, "when I would do absolutely anything. I'm appalled you remember." His attention was diverted; he looked over Andrew's shoulder, and waved to someone entering. An extremely handsome young brunette: "Kit Cohn, of the New York office. My agent."

Andrew and Alida were led to their table. "Do you think Tom will believe you're my lawyer? Do you think he'll phone the Coast and start gossiping?"

Andrew was surprised. "Why shouldn't he think I'm your lawyer? I am."

"You're so handsome."

Andrew was at a loss for words. Perhaps he was unused to compliments; perhaps she had been too daring, too personal for a professional relationship. He merely said, "Alida!" in a mock-scolding, deprecatory tone.

"We didn't really need to meet, because I've changed my mind," Alida said. "I see that you're right. I didn't call and let you off because I'm so grateful to you, I wanted to buy you dinner. And champagne."

Andrew was again nonplussed. "Grateful for what?"

"Everything. Your patience. Your helpfulness. Your good advice. And making me sensible."

"All in a day's work," Andrew said. "And seeing how far you've come, I'll buy *you* champagne and dinner."

They argued; in the course of the squabble Andrew's mood lightened to match Alida's gaiety. "Mr. Frank and his agent—if she *is* his agent—just sat down. I can see them—you can't—and they can see our table. Would you like him to telephone the West Coast with the story that you're buying dinner for a handsome stranger you introduce as your lawyer?"

Andrew studied the wine list, gave his order, and then said, "That's an enchanting hat. But let's get our business out of the way. Have you brought Amelia's expenses?"

"I have"—Alida took the envelope from her handbag—"and it's practically nothing. Her tuition. I couldn't figure out her clothes; they're all mixed in with my and my mother's accounts. Once to the dentist. Once to the doctor. Now *there's* something, Andrew. Amelia hasn't been sick a day this year. *I* got the flu, but she's never had a sniffle. I've never known a child so healthy. Maybe we're making a mistake to think of my moving to the city. If Amelia's so healthy, doesn't it mean, psychologically, that she's happy where she is?"

"Alida," Andrew said earnestly, "you are a remarkable woman. You think of everyone except yourself. You tried to spare this wretched man paying what he owes . . . And here you are, a young woman, a beautiful woman, a gifted woman, ready to bury yourself in the country just because your child hasn't had a cold. It's time you thought of yourself. I didn't understand you so well at first," he went on. "I thought you were unreasonable about Hugo seeing Amelia. That was forgivable. You were hurt. But I told you how you seemed only a month ago—sore, sullen. The idea crossed my mind that you might be spoiled, that you might be, or become, one of those dangerous people who feel that a single disappointment excuses anything they do." Here Andrew sighed. "I've seen vindictiveness so terrible you'd think the devil was in it. If you believed in the devil."

"Do you believe in God?"

"Probably not. Why do you ask?"

"No reason," Alida said. "It's none of my business, anyhow. I suppose because you mentioned the devil. I'd forgotten all about religious people until I moved back with my mother."

"Well, one reason you could say I'm not a believer is that, though I admire your mother, I think her religiousness is compensation."

"For not marrying again?"

"I think so. I think she was scared."

"I would have had a stepfather."

"It might have been good for you. For Josiah, especially." Andrew shrugged. "That's past. I direct your attention to the immediate future—the menu."

After they ordered, Andrew mentioned that one reason he liked the restaurant was its old-fashioned spaciousness. "It can't last," he said. "Rents go up, and they add tables. Most of the so-called 'in' places are as jammed as the subway."

That reminded Alida how little she had been in the city in recent years, and she began to ask questions. Noisy? Dirty? Dangerous?

Andrew asked if she had written the Gibsons. Alida admitted she had not; she wanted to be sure of Amelia's school before she worked on plans to move in. Andrew thought her worry was nonsense.

"It's real to me."

"I don't know much about children," Andrew said. "Janet has

132

explained that to me. I don't have a natural feeling for the young, especially the modern young. But I'd bet on Amelia sight unseen. Janet has a meeting tonight, but she'll be home early. I'll ask her to talk to you about schools. I'll call you tomorrow and tell you what she says."

They chatted as they dined, very much at ease, not talking business or family or any of the immediate and practical subjects they had usually discussed, but food, and travel, and how Andrew had got interested in old silver. Tom and Kit came to the table to say good-bye, and, after they left, Alida commented on the coincidence that she had met Tom immediately after deciding she could not pretend Hugo did not exist. "Coincidences are sometimes useful," Andrew said.

"Of course it's not wholly coincidence; it's logical that Tom would be looking for work after the show closed. But I'd imagined meeting somebody from the Coast would be—I don't know—upsetting. It wasn't."

Andrew looked up from the check. "It's a symptom. You're getting over it."

His last words, as he put her in a taxi, were "I'll call you tomorrow morning about seeing Janet."

He did, and asked if she could bring Amelia to lunch at their apartment on Saturday.

When Alida and Amelia presented themselves at the old fortress of an apartment house on Park Avenue where the Camerons lived, shortly after noon on Saturday, mother and child were in different states of mind. Amelia was mildly curious about lunch with her mother's friend, but Alida was anxious, knowing that Amelia was to be inspected and wondering what Janet Cameron would make of her, Alida. Worshiping Andrew, Alida was ready to idolize his wife, but feared failing the standards of that paragon of womanhood. A maid answered the doorbell, helped them with their coats, showed them into the library, said, "I'll tell Mrs. Cameron you're here," and left them to wait for their hostess, who seemed in no hurry to appear. The room disappointed Alida. There were two good pieces in it—a large old partners' desk with its back to the window, and, just inside the entrance, a handsome, conceivably eighteenth-century tall clock. The walls were lined with glass-fronted bookcases of a dismal, dark wood, enclosing sets bound in dull colors. The rest of the furniture was a graceless assembly of hand-me-downs and leftovers: heavy, bulging sofas and chairs of some period before the First World War, all covered in a peculiarly somber shade of red damask with matching curtains at the windows. The carpeting was an unfortunate beige that looked sallow. Though the gray light of the overcast, wintry day may have increased the pessimism of the colors, hue alone was not to blame for the impression of indifference to—or even dislike of—decorative amenity: the forms themselves were irretrievably ugly, and they were arranged any which way, like a sales floor. While they waited, Amelia looked out of the window— she was still fascinated by the existence of apartments, by the excitement of living at a height. Alida used the time to make mental excuses for the ugliness around her: Andrew, like many men, may have left domestic matters entirely to his wife, and Janet might be just on the point of fixing up the room.

Hugo's lessons in drama had been extensive. He once pointed out to Alida that the principle of drama (by contrast with life) was efficiency. In dramatic exposition, character must reveal itself immediately, subtly or not as the dramatist can manage, whereas, when strangers appear in our real lives, we meet them with so many possible feelings and combinations of feelings—all the way from indifference to awe—and with so many preoccupations apart from meeting them, that we rarely know who they are or even what we are going to feel about them in the way that we know, within minutes of the curtain's rise, that X is the heroine and Y her enemy. Alida had often noticed the truth of Hugo's law in the days when she was newly married and meeting many new people. She realized, too, that there were rare exceptions in life, if not in art. For Alida, Janet Cameron was one. Within moments, Alida felt that Andrew's wife was a self-righteous, self-important, ill-mannered frump. She entered at last, bustling as if the company she had invited were unexpected. She was a large woman, fair, tall, and heavy, with large features. She wore no makeup, and her graying blonde hair was screwed into a small topknot from which wisps dangled. She wore a shapeless, gaudy, printed-cotton garment, like a Mother Hubbard ordained by missionaries for a tribe exceptionally gifted in textile design, a full complement of native, or savage, beads and bracelets, and, incongruously, a large, old-fashioned diamond bar pin that reminded Alida of something or somebody. Janet's manner was self-assured, her voice cloyingly soft, and her approach inquisitorial.

"Ah, Alida," she said, "Andrew has spoken of you," and then: "and this is Amelia." Well-trained, well-behaved Amelia came from the

134

window and held out her hand. "Does she *always* behave like that?" Janet asked and, without waiting for an answer, went on, "Does she *like* to dress up like that? Does she wear dresses most of the time?"

These low-spoken inquiries were followed by a few more brusque comments, ending with the promise that she and Amelia would have "a little talk by ourselves" after lunch. Then Janet remarked, as if reporting hearsay, "Some people have a drink before lunch."

Alida realized that she was supposed to reply that she was not one of those people, but she hoped that a little alcohol might blur Janet, and asked for sherry. Janet unexpectedly lumbered off and returned bringing a tray. On it were an unopened bottle, a corkscrew, and a wineglass. "I can't ask the maids to do everything," she said. "We're very simple on Saturdays, especially since Andrew has got this silver madness. And we have no sherry."

Janet expected Alida to open a bottle of red wine. On the label, Alida recognized the name of a great French vineyard, wondered whether Janet cared for her *that* much, whether she, Alida, was mixed up about wines, and then how she would open the bottle with the basic corkscrew Janet had provided. Opening wine was a task that had rarely fallen to Alida, but whenever it had, she used elaborate gadgets that did most of the work. Alida bent over the bottle on the heavy low coffee table, centered the screw in the cork, and tried to ascertain how much physical force Janet's corkscrew required—more, she discovered, than she had expected, for at her first, inadequate, pressure, the tool slipped sideways. During Alida's second attempt, Janet continued lamenting her husband's extravagance. Alida, who had heard a modest account of Andrew's interest in silver from Andrew himself, now learned that, over the years, Andrew had received a few pieces of family silver from a spinster great-aunt who had been distributing heirlooms among the males of the family. Miss Cameron had died (Was it Lucy Cameron? Alida asked herself. Was Janet wearing Miss Lucy Cameron's diamond pin?), and her feelings would not be hurt if Andrew sold the objects (Janet never said what they were) but instead he had been studying up in museums and browsing in silver shops and visiting auctions, and from time to time adding to his hoard. Alida did not try to stanch the flow of Janet's grievances because she was concentrating on her struggles with the cork. Just as she was thinking she could never persuade the corkscrew to go in, it drove through the recalcitrant cork, pushing pellets of cork into the wine, and then refused to let itself be withdrawn. Janet observed the disaster without comprehending it. She said, in the role of tutor or coach she had arrogated, "There now. You see, you've practically done it." While Alida labored to free the cork, Janet talked about "a little more effort—there, there, now, it's coming"—congratulating Alida on retrieving the largest lump of the shattered cork. Janet was so carried away by her own approbation that she said she thought she would join Alida, though she added that she did not want to be "tipsy" when she "interviewed" Amelia.

Janet returned with a wineglass and with a girl as well, a skinny adolescent whose tangled long brown hair hung down her back, showing a small, pallid, expressionless, bony face whose features seemed squeezed together. She wore something like tights below, and a loose, unidentifiable Asian jacket above. "Little Janet has just finished meditating," her mother explained, "and would like to join us."

Little Janet herself betrayed no such liking; she merely nodded on being told the guests' names, and sat down. She was as silent as if she had still been meditating, but she had a malicious liveliness in her eyes, particularly when they were directed at her mother, who was boasting about her, saying proudly that little Janet had found her *own* way, which was not everybody's. The incongruity of the older Janet's attitudes struck Alida as something beyond bad manners; the woman was ignoring Amelia, treating Alida like a backward adolescent, and deferring to what was, if not a backward, an outré adolescent, who refused to accept her homage. Having presented one cherished achievement, a meditating daughter, Janet returned to spreading her ego in other ways, explaining what Andrew had already explained—that she was on the boards of two day schools, one a fairly conservative institution from which she had withdrawn her own daughter, and the other a more progressive, or, as Janet said, "innovating" school for more "creative" young people, from which young Janet had recently withdrawn herself. "They didn't mind," the mother said. "They try to help the students strike out for themselves. Of course, it only works with very special people"—here she nodded toward her daughter, who dropped her eyes as if in modesty, concealing from her mother a look of contempt that Alida spotted and that made her feel momentary pity for the dowdy, self-deceiving parent and loathing for the sneering child.

Janet now asked Alida what she was doing, and Alida said she had enrolled in school, for she had; Dr. Talbot had admitted her.

It was the right thing to say to Janet, who droned on about self-improvement and self-enhancement, and it being never too late to learn. She brought to every cliché a sense of discovery that must have made her extremely interesting to herself. Pleased to be delivering such favorable opinions, she decided on a second glass of wine, offered one to Alida, and asked, "And what are you studying?"

Here Alida decided to lie. "Interior Decoration Two" might not strike this humorless, tasteless woman as (a word Janet had used) "worthwhile," and Alida wanted her goodwill and good offices for Amelia. "I've taken up my old studies in art," she said.

Janet nodded and asked no more. She was ready with a new collection of banalities: art as therapy, as self-expression, as the voice or vocation of the downtrodden—everything, in short, that opposed Alida's notions of art, which had to do with discipline, craft, polish. Just before they went in to lunch, Janet remembered to ask after Alida's mother. She could not recall exactly when they had last met.

Lunch itself was two lunches: little Janet nibbled at a mysterious brownish mess, and for the others, a maid set down a sort of delicatessen platter with cold meats and potato salad—not precisely the ideal food for a winter's day. Amelia, who had so far spent all her life as a child and had not yet learned to resent being patronized, responded to Janet warmly. She did not know, or mind, that she was being cross-questioned throughout lunch; she enjoyed the attention. Alida wanted to draw little Janet into conversation, but she was given no opening: the girl looked down at her plate steadily. Toward the end of the meal she suddenly asked Alida, "Are you one of my mother's lame ducks?"

Alida was taken aback by the question, the more so by the fact that the girl's speech pattern recalled Andrew's. "I don't know," Alida said. "What is a lame duck?"

"Almost anyone my mother asks to lunch," little Janet replied, and returned her eyes to her plate.

When they finished eating, Janet, the mother, directed Alida to return to the library, and went off somewhere with Amelia, while Janet, the daughter, disappeared. Alone, Alida stood at the window and looked up at the inveterate sky—the clouds piled atop the city's buildings reminded her of dirty absorbent cotton, or one might think that all the citizens' soiled laundry had transposed itself on high—and down into the avenue, where no one was out except doormen getting taxis. She wondered what she had got Amelia into; whether they should go and visit Betsy Weinstein later, as Alida had

137

half-promised, and, most of all, whether she, Alida, was wrong in her deep-seated feeling that Andrew's wife and daughter were catastrophes. The insides of marriages were often very different from the outsides, and Janet might offer Andrew blessings no observer could imagine. But little Janet was *too* odd . . . Here Alida corrected herself. Too odd for what? She shrugged, sighed, walked around the ugly room, studied the backs of books, the dial of the clock, and then went back to the window and waited.

The clock began an elaborate series of whirrs, and then struck. Alida turned; Amelia was at the library door, smiling. Behind her loomed Janet, saying, in her soft, determined voice, "I think this young woman is going to test very high. I shouldn't be surprised if she were a genius."

Alida's estimation of Janet soared; perhaps there was something to the woman after all. But then Janet continued, "She's not very free, though. Not imaginative."

Alida was enraged. Imagine criticizing Amelia—unfairly—and in front of her, too! But Janet went quickly ahead. Her soft voice was noticeably softer; though Alida had thought it boring, she allowed it might be considered caressing. "There is often a tendency, when a child has been subjected to change, to freeze. You find that exaggerated in sick children—Amelia isn't sick, not a bit of it, but she may be looking for safety. Not daring to be different. It's too soon, really, to say she's not imaginative. I'm just wondering where she'd be happiest. I think, for the time being, we'll put Amelia in Fanny Burney."

Alida was amazed by the woman's assurance: "we'll put" suggested she was not merely on the board but ran the place. Janet leaned forward. Then she noticed Amelia, and said, "Amelia dear, would you go back in our room and bring some of your drawings to show your mother?" As soon as the child left, Janet said, "I know it's a personal question, but I'm thinking about Amelia. Is there a chance of your getting back together with your husband?"

Alida shook her head no.

"It's so much better for—"

"There's someone else."

Janet looked shocked. "Do you mean you—?"

Alida said, "No, Hugo." A pause. "He has—has another woman. A mistress."

"I'd find that unforgivable," Janet said. "One does have to make compromises, sacrifices, even . . ." She paused, as if reflecting how much she sacrificed to Andrew's deficiencies, and went on, "but if my husband were unfaithful . . . Yes, yes, I see it wouldn't do for you."

The conversation ended when Amelia returned. Janet was wholly sympathetic, exclaiming, "My, aren't these lovely!" as Amelia produced routine, though deft, crayon portrayals of a man, a woman, a child, a house. "I'll call you Monday," Janet said.

Class dismissed.

"I liked that lady, that Mrs. Cameron," Amelia said, as they got out of the elevator. "Will we see her again?"

"If you like," Alida said. "Would you like to visit some more friends of mine?"

"Right now?" Amelia asked, as if that were too much to hope for—as if, by its very nature, pleasure had to be rationed.

"Yes, I think so."

Back in December, Alida had scrutinized the Christmas cards she received in response to those she had sent out like a Roman augur examining entrails, attempting to read her future in scrawls that wished her well or expressed hopes for meeting in the new year. Her flu and her multifarious January had driven from her mind her worry about her social acceptability as a lone woman. When Alida remembered what an emotional effort it had cost—the courage it had required—to send her cards out, she was, for once, relieved by a phenomenon we often resent: others do not share our intensities, and often do not even suspect their existence. No one thought her cards were anything but cards. So far, Betsy Weinstein was the only friend who had immediately followed up the Christmas promise to "get in touch." She had written a note after sending a card, and she had telephoned several times. Out in California, Alida had heard Jews congratulating themselves or each other on their characteristic warmheartedness, and perhaps that was all. Alida was slightly suspicious of the Weinsteins, however, because they had originally introduced her to Hugo. She had delayed calling Betsy back in fear that the Weinsteins might blame her; might somehow meddle; might ask questions; might talk of Hugo. But she did not want to cut them entirely, so, late on Friday, she called Betsy and told her they would be in the city the next day. Betsy was thrilled at the prospect of Saturday company for her own reasons: her eldest child, her daughter Debby, a graduate student in mathematics, was studying for some horrendous examination and had asked her

139

mother to baby-sit Monica, Debby's three-year-old, over the weekend. "The weather's so horrible," Betsy said, "I don't want to go out. I'd be frozen and Monica would get the sniffles, so I'll be home all the time. Would you like to have dinner here on Saturday?"

Alida, still wary, alleged an evening appointment in Flat Rock, and explained, besides, that she had no idea what Janet planned; they left it that Alida would phone after Janet. When she did, Betsy said, "Of course, Alida, come right down. We're expecting you. Monica's looking forward to Amelia."

As the taxi went down Fifth Avenue, Alida began remembering the Sunday afternoon in April, 1962, when she had gone to the Weinsteins' cocktail party. Starting over entailed so much visiting the past!

The Weinstein acquaintance had begun when Betsy had asked Alida to lunch in a restaurant after their classes; Betsy and Alida had become school, or weekday, daytime friends, their conversation almost wholly devoted to the courses, the assignments, the teachers, and art shows they had seen. Alida had not understood at the time, and did not understand until much later, after she knew the Weinsteins well, that Betsy sought her out because she had admired Alida's performance in class, her taste, her quickness, her knowingness—her brains, in short. Nobody had ever suggested that Alida had any brains, and she would have regarded the notion that she had as farfetched, if not comic, never understanding that appreciation and enthusiasm had unlocked her abilities. Besides, in so limited a friendship—a friendship of convenience—it would not occur to Alida to ask what Betsy saw in her, any more than she discussed Betsy with herself. She knew that Betsy was married, and had a family, but she never expected to meet them. The invitation to the Weinsteins' cocktail party had taken Alida by surprise. Her uncle and aunt were abroad, and she was lonelier than usual. It was an attraction that the Weinsteins lived in Greenwich Village.

Alida did not know what to expect on that pale spring afternoon when the taxi drew up before a red-brick period house, a restored bandbox, on a handsome, tree-lined street of similar houses. She hesitated on the stoop. She was all in gray—a gray spring coat, a gray silk dress with white collar and cuffs. Her hair was very short, and her heels were very high—both in that year's style. In those days she wore little makeup and timorously applied the slightest of floral scents. How young she was! And how young she must have appeared! A white-jacketed man answered the bell and let her in. The parlor floor was furnished to period, though in no doctrinaire way. The mood achieved was that of mid-Victorian domesticity, without flamboyance, and

140

without the astringency Alida liked: the middle-class family and its interior as they had been a century earlier. She noticed five or six old American blown-glass flasks on the front-parlor mantel before she became immersed in the party. The rooms were just full, not crowded, and the guests were people from the theater and people from the art world—some patrons, some connoisseurs, some on the business side, and one or two, like Hugo, originators. Alida had much greater success at this party than she had among her peers. The company was older than she but shared her interests; Alida forgot her shyness, and they found her eagerness and her youth engaging. Hugo was probably the nearest in age to her, and though, as he told her later, he was absorbed in several heart-to-heart theatrical gossips, he was aware that this demure young woman was making a stir, and dedicated himself to maneuvering to her group. When he joined them, they were talking pottery and china. "Everyone was saying 'Creil,'" Hugo remembered, "and I didn't know what you were talking about. I felt like a salmon who'd fought his way upstream over waterfalls and rapids only to discover his beloved was really a can of tuna fish."

Hugo improvised a few lines to wedge himself into the conversation, and gradually appropriated Alida. He took her out to dinner to a local Italian restaurant, and, when he left her in front of her uncle's apartment house, told her that he was going away but that he hoped to see her when he returned, and asked for her telephone number. At that moment, Alida was not looking forward: she thought a party with so many interesting people followed by dinner with a genuine playwright was glamorous enough. While Hugo was away (he was in California for six months), she saw more of the Weinsteins; she became a sort of extra girl, young friend of the family. Their friendship was active enough so that, when her aunt came back, Alida mentioned it. "There's no harm in it," her aunt said. "No harm at all. We're not bigoted. There is a problem, though, that can be painful, and you should bear it in mind. When you get friendly with Jews, they can be hurt when you go places they can't. And sometimes—it happened to a friend of mine—they expect you to take them, and you can't—it'd only make everybody miserable if you tried—and they don't understand."

The Weinsteins, however, never expected Alida to take them anywhere; the hospitality was all theirs; they rarely asked questions about her world, and indeed, acted as if she had no connections apart from them. After her engagement to Hugo was announced, she learned from him that the Weinsteins were surprised to read of her family; they had somehow assumed she was a poor relation, an indigent dependent of her New York City relatives. The subject was never discussed after Alida's marriage, but Alida sometimes pondered the quality of orphanedness, or forlornness—of pathos—she must have exhibited, though how, she did not know. Did she seem lost? Alone? Was it the absence of a father? Her fear of her uncle?

At the Weinsteins' door, now, shivering with Amelia on the stoop, Alida rang the bell, and—happy homecoming!—George, their houseman, recognized her. He led Alida and Amelia downstairs to a ground-floor room, a sort of summer-printed quasi-winter garden that had been a children's playroom years before. It struck Alida as too bright, affected, unsuited to the city, but all she said was that it was new. Yes, Betsy said, they had had it redone after their daughter's—Debby's—marriage. The boys were away at school; Debby and her husband were at graduate school in the city. "On a day like this," Betsy said, "I'm not sure a glass wall on the garden, as we are now supposed to call the backyard, makes sense. Shall I pull the curtains?"

She did. They settled into white wicker chairs, and, after a discussion with George about tea for the ladies and cocoa for the children, Betsy and Alida sat wondering where to begin. With the last time they had met, nearly two years ago, when Alida and Hugo had been in New York and had had dinner and gone to the theater with the Weinsteins. Both women remembered that it was an O'Neill revival that the men had liked and that they, the women, thought dated. They admired one another's child and grandchild. Monica, just three, was not precisely a playmate for Amelia, but the girls invented a sort of school or house game with Monica's dolls. Amelia enjoyed the role of parent or teacher; to Alida's dismay, she was reproducing some of Janet's governessy phrases.

As the conversation moved to where Alida and Amelia had just been, Betsy volunteered that she did not like Janet Cameron. That surprised Alida, who could not remember Betsy disliking anybody. She was a medium-sized, pretty, blue-eyed blonde with wide cheekbones and slightly slanting eyes suggesting the Slavic. In the years when Alida used to see her often, Betsy had been harassed by the demands of the house, three children, and an indefatigable husband. She spent very little time and thought on herself (she wore what "did"—this afternoon, a blue sweater and brown skirt), and, in her approach to others, tended to be welcoming. She was sometimes wry, as just now about the garden, and she was often tired. She may have avoided judging other people out of fatigue, finding that the sustained reflection required to devalue other people's characters demanded more time than she had. Alida questioned Betsy, who

142

assured her that if Janet said she would put Amelia into Fanny Burney, there was no doubt she would; Janet was a steamroller. "I shouldn't be so unkind about her," Betsy said. "I don't know her that well. The Camerons are part of what we'd call our public life— charities, boards, so on. What Larry calls our 'civic duties.' But you're lucky to have her with you, is my feeling. Not against you. She's known for getting her way. Everybody loves Andrew," she went on, "and Larry sees a lot of him. They went on the museum board at the same time—"

"What museum?" Alida asked.

George interrupted and told Betsy her daughter was on the telephone. Betsy excused herself. Alida watched the children play. They were spanking a small doll.

"Bad, very bad"—Monica.

"She tags along"—Amelia.

"Never obeys Mommy"—Monica.

"Destructive"—Amelia-Janet.

Betsy returned, disturbed. "After all these years," she said, "you walk into *this*."

Debby had just told her mother that she and her husband had had their final, definitive quarrel. She had forgotten to go to the bank on Friday, and, when she looked into her handbag before going out to buy cigarettes, she discovered she was penniless. Danny had left the apartment. She wanted somebody to bring cash. Betsy dispatched George to bring Debby.

Alida wondered if she should leave, but she could see that Amelia's occupying Monica was helpful, and perhaps her own presence gave Betsy some support. Betsy was really waiting for Larry, who was due any minute from tennis. "He was so looking forward to seeing you," Betsy said. "A nice, good visit and chat. Instead . . ."

Larry entered then, as if on cue. He was tall, dark, and, on the whole, handsome. His color was sallow, but his lips were red; an aquiline nose lent distinction to a face that would otherwise have been too bland; his black eyes were merry. He radiated vitality to the point that Alida sometimes found his mere presence exhausting. He bounded in, kissed both women, and, saying, "I'd like a Scotch," rang for George.

Betsy mournfully explained why George was not there. She concluded by repeating that it was unfair to happen when Alida was visiting. Larry said, amiably, that he remembered Alida as tough enough to stand a little uproar. All she ever needed, as he recalled,

143

was a net game. Alida decided it would be helpful to live up to Larry's appraisal and show toughness. "Betsy," she said, "don't be so upset about Debby or you'll hurt my feelings. Just now I'm *my* mother's Debby."

Betsy was perplexed. Larry laughed. "Betsy never learns," he said. "Troubles are what we call life."

Betsy calmed down. "It's having things come unstuck," she said. "I thought I was through, at least with Debby."

"You're never through with children," Larry said, and went off to find whisky.

When Debby came, he greeted her casually, remarking that he was delighted at the prospect of a really good chess game that evening, and then commanded Debby to pay attention to Alida, who had to leave shortly. "My, Alida, how you've grown!" Debby said.

Debby, plain and bespectacled, embodied the concept of "brainy" girl as it had been in the days when Alida escaped college, and Alida thought uneasily of Janet's use of the word "genius" to describe Amelia. But Debby was friendly and funny. They talked about what Debby and Alida could remember of each other, and Debby (at Alida's request) tried to explain her recondite mathematical specialty. Not a word was said about the young Mahons' (that was Debby's married name) marital crisis, and, as Alida rose to go, Debby made the afternoon's only reference to Alida's circumstances: "Now that you're living back east," Debby said, artlessly, "I wish you could find time to shop with me. You're always so well turned out, and no matter what I buy, it comes out higgledy-piggledy."

Alida nodded a promise, and Larry saw her and Amelia out. He whispered in the hall, "Betsy never learned to psych herself. That's why she's no sort of competitor. With children, the trick is to persuade yourself you don't take them seriously."

When Alida got home, she found the morning's mail. There was nothing of interest, except a letter from her tenant, Mrs. Gibson, that had been sent to California and readdressed by Hugo. Mrs. Gibson was asking if it was possible to be relieved of their lease before it expired in the fall. Her husband's company was in difficulties, and he was taking early retirement. They owned a house in Vermont, they could move out anytime, and would like to do so immediately; if Alida preferred, they would attempt a sublet. "Perhaps you have read about Divco's reorganization in the newspapers," Mrs. Gibson wrote, as if in support of her plea. Alida recalled old Mr. Jones talking about Divco on New Year's Eve, and was amazed that he was right about something.

Alida called Mrs. Gibson on Monday morning. Around eleven, Janet called and said that an interview with Mrs. Moulton, Fanny Burney's director of admissions, was arranged for mother and daughter at eleven o'clock the following day. Alida thanked her, and Janet added, "They're on intersession, so I don't know who'll be around; the administrative offices are on the left as you enter."

Monday was the first day of Amelia's intersession. Alida and Amelia prospected in the Old Bridge shops, lunched at Martha's, an imitation old-fashioned ice-cream parlor on Main Street, and then Alida took Amelia to an ice-skating lesson. Driving home after the lesson, Alida said, casually, "You know that Mrs. Cameron we saw on Saturday? She knows about another school for you, in the city. We're going there tomorrow."

"Does Daddy know?"

"Not yet," Alida said. "You can tell him. The name of the school is Fanny Burney."

Amelia said nothing. Alida, with her eyes on the road in the winter twilight, wished she had waited to mention the interview until they were home so that she could see her child's face. In a little while, Amelia said, "But I like Flat Rock."

"Of course you do. It's just that I've been thinking of moving to the city next year, and Fanny Burney's the best school in it."

"I would live in the city with you?" Amelia asked.

"Yes," Alida said. "High up. On the fifteenth and sixteenth floor." She added, "But nothing's certain. We're only thinking about it. If you *hate* the idea, we'll think of something else."

"How can I hate it when I don't know what it's like?"

When they were home, Amelia seemed restless and uneasy; she came into Alida's room and sat on the bed, kicking her legs and fidgeting while Alida combed her hair. At once irritated and sympathetic at the indirection of her shy, worried child, Alida asked, "What is it? Do you have some questions?"

"Yes," Amelia said. "May I phone Daddy?"

"He may not be home, but you can try him."

Amelia's talk with Hugo resolved whatever doubts she may have had. She said, "Daddy *wants* me to go to Fanny Burney."

"I shouldn't wonder."

145

It was pouring Tuesday morning, and Alida decided to have James drive them in to the school. Under dripping umbrellas, they waited for a guard to let them in. Though, in the circumstances, Alida could see little of the building; it was no architectural statement and—another contrast to Barlow—had no signs in the halls: Fanny Burney had not prepared itself for strangers. The guard scanned a brief list of names and led them part of the way to the offices, a courtesy that had in it an element of precaution. There was no large office comparable to Barlow's, only a room with plants in the windows, three secretaries' desks, and one pretty young secretary, who showed them an umbrella stand and helped them hang up their coats. But differences in architecture mattered less than similarities in approach: Mrs. Moulton belonged to the same tribe as Miss Kurtz. Educational administrators, torn between exerting power and demonstrating sympathy, were deliberately sharp and soft, sweet and sour, hard-edged and fuzzy. Mrs. Moulton, who was probably in her forties, had short brown hair disciplined into waves; wore eyeglasses and pearl earrings, a tailored gray suit and a ruffled white blouse. Like her appearance, her remarks alternated crispness and uncertainty.

"We're so glad you could come," she opened, cordially. "Mrs. Cameron has spoken highly of you." She motioned them to seats beside her desk, and said, professionally vague: "It's very doubtful that we'll have any room in the fifth grade next fall."

Something had been happening in, as well as to, Alida in January; she was beginning to trust herself more and other people less. She decided to call Mrs. Moulton's tiresome bluff, and inquired, with false innocence, "Do you mean it's a waste of time to apply?"

"Oh no," Mrs. Moulton said, rapidly, and then, as if abashed at her own tricks, turned to Amelia, and asked, "Why do you want to go to Fanny Burney?"

"My mother wants to live in the city and my father says it's the best school in the country."

Amelia's answer was conclusive, and since Janet had apparently been exhaustive in her discussion of the Kellys, Mrs. Moulton asked only one or two verifying questions before she started going over the application form with them. Alida expressed concern about letters of reference. "There are so few people in the East who know Amelia well," she said.

"You have Mrs. Cameron," Mrs. Moulton answered, "and of course we'll have the Country Day School records and we'll talk to

Miss Blossom. I doubt we'll have to go all the way back to California. Is there some other adult in Flat Rock who has seen a good deal of Amelia this past year?"

"Father Peele," Amelia said, without hesitation.

The child was really managing the interview: Alida began to see the benefits of a year's exposure to Mrs. Waterman's efficiency. As the car splashed homeward, Alida told Amelia that she had acquitted herself magnificently. "You said just the right things."

"That Mrs. Moulton talked too much," Amelia said.

Alida was pleased at Amelia's crust. She wanted her child to grow up less timid and more self-assured than herself. Because, when you came to think of it, everybody needed a tough skin to get through life, which, long after school was over, went on being a series of auditions, a fact acknowledged only in the theater. Only performers were allowed to discuss frankly the humiliation and defiance and exhibitionism that went into selling oneself.

The rest of the week was all arrangements and errands, each day a little busier than its predecessor. Events had moved faster than Alida had expected, chopping up her time. Amelia played with Helen Richardson more often than Alida would have wished; she had looked forward to mothering during intersession, feeling premonitory guilt for her prospective absences in the spring. On the Friday afternoon, after they returned from Dr. Plum, a psychologist who gave Amelia an I.Q. test for Fanny Burney, Alida had begun to ask Amelia whether she could think of a bang-up treat for the two of them that weekend when Betsy Weinstein phoned. They had just arrived at their country place, about twenty miles from Flat Rock. Could Alida and Amelia spend the weekend? Betsy apologized for short notice. Their own arrival had been a spur-of-the-moment effort to entertain Mark, their younger son, who had expected to visit Mexico during intersession with a friend who had fallen ill. "Does she skate?" Betsy asked. "The pond's frozen."

The prospect of skating decided Amelia. They left after lunch on Saturday. The Weinsteins' country house was a recent acquisition, and Alida had never been there. She drove slowly lest she lose her way, and the slow pace made her see winter in all its country bleakness; its natural colors were grays and browns. The evergreens supplied the only hint of life on the planet. Man's presence was marked by red roofs and colorful cars and occasional brightly painted houses, but the human species itself was rarely in evidence. As Alida passed beyond Flat Rock's zoning, she drove through intermittent concatenations of tumbledown houses, sheds, and sagging barns that centered, as a rule, around a gasoline pump; aging, moribund, or dead machines served as the equivalent of civic ornaments around these hamlets. They were separated by brown fields so stark that it was impossible to believe they had ever been, or ever would be, green. The nuances of smoky grays and duns that distinguished the various barks and branches were delicate and fragile, and emphasized the mood of death and desertion that winter brought. Then the route entered an area of gentlemen's farms and farm estates, like the Weinsteins', which was a sprawling old clapboard house painted white with black shutters. It sat in its own spread of winter fields at the end of a long driveway bordered by leafless trees. A maid showed Alida and Amelia to a guest room, and pointed out the window to the steel gray pond, where there was a small group, some skating, some watching, bringing life to the scene by their movement and by the bright stripes of their caps and scarves. Alida had not been able to find her old ice skates, but Amelia had her new ones. They walked down the long slope behind the house. Betsy and Monica were watching Larry, Debby, and two youthful males skate. Amelia put on her skates and wobbled to join them. Monica, in snowsuit and rubber boots, broke away from Betsy to follow Amelia, slipped on the ice, fell, righted herself without a squeak, and continued to pursue her glamorous grown-up friend. Betsy smiled. She looked tired and older in the out-of-doors; what the light showed, more telling than wrinkles, was resignation.

One of the young men on the pond was a remarkable skater. He had been teaching Larry a figure that Larry went off to practice alone, and then the younger man exploded in a series of leaps and turns worthy of Olympics and ice shows. "Danny's from upstate," Betsy remarked, explaining his skill on the ice, and forgetting that she had not explained how Danny and Debby were together after last Saturday's final parting.

Debby was distracted by Monica, who, torn between admiration of her father and Amelia, skidded this way and that, and threatened to collide with the skaters. Debby failed to persuade her to leave the ice, and Danny, seeing the difficulty, ceased his exhibition, skated over to his daughter, picked her up, and placed her on his shoulders. He then toured the pond, whirling occasionally to thrill the child, but for the most part idling, incorporating her in events. Alida thought Amelia was rather out of things, for Debby joined Larry. But the other young man, who was Betsy's younger son, Mark, came to her rescue. Betsy told Alida that before Mark's disappointment about his trip to Mexico, she and Larry had planned to go away. (His older brother had remained in Cambridge, unable to tear himself away from the laboratory where he had a part-time job.) "There's always something," Betsy said. "It was nice of you to come."

Alida wondered if Betsy's depression was the result of too much— too much noise, people, talk, family. Or perhaps it was only Alida who found the full force of family life trying. Emerging from loneliness, she missed solitude. She had never before shared a room with Amelia. They got in each other's way, changing after skating, and though their closeness and companionship was amiable, Alida would have liked time to herself before going downstairs to the bustle in the living room.

The room was large—Alida thought it must once have been several rooms. Its ceiling was low and beamed, and the furniture mingled comfortable city modern with old country authenticity. A fire was going in the fireplace. Larry rose when Alida and Amelia came in. Halfway inviting inspection, he said, "I wanted a place for my American things."

Alida looked at the mantel, and saw the glass was there. She said, "The first time I visited you in the city, you had blown glass on the mantel."

"So you remember," Larry said. "It's all around here." Larry was pleased, and Alida, who had been finding so many of her own memories saddening, realized that remembering might also create happiness. "Come look," Larry added.

He took her on an abbreviated tour of several rooms, and when they came back to the living room, Debby said, "That's a lovely dress, Alida"—Alida wore a floor-length wool dress in a pale print—"you must take me in hand."

Betsy said, "We'd know all about clothes if your father ever started anyone in boutiques."

"Why not, Pop?" Debby asked. "That's a great idea."

Larry said he never recommended anybody going into a small retail business. "And haven't I gotten us into enough?" He turned to Alida, and explained, "I was just trying to find out what was what as a young accountant. Theater, art . . . I wanted to know what people were talking about when they said this was good, that was bad. An accountant shouldn't take anything on faith. If he just looks at the figures he's worse than useless."

So that was how Larry had met Hugo and all the people in that cocktail party!

Larry got up to poke the fire, and Debby said, "I've noticed you don't wear much jewelry, Alida. Why is that?"

Debby's direct analytic approach—so like her father's wanting to understand what his clients were doing—was disarming. But, since Debby had raised a topic on which Alida had not thought much, she answered rather slowly, thinking aloud: "Well, there was—is—family jewelry. In banks, mostly, but I've always known about it. Then, of course, my aunt Jane has a lot of things my uncle Arthur gave her. Splendid things. But years ago, when I lived with her—when I first met your mother—I guess I always associated grand, great— you know, really impressive—jewelry with older women. Aunts. That's just as well, because there aren't many men who can buy the jewelry my uncle can."

Debby popped questions like firecrackers: "Who's your uncle?" (Larry told her.) "What about your family jewels?"

"You make them sound royal. They aren't. But I remember my mother gave my sister-in-law Margaret a necklace when she became engaged to my brother, and I thought it was awful. When my turn came, she took me to the bank and asked me to pick something—I suppose I could have had it all; she never wears it—and I had a terrible time. I didn't want to hurt her feelings, but it wasn't my taste. Still, it might be now."

"Has your taste changed a lot?" Debby asked.

"It's broadened, I think. One grows more tolerant with age, maybe, sees virtues or attractions where one had been scornful or impatient. Don't you think so, Betsy?"

Betsy said, sharply, "I've grown more nervous, and I find I'm less tolerant of people."

"Oh, Mother, that's not true—" Danny entered the conversation. He was an exceptionally handsome young man, very large and very blond—all freshness and decency, country niceness. His consideration was inclusive: when Debby and Betsy departed temporarily to see Monica fed early, he said to Amelia, "I bet you like being grown up and dining with the grown-ups."

That gave Amelia a chance to star before she followed Mark into another room to watch television. Alone with Danny and Larry, Alida pursued the earlier theme: "What were your tastes like when you were young?"

"I had none," Danny said. "I'm a country boy."

"And I was a country boy from New York City," Larry said.

Danny recalled that where he had grown up there was nothing to look at but the country, and nobody thought of having opinions about anything except, of course, other people. "You could say we didn't have tastes; we just had gossip."

"It's a big change in your life," Larry said, "when you feel entitled to have a critical point of view. No doubt about it. When I was a kid, I went to the theater all the time—tickets were so cheap, it seems unbelievable now—and I sat in the balcony and I saw all the great stars, and I was thrilled. It never occurred to me that, most of the time, I was seeing junk, utter junk. Vehicles, they called them. They were terrible, but I didn't begin to question a play until—"

"When, Pop? You told us to question everything."

That was Debby, who had returned with Betsy.

"So you could learn from my mistakes."

Larry made drinks, and sat down. The evening proceeded thereafter as a duet—Debby and her father—with infrequent interjections by the others. The two were so alike in the way their minds worked that they could not help, or did not know, how they excluded the others. It was a reason that Danny and Betsy might find their marriages difficult. Though preferable to old Mr. Rush and Mary Anne because they were not drunk, not maudlin, and anything but complaining or defeated, this father-daughter team might be equally unlucky for everyone around them. Through gaps in their dialogue, which continued straight through dinner, Alida learned that Danny, who was in law school, hoped to specialize in environmental law, and that Mark was interested in archeology—hence his planned, unfulfilled trip to Mexico. Alida noticed that Amelia was rapt, listening to father and daughter. Might she talk that way with Hugo some day? Yet it was chat that omitted Alida, Amelia, Betsy, Mark, Danny. Chess arcana. Then they started talking about someone named Martin Gardner, who, Alida gradually realized, was not a person they knew, but someone who invented puzzles they solved. When there was room for others, father and daughter listened, and then their conversation closed over the new offering, incorporating it like a minor ingredient in a complex recipe. God knows how much intelligence was flying around the dinner table, but all it proved was that extremely intelligent people could be emotionally obtuse.

Larry was obtuse the next morning when, on the pretext of showing Alida his theater-design collection, he led her into a sitting room where the walls were covered with watercolor drawings and sketches of sets and costumes. Most of them came from plays with which Larry had had some connection, but he had also bought some gems from ballet, Bakst and Benois. When he had allowed Alida to look and comment, he thanked her for coming over. He hoped they would see more of her—Betsy, particularly, needed her. "I think she's lonely," he said. "She hasn't a really close friend, and you've always cheered her up. I don't know what troubles her. She has everything a woman could want—houses, children. And I took her—take her—everywhere. But then I am mother and father to so many . . ."

Before Alida could make up her mind to suggest that it might be precisely how much Betsy had—houses and children—that was troubling her, Larry had changed the subject. "What do you hear from Hugo these days?" he asked.

If he saw Alida flush, he did not take the silent hint. "Not much," she said. "Nothing. We don't correspond."

"I'm sorry his show ended," Larry continued. "Not surprised, though. I know it's wrong to say 'I told you so,' but I reminded him when he came in at Christmas that I'd begged him not to go to California. You remember."

"I don't," Alida said.

She was not lying; in fact, she did not.

"I thought very highly of his talent," Larry went on. "I wanted him to stick it out in the theater. But he was obstinate."

Alida resented Larry's paternal reminiscences. If he thought he had an important relationship with Hugo, well and good. But it was nothing to her. Nor did she like learning that Hugo had seen Larry last month. She had no particular recollection of Hugo's and Larry's professional intimacy, but Hugo rarely discussed business with her. When she pushed her mind back, she could remember that Larry had been Hugo's accountant when they lived in New York, and had had something to do with financing his plays, and that Hugo had always spoken with respect of Larry's judgment. And she recalled, too, that he had described Larry as an adviser, not only to himself, but to many other people, and not only about money. Larry was an all-purpose sage or guru to a troop of "creative" people. Perhaps Hugo was seeking Larry's advice again. Yet for Alida, the primary friendship had always been hers with Betsy. It had never crossed Alida's mind that the Kellys' move to California had been a subject of discussion, let alone dissension, between the two men. "There are always careers in the theater," Larry said, "for the handful who are genuinely gifted. Hugo is. Perhaps he'll come back. You must tell him so."

Alida objected that she was in no position to tell Hugo anything. "And vice versa," she added.

"So that's how it is," Larry said.

"That's how it really is."

"And yet"—Larry would not give up—"you were responsible for his decision. Hugo didn't want to hang on in the East and risk one more so-so success. He wanted money very badly. He hated having a rich wife."

"But I'm not—" Alida began.

Larry merely gave her a look. Then he sighed, everybody's father and mother contemplating the wayward young disregarding his advice. They went back to the others and he started complaining that Debby had selfishly done the *Times* puzzles, leaving nothing for him.

The following week Amelia was to leave on Friday for a long weekend skiing in the Berkshires with the Richardsons. Time vanished as Alida shopped for herself and Amelia, registered at Barlow, visited Miss Blossom to talk about Fanny Burney, and planned a thank-you dinner for the Richardsons, to which she asked Father Peele. The Richardsons were dull, useful only in confirming arguments in favor of Alida's leaving Flat Rock. Tom was on his best behavior, but the childish eruptiveness that had exploded on New Year's Eve underlay his civility; he was, perhaps, not naturally an indoors animal. His wife was effusive, but Alida thought her molasses did not wholly cover a naturally envious disposition; she had little to say beyond the dreariest kind of gossip about people they knew at school or at the Club, and Alida found her malice boring. Father Peele performed his usual binding function, and drew disparate personalities into little oases of common interest in what would otherwise have been perfect conversational aridity: the Berkshires for skiing, say, as compared with the Sierras; and proposals afoot for Flat Rock's Bicentennial celebration, which had split the community in almost as many ways as there were suggested courses of action. Snow was falling, and the Richardsons left early. Alida enjoyed a brief tête-à-tête with Father Peele, who wanted to know all Alida had done since he dined there the evening of her first visit to Barlow. Though she disliked or distrusted his influence on her mother, she began to appreciate him as a confidant. Like Morgan,

153

he concentrated on his companion, but Father Peele suggested detachment rather than flirtation. And, despite his simplicity, he seemed to understand—both to visualize and comprehend—everything Alida told him. "A warehouse can be an autobiography," he said, when she described her future job.

The snow fell all night, and was still falling the next day when the Richardsons' station wagon came by for Amelia. Mrs. Gibson, Alida's tenant, called soon after to say that a moving van had just taken the last of their possessions, and that, despite the bad weather, they would try to drive to Vermont that day. She raised business questions, asking for a formal legal discharge and mentioning the security deposited against damage or default. She hoped Alida would examine the premises and remit the money, et cetera. Alida promised, et cetera. It seemed as if they talked forever; important communications—"I love you"; "He's dead"; "You're hired"—are brief; unimportant ones niggle for hours. After Alida hung up, she realized she was free to inspect the apartment the following day— indeed, with school and work about to start, the empty Saturday was her likeliest time. She could also visit the Galleries and find a thank-you present for Janet Cameron.

The Saturday was frozen. Even the light suggested images of hostility: the sun glinted briefly on the icicles at the Flat Rock station as if picking up the highlights on armor. Winter was implacable. Alida thought she and everyone else on the train were at odds with Nature; their activity defied the commands of climate. The contrast between the temporary death of winter and Alida's own January animation was characteristic of the Northeast, which had been founded, and survived, on defiance. Thus Alida reflected once more on having come home—that decision she had taken so impulsively in June—and then considered the homecoming ahead. Was she again acting incautiously in returning alone to the apartment, to the scene of her first years with Hugo? She was finding these returns disquieting, for wherever she went, she kept meeting herself in strange guises—her uncle's and aunt's neglected daughter, say, or the Weinsteins' brilliant waif.

The train ground to a halt. The decay of service had taken place while Alida was away from Flat Rock. She had resumed her girlhood pattern of relying on the trains, and had so far been in luck. Now, on this frozen morning, she remembered all the lamentations and anger about commuting she had heard in the past months, and began to imagine herself stuck fast all day. Another train, long, silver, and sleek, whizzed by, and a slow freight chugged past, and then their own train began to emit a variety of metallic sighs and gnashes, gasps and grindings, and in a matter of minutes, it was off again, hurrying to make up lost time, racing in rebellion against winter, hurtling Alida toward her destiny, which, as far as she knew, was to become a divorced decorator with her own apartment in New York.

Morgan was back from California, and in the shop. He was talking to a customer, but interrupted himself to ask Alida to wait. When he was free, he thanked her warmly. "We're giving young Hardman a show," he said, "and, besides, I had some interesting conversations with his sister. We'll be carrying some of her pottery. And then, those names you gave me in southern California"—Alida had mentioned on New Year's Eve several painters she had known there when Morgan was encouraging her to talk about herself—"some of them are very promising. You've been a great help. I was going to tell you Monday, when you came in." Morgan thanked Alida further, told her how wonderful she looked, and asked after her mother and child. Then, "Any special reason you're here today?"

Alida presented her problem: a gift for Janet Cameron.

Morgan agreed Janet was difficult. He told Alida that Janet had given Guthrie another job, doing the offices of one of her charities. "She's had so many compliments on the day-care center, she thinks she did it herself. The first time, she left him alone; now she's making suggestions. Janet Cameron is a funny woman. She thinks she's all sweetness and light, pacifism, love, charity—that sort of thing—yet she's actually a Roundhead, an Ironsides. I don't much want to give her one of our treasures. Why not send her flowers or a plant?"

Alida objected that it was their duty to nurture the seedlings of an esthetic response that Guthrie had sown in Janet's Puritan soul. Besides, for Alida's own satisfaction, she wanted something that expressed gratitude in a striking way.

"Janet won't know," Morgan countered.

"But I will. Have you anything useful? Something that works?"

Morgan had a few nineteenth-century wooden workboxes. They considered those; they considered other things. The time flew. They were back to the workboxes again, when Morgan remembered a letter-opener, a lovely little Victorian object with a mother-of-pearl handle and, he took care to add, a working blade. "The trouble is, it isn't big, and it doesn't look like much, and it's really rather delicate."

Alida suggested they add a paperweight, and Morgan, in a burst

155

of enthusiasm, told her about some marvelous reproductions he had found. He was lamenting his stupidity for not having thought of them sooner, "but one doesn't immediately associate Janet Cameron with millefiori." And then he complimented Alida. "Now it's right," he said. "You've *made* it right. Whatever she sees in these things, she'll see the gift as a tribute to her importance."

Alida wrote a card, and Morgan said there was a possibility they could have it wrapped and hand-delivered in the course of the afternoon. Morgan asked where she was going. She told him and, as an afterthought, asked if he would be willing to look over her apartment and make some suggestions.

"I'll bring Guthrie. One day next week after work. Wednesday. Come up from the warehouse. Let me check and tell you Monday."

So that was done. Alida bought a sandwich at a crowded counter and started down the avenue toward her apartment. She would have dawdled if the cold had not been so punishing. She was reluctant to arrive. She *had* been hasty. She should have taken time to find someone—Aunt Jane?—to go with her. Mrs. Gibson could have waited for her security. Everyone was talking up independence nowadays, yet there was something to be said for dependence— extra arms and shoulders to lean on. Or even the uses of a dependent (a child, a servant) whose presence demanded composure. She was going to have to face the apartment alone, but (changing her mind) alone had advantages. If she felt sad, she would cry.

Someone called her name. A man. The avenue was so crowded, and her mind so unfocused, or so focused on the apartment, that she could not at first identify the voice. She turned, and it was Andrew, behind her, coming out of a record store.

"Hello, Alida," he said. "What are you doing sneaking into the city on the weekend?"

"Serious business. Affairs of my own. I've just bought Janet a present, and now I am going to look at my apartment."

"Did you get my letter to forward to Mrs. Gibson?" Alida had not. "I reminded her that you would return her security only after you had inspected the premises. You really should have a professional do that. I hope you brought your inventory." Alida had forgotten she ever had had one. Andrew shook his head. "I suppose you brought a flashlight." Alida had no flashlight. "Actually," Andrew continued, "they're not likely to have stolen the copper pipes. But there have been some appalling shenanigans at Divco. When you think of it, making off with the parquet would be small potatoes."

Alida was conscious that, standing, they were blocking the side-walk, and, with a nod of her head, started across the street to a housewares store to buy a flashlight. Andrew went with her, still talking, arguing, really, with himself. "Lawyers are taught to take a dark view of human nature." (On the one hand.) "But I don't think they would mess up a place they had been using for business enter-tainment." (On the other.) "But apartments have been terribly bashed up, even by so-called nice people." (On the other hand again.) He seemed to have settled something. "I'd better go with you. You're a trusting child, Alida."

After they had left the store, Alida replied, "Debby Weinstein—Debby Mahon—thinks I'm a woman of the world."

"Who's Debby what's-her-name?"

Alida identified her, and Andrew said, "Her father knows his stuff."

Alida mentioned her annoyance with Larry, and Andrew said, "If he worries you, don't see him. He has allegiances, and it's right he should. But if he chooses Hugo . . ." Andrew changed topics. "It's very good of you, Alida, to get something for Janet. Not that I'm surprised—you're naturally kind and sensitive. But Janet has helped many people who haven't been grateful, and I know it's hurt her. What did you get?"

Alida told him and Andrew was delighted. "It's just right, Alida. Perfect. I know she'll be pleased." Then he said, "And you're perfect, too. Come to think of it, isn't the perfect combination to appear to be a woman of the world—stylish, assured, doing and saying the right thing—and not *be* one, not be hard or selfish or careless about people?"

"Do you think worldly people are hard?" Alida asked. "I think they're apt to be tolerant—at least in big things. They can get very worked up about the wine, but they're indifferent to fibs."

As they walked along, they fell into a discussion of "hard" and "soft" and how it applied to people, and who was what in what circumstances, and when hardness was appropriate—when to spank and when to sue. Their topic was ethics, although, since they brought in the names of people they knew and instances from their own lives, they thought they were gossiping. The conversation di-verted Alida to the point that she forgot to be anxious about going to the apartment.

Mrs. Gibson had alerted the staff. The doorman passed them along to the superintendent, who had the keys, and who volunteered, though not eagerly, to accompany them. Andrew said, "Perhaps later. If we need you. Enjoy the game," and pressed a bill into his hand.

"Thanks, Mr. Kelly."

First off, Alida decided the entry was dark. Andrew, however, stepped forward, and called back to her, "I didn't remember you had such a handsome living room. Is it possible I was never in it?"

It was indeed a fine room, a well-proportioned two-story room that seemed correct in every dimension. But Alida disliked the two sofas that faced each other on either side of the fireplace. And the whole room needed painting.

"Everything in New York City always needs painting," Andrew said.

They had exchanged roles. *He* had been the one who was going to look suspiciously at everything, but instead he was telling Alida how beautiful it all was. He suggested they look at the kitchen and, as they went through the dining room, he asked if the table was valuable. When Alida said it had come out of storage from a Clark house—"my grandparents' country house, I think"—he looked again and pronounced the top in excellent condition. The kitchen was larger than Alida remembered, and some of the appliances were unfamiliar. "That's my stove. I remember it from when I was taking cooking lessons. But that refrigerator looks new." Mrs. Gibson had left a paper for Alida on the kitchen table, recapitulating her address and phone number, along with the name, address, and phone number of her cleaning woman and a few recommendations about local shops. One of the maids' rooms had been turned into a laundry, and when Alida looked in she was almost certain that the Gibsons had installed new appliances and had neither removed them nor attempted to sell them to her. "Andrew," she said, "I'm not going to hold them up for security when she's left me all this stuff."

Andrew objected that they had no way of knowing if any of it worked, but he seemed halfhearted; the place *had* been well cared for, and he was ready to move on. The kitchen looked out onto a court, and the sun had shifted as the winter afternoon moved along. The room was not dark, but the thinning of the light was like a host's hint to speed his guests. They went to the front of the apartment again, and stood in the library where Hugo had worked. He had had a superstitious attachment to his working furniture—his desk, his chair, his "thinking sofa"—and it had been moved to California. Whatever the Gibsons had placed in the room was gone. Paler areas on the pale-blue carpeting showed where their furniture had stood.

Suddenly the young woman Alida had been avoiding all afternoon was there, in the room with them—that bride full of joy and expectations of further joy. Alida remembered bringing home her triumphs to Hugo. When she had found that blue ready-made carpeting whose color was the color of Chinese *clair de lune*, Hugo reveled in her use of the term, and was proud (possibly because he knew nothing about porcelain and pottery) that his bride had such arcane knowledge. At the time, Alida had thought their delight in each other was reciprocal, but now it seemed that she was always bringing her little doings to him like a dog bringing back sticks. Alida's memory began perversely retrieving, word for word, her conversations with Hugo about every object in the apartment, and the person she hated in those remembered dialogues was not the lordly husband but the canine bride. She would have to be exorcised if Alida were to live in the apartment again. She thought that if she got rid of—sold, stored, gave away, threw out—everything in the place and made it over totally, she might find herself ready for a fresh start. She said, "Larry Weinstein said I was rich."

"Damn Larry Weinstein! What is he putting you up to? I will not let you invest in plays."

Then Alida began to explain, with her own kind of coherence that might have sounded to Andrew like incoherence, why she wanted to redo her apartment. All her instances and illustrations were bound up with things, and not, as she usually talked or thought of things, for themselves, but as symbols. She was not speaking as a student or connoisseur. Suddenly objects expressed all the meanings in her past: every wineglass was a grail. But Andrew did not see why she could not simply have the blue rug cleaned.

She told him she knew she could not spend money like Mary Smith, and then, since Andrew did not recognize her name, out came the events of New Year's Eve (omitting the part about Alida's infatuation with Morgan). Andrew retorted that, while Alida might be disconcerted when a woman made a pass at her, it was no reason to remodel an apartment. Alida, seeing he still did not understand, went back to her mother's Canton bowl, the bowl Alida had broken, as a symbol of living in the past.

Andrew interrupted. "We've never felt that spending money was a solution to problems."

Alida was furious. "Who's 'we'? Just because your life has gone so smoothly and you've never had disappointments, you've no right to preach."

159

By now they had returned to the living room. They sat down and faced each other, each on one of the sofas Alida disliked, and Andrew, nettled, said, "Alida, you know you can spend money on the apartment. The 'we' referred to our families, yours and mine. Watermans and Camerons have known each other for more than a century. And the Clarks aren't that different. Your mother is generous. This is a lovely apartment she gave you. And she lives well, very well, but she's not extravagant. She's not showy. She had a tragedy. She lost her husband. Perhaps she made too much of it, but she didn't try to cure her sorrow by flashy spending. And your father. I remember telling you he was a flirt, but he had a serious side. He volunteered for the navy. He gave his life for his country. And I remember hearing him say—remember, I was so young that *he* must have been very young, too—that what this country needed was 'a responsible aristocracy.' It's a phrase that sticks in a boy's mind. And there's meaning to it."

Alida was depressed. It looked as if Andrew were going to talk politics. But such moments of hiatus in conversations often allow time for reflection (I am being foolish; he does not know what he is talking about), and Alida recognized that she was taking advantage of Andrew. Despite a century's family connection, this particular Waterman-Cameron relationship was essentially professional. All professional relationships have moments of intimacy—one displayed oneself in varying states of helplessness or disarray or dubiety to doctors, dentists, lawyers, accountants, priests, and they did whatever it was their business to do—but then it was over. Andrew had given her his afternoon because he was kind. Apartment-fussing was no part of his job. He was acting as a friend, but he was only a friend in the most general sense of the term, not a best friend, not a personal friend. "Andrew," Alida said, "I'm sorry. I seem to want to fight with someone this afternoon." She rose, and added, "I might as well go home. Morgan Davies is coming Wednesday and bringing Guthrie. They'll know what I should do."

"Ah, Guthrie, the famous Guthrie," said Andrew. "Is that his first, last, or only name?"

"I haven't the faintest idea," said Alida.

"Well, sit a moment and calm down."

She did, and they began to talk quietly and soberly, going over the ground of her anger again, and Andrew pointed out that what he was really objecting to was not this or that expenditure, but the notion of spending as a solution—people could buy company, but

160

not friendship or esteem, let alone happiness or fulfillment. And then, apologetically, "I wish I didn't always seem to be lecturing you or preaching. It's age, of course, and my professional role. I feel I must correct you. For instance, your saying I'd had no disappointments. Alida, don't you know that nobody, *nobody* lives past a certain age without disappointments? Many of us (I mean human beings, not lawyers, or men) are going on day after day, wondering where their lives went wrong. Not, perhaps, after an event as acute as yours. A slow leak rather than a blowout. Like my secretary, Mrs. Southern. And I myself remember . . ."

"What?"

"Nothing."

Alida thought of little Janet. She could understand that Andrew would not want to talk about her. The February-afternoon light was beginning to fade in the living room. It was not dark—had there been lamps, Alida would not have felt the need to turn them on— but, as in the kitchen, time passing recalled the journeys and duties that waited. Relaxing, putting off parting, now that she and Andrew were on good terms again, Alida looked at him across the coffee table. Against the tall, uncurtained windows, his outline was dark. A solid flat almost black against the blue-gray background of the glass. Degas or Manet. Andrew, still apologetic, was taking back some of what he said about the Waterman-Cameron connection. All Camerons did not worship all Watermans. He mentioned her aunt Isabel, her father's older sister, whom he detested, and Alida, partly listening, partly not, looking at Andrew turn into a painting (she, too, detested her aunt Isabel, but Isabel lived in France), became aware that she was alone, cut off—no one knew where they were— in the beginning of twilight with a man. Andrew. And quite suddenly, she felt a sweet tingling in the loins, a stiffening of the breasts, as desire took hold of her. It was shocking, unexpected, uncontrollable. She was unable to speak. Her body went off on its own mania for Andrew, Janet's husband, Alida's lawyer, her father's friend. She was shaken as the terrible, delicious feelings rolled through her, surged, broke, eddied, and surged again. She—her personality, her respectability, her self—was drowning in her own sexuality. She bent her mental energies to control it. When, for example, Andrew raised his arm in a gesture, she concentrated on thinking of other flat painters as the dark-suited arm was extended before the graying window. Whistler. But immediately she felt moistness between her thighs. She reminded herself that new curtains would cost a fortune.

But it was no use. She could only hope that Andrew could not guess from her face what was happening to her. Perhaps her silence sounded like unresponsiveness, like boredom. Andrew seemed restless, making brief moves—hands in and out of pockets, legs crossed and uncrossed—that suggested anxiety (which was not typical of him) or, more likely, *his* boredom. He wanted to be gone. That was it. He stood up and asked, "Is there anything else we should look at?"

It was better that they go. The kind of pleasure Alida found in sitting with Andrew had to be suppressed and forgotten. There were things that Watermans, even her detestable aunt Isabel, did not do. With a last effort, she pulled herself together, and answered, in her normal, casual voice, "Nothing much upstairs. The master bedroom, Amelia's room. The nurse's. And a guest room."

"Did you leave the nursery furniture for the Gibsons?"

"No, their children were older. Amelia was outgrowing it. I must have given it to Goodwill." Then she said, "This staircase is lovely," and, by no great leap of the mind, "You're right, Andrew, my mother *is* generous."

Andrew seemed to have run out of conversation. They looked in, briefly, at the smaller bedrooms and baths, all empty, bare, and clean. A hall led to the master bedroom, which was approximately over the living room. The Gibsons had left blinds on the windows and carpet on the floor. The bed, stripped to the mattress, looked immense. It had been one of Alida's "finds," but she was beginning to tire of it by the time she and Hugo were moving, and it was so unusually heavy that they left it. Now she wondered what she had ever seen in it. She had been snared by a temporary vogue for outsize pieces of furniture, and her bed was a huge carved-rosewood four-poster, from Spain, she had been told, a nineteenth-century reproduction of the eighteenth that betrayed the incomprehension of one period for another: grossness had crept in where virtuosity had been intended. What Alida had just been feeling for Andrew had erased Hugo from her mind—yesterday's lesson washed off the blackboard. He might never have existed. As she looked at the bed, she was not thinking of it as the bed in which Amelia had been conceived; she was wondering whether she could do anything with it, or whether she could persuade Morgan or Guthrie to palm it off on a client for whom there was charm in esthetic failure. Andrew, perhaps misunderstanding her concentration, and thinking of her earlier distress, put his hand on her shoulder, in a gesture of consolation that would have been no more than that, coming from Josiah. But Andrew's touch, the weight of his hand, and Alida's sense of his palm and fingers destroyed Alida's poise. Her too keen physical awareness of Andrew was no longer suppressible; she turned, stood on tiptoe, and kissed him on the lips. There was, perhaps, a brief moment when that kiss, too, might have remained a simple social gesture, but it changed on its own; it metamorphosed into an embrace that did not prefigure, but already was, union. Andrew broke away, and Alida feared he was leaving her. No, he was closing the blinds. They moved in slow, wordless, uncertain tenderness, undressing and looking at each other; caressing silently, earnestly, deliberately, as if haste, speech, or any sign of their eagerness would break a spell. They were enchanted and shy, but they were also passionate in the fulfillment of hopes they had not allowed themselves to imagine. Behind their rapture lay desperation. An accumulation of sorrows had created two solitudes that were now ending. They had been living no; they were mining each other's bodies for yes.

It was dark in the room. Andrew said, "I wish I could see you."

Alida took his hand and placed it on her heart, and said, "Dark is better. I love you."

Andrew's reply was a confession: "When I glimpsed you this afternoon through the record-store window I was thrilled. Like a boy. I ran out on the street to follow you." And then, after a pause, "Oh my God, I forgot the record."

Alida, wishing to know everything about the man who had become hers, asked, "What was it?"

"*Tristan.*"

An ill-omened name to hear beside a lover.

"Do you like Wagner?"

Andrew, drowsy, dazed with happiness after possessing the woman he adored, was wholly unguarded: "Not a bit. Janet wanted it."

Easter

The next day began like an ordinary churchgoing Sunday in the Waterman household. At eight-thirty, Jenny brought a cup of coffee, drew open the curtains, and began to run a bath. She tidied and maided, and, when Alida emerged from the tub, presented a brown broadcloth suit and a white blouse with a wide, flat collar and deep turned-back cuffs, a churchgoing costume befitting Priscilla Alden rather than Hester Prynne. Alida dressed, went down to the breakfast room, and leafed through the Sunday papers while Sally served. There was a sudden catastrophe—an earthquake in Guatemala— and lingering calamity—New York City's finances—but no disaster could compare to the havoc Alida had created. She could not imagine how she would ever face Andrew again, and she was horrified that, even as she recognized that she had touched the profoundest depths of sluttishness, her pleasure at recalling the weight of Andrew's body on hers was keener than her guilt. She had thrown herself at him, seduced him, breached every decency—honor and reserve alike; she remembered telling him that she loved him—and awoke incorrigible. The telephone rang. Sally entered and asked if she would speak to Mr. Cameron.

"I must talk to you," he said. "We must talk."

"Yes," Alida replied.

"Now," he added.

"Where are you?"

"At the Old Bridge station parking lot."

Alida was astonished. "When—how—did you get there?"

"In a Hertz. I'm calling from a phone booth. Meet me there. How long will it take you?"

"Twenty minutes."

"When you get there, follow me."

"What kind of car have you got?"

"Oh damn. I don't know. Wait a minute. It's black. Some sort of Chevy, I think. You'll see it. There's nobody around. Or I'll see you. Just follow me when I leave."

Coins thunked as he hung up. Alida looked at her watch. It was more than an hour before the family usually left for church—what would the staff make of her departure?—but she was afraid to keep Andrew waiting, as if tardiness could aggravate the offense of having seduced him. As she started the car, she reminded herself not to speed and to beware of ice on the road. She thought of the horrible double curve and of Fred; wicked as she was, she did not want to die. Her palms were sweating within her gloves as she inched out of the driveway. The car radio was playing a hymn that was succeeded by a sermon on self-sacrifice. She switched it off. At the station there was only one black car in the almost empty parking lot. She tooted her horn; the driver looked up. It was Andrew. She followed his car southward and then westward on a highway. Traffic was light and following easy; she was free to concentrate on uncertainty, to pick at her guilt, to scratch her anxiety about Andrew's anger, and to dread the confrontation that would occur whenever they arrived where he was leading her. They turned north just short of the Hudson, and after another ten miles left the highway for a blacktop road that paralleled the river, running most of the way between brick estate walls, some with institutional signs at their gates (convents, schools), others marked as clubs, a few calling themselves farms. Some five miles farther, Andrew slowed, signaled left, crossed the road, and entered an unmarked, gateless opening in a red-brick wall. They were apparently on a property that he knew well, for he drove unhesitatingly over narrow, winding paved roads until he pulled up in front of a sizable fieldstone building with a brown-shingled roof. Alida stopped and got out. She waited for him to speak. He opened the door with a key, and she followed into a dark, cold entryway. "I hope you don't mind the smell of paint," he said, as he turned on a light switch on the wall.

There was a jumble of builders' equipment—ladders and sawhorses and paint buckets—at the foot of a raw, new wooden staircase. The thermostat beside the switch registered 40; Andrew turned it up, saying, "The system is brand-new. It'll be warm in a moment."

165

He led her through a door on the left, into a room in semidarkness that was very large and, like the entry hall, confused and crowded. Huge white wooden shutters stood on the floor leaning against the windows, like a frieze of tipsy ghosts, and kept out most of the daylight. Andrew stepped forward. His hand was up, reaching for a light cord from a ceiling fixture. "Goddamn" marked his collision with some heavy, low object. The light came on from a large brass chandelier. Alida was standing at the bottom of the downstroke of a big pine-paneled T-shaped room. There was a huge stone fireplace on the wall on the right; the cross-stroke of the T was a broad expanse the width of the building, with a stage at the rear that was piled with partly dismantled old servants' room furniture—metal bedsteads and small pine chests. Thin mattresses were stacked in a corner beside folded blue-velvet stage curtains. Alida could discern the outlines of irregular rows of auditorium chairs as well as sofas and upholstered seats beneath painters' tarpaulins.

"They'll be finished upstairs next week," Andrew said. "Then they'll come down here."

Alida looked around for a place to sit, but the drop cloths were covered with a mixture of dust, granulated plaster, and paint flakes. The room was warming up, though, and she pulled off her gloves and opened her coat. She picked her way through the maze of shrouded furniture, ran her finger along the edge of the stage, and, finding it less soiled than she had expected, half-sat, half-leaned against it, staring at the floor past her hands holding the handle of her pocketbook, awaiting with resignation Andrew's condemnation. He did not speak immediately. She began to tremble.

"Are you cold?" he asked.

"No, no, not at all."

"You're shivering."

"Am I?"

"Look at me. Please don't be angry. Forgive me."

Alida felt her face go hot; ashamed of blushing, embarrassed at Andrew's apology for her guilt, she gazed at her shaking hands in perplexity.

"Are you angry?" Andrew asked.

She shook her head no.

"Then look at me," he implored.

But she did not, for, once she grasped that he was not angry at her—and that he feared that she was angry at him—she realized how much she desired him, and was afraid to show him her face. He took her chin in his hand, turned her face up, and looked into her eyes. Her lips were parted, but not to speak. As they kissed, their exploring tongues sent urgent signals to themselves and to each other. In a harsh, dark, ragged voice, Andrew said, "Pull up your skirt."

She wriggled onto the stage, onto the pile of curtains, kicked off her shoes, struggled out of her panty hose, and felt him fall on her and drive into her. The little delights gave way to a grand one: she felt she was cleft in two by a grand sword—an executioner's sword—of pleasure, and then self was extinguished. They lay entangled until the sound of a church bell nearby roused them. Alida turned her head and encountered Andrew's lips. They sucked each other's mouths, lying on the stage where generations before them had disported themselves through tableaux, charades, plays, puppet shows, and, lastly, the performer yielding to the *voyeur* and *auteur*, movies of travel and homemade efforts at cinematic art, forms of fulfillment more elaborate than the direct satisfaction Andrew and Alida extracted from each other. The demon who had taken command of him now ordered, "Everything off. I want to look at you."

Nude on stage, they nibbled each other with their eyes, and, holding each other at arms' length, turned each other as if examining statues; they began patting, touching, feeling, fingers exploring as if hunting for nicks or repaired cracks, and finding crevices; a kind of open-eyed blind man's examination, a connoisseur's caress, a dealer's appraisal. But of course they were not curios, vases, or statues, and could not be passive under such fingering; they began, almost playfully, to probe, to nip, to bite, to lick, to kiss, and the tempo of their game increased as their pulses speeded; down on the curtains they fell, rolling over and gasping and panting, and, once more in union, cried, "Ah!" and then subsided in trance.

They heard a car slow outside, and held their breaths until it went on after pausing. Andrew looked at his watch. "They'll be showing the place any minute," he said.

He pulled her up. They sought their dusty, crumpled clothes and began to dress. Though trying to hurry, they could not help playing—dusting each other off, kissing, laughing as if they were children; each hated to see the other—skin, stomach, breasts, hips, genitals—disappear beneath layers of cloth. "Do you need a mirror?" Andrew asked, when they had at last resumed their garments and the adult personalities that went with them. "I'll see if there is one." He darted out. Alida heard his footsteps overhead, and then he called, "Up here. We're in luck."

A newly installed bathroom upstairs boasted a tape-crossed,

plaster-daubed mirror; Alida combed and powdered and painted while Andrew sat on the edge of the tub, scanning the motions that led to the return of Alida's public face. He was not yet wholly the official Andrew, however, for, as they were almost ready to leave, he surveyed her in the downstairs hall, and giggled. "What a little Puritan you look like in that white collar."

He turned down the thermostat, turned off the light, and, just before opening the door, said—this was the voice of her serious, responsible lawyer—"We must meet again and talk, really talk. The men leave at four. Where will you be tomorrow?"

"In the city," she answered. "I don't even know where the warehouse is."

"Tuesday, then."

"I'll be here at five, after classes."

They met on Tuesday, but they did not talk.

Andrew and Alida were descended from rapacious, aggressive, esurient stock, men and women who did as they pleased and took what they wanted and justified their ease, their power, and their misdeeds by whatever authorities were fashionable, the Will of God, the intent of the Founding Fathers, the Survival of the Fittest. These swaggering forebears had bequeathed them the healthy nerves and first-rate coordination that they demonstrated in sport. But Andrew and Alida played by different rules from their ancestors, because the buccaneers' gross assurance had been undermined by the Social Gospel and Freudianism; by new concepts of gentility, sincerity, and civility; by inheritance taxes, boarding schools, and gossip columns, which successively and together had instilled a conscience more given to renunciation than to assertion—a restrictive conscience, a prudent *rentier*'s conscience that counseled against show, risk, greed, and insistence on self. Therefore they could not talk, for by doing so they would have had to admit that their relation was a tapestry of betrayals. Alida at first pretended to herself that they *were* just about to talk, and her self-deception made it easier for her everytime she turned into the breach in the brick wall. She did not acknowledge the truth, even to herself: when she decided to buy a car, she alleged that, as she was driving into the city as well as to school, she ought not wear out her mother's; in fact, she did not want another driver—James or her mother—to notice or question the extra mileage. Even when she began to bring sheets or a change of underclothes to their rendezvous, she never admitted to herself why. Andrew mailed her a copy of a map, a survey of the property where they met, drawn, as the legend read, for the heirs of Lucy Maitland Cameron, deceased. Alida never asked him the precise relations between himself, the property, and the dead woman, but was sure that the domain had belonged to the old lady of her childhood Thanksgivings.

When the workmen finished the playhouse (for whose occupation, she did not know), Alida and Andrew moved over a knoll to a cottage beside greenhouses. Though dilapidated and dark inside and still somehow permeated by the Burgundy-wine smell of moist earth and potting soil, this rendezvous was more habitable than their first. There were beds. In their haste, they did not always remember to use them. Their lovemaking was savage; their desire to incorporate and to be incorporated expressed itself without delicacy, and, as February's cold turned toward spring, they met and coalesced as brutally as the archetypal primitive pair copulating in fields to insure their fertility. This couple needed no hints from books, no tricks to enhance attraction or increase pleasure. In their violence, they sometimes lived bawdy jokes (when Andrew's tumescence took him unaware and he stumbled disrobing, or when they huddled against each other naked in a tiny bedroom closet while a watchman cursorily cast his flashlight over the adjoining room, the cottage parlor), but they did so with the utmost gravity. Their busy fingers, tongues, and mouths were not audacious assaults on, but efforts to become, the other. When Alida took Andrew's penis in her mouth, she would have wanted to swallow him entire and become him, just as, when he entered her, he would have wanted to follow his penis into her and be her. Their doings were not experimental or modern, but before history, before literature, before art, when there was only religion, when gods coupled with humans, spawned through their heads, swallowed their young, and when any being might be a god in disguise. Nothing they did seemed to them funny, sweet, sportive, or merry. Their sex was archaic, timeless, mythical—as rough, serious, and unreflective as paganism itself.

Their speechlessness was a truce that offered Alida a surcease from thinking about their doings—their adulteries—but at times, when they were apart, their muteness frightened her. As winter dragged toward its end, rallying at last with snow that melted and sleet that glazed the roads and then disappeared, leaving the soil pullulating, germinating, moist, soggy, spongy, she remembered how hard Andrew was. His bones were huge. Often, when his strength embraced her, she imagined being smothered by his

169

physical power—dying, disappearing. The thrill resembled a child's pretense when Daddy lifts him high in the air and both pretend he will let Baby drop. It was the father in Andrew who worried Alida; she had no experience of the sterner parent, and she sometimes wondered what Andrew thought of her ardent response to his ferocity, and, imagining him in paternal judgment, in imagination heard herself speak a stale, timid truth: "I've never done anything like this before."

There was a stratum of tenderness beneath his force—he called her "Lida" or "little Lida"—and there was (or so it sometimes seemed to Alida) unhappiness as well, though she could not have explained what made her suspect that, and frequently doubted her intuition because Andrew was making her so happy. Their meetings, though frequent, were brief—the hours they spent together were, in duration, the smallest part of her week, yet they became the most important part of her life; they changed her and her approach toward everything and everybody else in her existence. These others grew pale, lost reality, significance. Nothing mattered except being with Andrew, and therefore all else became easy. She did not fret while waiting to hear from Fanny Burney; she took Amelia's acceptance (which duly came) for granted.

As for Alida's own education, she had forgotten how boring school was, a lot of time-wasting, record-keeping, paper-shuffling. Textbooks and drawing paper. A brief review. She bought the fall-term textbook, a paperback devoted to every conceivable shape of interior, from the double-cube room at Wilton and the interior of Saint Peter's to the minginess of mobile homes. The spring was to be dedicated to learning how to borrow devices from handsome spaces to disguise small and ungracious ones. Most of her fellow students were recent graduates of manual-training or commercial-arts high-school courses, and there were very few points at which their experiences intersected with hers—she had visited Saint Peter's and they mobile homes—but, having Andrew, Alida was incurious about other people. The teacher, Miss Kinsky, who looked about Alida's age, brought such enthusiasm to teaching optical cheating and spatial falsification that Alida suspected she was battling her own boredom. Her inexpensive clothing was always slightly original; Alida invented (correctly, she found out) that Miss Kinsky was, or meant to be, an artist. (She painted.) Not caring, Alida did well, and tore through the simple assignments without effort.

The warehouse was more engrossing. On the first day, Alida was daunted by the jam of furniture shrouded in varieties of protective covering on the ground floor; she stood just inside the door, and said to Johnny, who had come down to help her, "We'll never get in!" But presently they did edge into spaces and find little passages between the bulky pieces. Then Alida picked up the edge of a mover's pad and uncovered what appeared to be a collection of decorative screens propped between two large objects—breakfronts, perhaps. She said, "We might as well start here. Where's the best light?"

Thereafter she worked with that concentrated absorption that was her gift, her blessing. Johnny was not only handsome and graceful, but strong, willing, and tireless. She was surprised to learn that he had no interest in decoration or decorative objects, but that was no drawback; as usual, the objects themselves became her companions. Their variety fascinated her; every day she made an unexpected find, a sample of a past taste or a bygone vogue from Mrs. McKinley's heyday, and sometimes she found real beauty. She very quickly ceased to notice the discomforts of her peculiar workplace; the sordid warehouse was a treasure house.

After the first consultation about her apartment, she saw Morgan and Guthrie infrequently. They thought she should develop some ideas of her own (all she had developed was a decision to keep the outsize bed) while they went on remodeling the Galleries. Alida visited Morgan periodically to go over her lists of objects in the warehouse and discuss those that baffled her, and on one such occasion, in the latter part of a Wednesday afternoon in mid-March, when they had taken a little longer than usual, Morgan, having complimented her on her work and put her lists in the appropriate folder, suggested a drink in the horsy bar. Alida disguised her eagerness to be on her way to Andrew. "Oh no, Morgan, thanks, but I've got this blessed drive ahead of me in all this traffic."

Something about her alerted him: her good-humored, offhand manner, a new glibness, and he said, "Alida, you've changed. Are you in love?"

Last year's fantasy became this year's fib: "Ah, Morgan, darling, only and forever with you."

Alida feared her mother's return, and the ordinary maternal awareness of a daughter's comings and goings, but the Gertrude who arrived home in March was different from the woman who left in January. Like the earth itself, she was wholly absorbed in her own doings. Alida had seen her mother in summer—satisfied fruition—

171

and fall and winter—seasons of obsequies and probate of gardens. Now, on the edge of spring, dormant Gertrude was not merely alert but agog. When she was not working with James and his boy, she was haring off to nurseries. Alida had picked up, at Barlow, a fistful of folders from historic-preservation sites; her course required that she visit some, and she planned to explain absences or latenesses by claiming that she had been studying this or that period restoration miles away. She found no excuses necessary. Her mother was not concerned with Alida's whereabouts and, atypically, talked a lot about her own projects, cascading Latin botanical names through her conversation. Her excitement communicated itself to Amelia, who began to spend more of her spare time with her grandmother and seemed not to need her mother. Their only joint expedition was a Saturday lunch at the Weinsteins' country house. Betsy was once more caught up in a last-minute family upset. Mark had turned up unexpectedly, announcing that he was quitting school. When Alida and Amelia arrived, Debby was in the living room, trying to help her mother quell the boy's mutiny, but Debby had too direct a mind. She could not see why every dispute could not be settled logically nor could she appreciate that other people did not always want to settle matters. Mark was reveling in the uproar he had created. Luncheon was announced. Debby went to look for Monica and Danny, while Betsy said wearily, to Alida, "His father will have to handle it."

"Where is Larry?"

"He had to go away on business," Betsy said. "Suddenly." She paused. "To California."

Her pause told Alida that Larry would see Hugo. But Hugo was very dim these days, and Alida would have been surprised if anyone had reminded her that he was her husband.

Portents of spring began calling attention to themselves. After a warm spell, the willows suddenly grew golden haloes, and one morning, before Jenny opened the rosebud-strewn curtains, Alida was awakened by the chatter of birds debating on the lawn. City streets became more colorful as dark winter coats yielded to bright spring clothes; the people who figured in urban scenes foretold the flowers about to bloom in the country. Alida took pleasure in this revivification until, looking at her school calendar, she realized it was all speeding inexorably toward Easter, a holiday that would interrupt the everyday routine in whose interstices she and Andrew hid. Her school and Amelia's would close, and she had arranged with Morgan to stay home from the warehouse to keep Amelia company. Later, it had been decided that David's show was to open at the Galleries some time during Easter vacation, and that he would come to New York, bringing Teeny to Flat Rock as Amelia's guest while he worked in the city hanging his pictures. This complex of circumstances would shrink Alida's liberty. The historic-preservation ruse might serve to free her for an afternoon, but the trouble was that she really did have to inspect at least one of those houses for a class paper due immediately after Easter. Before Andrew, holidays had been threatening and painful because she felt superfluous. Now that she did not, a holiday was time intruding on timelessness: not a festivity, but a demand. The calendar was an impersonal grid, clamped down on every living being, chopping up privacy in the name of public, communal existence with all its frauds, lies, shams, and mistaken assumptions about families and about seasons. Alida waited for Andrew to say something about Easter, to suggest contrivances by which they might meet during spring holiday. She found it impossible to open a conversation in which she would have to put into words that they were outlaws plotting. Days vanished before she realized that Andrew was not as intimately involved with school calendars as she; Easter, to him, might mean only a weekend, and since, after their first rendezvous, they had never attempted to meet on weekends, he would have no sense of impending separation. Thus she came to the ninth of April, a Friday, when, turning into the Cameron property, she knew she would have to force herself to say something, because it was the last day of Flat Rock Country Day School, and Teeny and David were arriving for dinner that night. Her day had been a mass of trivial incidents and duties, each taking longer than planned, so that Alida was a little late, and was surprised that Andrew had not arrived. They had migrated from the gardener's cottage to living quarters above a carriage-house-garage. Apprehension—where was he? when should she start talking?—mingled with anticipation as she left her car and climbed two steep wooden flights up past the onetime hayloft into a garret that had been cut into three tiny rooms illuminated by small dirty windows. As she put a sheet on the old metal cot, she felt a momentary panic at Andrew's absence. Then she undressed without thinking of anything.

Nude, she lay on her back beneath her navy blue spring coat. She pillowed her head on her arms, closed her eyes, and began to evoke the image of Andrew. She heard his car. She heard his steps on the stairs—they sounded slow and heavy rather than eager—but she was relieved to open her eyes and see him, handsome as ever, filling the narrow doorway. He did not smile, however, nor did he move toward her. In a tone of barbed patience, like a teacher's, he said, "I suppose you know a banker named Jones. Of course you do."

Who could have told him? Alida nodded and gaped. Andrew looked at her briefly, fetched a wooden chair from the next room, placed it at the foot of the bed, looked away, and began talking. She did not know if he was avoiding her face to escape her interruption or justification, or if, having learned about her and Eliot, he was so disgusted that he could not bear the sight of her. Andrew remained clothed; Alida tried to pull her coat around her. She had difficulty concentrating on what he was saying. She heard him mention Eliot's father. Could that stupid pimple have confessed to the old man? But how or why would Eliot's father have told Andrew? Belatedly, Alida began to listen and understood that Andrew was talking about business. She felt weak with relief. Perhaps her intermittent sense of Andrew's unhappiness had been accurate, but perhaps it had something to do with business or money. This year everybody was worrying about money or talking about worrying about money; older people were recalling the depression. But no matter what the stock market or inflation or OPEC meant to the world, none of it could have anything to do with them. Yet Andrew was extremely agitated. He wanted to tell her a story for a purpose, but his telling was disconnected. He repeated himself; he searched for words; he corrected himself. As far as Alida could follow, Andrew had dined the previous night, Thursday night, with a lawyer from Connecticut who had come to New York on business. They had talked about the national economy, and the Connecticut man had said that he expected more and more nasty revelations. As an instance, he mentioned a family that had consulted him after the accidental death of a young builder, when they had found that he had left practically no business—all debts and loans. They wondered if there was anything he, the lawyer, could do. He had gone through the papers they brought, and discovered that a local banker had drawn the decedent in over his head, pyramiding loans on loans, inciting him to create new corporations to borrow more. The pattern of banking was so risky, so imprudent, worse, so irresponsible—particularly since the relationship between the men, as the family had described it, had been one of confidence: on the part of the builder, of utter

174

trust—that it could only be called vicious. "He peddled loans like a pusher."

Andrew's informant had been discreet, but he had mentioned that the villain was the son of a moralizing, tiresome old bore of a country banker, famous for his stuffiness and his integrity, for his pessimism and his prudence. Several references suggested to Andrew the locality of the bank, and, besides, the elder Jones had long been famous beyond his own state: there could scarcely be two such living caricatures of the proverbial Yankee: thrifty, gloomy, ungracious, shrewd, and honest. The Connecticut lawyer had described these people to support his argument that the national decline in moral standards—possibly caused, and certainly concealed, by a long period of prosperity—had affected men and families whom communities had long, and with reason, expected to be above suspicion. "Seduction" and "self-seduction" were words the lawyer used. Corruption, he believed, had sifted into every joint and corner and crack of society and soiled it, perhaps indelibly. Watergate was not isolated. Everyone had been doing anything he could get away with; it was worse than the twenties, the lawyer thought, when, in his phrase, people had been "innocently wicked."

At all events, Andrew was not talking about what Alida feared, and while she was puzzling why he was so upset by a secondhand suspicion of a man he knew only by name, hearsay, or perhaps correspondence, she realized that, if the banker was indeed Eliot Jones, the dead builder was, inevitably, Fred Palmieri, and she burst into tears. Andrew's story meant that Fred's life had been wasted: all his sacrifices had been useless. He had renounced his own ambitions for the good of his family—and to no purpose. "Live all you can. It's a mistake not to," Fred cried from the grave, repeating the most desperate injunction ever spoken. Was there a sadder message? Only one, and that from a scaffold: "Remember."

The meaning to Alida was plain: Andrew should stop talking and take off his clothes.

"You see what I'm driving at," Andrew said.

Alida's nose was stuffed, her face was wet, and her handbag was across the room on top of a chest of drawers. "I don't, I don't," she answered, sounding querulous rather than bewildered amid her sniffles.

Andrew reached into his pocket and passed her a handkerchief. "Why are you crying?" he asked.

She tried to tell him about Fred, but between her emotional

175

disarray and her sobs and hiccups, she could not easily make herself understood. Andrew thought, at first, that she was telling him about a fellow student, and when he comprehended who Fred was, began to question her. How well had she known him? Why had she never mentioned him? Alida realized that her tears had made him jealous. "He's dead, Andrew," she said. "I'm sorry. He was my age. He wasn't my lover."

"My God, Alida, why can't you listen to me?"

Alida was seized by another outburst of weeping. Andrew waited and then began, very slowly, explaining the connection between his tale and their wrongdoing. "When I heard all this, my first thought was 'Lida's friendly country banker is a plain crook.' And then I thought, 'And what am I?' If I'd heard that Charlie Saunders had seduced you, I'd be furious."

Alida began to titter, though she saw the connection in Andrew's mind. Mr. Saunders was a bank trust officer in New York, who helped look after some of her money. He was a bald, stout, slow, stuffy, pontificating man, impossible to imagine as a lover. Alida's laughter seemed to depress Andrew; he looked unbearably sad in half-profile. Her impulse to comfort him was uncontrollable. She was sitting up, clutching her coat with one hand and wiping away her tears with the other, and when she reached out to touch his shoulder whose outline, in an unself-conscious pose, was a sketch of unhappiness, her protecting coat fell away. He glanced up, removed her hand, and said, "Don't tempt me, Alida."

"I'm not trying to tempt you; I want to console you. This isn't bad."

Her voice carried more plea than conviction.

"Of course it's bad. It was bad from the beginning. There you were—charming, smart, young, beautiful, trusting . . . I couldn't resist you. I took a bite. Like a shark. I've nothing to offer you, Alida. I took what wasn't mine. I don't understand myself. I'm no different from an embezzling banker. They always tell themselves they're going to put it back. When we met the first time, I was going to ask your forgiveness. I was going to tell you that, if you couldn't forgive, there's a new man in the office, Frank Hooper, you could see, but that I'd take care of your business anyhow. And what did I do? I fell on you like an animal. I've dragged you all over my great-aunt's property. What would she think of me? She was a gentle-woman. You never knew her—"

"Yes, I did," Alida interrupted, softly.

He took no notice. "You shouldn't be hiding in sties like these. And it's all I can give you. I can't leave my family. My son keeps vanishing, I think my daughter is crazy, and Janet can't handle it. I want her to see somebody, a doctor, but she won't go, and . . ." He stopped. He was not going to confide the rest. "What am I doing? Humiliating you, ruining your life because mine's been wrecked."

"You're not ruining my life, you *are* my life; you're all I have."

She could say no more, she could only sob. This was the "talk" they had so rightly avoided, so justly feared, and she was speechless. She covered her face as she cried. Then she looked up and tried to catch her breath to tell him that she wanted him anywhere, on any terms, trying to assure him that she was not suffering. She was almost inarticulate, gasping and weeping. He stood up, and said, wearily, "I must go."

"Don't leave me. We must talk. At least that."

He moved toward the door, and said, grimly, "I said that before."

He left. Closed the door. Really left. Still clutching her coat, Alida jumped up to follow him. He had disappeared around a turn in the stairs. She cursed her nudity. She heard the sound of his car, and stood for a moment, listening to the motor as he drove away. The sound dwindled, and in the silence that followed she began to think of what she should have said. That if he was unhappy with his family he needed her. They were justified by their necessity. And by their happiness. Some good had come out of their long-deferred "talk." Before Andrew had spoken, Alida agreed with everything he said; she had felt guilty and ashamed, as he did. Yet when she heard Andrew put into words the reasons that their pleasure was culpable, she realized she believed none of it. She had been tormenting herself for months with secondhand, worn-out notions, a spiteful morality that, she was certain, Andrew could not really accept, either. No one was injured by their love. They were entitled to it.

She sat on the bed, and the words formed in her mind: "He doesn't mean it. He isn't leaving me." It was not only wish but experience that told her the scene just past was not a parting. It was too truncated. A real break would take longer. There was more to rupture. Accusations. Rage. Hugo had hit her. But Andrew was not angry with her, any more than she was angry with him. He had had a momentary qualm—perhaps the approach of Easter was some-how troubling *that* family, his family—but it would pass.

Within the room, now half in shadow, Alida formed a conventional academic painting as she sat on the cot: "Interior with Nude."

She had to coax herself to dress and leave the room where Andrew had been. The chair on which he had sat seemed forlorn in his absence; its splayed back and legs, covered with chipped pale green paint, looked impoverished and deserted in the room's twilight. Yet the metal frame of the cot still glinted in the sun. The room and its contents were not orphaned, not abandoned. She would see them again; she would call Andrew at his office on Monday.

Alida reached home before David and Teeny arrived from the airport. She dressed and joined Gertrude and Amelia, who were playing checkers in the television room. "I've been keeping Grandma company," Amelia said. "Will you finish my game for me?"

She went out to wait for her guest at the gate.

Picking up her needlepoint, Gertrude said hopefully, "He wouldn't bring her if she weren't better."

They discussed how uncomfortable one felt disliking a child—especially a child one ought to pity—and Alida remarked that she was spoiled, as a mother, by having so remarkable a daughter. Mrs. Waterman suggested that the Rushes and Hardmans doubtless thought Teeny remarkable, too. She was right, of course, but Alida could not help her premonition that something would go wrong on Teeny's visit.

Unconscious of these forebodings, the child and her father entered the hall with Amelia and a bustle of baggage. Teeny was a trifle self-important to cover her shyness, but otherwise well behaved and as eager to see Amelia as Amelia had been to see her. Their first thought was to be allowed to share a room. "You'll keep each other up all night," Mrs. Waterman objected.

They pleaded and promised until they had their way. Mrs. Waterman gave orders, and they all went upstairs. David, who was only staying overnight, was back almost immediately. "The girls are telling secrets," he said gaily. "Have we any?"

Over cocktails, he offered the women news of Josiah and Margaret and their sons. "Josiah is so generous," David said. "Do you know, he offered to pay Teeny's fare?"

Alida was pleased that David no longer resented Josiah. There was not a trace of bitterness in David today. Instead, there was an optimistic/anxious, euphoric/suspicious obsession with his show. He reminded Alida of actors she had seen on the eve of an appearance: one moment assured, the next uneasy; hopeful, yet trying not to hope too much. He made his concerns theirs. He wanted to know what *they* thought of Morgan and Guthrie. He recognized their taste and he liked them, but wondered if they knew how to push pictures. He appreciated the Galleries' natural light, but the windowed wall subtracted from the space for paintings; he did not want to crowd his pictures, and was thinking of putting several, instead of just one, in the shop window downstairs. Some of his frames looked wrong. At dinner, David and Teeny continued to be the easiest of guests; Teeny was absorbed in Amelia, David in himself. The only difficulty he presented was asking Alida and Gertrude for opinions they were not qualified to give, as when he reverted to wondering if McKinley carried weight in the "serious" art world—in effect, whether his showing there was a mistake, like an actor asking whether doing such-and-such was "exposure" and hence good, or whether it was the wrong kind of exposure and hence bad. He asked if the state of the economy would stop people buying pictures by comparative unknowns. Mrs. Waterman said, half-laughing, "You're asking me to be an oracle."

He was partly laughing, too, when he answered, "Why not? My sister is," which reminded Gertrude to ask what Rosa thought. David said, "She's so oracular, I never understand what she says."

Immersion in David's problems was a lucky distraction. After he left, on Saturday morning, the party milled about in the hall, planning the day. Alida heard them as from a distance, for all the details of the scene with Andrew came flooding back into her mind. She began reexamining every word he had spoken, every gesture, every expression. She was still certain that he was suffering only a temporary spasm, the death throes of erroneous conscience. And yet—there was always a little doubt to calm—a lover should have been more responsive to tears. Unless weeping had disfigured her. While Gertrude and the children were agreeing that they would not accompany her on her morning errands—like lovers, the girls wanted to be alone—another doubt arose in Alida's mind. Andrew sounded annoyed with Janet, but annoyance did not mean the absence of attachment. Though often annoyed with her mother, Alida loved her dearly: indeed, it was the very closeness that bred annoyance when they differed. She was so possessed by these thoughts that when she heard her mother question her about what she proposed doing, she almost answered, "Call Andrew Monday morning." Instead, she plucked the dormant excuse from her memory: "I'm going to the Grindall Homestead for my term paper."

179

The Grindall Homestead was thirty-odd miles away, and Alida rejoiced at the prospect of a drive through spring and the respite of a few hours' intent looking. From the outside, the Homestead was a sparkling white collection of rectangles—additions and wings built over the years—squared off against a very blue sky, its angular challenge softened by the pillowy luxuriance of a few large trees. It promised well: the parking lot was uncrowded, there was no tour guide to ration information, but instead an intelligent pamphlet for sale calling attention to important architectural or decorative features. Yet thoughts of Andrew—the psychic equivalent of an invisible force, like magnetism or gravity—destroyed Alida's faculty for absorption in things. She did not see the Grindall Homestead and its contents as a representative procession of New England styles; instead, everything about the place assumed another meaning. She saw either the transcript of a terrible reality or a symbol of something horrifying. The oldest part—the original home—was scarcely more than a hovel assembled around a huge fireplace. Though its intactness (as uncovered and restored) was one of the prides of the exhibit, what it showed was a revolting existence: everyone crowding for warmth, undoubtedly smelly, probably lousy, grubbing porridge with wooden spoons. The larger spaces, telling of the Grindalls' increasing prosperity and the country's growing amenity, looked bare, suggesting a cross-grained resistance to comfort. The parlor, the acme of Grindall flamboyance, boasted a chair rail hand-carved in a sunflower pattern, but how scanty the furnishings! Upright chairs for upright individuals only recalled Andrew's appeal to rectitude. Alida began to resent how deeply she had given herself into captivity—how, even in his absence, Andrew dominated her—so that she could not escape into seeing as she had used to do. There were Grindall portraits on the parlor wall, likenesses taken by some stiff-fingered sign painter before the Revolution. Once she would have noted only such matters as the excessive cautiousness, the lack of fluency with which the paint was laid on, but now, in thrall to Andrew, Alida saw artistic incapacity expressing ascetic rejection of the body and its delights, for the painter had been unable to make flesh breathe or fabric fold, so that bony Matthew and rigid Elizabeth Grindall were not a man and woman wearing their best clothes, but effigies encased, as in armor: the armor of Puritan righteousness. Alida gave the couple a dirty look and drove home.

The next day was Palm Sunday, an occasion new to Teeny, who

did not go to church or Sunday school. "What do you *do* on Sundays?" Amelia asked.

"I see my father."

The grown-ups hurried past that remark to church, where, to Alida's surprise, Teeny was not restless but rapt. She did not seem to notice the shrouded statues nor understand the service, but was enthralled by the procession, and by getting to keep her palm leaf. Waving it as they crossed the church parking lot afterward, she said, "You know, they really ought to have this in California."

That evening, over dinner at the Club, Teeny, who had been impressed by Mrs. Waterman, now wanted to impress. The child knew of church as a place for weddings. She had recently been to a wedding, and wanted to describe it. The bride was, naturally, the central figure, and Teeny began confusing the bride with any girl, every girl, herself. "You are all in white," she said, "and you are beautiful. Everyone stands up to look at you when you come in. And there are lots of flowers and everyone kisses you and cries and tells you how beautiful you are." Teeny went on from the church to the wedding cake, which, after the bride, had been the most striking feature of the event. "All white, and very, very sweet," she remembered. "And then you throw your flowers away and whoever catches them is a bride."

Teeny enjoyed the attention of her borrowed grandmother while recalling the glorification of a girl. The bride she had seen had worn a coronet, "like a princess." The chatter stopped for a moment while the word "princess" resounded in the little girls' minds. Both women smiled, half remembering their own childish daydreams about princesses, storybook images of crowns and of scepters that looked like fairy wands. Princesses were surrounded by admiring eyes and obedient hands; there were no scoldings and no bedtimes, and, kneeling in adoration before them, there was a handsome prince. Musing on this old reverie, Alida momentarily contrasted the silkiness of fantasy with the rigors of reality, and thought of Andrew, her beloved, her prince. She could not imagine him kneeling. When her attention returned to the little party, the topic had changed: Amelia and Gertrude were engaged in theology. Cloudy words like "atonement" were scudding past as they examined (insofar as a child could) the meanings of Holy Week. Gertrude's love for her granddaughter was leading her socially astray. She was making the mistake, rare for her, of excluding. Gertrude's and Amelia's mutual absorption resembled Larry's and Debby's. Alida minded because

181

she thought it all foolishness, but Teeny, who resented being out of the limelight, demonstrated her annoyance by physical restlessness, by tearing her roll into little bits and scattering the morsels on the tablecloth. Gertrude reproved her gently, and then made an effort to restore the balance that her partiality had upset. She asked if Teeny enjoyed coloring Easter eggs, but the attention came too late. Rivalry had sprung up between the girls, a competition for Mrs. Waterman's attention and approval. Teeny seemed the more inveterate, returning to attack repeatedly, insisting harder on what she did or knew or had; she threw in her last reserves with the announcement "My father has promised me a dog."

That assault told: Amelia demanded a dog, too. Alida explained that a dog was too much trouble in the city, and Teeny asserted that cities were crowded with black men who robbed and killed.

"Nonsense," said Alida.

"My grandfather says so," Teeny insisted.

When Amelia came into Alida's room that night, crying, and crept into her mother's bed, Alida's first thought was that old Mr. Rush's summary of urban life had given the child a nightmare. "What is it? What happened? Tell me. What can I do?" Alida asked. She switched on the light and looked at Amelia carefully; there was no visible physical injury. "What did Teeny do to you?" Alida asked, betraying expectations she had been concealing.

"Why didn't you tell me you divorced my daddy?"

Amelia just got that out; it was a bit of a scream, a bit of a gasp, and wholly an accusation.

"Because I didn't. We're not divorced."

"Teeny said you were. She knows."

"Teeny is a stupid little girl who doesn't know anything," Alida said. "She's full of taradiddles and she's nasty besides."

Amelia had another accusation: "You invited her."

"I had to. I couldn't get out of it. She's my brother's—your uncle Josiah's—niece."

Limitation of adult freedom was a new idea to Amelia. Alida remembered when she, too, thought that the main difference between children and grown-ups, apart from size, was that adults could do anything they wanted, so she was not surprised when Amelia asked who made her invite Teeny. Grandma? Alida said Grandma was as helpless as she was, that Teeny's father was coming to New York, and—

"That's it, that's it," Amelia interrupted. "*They're* divorced, aren't they? And don't we live like that?"

182

Alida had never seen Amelia attacking; her mother parried by seeking information. "What, exactly, has Teeny been telling you?"

Amelia was angry and perplexed. She was shocked by Teeny's assertion, which she did not doubt; she was furious at her mother while wanting her mother to comfort her. "About divorce," Amelia said.

"But you *know* about divorce," Alida answered. Remember—" and named children Amelia had played with in California whose parents were divorced and, referring to Flat Rock, added, "The Lewises are divorcing, I hear. Frances Lewis's parents."

"She's not in my class."

Alida looked behind Amelia to the clock on the table beneath the lamp. It was twelve-thirty, and she suddenly felt very sleepy. "Why don't we talk about this in the morning?"

But Amelia was not to be put off; she said, "First tell me when we are going to live with Daddy again. Will he live with us in New York?"

"No," Alida said. "I don't think so. We may never live with him again."

"Why didn't you tell me? Why didn't you ask me?"

"Tell what? Ask what?"

"What happened. What *I* wanted—" here Amelia began to cry again, tears of self-pity and rage at having been ignored.

"Well, I didn't know what to tell you."

This second revelation of her mother's inability to control life unsettled Amelia further. They were lying side by side, facing each other, and Amelia's expression was skeptical, suggesting that she still felt grown-ups could if they would. She looked, too, as if she resented her mother's pretense of incompetence. The child's expression of wary sulkiness annoyed Alida, who saw herself blamed where she was blameless. She had intended to protect Amelia, but she would not go on protecting Hugo.

"Do you remember Thanksgiving?" Alida asked. Amelia nodded. "Do you remember the lady who was with Daddy?"

"Oh yes," Amelia said, matter-of-factly, "Yvonne. She told me to call her 'Aunt.' Daddy called her a bitch."

"To you?" Alida asked in amazement.

"Oh, no," Amelia said, "that was when they were fighting."

Alida remembered Andrew's assurance that Hugo did not want to marry Yvonne, and her thinking it odd that good Andrew thought he understood wicked Hugo. She said, "I think your daddy wants to marry Yvonne. We're not divorced, mind you, but it's my opinion he's in love with her."

Amelia looked at her mother steadily and almost contemptuously as she informed her ignorance: "Oh no. He sent her away."

"When? On Thanksgiving?" Alida asked.

"Yes," Amelia said. "It was at the end of the fight. He told her to go away. He said, 'Get out, you bitch.' "

"And when was that?"

"After dinner."

"What dinner?"

"Thanksgiving dinner."

Alida said, honestly, "I'm surprised. Very surprised. Did you see her again?" Amelia said no. "Tell me," Alida asked. "What did you think was happening when we came here?"

"First you told me we were going to visit Grandma. Then I thought you and Daddy picked Country Day for me because Daddy always used to make fun of my California school. Remember?"

"Indeed I do," Alida answered, recalling Hugo's description of Amelia's progressive school as a training institution for dropouts. "And when you went to Daddy for holidays?"

"Teeny says that's how you know it's a divorce."

"But you didn't think that."

"I thought Daddy and Grandma were mad at each other."

"Not Daddy and me?"

"No. Not Daddy and you. You never fought. I never saw you quarrel. And Daddy asks me about you. He doesn't sound angry. He sometimes says mean things about Grandma. I don't think he likes her." Amelia's face was glum. "But you *are* mad at Daddy, aren't you?"

"Yes, I am," Alida admitted.

"But you always tell me to make up and be friends."

Alida did not want to rouse hopes that were bound to be dashed; Hugo might have discarded Yvonne for someone else; he had certainly made no gesture toward Alida, who, in any case, loved Andrew. Determined not to bear all the blame, Alida said, "I don't know what your father wants."

"I'll call him up and ask him," Amelia offered.

"Don't," Alida replied. "He loves you, and it might upset him to tell you he doesn't love me."

"But what will happen to *me*?" Amelia asked.

"Nothing," her mother said. "You'll go to school like every little girl."

That was an unsatisfactory answer, but Amelia was exhausted. "May I sleep with you tonight?"

"Of course."

They were surprised to wake up and find each other in the morning. Alida, who had nothing to add to their earlier discussions, simply embraced her child and held her. She felt the fragility of the girl's body contrast with Andrew's remembered strength. Amelia understood her mother was unhappy. The child wanted to blame and to solve; she wanted to learn there was a happy ending in sight, yet she suspected her mother would not supply it. As they clung to one another, each resolved privately to speak to Gertrude. Jenny came in. She pulled back the curtains, and said to Amelia, "So there you are. Your friend has been looking for you."

"Oh, Mother, must I?" was all Amelia said.

"I don't see how I can shoot her," Alida answered. "I don't know about Teeny. I don't know if she was being mean on purpose last night, if she was showing off, or if she knows what she's talking about. She's much stupider than you."

"Will I like Fanny Burney?"

"I hope so. It's supposed to be very good."

"Will I make friends?"

"You always do."

"But a lot of them are boring."

"Most people are boring sometimes," Alida said, "and sometimes not."

Breakfast was difficult. Amelia was silent, Teeny fraudulently sprightly. "Is anything the matter?" Mrs. Waterman asked.

"Oh, no, no," said Teeny, too loudly.

Amelia said nothing.

"Did anyone have a bad dream?"

Amelia shook her head no.

Mrs. Waterman offered marmalade. Amelia was not eating. "At least drink your milk," her grandmother said.

Teeny ostentatiously picked up her glass.

The meal dragged on until Sally told her mistress that James was waiting, and the exigencies of the land hurried Gertrude away. The girls were expected to lunch and to spend the afternoon at the Richardsons'. Alida rose from the table, intending to telephone Andrew, but Amelia followed her to her room. The child did not want to be alone with Teeny and, though she did not reopen the subject of her parents' relations or mention her anxieties about her

185

own future, she wanted to be with her mother. She demonstrated every child's trick of ubiquity and adhesiveness; when, in despair, Alida told her to go away and let her mother have some peace and privacy, Amelia lurked just outside the door so that a splinter of her profile remained always in view. Alida had not planned to say anything indiscreet—Andrew's was an office line, and there were extensions all over her mother's house—yet Amelia's presence inhibited her from telephoning her lover. She was not able to chase Amelia away before they all left for the Richardsons'. By the time Alida came back, it was getting on for office lunch hour. She called, anyhow, hoping she might catch him before he left. Mrs. Southern answered; Andrew was at lunch, but she took Alida's message asking Andrew to call her at home that afternoon.

Alida waited and wondered. When did he finish lunch? Was it a business lunch? Where? In the club in his building? With a client? Absorbed in business? Or alone, thinking of her? It was after lunch. Was he engaged in a difficult piece of work? Locked into an appointment and unable to telephone? Office hours had the same tyrannical quality as holidays, preventing people from doing what mattered most to them. In between thinking of and waiting for Andrew, she looked over her notes on the Grindall Homestead. As the afternoon wore on, she told herself that he might be waiting until the office had emptied, when, alone, he could risk speaking endearments. So she lingered long after she should have left to pick up Amelia and Teeny, and found three girls bored with each other, and Ethel Richardson irked at Alida's lateness. No one had telephoned during Alida's brief absence. The girls watched *Galaxy Guards,* Mrs. Waterman worked needlepoint, and Alida told herself that office Mondays were apt to be rushed. On Tuesday, she went to her room immediately after breakfast, and had just lifted the receiver when her mother knocked and entered, looking grave. "Amelia has been talking to me," she said.

Amelia had expressed her relief that her father and grandmother were not enemies, and then had told her much the same story she had told her mother. The child wanted her grandmother to order her mother, as a parent orders a child, to return to her husband. Amelia told her grandmother frankly that she loved her and loved being with her, but that she wanted to live with both her parents. Mrs. Waterman reported Amelia's forthright plea: "You tell her," Amelia had urged. "You make her go back and live with Daddy. That's how things are supposed to be."

"Why tell me?" Alida said. "I know she's unhappy, and I'm sorry, but I can't make Hugo love me."

"Amelia told me he quarreled with that woman."

"I know nothing about it. He may have another one by now. I was afraid Teeny Hardman would be bad news."

"Teeny is beside the point." Her mother was stern. "Amelia is not a child who takes things lightly. You know that." Gertrude was perhaps regretting her granddaughter's resemblance to herself. "She doesn't make trouble for trouble's sake. She's capable of suffering, and I think she's suffering now."

"I know it was a mistake not to have told her more when we first came here, but I was so confused myself that I didn't know what to say. But you aren't thinking"—Alida meant to be sarcastic—"that I should beg Hugo to take us back."

Gertrude, all earnestness herself, could not hear the sarcasm, and after a moment's reflection suggested, "I could ask Josiah to talk to him."

Alida was appalled: "You'd expose me to another rejection, another humiliation?"

Gertrude now put forward the theory that Andrew had once propounded—that Yvonne was a shrewd, tough, ambitious siren who had entrapped Hugo, and that Hugo deserved sympathy.

"I don't know, Mother. I'm no expert in snaring and luring and trapping, but I don't believe in it. Maybe when you're talking about youngsters. Teenage girls can be taken advantage of by older men. And sheltered youths by sharp females. But Hugo's not a boy. He knew what he was doing." Alida, playing a part, strove to reproduce her bitterness and hurt of last June. She found the words: "Hugo knew what he was doing. He wanted to wound me and he did. He picked a woman who was cheap, coarse. Uneducated. Grasping. Pushy. On the make. Pretentious. And he flaunted her to hurt my pride. If that were all—my pride hurt—maybe I'd feel this crazy conversation made sense. But if he can have anything, anything at all, to do with someone like that, what could he have to do with me? Or with Amelia?"

Alida needed more rehearsal. She did not speak these words, invented for the woman she had been the previous summer, with enough sincerity to fool her mother. To Gertrude, Alida sounded merely peevish, not like a woman talking about the most important issues in her life, but like a customer annoyed at an error in computer billing. Unable to understand why her daughter would not be

187

candid about so serious a matter, Gertrude made no reply. Alida went on, "My happiness counts for something," and closed her tirade with another rhetorical question: "How much should I sacrifice for my child?"

Gertrude said, flatly, glacially: "That reminds me. I've spoken to Father Peele. I'm going to your parties."

Alida sighed. An entire year's omissions and negligences were suddenly coming due at Easter. Certainly she should have spoken to Amelia. Not doing so was partly depression and partly cowardice. After she had begun her affair with Andrew, these had been replaced by a careless euphoria; Alida said "yes" to everything—to David and Teeny, for instance—and then forgot. As to this fast-approaching birthday party. While her mother was still off on her cruise, Aunt Jane had telephoned to say that her uncle Arthur wanted to give Alida a birthday party. Alida agreed; her birthday—April 15—had seemed very far away then. Later, she was amused that the same date was chosen for David's opening, and only after her mother had been home for a few weeks did Alida remember to tell her—and only her mother knew that the date this year fell on Maundy Thursday. Gertrude was more than distressed; she was outraged. She could not comprehend such thoughtlessness and said she would not go. Alida, distracted and enchanted by Andrew, had forgotten all about the proposed boycott until this moment, when her mother lifted it.

"I'm glad he let you come," she said.

"I still can't understand it. Who ever heard of opening anything in Holy Week? How could your aunt—my own sister—forget? And you—I'd think *you'd* remember the Last Supper. It's been painted."

Their conversation was interrupted by the sound of a car: in retaliation for Alida's lateness the day before, Ethel Richardson was bringing her daughter to lunch too early.

When Alida was at last free to telephone that afternoon, Mrs. Southern apologized that Andrew had not returned her call; he had been very rushed because he had only been in the office for a few hours in the morning and now he was gone for the day. Alida wondered where he was. What could he be doing? He might call her from outside the office, and for a while she sat in her room, again looking over her notes on the Grindall Homestead, waiting for his call, until her boredom and restlessness turned to something like rebellion against her enslavement. She thought, let *him* call and wonder where I am, and went out to walk over her mother's pretty paths, inspecting the unevenness of nature, so different from the organized, finished quality of human work. The early bulbs were up, most of the flowering shrubs were in leaf—the forsythia was yellow—but some trees were still covered with a pale yellow-green fuzz along their branches. "Spring" in art is always a perfectly formed maiden, but in reality, Alida thought, she is a disorganized adolescent, always forgetting and having to go back, unreliable in her annual procession northward, darting here, lingering there, with no sense of time or responsibility. Spring had all the characteristics of the teenager—fitfulness, caprice—and yet believers (and unbelievers, too) insisted upon the predictability of nature as proving either the existence of God or the rationality of the universe. Still, spring air was undeniably lovely; Alida felt caressed by the breeze that ruffled her hair and stroked her cheeks. She followed a turning, and saw her mother come out of the greenhouse with the three girls. Mrs. Waterman was saying, "Everything has a time. It's not one season, but three, and you have to get ready for each season and every kind of plant."

Whether the girls understood or not, these words intrigued them. What she said may have meant no more than "abracadabra," but, as apprentice magicians, they wanted to learn. They greeted Alida, who turned and followed them, musing how her mother, though she did not live off the land, was as closely bound to the natural year as a serf or a Grindall, and so, perhaps, to the church calendar, part myth, part agriculture. But there was no escape from calendars— the school year dominated Alida's life, and even madhouses celebrated holidays. The girls ambled after Mrs. Waterman toward the cutting garden. She stopped at a bed where nothing showed but turned-over earth, and bent down, saying something. The girls sat on the freshening lawn, and, at her suggestion, put their hands in the soil and ran it through their fingers. When Alida came up to them, Mrs. Waterman was extolling earthworms. Alida's impression of a lesson in magic recurred at this scene of immemorial antiquity, a woman teaching girls to grow things. Gertrude might have been a priestess of the old Mother Goddess, yet she had chosen to believe in a Father God, Who, as this week recalled, had sacrificed His Son. But those Great Mothers, too, had blood on their hands. Alida's gaze fixed on these girls of modern suburban America while she tried to sort out rescued daughters and slaughtered lovers, castrated priests and temple prostitutes, wild festivals of dance and drink. Mother religions belonged to all the red-light districts of the world. Mothers were easiergoing than fathers, and paganism had doubtless been sloppier than Christianity. Still, the message was the same. Someone suffered. Someone had to die. A child sacrificed, a young man torn to shreds. Actaeon. Abraham and Isaac. My daughter in the Underworld. But it was all rubbish, all of it, not fit for civilized people. Alida wandered back to the house to wait for Andrew.

On Wednesday morning, she called early. Mrs. Southern explained that Mr. Cameron had not yet come in; that he had a meeting at ten; that she would once more give him Alida's message. Alida settled at her desk to work and wait. "The Grindall Homestead (1723–1788)," she wrote, "is a rare example of a perfectly preserved Connecticut farmhouse built, enlarged, and furnished over three generations." Logic demanded that she begin with the earliest portion. "A large double chimney divided two rooms"— here she checked their dimensions—and found herself thinking of the miserable existence of the first Grindalls, and wondering if they were aware of their wretchedness or if they thought of themselves as pioneers and looked hopefully to the future. She tried to forget these rude forefathers and continue with the details of the kitchen, but the Grindalls' ghosts continued to intrude while she mentally turned over their possessions and acquisitions. As she waited for the phone to ring, she was yet again uncomfortable that Andrew, or her love for him, had alienated her from her predominantly esthetic nature, which had always been detached from the "story"—the social history, the human uses—of objects of art and architecture. Hugo had not changed her that way, and perhaps she had more in common with him, for he looked out at the world in search of raw material, and saw, not human individuals but characters. When the Grindall Homestead was first enlarged, a front room in the new wing served both as the parlor and the master bedroom. Even so, Grindalls increased and multiplied. Alida wished she had not put off having another child. Surely Andrew would call. Lunch. She tried to pay attention to the chattering children, who seemed to have become friends again over a secret. They looked sly. Teeny asked what was Alida's favorite perfume. Alida asked to think it over. Her mother said she had performed some devotions that morning and would take the girls shopping that afternoon. Was that all right?

"I'm having a terrible time, Mother," Alida said. "The tests were easy, but I can't seem to get into writing a paper."

Mrs. Waterman was sympathetic, but she had no advice except sticking to it.

So Alida stuck to it. Coarse fabrics and fine ones. Secondary woods in the late Colonial period. She ought not be so annoyed at the Grindalls in the Bicentennial Year, but they were so prudent! So foursquare! Generation after generation they rose to such pomps as looking glasses and a Turkey carpet, and never put a foot wrong. Grindalls added and Grindalls multiplied and never a sign of whimsy or freak or fantasy or naughtiness or sin, just a remorseless, slow accretion. Yet their house was a museum. What had happened to them? The afternoon wore away as Alida toiled amid the hyperactive rosebuds and bowknots of her girlish bower, growing even angrier that Andrew did not call and that she cared so much. At four-thirty she could wait no longer. She called. Andrew had left for the day. Mrs. Southern sounded truly distressed. "I gave him the message, Mrs. Kelly. I'll remind him tomorrow."

Alida began to be frightened. Was Andrew avoiding her? Did he mean what he had said on Friday? His barbarous conscience might not be an aberration, after all. Perhaps he was a Grindall. Alida could not believe it. Something else was the matter. His daughter was going crazy, and he had not told Mrs. Southern.

Mrs. Southern asked if Alida had something urgent on her mind, and if she wished to consult another member of the firm.

"Oh, no, it can wait till after the holiday."

"I'll remind him in any case," Mrs. Southern promised.

At drinks the girls were whispering and tittering. Alida told her mother, "I'm at sea, completely at sea," and asked Sally to bring a martini, gulped it, and had another. Her mother looked at her doubtfully.

Was there time for a third?

"If you insist," Gertrude said, and bent her head over her needlepoint.

So, dinner.

And a curious night in which Alida could not fall asleep but hallucinated the texture of a homespun coverlet, the sound of Andrew panting at climax, the carved knob of a stair post, and the shape of Andrew's hip joint. At one in the morning she went to the stock of sleeping pills she had brought with her from California. So far, she had not needed any in the East, and before the chemical closed her down, she remembered that Hugo's inexplicable fault-finding—the carping that accompanied his affair with Yvonne—had first destroyed her sleep.

Her birthday morning was clear. Still drowsy from her pill, Alida discovered that the girls' secret was presents; there was a heap of

191

little packages at her place at breakfast. Her mother's gift was an art nouveau necklace of golden lilies, sinuous, subtle, and sophisticated, a relief from Grindall angularity. Margaret and Josiah had given matching earrings. The girls' offering was a variety of scents and scented preparations. Teeny was still giggling over the words "toilet water," while Amelia, superior to that childish jest, anxiously awaited her mother's approval of their choices. The girls dawdled over breakfast, nourishing themselves on Alida's thanks. Just before Alida left for the hairdresser, the telephone rang. Her heart jumped. Josiah and Margaret were calling their birthday wishes.

In late morning, the last of the pill-induced somnolence wore off, and Alida, leaving the hairdresser, was normally alert and furious at Andrew for leaving her to the consoling embrace of sleeping pills. Hugo. Eliot. Andrew. Was she abnormally a victim? She would have liked to cause, rather than suffer, pain. Home for lunch. A huge florist's box had just arrived.

"Coals to Newcastle," she said to her mother, who was holding the box, and examining the card, which read, "Happy birthday. Hugo."

"How good of him to remember!" Mrs. Waterman said. "Aren't they lovely?" She was cajoling. "You *will* thank him, won't you?"

"Yes, Mother, if you'll arrange them."

What was Hugo doing? Thickening the plot, Alida thought, as he had told her he always did, putting in an unexpected little complication to keep the audience alert and engaged. This time only his mother-in-law responded, and only because she was intent on reading something beyond trickery into his tricks.

The phone rang just after lunch: Uncle Arthur's secretary was verifying the time a car would arrive. Alida's rage increased while she dressed, thinking how women confined to the home, as she had been this past week, could only destroy themselves or their families, while men were free—as in that typically masculine activity, war— to destroy strangers. Was Andrew deliberately willing her destruction? If not, what was he doing? Making mischief, like Hugo?

Fury was an unsuitable mood in which to set out to parties, and Alida tried to subdue it. She sent Jenny away to help dress the girls, and thoughtfully renounced a bright new spring print that detracted from her mother's gift in favor of a cream-colored silk dress. As she made herself outwardly presentable, she concentrated on all the conceivable gaieties ahead, from the sheer fun of being out to the possibility of meeting a fascinating stranger who would temporarily drive Andrew out of her thoughts. Just as she got into the limousine her uncle had sent, she remembered that both parties were in truth likely to be filled with strangers, for she had forgotten to respond to Morgan's and her aunt's requests for a list of her guests. When Morgan had reminded her, she had suggested he ask her teacher, Miss Kinsky, to David's opening. Alida felt sorry for the woman, who seemed to her betrayed by unknown circumstances into an inferior situation, like a nineteenth-century gentlewoman forced to become a governess. Jane had not asked twice. The car drove off, and Alida told her mother, "I've been so distracted all spring I never found out who's coming. Not to the Galleries and not even to my birthday party."

Gertrude received Alida's remark as yet another apology for having forgotten Maundy Thursday. Mrs. Waterman had promised herself to try to be in good humor, but she could not help her annoyance at her brother-in-law's sending a car. She disliked what she called "dowager style," a phrase that expressed her own youthful annoyance at some of her elders: their demands for too much service, pomp, or attention, patterns of dependence that seemed to her fuddy-duddy, anxious, or manipulative. She thought of herself as a secure driver, and when, for any reason, she needed to be driven, James or his boy were available. She did not know (though Alida did) that, Gertrude being who she was, Flat Rock regarded her arrangements as "dowager style," simultaneously eccentric and exemplary. She replied to Alida, "We'll have to take it as it comes, I suppose," and began to talk of her grievance: "Have you noticed yet that a woman alone is always bullied? I was surprised at first, years ago. When I was a girl, I thought that, once you were married, you were grown-up for good and all. I didn't, of course, think about being a widow, but that was when it started. Advice I never asked for. Plans made for me. Your uncle Arthur has never stopped. He imagines he's the head of our family—my family."

"I wonder if he knows how bossy he is," Alida remarked.

"My sister isn't likely to tell him," Gertrude said, "and nobody else dares."

Attempting to start a happier current of ideas, Alida gestured to the necklace and earrings, and said, "These are the most beautiful I've ever seen."

"Morgan found them for me. I'd been looking at an art book of flower motifs before I went away. That gave me the idea." She returned to her annoyance with Arthur: "I was thinking of celebrat-

193

ing your birthday on Easter Sunday. I didn't expect my brother-in-law to make his own plans for my daughter."

When they approached the city, Teeny said, "Ooh, look at the lights!" and then, "Will I see my daddy soon?"

"Very soon," Alida replied.

The child began to ask questions about the show. It was evident that she had been told, and had understood, and simply wanted the assurance of repetition. When that was gained, she started to talk about "my father" and "Daddy" in a way that made Alida uneasy on Amelia's behalf. Was Teeny deliberately bragging to hurt the feelings of Amelia, whose father was absent? In the midst of Teeny's chatter—and in the wake of Amelia's unhappiness—Hugo's flowers became troubling. They called attention to a father's separation from his daughter during a holiday season.

The sound of the party filled the shop downstairs with the noise of a heterosexual group in which the low timbre of masculine voices predominated, a rumble welcome to Alida after days of the shrillness of little girls. Johnny sat just inside the door overseeing a guest book and a coatrack. He was pleased to be introduced to Mrs. Waterman, whose work he knew, and he was gracious to the little girls, telling Teeny, "Your father's waiting for you upstairs."

The shop counters had been moved back to widen the center aisle, and a new, broad staircase had been installed. Several attractive couples, overflow from the party, were conversing on the steps. Other guests congregated around a bar set up in a newly created hall at the top of the stairs outside the exhibition room, which was a mass of bobbing heads, suggesting summer at Coney Island. They had arrived at the high tide of David's opening, but somehow word of their arrival permeated the crowd. They could see it parting and David laboring toward them looking happy and, when he noticed guests staring or nodding or gesturing toward him in recognition, also looking slightly embarrassed. Teeny flung herself at him, hugging and kissing, a very different demonstration from her howling rejection of last Thanksgiving. "She's not angry at me anymore," David said.

The women acknowledged the change, and then debated whether to try to bring the children into a room where they would be chest-high to the crush. Morgan appeared and suggested taking them upstairs to the studio and encouraging them to draw until the party ebbed. He consigned Gertrude to David's care, and led Alida and the girls away. The children began to work; Morgan and Alida lingered a moment to see how they did, and when they saw they were happy, left them. Going back downstairs, Alida asked Morgan if he had expected such a turnout and who all the people were. Morgan said they were everybody he and Guthrie had ever known—practically their entire life stories. They had miscalculated, sending out too many invitations because they had feared their reputation as art dealers was so slight that no one would come. "It's just as well you let me down about your list," he said, "but don't forget, next time. You're working for us, and everything counts." A woman entering caught his eye, and he said, "I wonder who *she* is."

The stranger toward whom he was glancing wore a scarlet cloak that seemed to swirl or float as she surveyed the hall, the bar, and the crowded room with an air of curiosity and assurance.

"That's Miss Kinsky, my teacher!" Alida exclaimed. "She doesn't look like that in school."

"I should think not. I must find Guthrie, wherever he is, and relieve him of the strain of being polite."

Those words sufficed for Morgan's adieu. He plunged into the mob and disappeared. Alida looked wistfully at the throng around the bar, and then braced herself and followed Morgan. As she wriggled through the crowd, she could glimpse the tops of David's picture frames, about which he had worried. She spied the top of Guthrie's head, but she could not see her mother anywhere. Nor did she recognize any of the guests, some of whom were, as at so many art parties, dressed and others costumed. None betrayed any interest in her, not even the transitory glint that is an unconscious response to attractiveness; as far as she could tell, as she moved eelwise in search of her mother, conversations were earnest and, usually, centered on self. An awkward step, almost a stumble, and she found she had broken into a little circle around Miss Kinsky, who was holding court. David had joined her audience. Miss Kinsky was recalling her work with someone whose name several of her listeners recognized, a man, Alida gathered, who had been obsessed by a scheme to reconstruct late medieval Flemish formulas to achieve a high glaze. Miss Kinsky was describing their—chiefly his—endeavors as comic laboratory fantasy, part college humor, part science fiction, but it was clear, nonetheless, that she knew a good deal about paint chemistry. She interrupted herself to introduce Alida as her best student. The conversation resumed on less esoteric topics, with universally recognized nouns ("casein," "acrylic") and brand names. Painters, teachers, whoever, they all knew about discount art-supply shops and were all concerned about living and working space, whereupon Miss Kinsky described her enormous quarters in a renovated factory not far from Barlow. Morgan, standing behind Alida, whispered how pleased he was with "her" Miss Kinsky; as they turned partly away, he added that the way to catch collectors was to snare the painters, for he was convinced that artists, far more than critics, dealers, or curators, formed the taste of a period.

"That's a fascinating idea," Alida said: she recognized its truth; she also recognized that this was not the place to explore it. Through a parting in the crowd she saw Guthrie's sharp face, like a carved martyr's, listening to a white-haired woman with a hearing aid. Morgan had disappeared—how could he maneuver in this crush?—and then she heard him behind her, greeting someone. A voice detached itself from the indecipherable mélange of speech, the voice of Janet Cameron, cloying and demanding: "You must explain all this to me." Possibly Morgan said something. There was a pause. Janet again: "Oh, never mind. That's Alida over there. She can tell me. She knows art."

Alida waited, her head bowed, for the affliction of meeting her lover's wife. She had given no thought to the likelihood of Janet's presence at this party, though, as a patron of the firm, she was more than likely to have been invited. Janet arrived at her side, exclaiming, "How lovely to see you! Happy birthday! We're all so pleased you're working with Guthrie, aren't we, dear?"

Who was "dear"? The room was hot, but Alida shivered. She turned and saw little Janet. As they greeted each other, Alida studied Andrew's daughter for signs of the madness he had mentioned. Last Friday seemed an eon ago. The girl spread her lips in a smile as if the action caused pain, and nodded to Alida's greeting as if the movement hurt her neck, but her appearance had improved since the day they had had lunch. Had someone—surely not her mother—taken her in hand? The elder Janet, with wisps trailing from her topknot and incoherent ornaments on a navy satin sack, was much as she had been that day, but the daughter had had her hair cut and shaped softly, and she was wearing a cherry-colored, ruffle-collared, Pierrot-inspired party pajama. Still, the effect of these efforts was to emphasize the girl's pinched, colorless face, bare of makeup, its expression suggesting resentfulness. Janet, the mother, betrayed no sense of unease, and repeatedly congratulated Alida on her birthday and on her job. She spoke of their meeting at the Galleries as if they had planned the rendezvous. She remembered to thank Alida again for her gift—how could she guess it had been bought on the day Alida first went to bed with Andrew? She asked after Amelia, saying, "Fanny Burney will be just fine, you'll see," and expressed her delight that the child was at the Galleries and would come to Alida's birthday party. She then apologized that Andrew had not come to the Galleries. "He's been doing a lot of extra work this spring. He's in and out of the office and working late. We've scarcely seen him. When he's home, he's always loaded down with papers. I keep telling him it's time he let some of the younger men take over. You know, he didn't want to go out at all tonight. I told him he could skip *your* protégé's paintings, but he couldn't skip *my* protégée's birthday. So he'll be at your uncle's later."

Alida was aghast. She had been longing to see Andrew, but not at a party, not at her uncle's, and certainly not with his wife and daughter. How had the Camerons gotten onto Aunt Jane's party list? How should she greet him, act toward him, speak to him? She had forgotten the proper distance between a family lawyer and his client. The party pressed the two women together, and while Janet babbled warmth, Alida thought, I am like Yvonne, remembering how polite her husband's mistress had always been to her—as deferential and correct as Yvonne's egoism and stiff, brand-new manners allowed. There was no escaping Janet: Alida stood there receiving the affection and approbation of a woman she had wronged (and would go on wronging if she could), recalling Yvonne's false friendship, and promising to work for one of Janet's charities in the fall. Filled with shame at practicing the deception that had been practiced on her, she felt angry at Janet for causing these feelings: it was Janet's fault, not Alida's, that Janet was overweight and unkempt; but of course Yvonne probably thought it was Alida's fault that Hugo looked elsewhere. Alida began to comprehend some of Andrew's feelings: if she found a moment's deception so painful, what must he feel, lying and pretending every day, day after day? And Janet's physical unattractiveness could not excuse contempt while the woman was demonstrating qualities for which anyone might like or love her, such as loyalty, willingness to show affection, and pride in a friend's achievement. Janet's flaw was her obstinate adhesiveness. She clung to Alida physically, taking her arm, repeating how suitable it was for Alida to work for the Galleries, on the basis that it was "practical" rather than "frivolous" and just what everybody ought to be doing "in times like these." Alida saw her mother talking to David and an oldish couple Alida did not know; she tried to move in their direction. Janet followed her, and said, "I don't know any of these people. You must take me around."

Alida could not bear her own agony in Janet's company. She said, "I don't know anybody either. I'm going to get the girls. I've left them a long time."

"I'll come with you."

Janet followed her upstairs, asking questions about Teeny, her parents' divorce, and David's future. The girls were not up to much. They had littered the floor with their drawings, but they had tired of sketching and were ready to come downstairs. Janet, however, was not. She kept them there, winning them with the same caressing, patronizing, and, Alida suspected, insincere attentions that had beguiled Amelia at lunch in January. Janet's request to see their drawings, the comments she made, the questions she asked, and the explanations she elicited were the first attention anyone had paid them. The girls afforded her a refuge from the room full of strangers. Alida could not help thinking how different Janet was from herself—what did Andrew see in her? in either of them?— and how different they both were from Yvonne. It was conceivable that Yvonne, who thought of herself as an actress, enjoyed deception. Last June, though, there had been very little of it. Alida looked down at this tiresome, earnest, fat woman sitting between the girls, the trio leaning over a drawing board, and tried to imagine herself in the part of Yvonne, entering a party on the arm of Andrew, as Yvonne had entered with Hugo, and an entire party observing the spectacle of Janet's astonishment and humiliation as they had observed Alida's. It was a brutal vision. Alida fled from it, and from the room.

From the staircase, she could see Miss Kinsky in the hall saying complicated farewells to Morgan and Guthrie and David, while some of the artistic contingent waited for her. As in a Gothic romance, the governess had become the belle, and Alida envied her. Her party left at last, crossing Lady Mary, swathed in foxes and coruscating in jewels, who announced she had only a moment to spare before she left to meet her own dinner party. She marched up to hapless little Janet, asking, "What's going on?"

Alida slipped into the exhibition room and, skulking behind guests to avoid Lady Mary, began looking at the pictures. She remembered David's saying, "It comes from the hills" at Thanksgiving, and recognized that his palette recalled the Coastal Range in summer, when the dry golden fields of the slopes and valleys are

198

dotted with dark green live oaks. The forms were slightly more powerful than his words suggested, yet the work as a whole was primarily decorative. It was, perhaps, too humble, too pretty, not quite assertive enough for current critical taste.

Guthrie, beside her, said, "When you think what the poor son of a bitch has been through you'd think he'd come out fighting. Maybe he'll learn. It's lovely but it needs kick. Or punch."

"I'm buying that one, anyhow," Alida said, pointing: the impulse was not charity or pity but alliance, as between two of life's also-rans.

Guthrie looked startled. "Won't he give you one?"

Alida shrugged. "Then I'll have two."

Janet came in trailing the girls.

Guthrie announced: "Alida has just bought a picture."

"Are they for sale?" Janet asked. "Can anyone buy them?"

"That's the general idea," Guthrie said.

"Which one is Alida's?"

Guthrie pointed it out.

"Do you like that one best, Alida? Should I buy one, too? Will you choose it for me?"

"I almost took that one" (pointing) "but of course you may like another better."

"Oh no, Alida, you're the expert. Can I have it, Guthrie?"

Lady Mary bore down on them. To Alida, she said, "Happy birthday." To Janet, "You have some funny kid."

Just then, Morgan and Gertrude appeared—they had been out of the room, they said, for just a moment, talking business—and Johnny brought word that Uncle Arthur's car was waiting. Gertrude offered the Camerons a ride. "I'm going to stay to meet the artist," Lady Mary said.

Organizing was suddenly a problem: Teeny wanted to remain at the Galleries with her father, and come over to Aunt Jane's when he did. David was struggling with Lady Mary, who asked him loudly if there was anything in his work, suggesting that she could bring him to confess that it was all a bluff. Gertrude asked him if he would keep Teeny, who threw her arms around him. "Another funny kid," said Lady Mary wearily.

Janet collected her daughter, and they all collected their coats to the accompaniment of Janet's stream of verbal molasses: thanks for the offer of the ride, delight at seeing Gertrude, pleasure at having bought a picture warranted by the expert Alida, et cetera. Janet went on droning. Amelia, on the jump seat, shifted her weight,

199

jostled little Janet, and apologized. Little Janet said nothing in reply, and Amelia repeated, "I'm sorry" with an edge in her voice. The sharpness rang in Alida's ear. She reheard her child quoting Hugo: "He said, 'Get out, you bitch.' "

Had that been, in politer language, what Andrew had meant last Friday?

The elevator at her uncle's and aunt's apartment opened directly into a large two-story hall—anteroom, foyer, or reception room, as one chose to call it—its walls paneled in dark oak retrieved from some seventeenth-century demolition and recut for these premises. From two stories up, the chandelier could not shed enough light to dissipate the expensive, intimidating gloom with which Alida and her mother were familiar, but which slightly awed the two Janets. They lagged behind as the hosts' relatives turned toward the cloak-room under the staircase; Alida said quickly to her mother, "I'll take Amelia upstairs for a moment," and went to a guest bathroom there, with a long, well-lit dressing table with several chairs, and they began their primping. Amelia was passive, resigned rather than tired, as her mother brushed her hair. Alida asked, "You aren't having a very good time, are you?"

"I'm tired of behaving."

Alida sympathized; the same might be said of herself. "And there's more to come."

"I know."

Alida swiftly leaned forward and kissed Amelia's cheek.

"What's that for?"

"For behaving."

They dawdled until, Alida calculated, Janet must have had time to find a new object on whom to work her barnacle imitation. Downstairs, Alida's luck held; in one of the smaller drawing rooms, her two cousins, Paul and Arthur, Jr., and their wives were standing around the fireplace, chatting in a desultory, intimate way. They made a nice little fuss over Amelia; the sisters-in-law wanted Amelia and Alida for weekends (they all lived on Long Island) and blamed themselves for not having arranged visits. Paul made the point that, in families such as theirs, which ran wholly to boys, a girl—Amelia—was a prize, and then the five adults began comparing raising boys with raising girls. Alida's cousins had acquired assurance since the days when they had all lived, furtive as mice, in their father's house. Art referred obliquely to their panic-stricken youth when he mentioned his father's terror of his grandsons, whom Art described as "the little savages we were never allowed to be."

200

After reminiscence, Alida learned that her cousins had been given a somewhat grandiose account of her job, which she corrected, while their wives caressed Amelia. Champagne arrived, and Paul, picking up a glass, sipped it and said, "Father is doing us well tonight," and Art said, "To you, Alida."

Then Aunt Jane brought in two women with whom Alida had been at boarding school. During the introductions there was scrutiny, overt and intense but not unfriendly. How had time dealt with one's schoolmates? How (if one could read their expressions) did one strike them? Alida had no idea how her aunt had found Blanche and Mary, but though none of them had been particularly close in school, they were unusually pleased to meet each other—school really was, as teachers and deans and headmistresses prophesied, a bond in later years. Blanche and Mary praised Amelia, and remarked how greatly she resembled Alida. Both were taken by Alida's necklace and earrings, which led those in the room to deprecate their own presents—"Presents? For me?" Alida was truly astonished; she had not thought about receiving birthday gifts, and in her anxiety to escape Janet on arriving, had not noticed that a table in the entry held packages.

Her expression elicited laughter—surprise always seems irresistibly funny—and then Blanche, Mary, and Alida found themselves agreeing that they could not see that they were much changed. All during the conversation, Alida's ears strained to pick up Andrew's voice: he might be already contributing to the placid hum from the adjoining room, or he might be about to enter and say something in the hall. She furtively felt the sides of her neck to discover if the cords stood out.

The elevator door opened. Alida heard, floating high over the sedate rumble of masculine greetings, Teeny's shrill "Where's Amelia?"

In a moment she tore into the room, and cried, "Amelia, isn't everything wonderful?"

David, Morgan, and Guthrie followed. The conversation had divided into small units, so many amoebas out of the original cell, all thriving, when Uncle Arthur appeared and ordered them all— his sons and daughters-in-law, his niece, their children, and their friends—into the next room, exactly as he had commanded them in times gone by. That is, he looked pained and almost fearful while telling them that most of the guests had assembled in the larger room and missed their presence, assuring them that he knew they had not intended rudeness by lingering apart.

"We're coming, Father," Paul answered, and while the group began to stir toward the doorway, Alida caught his eye, and she and her cousins began to laugh.

The rooms themselves suddenly seemed funny. Her uncle's decor, like his personality, had used to frighten her, so that she had never dared examine his possessions closely in the years she lived with him, though at that time she had inspected almost every object everywhere else. The room they had just left was paneled in wood only a tinge lighter than the hall; the walls of the middle salon or parlor, where she now stood, were covered in dull green damask. The furnishings were of uncomfortable periods—Renaissance, Jacobean, Louis XIII—and were upholstered in an assortment of colors and patterns, authentic, Alida imagined, to the original fabrics (the duller and more tattered-looking, she assumed, *were* the original fabrics). As a youngster, she had privately called this the "horse room," because of its art, which was entirely images and icons of equines, gifts from her uncle to commemorate his wife's youthful equestrian prowess. The lack of overall orchestration suggested a sovereign's indifference to ordinary folk's notions of "home" and "parlor"; its sole common denominator—a reason that Alida, at last understanding it, found it funny—was its reflection of its owner's professional skill. Though robber baron in its harshness, the room belonged to a banker: every piece in it was very good value. Alida turned from her uncle's admirable if not precisely enviable chattels to the humans beside her. They were Arthur's fellow nabobs, invited to meet his niece. She suspected he had thoughts of "launching" her. His sponsorship was a mite overambitious, for his contemporaries, though kind, were the presidents and chairmen of the boards of everything in the universe, and she could not feel herself very interesting to them. Their wives, however, were welcoming, extracting Alida's West Coast committee credits; less obviously voracious than Janet, they were clearly filing Alida for fall reference. Locked in this elderly circle, Alida was still listening for Andrew. She happened to turn her head, and saw him standing in the door to the hall. He looked troubled or tired. She watched Janet come up to her husband, greet him, and look around the room until she saw Alida. The Camerons began to move in her direction. Her throat dried. She could not speak. While Janet attempted to propel Andrew toward Alida, Andrew was stopping to greet every guest he knew. By the time they reached her, her companions had melted away. She was alone.

Andrew's blue-gray eyes looked as if he were sad but did not wish to express or transmit much feeling of any kind. He said evenly, "Happy birthday, Alida."

Janet objected: "Andrew, you don't sound friendly."

"I'm tired, very tired." And then he asked if little Janet had been enjoying herself.

"I don't know why you always fret about her," his wife replied. "She's perfectly capable of taking care of herself."

"All the same, I'd like to find her."

"Just because she's not your ordinary run-of-the-mill finishing-school girl, you never stop thinking there's something the matter with her."

Janet's argument was a blow. It made Alida realize that these two were indeed married. The sound of a marital squabble demonstrates the reality of the bond like no other transaction: there is the assurance, the freedom, the intimacy—it is a relationship in which one dares to fight—and then, too, "you always" and "you never," by their reference to long-standing continuities, have the ring of genuine wedlock. Gently quarreling, or being quarreled with, about his daughter, Andrew sounded like Janet's husband, a role in which, though Alida might feel him miscast, he performed with conviction. Alida turned abruptly, and fled to David, whose expansiveness was a relief. Not that he wasn't worried; Guthrie and Morgan had been assuring him that the show was, or would be, a "success," but he still wanted to know of what kind. "I'm going to ask Miss Kinsky. Her name's Francesca. Did you know? She could tell me what's what."

Dinner was announced. Now Alida came upon a change in her uncle's ways. They had always used to sit at a single oblong table that might be extended to manorial vastness, usually covered in lace or damask and supplied chiefly with a roast. This evening there were four round tables for six, covered with French flower-printed tablecloths, bringing color and gaiety to the cavernous dining room. Alida was seated with David and Guthrie, the two little girls, and one of her uncle's magnates, Mr. Ellsworth. He was a slightly upsetting presence to Alida; though his hair was thin and all gray, and he wore eyeglasses, his size and alertness, his speech and manner, suggested an older Andrew. Guthrie said to Alida, "Your Miss Kinsky impressed me. There's something tough about her. She looks as if, like me, she likes a match. I wonder if it shows in her work. You remember, Rilke calls angels '*schrecklich.*' "

Who knew Rilke? Who knew German? Mr. Ellsworth. He took issue with Guthrie: "Rilke doesn't mean 'muse' when he writes '*Engel.*' "

"I like his connection of beauty and terror," Guthrie replied.

They thereupon embarked on a discussion of the purposes of art, to which David occasionally contributed, relying, Alida guessed, on ideas acquired from his father. He seemed entertained, though, by talk so brisk, articulate, sharp, and thoughtful. Her aunt's old-fashioned food had given way to remarkable French cooking, a menu a bit beyond the girls' tastes. They picked and grew restless. Teeny was whispering to her father; Amelia was kicking her chair. Alida, who had been seated between David and Guthrie, quietly signaled David to change places with her. She wanted to sit between the children, either to hush or divert them. Janet Cameron had arisen, too. She walked over to her husband, seated at another table. He stood up while she said something. After a moment (Alida could not see Andrew's face nor hear Janet's words) he picked up her chair, signaled a waiter, who moved her place, and they crammed her in at Andrew's table. It was a gesture of unparalleled rudeness, insulting one table and upsetting two, but Alida saw it as a dumb show of unity. Or perhaps of reconciliation: Janet might be attempting to make up after their disagreement. Whatever it was, Andrew was demonstrating his willingness to yield to his wife's whims; possibly he agreed to rescue her from the company of adults whom she could not dominate and charm as she bewitched children. The mime proved that Andrew *had* meant it last Friday, and that Alida's assurance that they—Alida and Andrew—were the couple, not Andrew and Janet, was wrong. They had not had a lovers' quarrel, a fit of his conscience. She had lost him. He had left her. Her response was a kind of paralysis. She could not whisper to the girls. She breathed; she was conscious; she saw and heard and did not fall down, but she was unable to summon strength and had lost control of some of her muscles; she sat, her mouth open, her eyelids beginning to prickle. Amelia asked, "Mother, what's wrong with you? I'm going to visit Grandma."

Amelia slipped out of her seat and went to Gertrude's table. There was a moment's talk there, and Alida saw her mother sending little Janet to Amelia's place. She sat down somberly. Mr. Ellsworth and Guthrie were disputing the relation between sexuality and fear. David said, "Talk to me, Alida. The grown-up conversation has gone over my head, and all Teeny can say is 'Where is the birthday cake?'"

"Just what we all want to know," said Mr. Ellsworth, "and are too shy to ask."

Alida's paralysis had lifted. "Don't you think I'm too old for birthday cake?"

"I'm not," Mr. Ellsworth said.

"Alida, how can you call yourself 'old'?" David asked.

"Stop fishing. You're young enough to look young," Guthrie said.

From little Janet, a dirty look.

From Teeny, a distressed and heartfelt cry: "Aunt Alida, do people really get too old for cake?"

"Teeny, I was teasing. And it's so much your father's party, I forgot it was mine, too. Honestly, though, my aunt Jane—you met her, Teeny, she's the lady in the pale purple dress, she's my aunt, you know, and she's giving this party—well, she didn't tell me what she planned."

David was impatient. "Teeny, you must learn to behave at grown-up parties. We're not at dessert, and sometimes we get salad and cheese first."

Little Janet murmured, "Cheese," fixed her mouth in a brief and rigid smile, and said that really important parties hired photographers. She was emitting that timid hostility of hers, so hard to define and to combat; the men ignored her. Guthrie asked Mr. Ellsworth about Germany in the twenties. The banker said he had not been sent there until after the currency had been stabilized, and that he had only worked in Berlin for two years. What he had seen was a period of remarkable optimism. Indeed, it seemed to him that, everywhere he had been, the late twenties were the most intensely optimistic era he could remember, and he found it odd that that time was now recalled, in history books, for its political or financial failures and in the popular mind as an epoch of uproarious wildness. "Perhaps no one can understand optimism today," he said. "I sometimes think the world has lost the habit of hope."

"Perhaps," said Guthrie, "they had the wrong hopes."

A waiter brought salad and cheese, and David called Teeny's attention to the accuracy of his prophecy. Little Janet declined to eat, but once again remarked, "Cheese," and asked for a photographer. It dawned on Alida that she was attempting a joke and might be trying to join the conversation. Alida said, "You remind me of our yearbook photographs, when the photographer draped us all with a sheet to make us look Grecian before we all said, 'Cheese.' Do they still do that?"

Alida's effort failed. Little Janet mumbled, "I don't know," and stared at Teeny as if she had never seen such an object. Yet Alida still had the notion that little Janet had been trying to be funny. She was such a bizarre disaster that she might need her father . . . Alida was beginning to tremble. David suddenly reached for, and held, her hand. He said, "Alida, this is the best party I've ever been to. Your uncle and aunt are the greatest uncle and aunt a girl ever had, and you are the prettiest birthday girl I ever have seen—"

"And you are the best painter at this party," said Guthrie, who found even two sentences of flattery unbearable.

He made them laugh, but Alida's laugh was forced. She had an impulse to go to Andrew. She had no idea what she would say—she was afraid she might sound crazy; she thought she *was* crazy. She could pretend to be flirtatious ("Why don't you visit *my* table?"), for Janet's example had led to more shifting around. Or alarming ("Your daughter is lonely"). But what she wanted to ask was "Have you really left me?" Andrew's maneuvers to avoid her—coming late, moving away so fast—argued that he really had, as had his more than gallantry toward his wife. But then he had seemed so unhappy. Not relieved, as one is when one is certain one has made the right decision. But perhaps his unhappiness was not about Alida, but about his child. Alida must have given some new sign of distress, for David, who had been holding her hand, kissed it and murmured, "And I have you to thank." That signal was clear as a flare. David, recalling his own misery of last fall, and sensing that she was unhappy now, was saying he was there for her support. His kiss and his thanks were not loverlike but familial—he was ranging himself, as a protector, among the men of her clan.

The waiters rolled a cart bearing a vast white cake to her table, her uncle rose, holding his champagne glass, and the room quieted.

"A toast to my niece Alida," he said. "May all her birthdays be happy and afford us as much happiness as this one."

Alida rose to reply. She was amazed that she could stand, but had difficulty finding her voice and pitching it; what wanted to come out was either a shriek or a mumble. She breathed deeply, started slowly, and, smiling, said, "Thank you very much, all my dear kinfolk and my loving friends."

Her eyes then turned to the cake, whose whiteness, like a bridal cake, seemed a horrifying symbol—the ghost of a hope, the wrong hope—and, as she held her breath to blow out the candles, her eyes flooded. She could not go on. She sat down, trusting that the guests would attribute her tears to birthday sentimentality.

Guthrie rose abruptly, and said, "And now, a toast to my painter, David Hardman."

That was unexpected, but David was equal to it. He rose, still holding Alida's hand, while he thanked the "trio at the McKinley Galleries, especially the beautiful one," and his host and hostess.

"Very well done," Guthrie said, "but Alida, you are too emotional."

Alida was losing control and adopting Guthrie's manners. She stammered, "But . . . but Guthrie—you're emotional."

He was furious. "What do you mean? In what way am I ever emotional?"

My God, Alida thought, now I've lost my job. But she said, "Aggressive—that's emotional. And enthusiastic. When you like something you're passionate. When you don't like, you hate."

"Game, set, and match to Mrs. Kelly," Mr. Ellsworth decided, with a finality that Guthrie could not dispute aloud. But later, as the party was dispersing to other rooms for coffee, Guthrie muttered, "You won't cry at work, Alida, will you?"

"Only on my birthday."

She had survived. The reshuffling of the party should have given her and Andrew a chance to seek each other, but first Alida was found by Aunt Jane, who told Alida how pleased Arthur was that Alida liked the party so much. Jane also reminded her that, since her mother wanted to leave early, Alida should circulate and not "waste time" on her old relatives when there were so many "interesting people."

"Oh, Jane"—Alida kissed her aunt—"you *are* darling. Mr. Ellsworth is fascinating."

"He's a terrific highbrow. Arthur was sure you'd appreciate him."

Then she was off, shepherding guests. Next came Morgan, who had been at the table Janet had deserted, and who said, "That woman is a pain," as if Alida would immediately know what woman. "They tell me her husband is nice, though."

"He's my lawyer."

Morgan shrugged and asked if she knew who had framed a specimen of antique crewelwork that hung over a side table in the hall. They went to look at it, and then returned to the large parlor. Alida's eyes followed Andrew moving around the room, demitasse in hand, trailed by Janet, and, at a distance, by little Janet, who, though she was unable to mix on her own, seemed not to want to dangle obviously after her parents. While Alida and Morgan talked of framers and framing, the current of the party drew Andrew closer. His back almost touched Morgan's shoulder. He was listening to Mr. Ellsworth, who had turned from Guthrie talk to lower-

Manhattan talk and politics; the early primaries seemed to fascinate him, and when Andrew spoke, he sounded composed and equally interested in the presidential campaigns. David, coming toward Alida, was waylaid by Mr. Ellsworth, who wanted to introduce him to Andrew. The group widened and opened as David drew in Morgan and Alida. Again seeing Andrew face-to-face, Alida had the impression that he looked convalescent. Mr. Ellsworth asked, "Do we all know each other?"

Alida introduced Morgan to Andrew and Mr. Ellsworth and informed the latter that Andrew was her trustee.

"Then you are in very good hands."

She made a pathetic effort to send Andrew a message. "But I somehow feel I don't see enough of him."

"You'll have to make a date fast," David replied. "I really came to collect you. Your mother sent me. She's ready to take the girls home. I'd better explain to Teeny that I'll be up Saturday."

The driver loaded Alida's presents in the trunk. Mrs. Waterman and the two girls took the back seat, and Alida sat on a jump seat. She looked forward to being alone in the dark, with nothing in sight but glass, night, and the right ear of Arthur's driver. Before they had gone a mile, the children fell asleep, and Mrs. Waterman spoke. "That Cameron child is crazy," she said. "They ought to take her to a doctor. I mean a psychiatrist." Alida had not wanted to converse; her mother was uncharacteristically voluble. "She's a very strange youngster, Alida. How is it you never noticed that?"

"I did, Mother, but Janet is an expert in child psychology. She'd know if anything were seriously wrong."

"Expert? She took some courses."

"She seemed very shrewd about Amelia."

"Everybody's shrewd about other people's children."

"But why does Andrew talk as if she knew all about children?"

"I suppose he loves her. He's always humored her and let her put on airs. *I* don't call myself a botanist. Andrew's aunt Lucy always thought Janet was, well, presumptuous. I wrote you that Lucy died two years ago. I used to visit her. She was alert to the last, over in that big place by the river, surrounded by nurses. Lucy was a sharp one—kind, but not easygoing. She couldn't stand Janet. And I remember I was surprised, back when they married. Janet wasn't so fat then, but she was clumsy. I could see—you *can* tell, even when nobody says anything outright—that none of Andrew's family was pleased; they were making the best of it."

"Where does she come from?" Alida asked. "Where did they meet?"

"Lucy told me all about it, years ago, but I've forgotten. All I remember is she grew up in a small town with one business that belonged to her family. Everybody worked for her father. She never got a proper notion of her own unimportance."

"You sound angry," Alida said. "For you, I mean."

"I am. I'm angry at Andrew. A man should take his wife in hand where a child's concerned. But you see how strange life is. Andrew is the devoted husband of a woman who probably doesn't know how lucky she is. I'm sure you really didn't need her help for Amelia. Now you're going to have to call and invite her or see her next fall. I don't envy you."

Alida did not envy herself.

Mrs. Waterman went on: "I'm angry for other reasons. I hate feeling this way in Holy Week. So discomposed. I could have given your birthday party on Easter Sunday. Why does Arthur meddle so?" Pause. Further explanation. "I forget you don't know my habits, how they've changed. We've lived apart so long, and I wasn't religious when you were a child. Now I'm getting old and set in my ways, and I don't explain. And sometimes I think I don't understand anybody anymore."

"Who don't you understand?"

"Everybody. And nobody understands me. The new nostalgia, for instance—the craze for a past that's my past. A couple of weeks ago I couldn't get out of driving with Katie Fowler. She turns on the car radio and talks through it. They played a program of music your father and I danced to. The announcer kept saying how 'sophisticated' it all was, how 'worldly.' Well, it wasn't. And we weren't. We were innocent—more innocent than people are nowadays. I was so innocent I didn't think your father could be killed. It's a terrible thing to lose your innocence to death. I used to hate your uncle Arthur for living. He must have guessed. Maybe that's why he likes to bully me. He ought to know that since I became a Christian I don't feel that way."

"*Became* a Christian?"

"Yes, became. I sent you and Josiah to Sunday school because I'd been sent. Your father didn't care one way or another. His family lived abroad so much, they weren't fussy about settled habits. I thought Sunday school was the right thing for children. You went to Sunday school, so I went to church. It was habit. Or convention. I just kept going. One day I found I was really praying. I came away refreshed. That's the only word I can think of for the feeling. Refreshed. It was nothing I planned because I didn't know about it before. But that's what it's like. The only person I've told is Father Peele. He explained to me about grace."

Alida grasped that her mother was confessing, and that she had changed inwardly, so that the visible, tangible things—the Canton bowl, the tôle tray—that had signified her changelessness to Alida meant nothing at all to Gertrude.

"And I've been angry at you, Alida. About Amelia and Hugo. I think I should tell you now. I try to think how I would feel and sound, and what I would do, and, Alida, you're different. And then I think I was married so long ago, my life is ancient history. But Alida, I'm afraid for you. And of you."

"Of me?"

"Of what you might do."

Gertrude's remark accused Alida, who knew what she had been doing. She guessed that her mother's confession was partly ritual, but even if it was routine, something ticked off on a spiritual calendar, it was certainly heartfelt. Alida would have liked to confess in return. She needed someone to talk to, someone to whom she could unburden her pity, her guilt, her anger, her love, her desire— someone to help her understand Andrew. Yet Alida did not feel free to offer her mother the truth, only reassurance and affection. She said, "Mother, don't worry about me. I have an interesting job. Maybe I'll have an interesting career. Morgan and Guthrie are talented people. And Amelia. Without Hugo she isn't"—Alida searched for a conclusive word, but none presented itself—"she's not exactly failing."

"She's unhappy."

"Won't she get over it?"

"I wish I knew," Gertrude said. "I'm not sure people get over things."

Alida slept badly, and nightmares woke her. When she turned on the light at three in the morning the wish formed in her mind that Janet would die. Or little Janet—the child was the real difficulty. Shocked at her own evil, she nonetheless went on imagining Andrew freed by some disaster for which no one was responsible. But earthquakes were rare on Park Avenue. When she fell back to sleep, her dreams were filled with corpses, the bodies of women and girls. Then she herself was a victim at an Aztec sacrifice. There were steps in the dream, and a stone knife, and the idea that someone wanted to cut her heart out. She woke in terror. The dream evaporated in the lamplight, but instead she remembered the living nightmare of Andrew and Janet, the married couple together.

Gertrude did not expect the girls to last out the full three-hour Good Friday service, so Alida followed the others to church in her own car, prepared to take the children away when they grew restless. Mrs. Waterman sang the first hymn in the unformed, uncertain contralto of Alida's earliest childhood memories; the Clark family was wholly unmusical, and both Gertrude and Aunt Jane had difficulty staying on key through "Rockabye Baby." Dr. Marshall, the rector, began to read prayers, and Alida's mind, as it had all the past year, began to wander. She remembered enough to say most of most prayers by heart without thinking what she was saying. She had studied the congregation (there never were any good-looking men in her age group) and the architecture, and tried to compare it with other Gothic reproductions. For the most part she thought about clothes. Today she suddenly understood that in repeating the General Confession she was admitting that she had sinned, and agreeing that she had followed "too much the devices and desires" of her own heart. What impudence! On the part of God? Or of the authors of the prayer book? Dr. Marshall was a different kind of clergyman from Father Peele, with a forceful, assured delivery, very much the Number One. No doubt Father Peele would have thought Alida sinful, but he would not have sounded, as did Dr. Marshall, like a man campaigning for office on an anti-Alida platform. Alida's mutiny was as silent as her mother's submission. Trapped, committed, responsible for two girls and a car, there was nothing Alida could do to signal her rebellion, no way to hoist a theological pirate flag. Father Peele came in now, reading the versicles to which the worshipers responded. She realized she liked him, not in his clerical role, and not because he was her mother's spiritual friend, but as a person. Compared to everyone she knew, he was what the world sees as a loser, but his apparent ignorance of this fact, his persisting earnestness—he read prayers almost as if he were discovering them—gave him sweetness. His contentment elicited respect that ambition rarely commands.

More prayers. Another hymn. Alida looked at her watch, then at her mother, then at the girls. Amelia was beginning to wriggle, but Teeny was steady. Alida began to juxtapose reds and greens. Starting, say, with a shocking pink and high-intensity poison green—in silk? or wool? And why had she never seen a dark purple linen? But say *that* were the dress, an olive-silk scarf would be too drab; try again, perhaps almond . . . No use. The gloom of the church today was oppressing Alida. And then she was angry again, angry at this mythic endorsement of mythic suffering to which she had let herself be shanghaied by daughterliness. Her mother had more staying power than the rest of the Flat Rock laity. They came, prayed, meditated, and listened for a while, and went away. Alida could not understand why Teeny was so well behaved despite the example of all these arrivals and departures. Amelia's restlessness had subsided; she had apparently disciplined herself to do whatever her grandmother did. Though Alida knew that her own angry unhappiness would follow her wherever she went—no attendant, no companion so faithful as misery—she wanted to leave. Teeny was her only chance. Alida looked carefully at the child and saw that she was not attentive but stiff, as if afraid. Alida touched her shoulder and she jumped. She turned to look at Alida with an expression that was fearful, woebegone, and confused: Alida whispered, "Do you want to go now?" and Teeny nodded. Amelia decided to stay with her grandmother. Taking Teeny's hand, Alida walked out. They were both immobilized by the sun's dazzle, which blinded them on the steps of the church. Teeny still held hands. Alida asked, "What would you like to do now?"

"I don't know."

"Would you like some ice cream?"

"Is that all right?"

"Certainly it's all right. Why wouldn't it be?"

Their vision regained, they walked toward the car, and Teeny skipped directly to what was troubling her: "It's all about dying, isn't it?"

"Yes and no," Alida said. "It's also about coming alive again."

"Like waking up in the morning?"

"Something like that. Coming out into the sunlight. Or being happy after you've cried."

"Then ice cream is all right."

Alida thought it ironic to be cheering up a child she did not like with answers she did not believe, but life was one patch or darn after another; human existence was always fraying or ripping, and one had to plunge into the ragbag of ideas or conventions, the accumulated odds and ends of the human race, to mend the fabric of life with whatever came to hand—theology, fairy tales, ice cream. They drove around and admired the countryside greening in the gleaming sun and discussed favorites—flavors, colors, and names for dolls. And what constituted a best friend. And agreed that you could have a West Coast best friend and another for the East Coast. And finally decided to have an elaborate confection—no mere cone, but a triple sundae, or even a super-duper banana split at Martha's ice-cream parlor on Main Street. The place was thronged with mothers and children on this school-vacation day. The youngsters were uproarious—laughing and quarreling and screaming. Babies were falling out of high chairs, and eight-year-olds were whining about their choices after they saw what somebody else got. Life was going on during Gertrude's prayers and Alida's despair: it was almost incomprehensible how the indifferent world went along.

Alida and Teeny worked away at their immense mounds of cold sweetness; Teeny gave up halfway. "Could we go home and start the eggs now?"

At the house, impatient Teeny took Alida in tow and headed for the kitchen. Alida had to slow the girl down by explaining that eggs were not hard *boiled* but hard *cooked*. The water was simmering when Mrs. Waterman came in with Amelia. Gertrude seemed remote: her mind, or maybe her soul, had been elsewhere. Amelia, released from darkness, constraint, sobriety, began chattering. Even Gertrude's state of quietude could not long withstand two piping, twittering little girls. They were all over the kitchen, into everything. They were naughtier together than either would have dared be alone; they opened the refrigerator and peered into the freezer. The cook, who returned from her devotions by taxi, was, like Mrs. Waterman, past resisting the assault of their high spirits. The phone rang. Mrs. Waterman picked it up. "Hello . . . How are you? Fine . . . Nice to see you and Janet . . . It's certainly been too long . . ." She handed the phone to Alida, and said, "Andrew Cameron wants to talk to you."

"Where have you been?" he asked. "Where was everybody? I've been calling for hours. Where are you now?"

"We were in church. Now we're all in the kitchen, making Easter eggs."

"Then just answer yes or no. I made a mistake last Friday. A terrible mistake. Can you forgive me?"

"Yes."

"Do you love me?"

"Yes."

"Are you flirting with that painter?"

Alida began to giggle; like the girls, she was past restraint: "Andrew, don't you know it's Easter? I'll call you Monday."

213

Memorial Day

Guided by the estate map, Alida drove along a winding road that ascended toward the main house, where Lucy Cameron had lived and died and where Andrew had asked her to meet him on the Monday after Easter. The road ran past the house front, where Alida stopped and stared at the large stone building, Queen Anne Revival in its general outline, but plucked of its detail. Pits in the ground and scars on the wall suggested that an imposing porte cochère had been removed. The vast front door had vanished and been replaced by a multicolored composition of dilapidated interior doors held in place by rough boards nailed crosswise. The building, stripped of all the exterior ornament that had once softened the facade, stretched handsome but sullen, like a mysteriously shorn lion couched unhappily in weeds. Alida regarded it for a moment, trying to imagine it as it had been, supposing that the trim had been wrought iron, and then thought better of loitering where anyone— a watchman, a workman—could see her. She began to drive slowly along the road. Just past the house, parked out of view behind it under shrubs that bordered a rough-cut patch of lawn, she saw Andrew's car, and Andrew himself coming toward her with both arms outstretched.

They embraced. He said, "Come," took her hand, led her around the house on an overgrown path between deserted flower beds where strangled rosebushes were losing their struggle against invading wild vegetation, and brought her to the remains of the porch that had spread across the west front of the house. On this facade, too, the door was gone and boarded up, and pits in the stone showed how much had come down, including the roof of the piazza. What was left were the weathered, and in some places splintered, dark gray wooden floorboards and a flight of stone steps that led down to the lawn. They sat on the stairs. The house had been sited on the highest point of the Cameron acres, and the porch commanded a proprietary view of the Hudson River. Andrew and Alida looked out over knolls rolling down to the sinuous, silvery blue stream, glinting as the westering sun's rays struck the ripples like sparks, and across to the opposite bank, where green hills folded gently into each other. On both sides of the water, the land lolled or lounged; the terrain was lyrical, sensuous, and serene, speaking, it seemed to Alida, of a world of gratification without woe. Through gaps where plantings had died, or where the trees and shrubs had not yet put forth their full screen of leaves, they could glimpse some of the estate buildings that had sheltered them, but it had clearly been the intent of the architect that the eyes of anyone sitting on the porch would be directed to the distant view, which at this moment appeared motionless. The scene was so empty and silent that Andrew and Alida might have been alone in the world.

Andrew took both her hands in his, and began, "I can't forgive myself, but I want you to forgive me." Alida was too happy to find words. She nodded and smiled and kissed him. "It's not easy to explain what happened," he went on.

But when he told his story, it was just as she had suspected: the approach of the Easter holiday had caused a small explosion in the Cameron family. Andrew had come home to change before going out to dinner with the Hartford lawyer and, walking down the hall to his bedroom, had met his daughter, who made a comment that implied she would not be accompanying her parents to the family's traditional Easter Sunday dinner at Andrew's oldest brother's. Andrew sought big Janet, who admitted that she had known of her daughter's mutinous scheme for several weeks. When Andrew complained that no one had informed him, the retort, from mother and daughter jointly, had been that they saw so little of him that they had had no chance to tell him anything.

"There it was," Andrew said, "the truth laid out like a corpse on a slab. I hadn't seen my daughter—not really *seen* her—in weeks, and when I looked at her she seemed to me to have gotten more peculiar. Squabbling with her is hopeless, because she keeps tossing out one idiotic word after another—'bourgeois,' 'materialistic,' 'hypocritical,' 'gross,' and, for a change, 'spiritual'—and her mother takes

215

it all seriously and tells me not to interfere with 'a young person's growth.' We had a couple of minutes of *that* kind of discussion after I told her she had to go to her uncle's. I couldn't help wondering where these females came from. What were they doing in my apartment? They were so bizarre, and so—so—irritating. And when I reminded myself that they were my own wife and daughter, I couldn't believe it. I'm ashamed of how I felt. I'm ashamed of what I did." Andrew paused before confessing. Alida squeezed his hand, and he continued. "I suddenly remembered how hard I found it to disobey my father, and I remembered, too, how he and my mother and my aunts and uncles all told us, when my brothers and cousins and I used to complain that they were strict, hard, mean parents, how tough *their* fathers, our grandfathers, had been, and I recalled a phrase everybody used about some Cameron patriarch: 'His word was law.' And I realized you could pretty much say that about most fathers down to now, and I was furious at all this back talk from my kid and her mother, both of them looking like freaks, and I said, 'I am the head of the household and what I say goes.' I told my daughter she didn't have the option of disobeying me, no matter what her mother said."

"I don't know that that's shameful," Alida said.

"Well, you couldn't call it understanding or sympathetic."

"Oh dear, oh dear, oh dear."

"What does that mean?"

"Me. My mother. Amelia. Teeny. It was a terrible week, last week. I don't know that I was very understanding or sympathetic."

"It was a terrible week for me, too. I left them not knowing what to think, and when I saw the Hartford lawyer and he told me about Eliot Jones, and he made me feel as if—"

"I know how he made you feel," Alida said, wryly.

"Like a thief. I have no right to you, don't you see? And then, a man is supposed to be the protector of his women. I had destroyed mine."

"Perhaps they were destroying you."

Andrew was not prepared to consider that possibility. He said, "I felt I had to give you up and repair them. I tried to fix up my girl. Janet was furious because I was forcing her sensitive child to go to a family dinner, and she wouldn't help. Anyhow, she probably couldn't. You know what she looks like. I wanted to call you, to ask your advice."

"I wish you had. Who did you call?"

216

"My sister-in-law Mary, my brother Duncan's wife. They have girls. I was ashamed I had to ask her where little Janet could get her hair cut and what shops had pretty clothes for a teenager. Mary's a thoroughbred. She went around with us and never said a word. She let little Janet make those faces and just smiled and said, 'How becoming!' Goddammit, I hate exposing how crazy, how cracked up, my family life is." Andrew shrugged. "I suppose they guess. But that's a reason I appreciated Mary's coming along and not saying anything."

"Why are you ashamed? None of this is your fault."

"I think it is. A man is supposed to be responsible. Powerful. Strong. He takes care of his family. I haven't. I've failed."

Andrew's feelings surprised Alida. She could understand that a man might feel ashamed of an unattractive wife, but not how he could feel guilty. Sitting beside him, holding his hand, Alida began to ransack her own attitudes for healing ideas. She remembered that, riding home from her birthday party, her mother had spoken as if Andrew were responsible for both Janets' eccentricity, but at that moment Alida had been so wretched that she could not think clearly enough to question her mother's assumptions. Considering the subject now, Alida found Andrew's and her mother's concept of manliness strange. Alida had never thought of Hugo as responsible for her, certainly not as her protector. She stared off at the river and down at the untended grass punctuated by clumps of dandelions and escaped daffodils whose brilliant yellows demanded attention like a visual cry. She did not know whether mentioning Hugo would be tactless, yet if she wished to cure Andrew of his absurd guilt, she should demonstrate the possibility of another pattern, one in which a husband is not a junior officer responsible for the troops' turnout. She said, very tentatively, "I didn't expect Hugo to be responsible for me."

Andrew's "Yes?" told her that he wanted to hear about her, he wanted to learn just as much as he wanted to impart. They had been silent these months past as if the absence of speech could deny that they were lovers and adulterers. They had been trying to conceal from themselves that their love was a lode embedded in an intractable social formation, almost impossible to extract yet too precious to abandon. But it was time—past time—for them to talk. Their talks, begun that day, streamed as copiously and as windingly as the river, and sometimes their confidences, like the acid yellow dandelions and daffodils, were cries.

217

Their rendezvous was the main house. Andrew had a key to a side door. They were shocked when they stepped inside that afternoon. The house had been stripped, rifled, looted. Not only the rugs and furniture, but the paneling, fireplace mantels and surrounds, and chandeliers had been removed for sale. "I had no idea . . . ," Andrew said.

They moved through ravaged salons that looked ghastly because the walls behind the missing paneling were a dirty gray-cream, like a ghost's robe, and these inner walls, too, were marked by holes where something—perhaps brackets for gas lamps—had come out. In one room the parquet itself had been lifted, revealing stout, homely wooden flooring. There was a lesson in the fact that the villas of nineteenth-century America were less lasting than those of Roman Britain, but Alida did not want to think about it, for she could see that Andrew was distressed. When they reached the great hall, she was almost as appalled as he by what had gone. It was darker here, and they needed Andrew's flashlight to see what Alida had not noticed from the outside, that the large second-story windows above the boarded-up front and back doors had lost their glass and were covered by boards.

"They were stained glass," Andrew said. His flashlight flickered along the forlorn walls. "The paneling in the hall was very dark. I think it was walnut."

What struck them both with a momentary terror was a gap where the front staircase had been. It looked to Alida like a screaming, toothless mouth. Andrew said, "It's terrible to see it this way. I suppose I should have imagined." He told her that the heirs had realized that the rise in fuel costs and the scarcity of servants had condemned the overspacious building, that the cousins had taken their pick of furniture and paintings and ornaments and sent the rest to auction, and that they had agreed that, before the house was razed, a dealer would remove all the period fittings, but he had not visualized the house vandalized. "It's worse," he added, "when you understand that you're responsible for the destruction. I knew the place couldn't last. You have no idea how much it cost to preserve Aunt Lucy's girlhood home, and she, poor woman, imagined she was economizing by staying on and not changing anything. But this . . ."

Alida had recovered from her shock. She was rather excited imagining how bits of century-old architectural detail would ennoble new buildings all over the country, and how strangers could incorporate morsels of the Camerons' past into their own lives. Working in the warehouse, where possessions had been heaped and hidden for years, she had begun to develop Morgan's peculiar combination of passion for and detachment from objects, whose beauty or meaning, as he had told her, afforded at best a life tenancy. Yet in Aunt Lucy's shattered hall, she had to admit that her acceptance of these partings between objects and owners had so far been only professional. She had yet to steel herself for a personal severance, such as selling her mother's house, and she understood why Andrew was disturbed. As they moved uneasily through other denuded rooms, he told her that he had not been inside the house since shortly after the funeral. "None of us ever liked this place," he said. "There was nothing children could do here. Nothing to play with. Nothing we were allowed to touch. I wonder how children lived here when it was new. We only knew it when our great-aunt Lucy was old. My cousin Bill called it 'the mummy's tomb.' But it wasn't dead till we killed it. The photograph albums showed everybody young. Great-aunt Lucy as a little girl with a bow in her hair, posing in the rose garden. But she kept those pictures in her room and we never saw them until after she died."

Alida interrupted his mourning with a kiss. She must try to cure his susceptibility to guilt. He had been leading them to the servants' staircase, and they climbed to the servants' cells on the third floor, which, having had no decorations to lose, remained more or less as they had been. There they found a cot and some exiguous bedding. When Alida lay down, she saw a small tarnished mirror, askew on a wall, reflecting a cloud and then a flying bird. Here under the roof they continued their conversations. Andrew, lying dreamily beside her and trying to envisage what Alida did when they were apart, said, half-aloud, "I'd love to see some of your bric-a-brac."

And Alida, equally dreamy, her soul as limp as her body, answered, "Why Andrew, you've seen it all."

So thereafter there was a never-ending exchange of "What soft gewgaws!"

"Show me your curios."

"What a pretty kickshaw."

"That is some *objet*!"

"Your bibelot is ticklish."

"These collectibles are sweet."

When their conversations ranged over the past, to the reasons for their mistaken marriages, they reviewed for each other—and for themselves—what they had been like when young. Andrew recalled coming out of the navy, going to law school, and feeling that his life had been planned for him before he was born. The bland young women he met, who held out as few surprises as a Mother's Day gift assortment of candies, seemed part of the plan. "I didn't expect much. I didn't think I was a genius with a mission, and I didn't feel above going into the family firm, but I wanted something else, too. Something less *given* than being a piece in a universal jigsaw puzzle. More daring, maybe."

"Did Janet seem daring?"

"Well, she was the first girl I met who expressed any ideas. It's funny, I could never remember anything impressive she said, but I can remember *being* impressed." There was a lull in the conversation, as they were gradually absorbed in other matters, and afterward Andrew recalled that Janet had talked so knowingly about sex (with the authority, he later realized, of all the how-to manuals of the day) that he was astonished to discover that she was a virgin and that, when introduced to erotic reality, she disliked it. "She seemed to feel sex as an infringement. When it was words, she had it under control."

When Alida tried to explain how *her* marriage came about, she was shocked to recognize how little she had willed it. "We're not as free a country as we're supposed to be," she announced. "There's a dictatorship of what's expected."

She recalled for Andrew the air of orphan or waif that the Weinsteins had descried about her and how, even this past year, her uncle and aunt were offering to make up for what they regarded as her mother's inadequacies. "But *I* never felt neglected. I *was* lonely, I suppose, but only because I didn't know many people who cared about the things that interested me. Marriage isn't a solution to that kind of loneliness."

"You married Hugo because you were lonely?"

"No. I married him because he went after me. He was persistent. And he was funny and smart. And when a man is after you all the time, and you know you're supposed to get married . . . That's what I mean by a dictatorship. People never thought of asking a girl if she wanted to marry. She knew she had to."

They explored their disappointments, each making the other wonder how a being so precious could have been so undervalued, how such a human treasure could have been so squandered. Andrew had found his verbally assertive wife dependent as well as

220

domineering. Uninterested in him, his work, his ideas, or his fancies, she was also uneasy with strangers, so that, little as they enjoyed themselves by themselves, going into company was never very happy, for the dinner-party Janet might be argumentative, aloof, or clinging. "Perhaps it's having been the only child, the apple of her father's eye," Andrew guessed. "She never had to try to please."

"Hugo's an only child, too. His mother's boy. But *her* way of cherishing was making him sing for his supper. He had to entertain, make up stories, perform." Hugo could never recover from his bride's inexperience, and continued to invent little ruses to persuade, wheedle, reassure a reluctant virgin. "He was always writing scenarios. I wasn't allowed desire."

"He didn't want a real woman."

"But was it any good for you, fighting for it?"

"After the children, it sort of tapered off."

"And what did you do?"

"Not much. A couple of times, not many, with other—oh, eager women who tried too hard to please. That kind makes you think you aren't very good. I thought Janet was right, I was a dull, clumsy fellow, meant to be a useful adviser, nothing more."

"You, dull?"

Once Andrew asked, "What did you do after Hugo . . . ?"

"I noticed when he left off . . . But I was more upset, I guess, about how he kept picking on me. I took sleeping pills in California. When I came east, I played tennis. And last year I had a terrific crush on Morgan."

What they were confiding, bit by bit, was the erosion of personality that results from mismating. In renouncing his rights to the body of his wife, Andrew had also yielded a broader range of entitlements, and Alida, restricted to the part of a sexual marionette whose strings Hugo had pulled, had been unable to grow up. She became ever more passive as she struggled against depression and incoherence. Andrew and Alida had managed to perform adequately in their expected tasks, but they had little pleasure and no joy. They never noticed when they grew into the habit of stifling their daydreams, for their respective unhappinesses came on them like subtle tyrannies, grinding them down gradually until they accepted dejection as their normal condition. Indeed, they had not even known they were dejected until they found each other and were suffused by gaiety. Other people noticed their cheerfulness, and when her mother commented, Alida told her it was spring.

221

The more they talked, the more they loved each other, for articulateness showed them to each other as full human beings—not fantasies, dolls, or pets, but genuine people who could hear and help each other. And they never talked enough. They wanted to tell each other everything about everything, and the little events of the day—a joke bumper sticker Alida observed on the road, a new waiter at Andrew's luncheon club—gained significance because they had someone to confide in. They also became each other's parents in worrying. The weather that year was exceptionally unpredictable—storms, hot spells, and near-freezes succeeded one another almost daily—and Andrew feared that Alida was insufficiently prepared for its vagaries. He bought her an extravagant raincoat, umbrella, and boots, and a still more extravagant lavender cashmere shawl. Like a doting father, he wanted to give her things. Alida, grasping the absent quality of his home life, grew concerned about his eating. She began stopping at a stylish SoHo delicatessen near the warehouse to buy tidbits to bring to their trysts. She wanted to feed him, to hover over his dinners like an anxious mother. Whatever they said or did with each other was never enough, and they spoke to each other mentally when they were apart.

Andrew also wanted to talk *about* Alida. He longed to hear her name and hear her praised, and he schemed to find someone who would admire her in conversation. He mulled over candidates, picked Morgan, whom he had met at Alida's birthday party, and decided to visit the Galleries late on a Saturday afternoon, when business would have slackened, so that a chat—silver would be his conversational opener—might be possible, and, with luck, he could maneuver Morgan into an after-closing drink and draw him out about Alida's perfections.

The project began with a difficulty, for the chosen Saturday brought pelting rain. Andrew sat in the ugly library where Alida had waited while Janet "tested" Amelia, looking over papers and wondering when the weather would clear. Enthralled by the prospect of conversation about Alida, he would get up restlessly, look out of the window, sit down, and stare at the clock, willing it to hurry. The afternoon wore on: so did the rain. There was no chance that he could bring off the meeting as a casual visit arising from an impulse during a stroll, yet he could not bear another week's delay. He looked at the curtain of falling water outside the window, and told himself that he had concluded an urgent errand, had been unable to find a taxi, and so had taken refuge in the Galleries.

Having persuaded himself that the foregoing testimony was true, Andrew put away the contract he had been reading, and shortly appeared, drenched and dramatizing his sopping state, at the Galleries. Kate looked up as he came in, and while he placed his umbrella in the stand inquired neutrally if she could help him.

He asked for Mr. Davies, and she said, "He's up in the picture gallery." She moved toward a phone and asked, "Who shall I say is calling on him?"

"Never mind. I'll go up."

Morgan was not in sight. The rooms were empty. Andrew was too impatient to appreciate their artful proportions and the artful decisions that formed them; his eyes sought doors, corners, or alcoves that might conceal the missing dealer. A door opened and a handsome, fiftyish woman came out, followed by Morgan. They had evidently just completed a transaction, for they exuded the air of slightly asymmetrical satisfaction that follows a sale—she proud of her acquisition, but rueful, as if suspecting that buying were a form of yielding, yielding perhaps too soon or too much, and he, with a courtliness exaggerated almost to the point of parody, disguising his triumph as he accompanied her across the floor and down the stairs while murmuring assurances of speedy delivery and enduring pleasure. He came back upstairs in a moment, though, focused on the new client: "Were you looking for me?"

"Nothing urgent," Andrew said. "I'm Andrew Cameron."

"Janet Cameron's husband? Did you come to see the picture she bought?"

Andrew did not know that Janet had bought a painting, but recognized a conversational lifeline stronger than the fiction he had prepared. "If I may."

"This one."

Andrew looked. It was a sizable canvas, recognizably a landscape, though simplified in outline and sweetened in color. Andrew was surprised that his wife had bought anything so pretty and so lacking any element of the pathetic on which to exercise her patronage. Though hypersensitive about letting strangers glimpse the black hole of his marriage, he was not as wary as he had wished, for his astonishment was evident when he asked how she had come to choose it.

"Mrs. Kelly helped her. One of our employees."

The conversation had landed exactly where Andrew planned. "Alida. We met at her birthday party."

"Of course," Morgan said. "How could I have forgotten! Do try to forgive me. My head was all in a whirl that night."

"Forgiven." Andrew smiled, and went on. "I didn't know Alida sold paintings."

"She doesn't ordinarily." Morgan seemed to begin a new conversation: "How do you know Mrs. Kel— Alida?"

"I'm her lawyer." Andrew sensed that Morgan was curious, that he, too, wanted to talk about Alida, and continued: "I've—we've—the firm's been her family's lawyers for generations." After a moment, he added, "And I don't mind saying I'm a great admirer of hers."

"As who is not?" asked Morgan dryly. "Have you seen her lately? If so, give her my regards."

Andrew had not expected a sour Morgan. Something was amiss. He was certain Alida was not at fault; possibly Morgan had an unreasonable side she had not seen. Andrew determined to discover it. A frontal assault seemed appropriate. "You sound annoyed."

"It's nothing serious."

"Come have a drink and tell me about it."

Andrew's tone, at once casual, brisk, and assured, concealed his concern on Alida's behalf and conveyed an authority he did not feel. It was adequate for its purpose, though. Morgan went back to his office for a raincoat and umbrella, led Andrew downstairs, said a few locking-up words to Kate, and drew Andrew across the street in the downpour to the horsy bar. They checked their wet gear in the coatroom. The bar was extremely crowded. They heard the crowd rather than saw it because the room was also pitch-dark. "This is a surprise," Morgan said. "It never happens on Saturday. Are they all sitting in a blackout waiting for the rain to stop?"

The headwaiter recognized Morgan, led them to a minute table in a far corner, and commanded busboys to wedge in a pair of chairs, taking care to mention, in a loud voice, "Mr. Davies' reservation." He bowed as he left, saying, "You're just in time."

"For what?" Andrew muttered.

"I don't know. Maybe a séance."

The question answered itself when two giant television sets above the bar came on in refulgent color and full voice for the Kentucky Derby. "I should have remembered," Morgan said. "I have three customers down there, though none has a horse running this year. Do you mind watching?"

Andrew suggested they honor the occasion with mint juleps.

Neither was a racing or a betting man, and both were bored by the long prologue, the commercials, the introductions of celebrities and of nonentities in funny hats. The race itself was a blast of excitement, a dramatic two-horse contest between Bold Forbes and Honest Pleasure. Andrew grew restless during the rerun, the ceremonies and interviews, and was irritated by the intensity of the crowd around him. Even after the sets were turned off, the room remained full. Bold Forbes' partisans crowed, Honest Pleasure's supporters divided blame between the trainer and the jockey, and other bettors and critics began talking of the Preakness. The customers dispersed slowly after the lights went up, their winners-and-losers' disputes about checks entwined with recapitulations of the race. Morgan looked down at his hands playing with his sprig of mint, and said, "Every time I see a race, which isn't often, I long for Degas. Racetracks are scruffy and horses are stupid—it's the deception that's so charming about art: it makes all that seedy nonsense elegant. Circuses are even sorrier, yet painters . . ."

Andrew mentioned that he recalled a racetrack Degas at Alida's uncle's.

"Are you trying to remind me that she's well connected?" Morgan asked. "Guthrie thinks that's the trouble. *I* think she's in love."

"What has she done?"

"She's changed since she came to work for us. We never see her. She's even taken to sending her lists up by Johnny. From the warehouse, that is. He tells us she's in a great good humor. She's efficient. I've no complaints about the work she's doing. But I thought we'd made it plain that she had a chance for a future here, and she never comes by. If she wanted a place with the firm—and I thought she did—she'd make excuses to visit, to nose around. She'd be all over us. She'd be asking questions. Guthrie and I expected to hear her ideas about her apartment. She never called us. Guthrie's hired an assistant, a poor boy who tears around the city matching fabrics. You can't keep him out of things in the office. He never goes home. I think he never sleeps. He's pushy and cringing, too." Morgan chewed on his mint stem, grimaced, and said, "You know, a perfect slave. Guthrie says that Alida can't help being a dilettante because she's rich. But I've worked with her mother, and . . . I suppose I *could* call Mrs. Waterman and ask her what her daughter's doing when she ought to be with me, or us, but if she's got somebody like a married lover her mother doesn't know about . . . I wouldn't want to do that to Alida, even if she has no ambition."

Andrew was aghast. He had never thought of himself as interfering with Alida's career, and, knowing where she was when she should have been with Morgan and Guthrie, he felt it his duty to repair the damage. "Her work, her real work at the warehouse, is satisfactory?"

"It's perfect."

Morgan seemed to dislike making that admission. Andrew suggested another drink, and sat quietly for a moment, meditating his plea. "I know that family," he said at last. "They're all shy. Alida's afraid of being in your way. I'll have a talk with her."

"Would you?" Morgan was relieved and grateful. "I never thought about her being shy." Then he was doubtful. "Do you think you can do any good?"

"I can certainly tell her to come by the Galleries. And find out if she has started work on her apartment." Covering tracks invisible to Morgan, he asked, "Does she have much to do there?"

"Everything. She had me and Guthrie over weeks ago, months ago, and promised to give us her ideas. Since then, not a word." Repeating this story brought Morgan's grievances and uncertainties to the fore again, and he said, "I'm not sure you're right about shyness. She didn't seem shy last year. She seemed brilliant."

"Did she?"

There followed the praise Andrew had sought. "In my store before Christmas. On New Year's Eve. You've no idea what a find she seemed. So sparkling, so outgoing, and so knowing. So witty." Morgan recalled his side of New Year's Eve (Andrew had already heard Alida's), and his praise was greater than Andrew had foreseen, for he explained that he had been impressed by her modesty—her unpretentiousness about her knowledge—to the point that, despite his and Guthrie's rule of consulting each other about personnel, he had offered her a job there and then without waiting to discuss it with his partner. "I didn't see her as a dilettante that night. I didn't find her shy. That's what makes me think she's in love. There's nothing like love for destroying a woman's usefulness. Women don't seem to understand that a lover is no excuse for neglecting their future."

Andrew was diverted by Morgan's priorities—it evidently had not occurred to him that, for many women, love *was* their future—but he was now as impatient to end the conversation as he had been to open it. "The warehouse is downtown, isn't it?" he asked. Morgan nodded. "Then I could easily take her to lunch."

226

"She's only there on Mondays and Wednesdays, and Johnny says she doesn't stop for lunch but leaves early."

"Never mind. I'll call her tomorrow and call you Monday afternoon."

Returning home, Andrew met his wife and daughter leaving the apartment. He looked at the heavy, pale woman and frail, pale girl with distaste, and immediately felt a prickle of guilt. Before she asked where he had been, Janet reminded him to leave his wet umbrella in the stand outside the door. He obeyed and told her he had been admiring the painting she had bought and talking to Morgan Davies.

"Oh do you like it? I meant to go back and look at it again, but I've been so busy . . ."

"Where are you two going?"

"To the movies. Little Janet wanted to see *One Flew Over the Cuckoo's Nest,* and we can just make it."

Andrew nodded, eager to see them depart. Janet looked down and said, "You should have worn rubbers. You'll wet the rugs. You'd better take off your shoes and leave them outside." Andrew was irked by her gesture—she pointed at his feet, making a sort of stabbing movement with her umbrella—but he obliged, and Janet rang for the elevator. As an afterthought, she mentioned, "Dolores may have something for you on the stove."

Andrew went to his bedroom without noticing that his daughter had not greeted him, took off his wet socks, and telephoned Alida, reaching her just as her mother's small party of middle-aged botanists was trooping toward the dining room. Alida took the call in the cloakroom and tried to grasp his account of Morgan's dissatisfaction. She was annoyed rather than alarmed, and pained when Andrew started blaming himself for interfering with her career.

"I can't talk now, Andrew, but don't *you* talk nonsense. What do you want me to do?"

"Lunch with me tomorrow. I know it's Sunday, but tell your mother it's urgent business."

At breakfast, Alida explained to her mother that she was going to the city because "Andrew Cameron found out that Morgan's upset about me, and seems agitated."

"That doesn't sound like Andrew," Mrs. Waterman remarked. "Or Morgan."

"I know," Alida said. "It's perplexing, and that's why I think I'd better find out what it's about right away."

227

"Certainly," Gertrude said, and asked, "Do you want *me* to speak to Morgan?"

Alida looked at her kind, loving, gracious, generous, unsuspecting mother, dressed for church, anxious about her daughter, and thought that this trusting woman did not deserve to be shut out of her child's life as totally as Alida had been shutting her. "Thanks for the offer. Let me get a grip on all this first. I'm pretty sure I'll need your advice."

The pleasure visible on Gertrude's face at that minute token of dependence pricked Alida with guilt, but, driving in and thinking about Morgan's grievance, she forgot her mother. Then she forgot Morgan at the sight of Andrew walking up and down in front of the restaurant. He got into her car to give directions to a garage, and they walked back to the restaurant hand in hand through a magnificent Sunday that had succeeded the sodden Saturday. Andrew had chosen one of a frieze of former workingmen's saloons restored for the affluent. The brunch population looked so young that Alida thought they should have been lingering over comics instead of bloody Marys, but, once seated, she forgot their neighbors. She was thrilled by this bonus meeting. Her giddiness took the form of interrupting—she wanted to know what time Andrew had got up and what he had had for breakfast. While he tried to make some sort of sequential narrative out of his encounter with Morgan, she kept reminding him to eat, but both of them had lost their appetites to excitement. They pushed the food around on their plates and forgot to lift it to their mouths. Presently the waiter presented the check with a perfunctory offer of more coffee, and stood by to be paid as a way of calling attention to a new cohort of hungry youngsters eyeing their table. They walked out into sunlight and, on the way to her apartment, Alida said, "It's never nice to be criticized, but Morgan's right."

Afterward, they lay and talked of her sense of her delinquency. "They did come over here," she said, "and I shouldn't have abused their time or patience. I've been thinking about it since you called. Morgan may sound hurt, or bossy, or demanding, or possessive, but, you know, I could have asked him out for a weekend to my mother's. And I forgot to think of Guthrie as he thinks of himself. That's why he's angry at me. And Morgan is probably angry *for* Guthrie. Guthrie sees himself as an important artist. He's filled with scorn and rage. A lot of creative people are like that. You don't think of it till you have to. But they're almost always angry. An artist has one idea. One vision. His. He gets appreciation. People say, 'My, how beautiful.' And mean it. And then they see something else, and say, 'That's beautiful, too.' And I'm like that." Alida buried her head in Andrew's armpit for a moment, and concluded: "Guthrie would say I have no artistic convictions. No," she corrected herself, "he would say, 'Alida has no convictions.' And he'd be right."

"You make yourself sound unprincipled."

"In Guthrie's sense I am. I like a lot of things. Anything— everything, practically, that's good of its kind. And eclecticism isn't considered a great taste." Alida sat up. "I'm just a consumer. A shopper. A customer. I'd be happy to do this place English, Japanese, Federal. I've always had a weakness for exotic rococo. You see, I'd like . . ."

She went on to describe her enthusiasms, and, transported by her imagination, got up and walked around the room, waving her arms and gesturing as she described the multiplicity of her enjoyments and ways of seeing the space around them. Andrew saw her breasts jiggling, stopped listening, picked her up, and piled them both back on the bed again.

Later, he said that he wanted her to be wary of accepting blame. After all, she was doing the job for which she had been hired, and she had to consider the possibility that her gifted employers might be exploitive. Some people, Andrew observed, live in terror lest anyone who works for them have a moment's liberty, a second's freedom. "One of my mother's cousins was like that. A slave driver. She was famous in the family. She could never keep help. They used to tell of the dinner parties she had to cancel when the cook quit."

Alida doubted that Morgan and Guthrie were slave drivers. The fault was hers. She could remember how important they had seemed to her last January. She could not have helped showing her respect and admiration—her awe—and they would justly feel surprised and wounded by her distance and silence. She had not deliberately planned to withdraw, but she had done so, and, when she looked back, she must have appeared inexplicable, for she had heard of their doings from Johnny, but even when he had told her of something interesting or lucky, she never thought of phoning congratulations or asking questions. The only man she thought about was Andrew. Though gratified when she said, "The only man I ever think of is you," he interrupted with instructions. "Never go into a negotiation thinking you're wrong. You have a child in Connecticut and you're attending school."

That was the line he took at the horsy bar on Wednesday when they met Morgan. Alida admired how Andrew assumed control of the meeting. The three were barely seated when he suggested, as a device to test the seriousness of Morgan's complaints, that they set up regular times when Alida would report to him and Guthrie.

"Oh, we don't need a formal schedule. It's just that we wanted"— Morgan sought a phrase with a wave of his hand—"to be in touch."

They ordered drinks, and Alida, following Andrew's scenario, opened with motherhood. "Morgan, I'm sorry I haven't been to the Galleries. Johnny can tell you that I keep chasing home to be with Amelia." She raised the academic. "And there's that course I'm taking." She promised for the future. "I'm looking forward to the end of school. I think I should finish the warehouse by the end of June, and then go on to work on my apartment."

Morgan was mollified but, wishing to justify his complaints, maintained his side of the quarrel by remarking that decorators were expected to handle more than one job at a time. Alida gave him an open-eyed stare, flirtatious and reproachful, and asked, "Do you really think I ought to take on another job now? Don't you think that's slave driving?"

Morgan laughed, and agreed it would be. "Guthrie, of course, wouldn't think it too much. I often have to remind him that everybody hasn't his stamina."

Alida looked sideways at Andrew, who was concealing a smile in his glass, and proceeded to the next bit of dialogue they had outlined together. It was time to parade her shyness. "Morgan," Alida sounded very tentative. "I've wanted to see you—you *and* Guthrie— and I thought of asking you for a weekend, but I didn't dare. We're very boring."

"I don't think your mother is boring."

"I mean it's quiet. Nothing glamorous or lively. Amelia and I do homework Saturday mornings and my mother gardens all day."

"It sounds restful."

"You mean you'd come? Both of you?"

Morgan could not commit Guthrie, and he reminded her, besides, that they worked Saturdays. Alida said, sadly, "We aren't really interesting enough for you," and then, as if cheering herself after a rejection, said, "I'll be in touch about the apartment."

Andrew intervened. "You're both unreasonable. Morgan, now that you see the demands on Alida, you must admit you've been unfair. Alida, Morgan isn't turning you down. He and Guthrie have to work, and you shouldn't be hurt if they can't come to the country—"

"I'd love to come," Morgan said, "but we don't close Saturdays until July . . ."

The conversation began wandering over times and possibilities. Alida suggested the Memorial Day weekend, and Morgan suggested she check with her mother, while Andrew suggested they fix a date for another council of war about the apartment. Again Morgan was loath to commit his partner, but before Alida rose, allegedly to hurry off to Amelia, Morgan had softened, and had settled on the following Monday.

Alida's tension relaxed in her car. Driving through Manhattan's end-of-day traffic jam was a relief compared to the strain of insincerity. She was relieved, too, that, with Andrew's coaching, she had won Morgan back, but her victory was infused with a melancholy that puzzled her. She had to concentrate on city traffic, but once she found herself safely on the way home and could wonder about her ruefulness, it came to her that she was dismayed by the appearance of Andrew in her workaday world because it reminded her of marriage. Drinking with Morgan, like a married couple out with a friend, was a comedown from their secret trysts. Such humdrum sociability had been a characteristic of her life with Hugo. Now, belatedly, it crossed her mind that Hugo's affair was his response to the mediocrity of their union. She could not explain to herself why they had given each other so little, but she could accept, without anger, that they had. As she turned off the highway and stopped for a light, she noticed a billboard for the Inn. It brought back memories of Fred and, worse, of Eliot, and, back in the past, the snickers and winks and whispers about the rumors of illicit couples upstairs that had titillated Flat Rock adolescents. Youthful ignorance had assumed those affairs were tawdry, but the Inn's lovers—if they really existed—might have experienced the kind of rapture she shared with Andrew. Her love for Andrew made her feel charity for Hugo. Turning into her mother's drive, she not only forgave Hugo for Yvonne, she accepted a justification for his affair that he himself could not give: Alida had never been with Hugo as she was with Andrew.

She sat in the car in the driveway for a moment, mentally saying farewell to Hugo, thinking of him as a collaborator on a project that had failed. The play that closes out of town, the museum display that never catches fire—these, too, brought explosions and

231

recriminations when disappointed people blamed each other, forgetting that they had all hoped, had all tried, and had all been disappointed.

She had somehow wiped a psychic slate clean. She began to inch toward the garage, and her car's lights moved through the twilight, picking up the brilliant colors of Gertrude's blooming borders. She thought of using all those improbably vivacious hues to decorate her apartment. She liked that idea, especially since it would give her a reason to bring her mother into her plans. Then she remembered, as she stepped out of the car, to mention that she wanted Guthrie and Morgan as houseguests for Memorial Day weekend. Gertrude and Amelia were already at the table, and Alida joined them, beginning by asking how they were, and dutifully listening to a somewhat involved account of a class discussion about Mother's Day—a lucky reminder, for Alida had forgotten its approach.

The telephone rang. It was Larry for Alida. He wanted to see her. He was calling on Hugo's behalf. He felt it was urgent. Tomorrow was not soon enough, but she delayed him till the Saturday, when she promised to visit him in the country.

Nature had so altered the scenery since January that Alida could scarcely recognize the way to the Weinsteins'; the earth's bones were concealed by trees, bushes, and grasses all in a competition of greens, and spring had embraced the Weinsteins' house, which, snuggled by lilac bushes, nestled on its rounded green lawn. Spring's gaiety had lightened her anxiety about her talk with Larry; she amused herself with the notion that the landscape's transformation demonstrated the importance of decoration, and wondered idly how her mother and Father Peele would react to a reference to the Great Decorator above. Larry had heard her car in the drive, and opened the front door. They had agreed that she would arrive around four—she had to spend the earlier part of the day with Amelia, shopping for a Mother's Day present for Gertrude—and that after their talk she would stay for an early family dinner. She was a little late, and apologized, explaining how spring had slowed her. "It's a beautiful day," Larry said. "Too lovely to sit indoors. I'll take you to Meadowland, as the family calls it."

They walked around the house and past the pond, on which Danny, Debby, and Monica paddled in a rubber boat. They waved. Alida asked after the boys: they were both at school and both, for the moment, doing well. On the far side of the pond, the meadow sloped gently upward to a ridge line that had been left wild; the path they followed briefly entered a wood, rose, and dipped, and then the scene opened out into a field in which earth-moving machinery stood like a herd of dinosaurs browsing amid heaps of soil and holes in the ground. At the far side there was a small house, a miniature of the main house. Larry explained that he was putting in a tennis court and swimming pool, and that the house, for changing and showering, included a kitchen and a second story with guest rooms to allow the children to give parties and to invite more company than the big house would hold. Larry had prepared for her coming with a pair of old-fashioned deck chairs set before the house, and, as they seated themselves, he said, "It was my answer to Debby's tantrum. You were there that Saturday. You remember, when she said she was leaving Danny."

Alida remembered, and remembered wondering how they had made up. "I'm a father first of all," Larry said. "My reward is my family. I told Debby I wouldn't permit her to leave her husband and ruin my grandchild's life."

"She obeyed you? Just like that?"

Larry said, guardedly, "Money came into it. I put on a little pressure. Then I thought about a little sweetening. The kids tease me about my extravagance. They don't know all this is bait."

"For whom?"

"For them. I want them and their friends and their husbands and someday their wives and all my grandchildren here. All of them, around me."

Alida was stunned by this confidence, and upset, too. Apart from the callousness of a father condemning a daughter, for all he knew, to a life of marital misery, she could sense, not very far off, a plea to return to Hugo for the sake of Amelia. She let her eyes range over the bit of wilderness, which in the sun seemed overpopulated, a veritable Hong Kong of insects with glimpses of squirrels, chipmunks, and, she thought, a rabbit; the rustles in the tangle of vegetation might be snakes, possibly, or toads. Despite the sun and the kindness of the air, the activity looked purposeful, not playful; insofar as a nonscientist could tell, life was, on every visible level, a desperate business. Larry continued with a tentative statement, just short of a question: "You don't disapprove."

Alida evaded, the better to protect herself when she became the subject. "I don't think I can have an opinion. I know so little about it. Other people's lives . . . ," she began.

Larry interrupted. "I can't think of my child or grandchild as 'other people.' They're mine, they will always remain mine ... There's a new myth that self is more important than family. I don't think self exists apart from family. Debby accused me of being a Jewish patriarch. Am I?"

At the edge of the trees there was a whirring of blues and a series of discordant cries: a couple of jays were fighting a grayish bird that fled before Alida could attempt to identify it. Once more she sensed that the landscape was an arena in which thousands of combats were being waged simultaneously, and she said, rather curtly, "I suppose so." And then she thought that all this natural ado was up to the same work as Larry; dandelions were founding dynasties and jays protecting their generations. She was struck, too, by the energy of it all. God knew what beetles were up to, but she knew that Larry had his work, his collecting, his boards—yet he was also trying to manage the feelings and the futures of his family and friends. "You men *do* so much," Alida said.

Larry was suspicious. "Is that a crack?" he asked.

"No, not at all. I mean it literally." She used herself by way of comparison, and gave him a brief account of her job and of her discovery that her bosses expected more of her. "I'm going to school, and living out here, and working in the warehouse, and Morgan actually complained to my lawyer because I wasn't hanging around the Galleries."

"Who's your lawyer? Oh—I remember, Andrew Cameron. I can't tell you how much I admire him. He's first-rate. What did he say?"

"He calmed him down. It's all blowing over. It just came to mind when you were talking, and I couldn't help thinking of all you do, and all *they* do, and how when I move back to the city I'll have to be at it all the time ... "

"Discipline," Larry said. "It's a habit men develop. But perhaps you don't need to. Hugo wants you back." He paused. "I was talking too much about *my* family affairs because I'm embarrassed to talk about yours. But Hugo asked me to. He's sorry about everything. He wants to start over. He misses Amelia. He feels he's losing her."

Larry waited for a response.

"I can't do much about that," Alida said. "I suppose I'm glad he cares for his child and sorry he's suffering."

"You could go back to him. He wants you very badly. He felt this way, he told me, almost from the moment you left, but he's afraid to tell you so. He's afraid to ask you to come back. He's afraid of rejection. I think he's afraid of *you*."

Alida shook her head in wonder at this preposterous notion. She sat and pondered, trying to imagine what Hugo felt. Larry's suggestion of fear did not seem right. Shame was more likely. Like Larry, though not quite as outspokenly, Hugo wanted to be in charge, a step ahead of his wife—not precisely commanding, but leading or teaching. Begging pardon and asking forgiveness were humiliating. His pride, not his courage, was at issue. She said, speaking slowly, and trying not to sound angry, because she was not angry at Larry: "Let's talk as friends. I think Hugo's using you unfairly. He's not your son. I'm not your daughter. The fact is, I can't think of—I can't imagine—going back to Hugo. It seems so long ago. Or far away, our being married."

"You don't miss him? You don't miss being married? Let me tell you what he had in mind. I've fixed up a movie for him. They're going to make it in Europe this summer. He was hoping you and Amelia would go with him. Spend time together when it was finished. It's supposed to be short and easy. It's a play he wrote, actually, and I'm not sure it wouldn't work *as* a play, though it needs some tightening . . . or loosening . . . Adjustments. Anyhow, his idea—his hope—is that the three of you could be alone together in Europe after the movie. Go back to being a family. I told him I thought he should ask you himself. But he begged me to try first. I think he's overcome with remorse. And afraid, too, as I said. But he's right. It's a good idea. A fair idea, to give the marriage another chance. That's all it is, really. It doesn't commit you. You're trying to retrieve more than ten years. You owe it to him. You owe it to yourself. And I suppose I have something to do with this—after all, I introduced you."

Alida was sympathetic to Larry, who had undertaken to do Hugo a favor and was about to fail, and she realized that his argument about trying to retrieve her investment of time—of nearly all her adult life—sounded like common sense, but she was annoyed, too, because he put her on the defensive. She looked at him. In the sunlight she noticed that the lines in his face had deepened; he was aging. Her irritation faded. "Everything you say is reasonable," she said at last, "but it's not how I feel. I was very angry at Hugo last year and very hurt, and I confess I wanted to keep Amelia from him. My mother and Andrew Cameron changed my mind. Now I don't feel anything about Hugo—he could be a stranger—but I don't want to keep him and Amelia apart anymore."

"How does your mother feel? What does Cameron think?"

"I suspect my mother thinks as you do. Andrew only wants me to do whatever I want to do in a legal form. I promised him I would see Hugo in June. That was the plan."

Larry broke in. "When this European thing came up, there wasn't time to wait for him to come. You'll need reservations for any place you want to go."

"*I* won't need them. I'd like Amelia to see her father again, although on Thanksgiving he took her out with that, that—his paramour. I was furious. But I suppose" (Alida was half talking to herself, with a tolerance born of her affair with Andrew) "after we're divorced, Amelia will have to get used to that kind of business."

Larry looked perplexed. "You sound so unconcerned about Hugo and other women."

"I wasn't before. I am now. Larry, let's not quarrel. You've done all you promised, all you could. Let Hugo know. We have to have a talk, I guess. Or our lawyers do. I want to have Amelia live with me, but Hugo can see her whenever she isn't in school. She could visit Europe this summer. He must let me know some dates, though, some exact dates. I'm working now and I must plan."

"He's supposed to be here around the first of June on his way to Europe. I'll let you know when I do." Alida rose, but Larry caught her hand, and said, "Stay a minute. Explain yourself to me better. You don't make sense to me. You really don't. You're breaking a family without regret."

Alida was tired of this conversation. She had had it with her mother, and both times her need to lie about Andrew had made her sound shallow or cold, abnormally detached from the father of her child. She longed for the freedom to say, "Yes, I am in love and having an affair with Andrew Cameron. *Now* do you see why I've lost interest in Hugo?" She was tempted to blurt out the truth, and momentarily perplexed at the speed with which her self-command repressed that impulse—for, after all, if everybody knew, what could anybody do to them? "Don't be sorry," Alida said. "These things can't be helped. I had a lot of feeling once. Now it's gone. Think of *me* for a moment. I'm lucky not to care. No one knows what Hugo would do. He could lure me back and start his games all over again."

Larry was still holding her hand as he got up. He sighed and admitted, "I meddled without thinking of you. I wasn't thinking

236

that much about Hugo. I was thinking of Amelia, and how, no matter what people promise themselves—or each other—a divorce costs children their fathers. I wish you'd think about that."

"My father died before I was born."

"And didn't you wish for a father?"

"I don't know. I can't remember how I felt when I was a child. I've thought about it this year, living with my mother. Perhaps I don't know what a father does. How he matters. But in any case, Hugo won't lose Amelia."

He started to walk toward the path. "Wait a minute," Larry said. He dropped her hand to fold up the deck chairs and nodded his head toward the pool-house/guest-house. "Come inside," he commanded, and began to show off the future of the unfinished interior—"All this open space, with that glass wall, will be the playroom. Game room. There'll be a TV and a record player . . . God knows what kind of music my grandchildren will be listening to. And this will be the kitchen . . ."

The playhouse abuilding reminded Alida of the playhouse on the Cameron estate; she had developed a store of memories she could share only with Andrew. She thought for a moment of the transience of dynasties—Larry's vast plans would have seemed entirely natural to the Cameron patriarch—but shook off her melancholy to adopt the tone of joking admiration that, she gathered, was the Weinstein family's: "This will probably be a grander Olympic Village than Montreal."

"You must promise to compete this summer."

They walked back to the house in silence. The Mahons had left the pond, and Alida began to wonder how much they knew about the purpose of her visit. She had a moment of panic when they came to the back door, fearing a trio agog to hear how the talk had ended, but there was nobody in the kitchen except a maid who told them that Mrs. Weinstein and the young people had gone to the village to buy milk.

"I want to look at your theater pictures again," Alida said.

They walked through the rooms and began looking. Alida's enthusiasm surged at an unexpected pairing of purples in a costume, and Larry said, "You haven't changed. Not one bit. You're the same girl who walked into my house in 1962. Do you remember how you started going over the glass on the mantel? Do you remember asking 'Is that Stiegel?' Do you remember?"

Alida smiled. "I must have been a funny youngster."

"Betsy prepared me for somebody more formidable. But I'm glad you haven't changed. I hate it when people outgrow their youthfulness, their eagerness." Larry turned her around and hugged her. "I'm sorry about the other thing."

They heard the car, the door, the noise of the family tumbling in. Betsy found them. She looked at Alida with the merest question in her eyes. Alida almost imperceptibly shook her head no. That was the end of Hugo for the evening.

During Dr. Marshall's Mother's Day sermon the next morning, Alida reverted to the question that had occurred to her while she was talking to Larry. Why were they, Andrew and Alida, hiding? She decided that she was avoiding conflict—arguments, scenes, emotional explosions—with her mother. That seemed to be the rule in her mother's house. That was civilization. Perhaps—she could not help thinking of Hugo and his habit of lecturing her about art—civilization wasn't art. Art heightened drama and conflict; art sought confrontation. Civilization was more like porcelain. Yet it was not *all* that fragile. Her mother would disapprove of her married daughter sleeping with a married man. Would she disinherit Alida? Would she change lawyers? And what could Hugo do? After all, he had carried on with Yvonne. What Janet would or could do, Alida could not guess. But everybody in this cast was civilized. None of them would do anything like pick up a gun or—more dramatic or operatic, and easier to come by—a knife. Tears were a weapon, though. She would hate to make her mother cry.

But this Sunday, Mother's Day, afforded no opportunity for tears or drama. Father Peele came for Sunday dinner, which featured a prodigious amount of unwrapping and giddy cries of "Just what I wanted!" and surprises. Gertrude thought nobody should be left out, so there was shaving soap for Father Peele, bubble bath for Amelia. They walked out in the gardens, and, in the sunlight, Alida remembered that she had been struck by the brilliance of flower colors in her headlights the other evening and had thought of getting those colors into her apartment. Then, beginning to think of using flowers themselves, she turned to her mother and asked if she would join the Monday confabulation at the apartment. Politeness required explaining to Father Peele, and he suggested that they take Amelia and let her help plan her future home. Thus, on Monday, Alida faced Morgan and Guthrie at the head of a team. Gertrude took Amelia on a tour of the apartment while Alida and Andrew and her employers sat in the living room, and Alida began to explain her feeling about flowers and flower colors. Guthrie was in surprisingly good humor. He said, "I'd been thinking about your making what we call a statement in your apartment, but I can see it's best for you to do what comes naturally. What *I* call the Kozy Korner. Old-and-new. It's everybody's bread and butter. The inherited look. Instant ancestors. In your case, it's real. You're entitled. You've got them. And even their furniture." Alida was partly relieved and partly disappointed. She was glad that Guthrie was not sulking or cutting, but sorry that he had relegated her to a lesser, lower place: safe, traditional, lucrative, but—in his eyes, at any rate—boring and lacking inventiveness. Guthrie went on. "I wonder what happened to all *my* family papers. I could probably cover a wall with my ancestors' eviction notices, notices of sheriff's sales, liens, writs of attachment. 'Replevin' is a funny word. I don't remember what it means."

Alida said, idly, "Truth in ancestry has its perils. Suppose my family foreclosed your family's mortgage."

Andrew, a quiet observer so far, said, reassuringly, "It's not likely," but Guthrie said, "I'd like to believe it."

Gertrude brought Amelia back. The little girl was excited at seeing what her grandmother had told her would be her room, and ran to the kitchen, returned, asked questions, and interrupted. Even so, she was understandable, containable, and attractive. Alida could not help contrasting her daughter with Andrew's, and wondering if he compared them, too. At the same time, she was listening to the comments and suggestions of the others, and clinging to her notion of flowers. She turned to Gertrude, and asked, "What about growing areas? What do we need?"

Gertrude replied, "I'm not an expert on indoors. I think it's hard to turn houses into greenhouses. Bathrooms are steamy, but they're not usually light, and houses are dry."

"Could we make a steamy garden in the master bath? Could we somehow wet up someplace else?" Alida began to chase ideas—a flower rug with growing flowers to match; a fernery in the bathroom; an herb garden. Or perhaps—this was the best idea—her mother could do a tapestry and the whole house could come out of it.

"That's good," Guthrie said. "That's it."

When they were getting ready to separate, Alida had a clue to the reason for Guthrie's atypical gentleness: Morgan and Guthrie both remarked how much they were looking forward to their Memorial Day visit. Alida realized that Gertrude's invitation meant something to them beyond anybody else's country weekend. She always marveled at her mother's power, whenever it came to her attention. Perhaps (she was mentally addressing Larry) Gertrude's strengths, which her children took for granted, had made the absence of a father less noticeable. For whatever reason—Gertrude's tapestry, possibly, but more likely her personality—Morgan and Guthrie felt honored to be asked as well as eager to come. Gertrude, obeying the law against omitting anyone present from an invitation, asked Andrew if he and Janet were free for any part of the weekend, but Andrew thanked and declined; they would be away for his son's graduation.

Andrew's potential departure worried Alida. "Are you really going away?" she asked, in bed in the Cameron house the following afternoon. "When? For how long?"

"I'm not sure when we go. Andy's graduation is June first. Janet wants to make an excursion. He's in New Mexico. She thought we should all leave early and stay at a ranch and fuss about the graduation and go back to the ranch with Andy, and do something. A rodeo, for all I know. A to-do. Because he's been thrown out of or run away from so many schools, and this time both sides stuck it out, Andy and the school. They've actually found a college that accepted him. Janet thinks we should let him know how proud we are. She says practically the only times we've seen him in recent years, it's been because he'd done something wrong. I fix it and scold him. She thinks we should show approval, for a change. She's right, of course. Andy probably thinks I was born with a scowl. But she's overdoing it. I'm not proud of Andy, just relieved that some place gave him a diploma. Actually the school's a cross between a rest home and a penitentiary. Going to Andy's graduation is like giving the bride away in the ninth month. 'Proud' isn't quite the word. Of course, we should reward him, encourage him, especially if he's willing to try college. But everything Janet does bothers me. I can't stand being with her. A week or ten days with her and little Janet would drive me crazy. Still, I can't abandon Andy. Or leave him entirely to Janet. She always puts his back up. She enrages him."

How could Alida help with Andrew's problem? What advice could she give? None at all. She thought to herself (still arguing with Larry) that an intact family was something more than simply hanging in there. She pitied Andy, though, as well as Andrew, and, as they were dressing, she said, "But you *will* go down for the graduation, at least."

"Of course," Andrew said. "I'm just trying to figure out how to show up and stage a circus for Andy but not put myself through another of Janet's family outings. Last Christmas . . . That ski trip."

Andrew seemed to cringe at the recollection, and Alida remembered that something about his expression when she had seen him in January had first suggested to her that he was unhappy. A little load she had not known she was carrying on her conscience was lifted: she was not responsible for dividing this father from his children.

Over the following weekend Alida made a systematic list of jobs to tackle at her apartment and the order in which they should go. She consulted her mother about Hugo's workroom. A "library" struck Alida as pretentious; a "television room" as suburban; a "music room" as ridiculous. A "small parlor" or second drawing room seemed the best solution, but because it was beside rather than beyond the living room, Alida doubted it would work at a party: a group of guests would not naturally flow into it. She was beginning to recognize limitations, as Guthrie and Morgan had hoped she would, and to glimpse the need for the disguises and accommodations that Miss Kinsky taught. She asked her mother again about indoor gardens: she fancied a jungle in the master bath. Gertrude cautioned against extravagance. Gertrude had trouble with words as she grew older, because the language of her girlhood muddled good taste and brutal class distinction. To her the outré, the spectacular were "ill bred," but she thought that expression sounded harsh or dated. In Gertrude's girlhood lexicon, "showy," except as applied to flowers, was the opposite of "solid." Still, stumble as they might on language, mother and daughter became close in their conferences. Father Peele, at Sunday dinner, suggested that Amelia might want to make decisions about her own room. The child objected: "I liked my room in California."

"Do you want it sent to New York?" Alida asked. "I'm not sure the furniture will fit. And, besides, you're ready for more grown-up things."

"Grown-up" should have been a lure, but Amelia was clinging to the past. When the adults questioned her, they learned she was not sure what she liked about her room in California, and was not too precise in her recollections of it.

Her grandmother suggested, "Maybe your father would take pictures of it and send them to you."

Gertrude's notion placated Amelia, but Alida was beginning to feel that Larry was a prophet: from the moment their talk had ended, the children—hers and Andrew's—had been putting in claims. She wondered if these worried Andrew, because he seemed, in their next few meetings, slightly withdrawn or abstracted, as if during their chatter he were thinking of another conversation. At last, on Monday the twenty-fourth, he met her in what was evidently a cheerful mood: he whistled as he got out of his car, and, finding her sitting on the veranda steps, looking out at the river, kissed the back of her neck and said, "They're going on Wednesday."

He meant that Janet and little Janet were flying to New Mexico, and the prospect of their absence made him, he admitted, irrationally jubilant. "I don't know why, but the idea that they won't be home, that I won't see or hear them for a couple of days, makes me feel like a kid out of school . . ."

On Wednesday, after his family had left, Andrew was saddened by Alida's needing to leave to dine with *her* family, and wished they could spend an entire evening together. They schemed and scheduled. As it happened, she was going to the city on Friday, when the air-conditioning crew was coming to her apartment. She might also, reasonably, plan to try out the kitchen, to see how well the equipment worked. Perhaps Andrew would come to dinner—a dinner she would cook. She could explain to her mother about wanting to cook and to stay over, just as a test of the apartment, and she could offer to drive Morgan and Guthrie out on the Saturday afternoon— did Andrew want to come, too? When was he flying out? On the Monday, on Memorial Day itself: he was delaying seeing his family by talk of needing to clear up some work before he left, and there was in fact some work he should do Saturday, but it was probable he could drive out for Sunday lunch.

They had never been able to make such elaborate plans, and Alida was enchanted. On Friday, though, she was almost overwhelmed, for after she conferred with the leader of the air-conditioning team, and the two men he left began work, she had to run in and out buying food and also knives and forks and plates and glasses and napkins and bathroom towels. And soap—hand soap, kitchen soap, dishwasher soap. The apartment needed so much. As she wandered the streets, she was struck both by the changes in the neighborhood and by the tenacity of the few stores that had survived after almost a decade. The liquor store, for instance. By late afternoon, she was afraid she was going to have to borrow from Andrew, for she was running out of cash; if a great new hardware-housewares store had not accepted her credit card, she would have been penniless. While she tore through her errands, stirred soup, and made mayonnaise, the air-conditioner men methodically cleaned, filtered, and oiled; they banged and scraped and chipped and bumped through their own unmelodious anvil chorus. Although they did not find a machine to junk, they occasionally called on her to warn of future trouble and to contradict something their chief had promised. He was supposed to return and examine their work, but he telephoned to report a delay that threatened to last until eight. They agreed to confer after the holiday, and the crew departed, leaving every air-conditioner on high, adjuring her to let them run for at least an hour. By the time she was ready to shower, the apartment was refrigerated, and she had to race around in her underwear turning machines down. At the last minute, she found she had forgotten to pack perfume and to buy something to nibble with drinks, but she was too exhausted and exhilarated to worry about these lapses. She had put together an adequate hot-weather meal (vichyssoise, chicken salad, and chocolate mousse); she had remembered wine and flowers (these had necessitated another trip to the hardware store for a corkscrew and a vase); the down-to-earth restaurant-supply-type place settings were not repellent, and although the apartment itself was not greatly improved since the day she and Andrew had first inspected it, her activity had made it, she thought, alive and welcoming.

But she was not ready to welcome an angry Andrew. His kiss at the door was a peck, and everything about him—even the way he walked, with his head forward as if he were butting or charging, expressed rage. "Janet called." He sat down on the living-room sofa. "Andy has refused to go to college after all. Mrs. Southern had to spend the day changing my flight so I could go out tomorrow. It's not easy on a holiday weekend. It seems there's some paper he has to write or sign and I have to make him do it. Janet says she doesn't know what happened. But I do. She cooed at him in that infuriating way she has. I called your mother, by the way, and apologized about Sunday."

"Perhaps you'd like a drink," Alida suggested.

"An excellent idea. Let me do the honors. Where is everything?"

"In the pantry. I'll show you." Alida apologized for the heavy glasses. "Make believe it's a picnic."

"Don't fret. I'm in a mood to smash everything anyhow."

"Drink first."

Andrew decided to make martinis. She emptied a heavy water pitcher that had been in the refrigerator. He carried the pitcher, she the glasses, back to the coffee table in the living room. He poured, and then they sat facing each other exactly as they had back in January. At the end of May, the windows behind Andrew were brighter, but the sense of something impending (for Alida, anyhow) was the same. Andrew sipped, sighed, sipped, and then said, "I don't know where to begin. With another apology to you. I'm always apologizing to you. I can't help myself. I think I'm so eaten with anger because I'm enraged at myself. I've known for years that Janet is a fool. I just kept myself—prevented myself—from admitting it. I pretended she had superior learning. I don't know that my children would have grown up to be ordinary, everyday, reasonable children if I hadn't given way to her crackpot ideas, if I hadn't effaced myself, if I hadn't let her drive me out of the family. Maybe I let her drive me out because I wanted to escape, because I couldn't face what I felt, that she was a nightmare. None of this is your fault. It's not even your business. And I'm ruining my last moment's pleasure—what you thought would be my pleasure . . ." Andrew poured himself more to drink, and got up and walked around the room. "Have you ever felt yourself boiling? Or churning? That's what I feel . . . Out of control. I'd like to beat someone up." He went on pacing, and, after a while, said, "I've never been so furious. And yet this is exactly the kind of mess that Janet has been cooking up for years." He walked up and down, and finally, getting no relief from motion, sat down again. Nothing he said called for any comment Alida could think of. She did not feel she ought to say anything against Janet, and while she did want to say something consoling, she could not decide whether "It may not be as bad as you think" would be pouring oil on troubled waters or throwing kerosene on a raging fire. She waited, looking at Andrew thoughtfully, hoping his anger would exhaust itself, blow itself out, but resigned, in case it did not, to the ruin of the evening. She felt helpless, not angry. She drank very little; she waited. Presently Andrew asked if he had upset her.

"Not really. Well, a little."

"Are you angry at me?"

"No, not at all. I didn't realize how strongly you felt about—"

"Neither did I. I knew—I've known—I wanted to leave her. To escape. Before I knew you, I was half-escaped and half-dead. I was living in the same apartment, exchanging information and pretending I thought she made sense, but I was absent. I don't know if she knew, or even if she cared. All week, ever since plans for Andy's graduation came up, I've been saying to myself, This is the last time. I will end it. Move out. And I really wanted to talk to you seriously, Alida, not when I'm disorganized by my own bile. But perhaps it's as well you see how foolish I am."

"You're not foolish, Andrew. You're angry and unhappy, and . . . I've been angry and unhappy. It's not unheard-of. I never thought of beating anybody up, but I was glad when Hugo's show closed. Now I don't care. People get over things. You helped me get over . . ."

"Do you think of me as a cure for Hugo?"

"That's foolish. Don't quarrel with me. Don't hurt me."

"I'm frightened."

"Not of me, surely."

Alida did not believe that Andrew could be frightened of anything. He got up and walked around again. The day was disappearing in the window behind him. Alida looked at her watch. It was past eight-thirty. She wondered if she should mention dinner.

"Frightened," Andrew repeated. "Embarrassed. I don't know how to tell you what I want. It's too absurd."

Andrew was beginning to fluster Alida. She could understand his anger and his bitterness at wasted years, because she, too, had felt those feelings. But she did not understand how Andrew, her Andrew, could be so fretful, so edgy, so—if he meant what he said—embarrassed with her. Andrew began again. "Did you ever dream—imagine, hope—for something magnificent and impossible? The way a little boy sets his heart on a red ten-speed bicycle for Christmas?" Then he stopped. He poured himself a little more to drink. "You sound ridiculous," he said to himself. "That's no way to propose." He looked at Alida. "You're not a bicycle. Alida, I'm such a bad bargain. I'm too old for you and I have two crazy children, but I want you to marry me after we get—"

Alida could do nothing but cry. She took hold of herself when she saw that her tears disturbed him. "If I say yes, will you eat dinner?"

Alida had to do a lot more taking hold of herself all through the Saturday. After Andrew left, she prowled the apartment and measured rooms. She threw linens, bedding, towels into the washing machine to see if it worked. She tried to master her raging joy by thinking over the explanations they had had. When, at dinner, she

245

had commented on Andrew's insistence on deception, he answered, "I'm trying to protect you."

"From what?" Alida asked, and went on to ask him what anyone could do to them.

"More than you think. Hugo feels he's in the wrong now, but he'd operate very differently if he knew you'd been seeing me."

Alida repeated aloud what she had told herself: everybody was modern, civilized; nobody was going to stab anybody. Life was not opera, not even theater. "What could they do?"

"Litigation and scandal. Either would be hard on the children. Andy's grown up—he's out of it, as far as domicile or custody are concerned—but I can't let Janet have complete control of little Janet, and you don't want Amelia torn and testifying. It's not necessarily the outcome; it's the process. The law leaves enormous scope for vengeful people."

These realistic considerations deferred the prospect of an immediate happy ending, but delay only slightly sedated Alida. In June, according to Andrew's plan, they would both begin to get themselves legally separated, but they should wait before appearing in public together socially, and should remain, as far as the world knew, lawyer and client. A lot depended on Hugo's and Janet's attitudes. Alida understood that Janet was inherently difficult, and that there was no sense in prodding her to make more difficulties by a flagrant demonstration that her husband had left her for a younger woman. But even with the vista of continuing precautions and surreptitiousness, Alida's Saturday in her apartment was a heady, giddy time. It yielded one practical conclusion: Hugo's workroom would, after all, be a library; Andrew would need a place to work at home.

Alida did not know whose plan it was, but somehow it had been arranged that, on Memorial Day, Alida and Morgan and Guthrie would drive over from her mother's house to lunch with Miss Kinsky and look at her paintings; afterward, Alida would leave the men at the railroad station in the town where Alida went to school and where Miss Kinsky lived and taught. They would take the train back to the city, and she would go home to her mother and Amelia and Father Peele, who were observing Memorial Day. Mrs. Waterman had helped decorate the old graveyard and was going to take Amelia to the parade and ceremonies in Old Bridge. Father Peele was some sort of chaplain to these rites.

At breakfast Guthrie teased Morgan and Alida, his theme being "the things you get me into." He pretended Alida had fixed up the expedition to toady to her teacher. "An apple would have done," he told her, and said, to Morgan, "You should have had Kinsky send in slides, like everybody else."

Morgan said, "There's a thrill, and you know it, seeing work *in situ*. Like archeology, but more telling. More like pathology. The studio's a slice of life, of the artist's own tissue."

"Hear the man talk!" Guthrie exclaimed. "Digs. Slides. It's nothing like that at all. It's jug wine and jug-wine esthetics, and some desperate wretch waiting to find out if you'll buy." Turning to Alida and Gertrude, Guthrie said, "Morgan likes to go out to studios because he's heartless. Don't you feel the anguish?"

Mrs. Waterman had not frequented studios, but Alida admitted she herself always felt panic: "I'm never sure what to say. I'm afraid I may praise badly."

"That's all right, Alida," Guthrie said. "You won't have to say a word today. We'll do all the talking."

Miss Kinsky lived in the same town where she taught, but away from downtown, where the college was, in a neighborhood near the Sound, a former industrial area being gentrified, a mini-bohemia, sub-suburban SoHo, and her address turned out to be a squat yellow-brick industrial building, a relative of the McKinley warehouse. Alida noticed a sign of prosperity in the street: a large brand-new station wagon, with California plates, parked just past the entrance to the Kinsky studio. They got out and scrutinized the door frame for a bell. There were two, neither with a name. Morgan said, "She wrote that she lives upstairs."

Guthrie rang the upper bell while complaining, "It had to be the garret. I suppose her little hands are cold. But who's the Rodolfo, I wonder."

They waited in the warm sun on the doorstep, expecting a buzzer to reply to Guthrie's ring and admit them. Instead, David Hardman, in jeans and shirt-sleeves, opened the house door. He wished them good morning, and asked if they had had trouble finding the way. Very much at home, he apologized for preceding them upstairs. "I'll show the way," he said. "Frannie's just finishing cooking."

Behind his back, the guests stared at each other, trying in a dumb show of shrugs and raised eyebrows to communicate their ignorance and surprise. They climbed a tall, steep, old wooden staircase, and paused for breath on a landing. David, who had continued

247

climbing, stopped, turned, and asked solicitously, "Is this too much for you?"

His ever-youthful appearance momentarily suggested a Boy Scout escorting a group of senior citizens, and Guthrie responded sourly that he did not know he had volunteered for boot camp and asked if David liked the heat. It *was* hot in the stairwell, and dim and dusty, too, but, as they resumed their ascent, light filtered from a skylight at the top of the stair, where the landing became a hall facing a large metal door that was open to a skylighted kitchen with a dining area visible beyond. Their hostess, a white chef's apron over her jeans, turned from stirring soup to greet them with what was, by Alida's count, a third face. In class, her small features, pointed but not sharp, like her brown hair and eyes and somewhat pallid/sallow complexion innocent of makeup, proclaimed a schoolmarm; at David's opening, her red cape, her makeup, her vivacity, had transformed the instructress into a princess of bohemia. Today Alida could see that Miss Kinsky was wearing makeup that enhanced and slightly slanted her eyes, suggesting the inscrutability that Westerners ascribe to Asians or the self-possession that dog-lovers ascribe to cats. Her face was a defense. Her manner was that of a relaxed hostess as she offered them their choice of looking or lunching. Morgan said that his huge breakfast still sufficed, and accepted David's offer to show them the loft. The dining area, with a trestle table and ladder-back chairs, was delimited by racks that stored paintings, and David went on to demonstrate how all the living spaces had been defined by such racks, so that there were a sitting room and a sleeping room (the visitors felt that their eyes were irresistibly, tactlessly, drawn by and riveted to the double bed). Most of the space—it appeared to be the entire floor of the building—was left open, with two painters' work spaces. There were many skylights but few windows. The walls were white-painted brick, crisscrossed by grids of pipes and wires, and the floors were old, sanded wood. The wires trailing across the floor, which connected large standing fans, were a summer hazard. When this tour ended, Miss Kinsky and Guthrie spoke at the same time. She asked if they would like some wine, and he asked if they could see her pictures. David, eager and effusive, told them he had brought some of his sister's wine. "Did you know Rosa made wine?"

His tone was so different from his Thanksgiving reference to Rosa's wine that Alida could not resist muttering that she did, but nobody was listening to her, and David was allowed to astonish them

248

with another of his sister's multiple talents. He went back to the kitchen and said he would join them "in the gallery."

His gesture waved them toward an area they had not visited. On the farthest side of the room from the entrance there was a row of cells, or exhibition rooms, made of white wallboard placed at right angles to the wall. Miss Kinsky led them to it, and bent over to turn on a switch that momentarily dazzled them with hanging track lights above and spots shining up from the floor. "It's a bit much at first," she admitted. "We start here," she began, but waited until David returned and served the guests their glasses from a tray.

Wineglasses in hand, the guests moved up to the outside wall of the first cell, where there was a hand-lettered sign: "Icons: Mother and Mistress." Beneath the title were pinned postcard reproductions of Raphael's small *Cowper Madonna* and Goya's *Naked Maja*. Miss Kinsky's paintings then followed from room to room, or cell to cell, the smaller pictures hanging on the wallboard, the larger ones propped against the building wall. Each painting was an enlarged rethinking, almost a caricature, of a detail of one of the two masterpieces: a version of Goya, for example, was all the Maja's sparkling black eyes, looking less inviting or sensuous than tigerish; in the parallel selection from the Raphael, the mother's gaze seemed overpowering. In each of her paintings, Miss Kinsky had taken a morsel of a feminine image and translated it into fierceness. Both women's breasts looked aggressive rather than maternal or erotic. The message was that women were forceful, even dangerous, beings. Whether or not that statement was true, Alida disliked opinionated art, and, as they processed through the little exhibition, she was glad that it was not her place to comment. They went through once, Morgan leading, and then began again. Carrying wineglasses and moving slowly without speech, they might have been engaged in ritual. Alida used the time to plan partial compliments to conceal her disappointment if she were called on. She decided that the work was visually ingenious, and the recombinations were consistently inventive: they made compositions. That praise arranged, Alida was free to think what she would not say: that she was more interested in what people made than in what they thought, because opinions were rarely original in the way that brushstrokes were unique, and that, in borrowing from great artists to express her ideas, Miss Kinsky devalued her own talent. Still and all, Alida had to recognize that, over the years, her rejections had grown less outspoken. Age had made her wary if not tolerant. The young enthusiast of 1962 whom Larry recalled would have spurned Miss Kinsky's painted feminism as trendy hogwash, but in 1976 Alida appreciated that it was deeply felt, and that trendy hogwash deeply felt had a validity, though not, perhaps, an esthetic one. She suspected Morgan believed, as she did, that art might move, but should not hector. By common consent, the party waited for his judgment. He spoke at last. "Ah," he said, "figurative work." He paused. "I expected it to return."

Miss Kinsky replied, "It is essential to bring back the body, to recover the physical."

Homemade wine, Alida thought, and homemade esthetics.

"This isn't decorative."

Miss Kinsky agreed. "Not primarily."

David interjected: "It's powerful."

Morgan ignored him, and pursued his thought: "And hence, perhaps, more difficult to sell than—"

Morgan tactfully stopped before the comparison, but Miss Kinsky continued: "—than David's landscapes?"

"To our customers, yes. It seems to me that these work magnificently together—as a total statement—but for a small museum, perhaps, or a downtown gallery." He paused. "I wonder about drawings. Perhaps we might try a few drawings."

Alida had thus far been envious of Miss Kinsky as a woman other people took seriously. Hearing Morgan's politely belittling offer, Alida began to feel sorry for the artist. She must have nurtured hopes of this visit; she lived in a warehouse and taught in a community college, and may have fantasized the power of women to compensate for her lack of it.

Her composure intact, Miss Kinsky said, "I didn't think it was right for you, but David thought you should see it."

Alida recognized that statement as a cousin of blackmail. David's show had sold out, and the Galleries were looking forward to handling the Hardman-Steins' output. Morgan did not reply in words; instead he began to walk through the show again. After a moment, Alida heard Guthrie, standing behind her, say, suddenly, "I like the blasphemy. Let's do it, the whole thing, the week after Labor Day, before our regular customers are back in town. Everybody—the papers, the whole city—is waiting for something to happen. We could make a hullabaloo. Don't forget; it's two kinds of blasphemy, artistic and religious."

Morgan was disconcerted. He said, "Guthrie always dreams of an old-fashioned artistic scandal, but they don't happen nowadays. Anything goes but nobody cares. You couldn't hire a bishop to protest. And there are no conservative critics."

Several arts besides painting had been on display: negotiation, blackmail, and Morgan's execution of the adagio known as letting down gently. Guthrie's intrusion smashed Morgan's delicate performance past repair, and he hammered on: "Maybe not, but there's no harm trying. You'll never make a stink with a few drawings."

Guthrie got his way because he was not afraid of scenes. He figuratively pushed his partner to the wall by forcing Morgan to admit that they had no particular show scheduled that early in the season, just a miscellany called a "gallery group"—"That's just where I thought we'd slip in drawings. Let people get used to—"

That was Morgan's last effort. Guthrie reiterated his insistence that drawings would not make an impact, would dissipate the shock. He challenged Morgan not to be a coward, and added that people scared by the oils might want to feel daring by buying a drawing. Morgan, overborne, turned to Miss Kinsky, and said, "Guthrie is probably right. What an effect you have! People are fighting over you already. Do you think you could get the show into the Galleries over the Labor Day weekend? To hang for two weeks?"

David answered, "Of course, Morgan. But I think you'll find two weeks isn't enough. There's a great deal in Frannie's pictures, and people will want to come back."

Miss Kinsky smiled at David, but decided not to push. "Two weeks in September," she said. "Lunch now."

Lunch came with more of Rosa's fruity wine, which made Alida drowsy and the rest of the party merry and talkative. They changed over to first names and began a spirited conversation that eddied around Alida without including her. She did not greatly mind, especially as she was still embarrassed at disliking Miss Kinsky's— no, Frannie's—paintings. Her withdrawal was very likely what Hugo saw as her remoteness; he always needed to be included, and would batter his way into any conversation. Alida wondered what Andrew was like in a group. He always had wisdom at his fingertips, but she did not know if he insisted on dispensing it unasked.

David was describing the neighborhood. He praised Frannie's acumen in finding it, reported his hunch that it was full of potential, and his discovery that his intuition was so widely shared that there was very little on the market. "I'm trying to buy this place," he said, "but the owner can't make up his mind to sell."

They were off on the all-American subject of real estate, which had bored Alida on both coasts. When did this passion for real property seize all our citizens? While Guthrie and Morgan were telling of the warehouse—their warehouse, where Alida worked—she remembered endless evenings in California devoted to stories of killings (on properties sold) and steals (on properties bought). Right now, Miss Kinsky—Frannie—was relating the saga of a painter she knew, who, in quest of cheap space, several years ago bought an abandoned farm in an area so godforsaken it was almost wilderness; at present he was fighting off or mulling over munificent offers, for his property abutted a new ski resort. David astonished Alida yet again that day: he recalled selling his house, when he was divorced, at a profit he could not believe; on his recent trip west, he heard that the purchaser had sold it at a price yet more dazzling. Alida remembered David's wretchedness on Thanksgiving, and could hardly believe that, six months later, he was turning what had been the keenest suffering into a tale of commercial success. Hugo used to insist on the importance of controlling one's characters, but life was uncontrollable. Alida's thoughts were muzzy, confused by wine, leading nowhere in particular, and she knew it. She heard the word "mortgage," and asked herself what real-estate dealers talked about at lunch.

She did not realize she had spoken aloud until she heard Guthrie reply, "That's easy, Alida. They talk about investing in art."

Alida's entry into the conversation had made the others aware of her silence. David asked after her mother and Amelia, and Morgan and Guthrie, as the most recent houseguests, took over the job of providing assurances and information. "Did you ever walk in those gardens?" Guthrie asked.

David admitted that he had not, and Guthrie urged Alida to invite him, or them, immediately. Turning to the woman Alida still thought of as Miss Kinsky, he said, "Frannie, they are an inspiration beyond words." He paused a moment as if recollecting, and went on: "It isn't only the gardens, it's everything. A way of life that's almost historic. There's nothing like it in the real world. It's like a beautiful dream. I understand now why Alida sometimes seems odd. She was raised in a fantasy."

Guthrie did not seem to mean that adjective unkindly, but Alida would have liked someone to come to her defense. No one did. She asked David about Teeny, who, David said without amplifying, was "fine," and mentioned that he had visited Josiah. When they talked of their California connections, Miss Kin—, Frannie, began to clear the table abruptly and ineptly. Her gestures had hitherto been fluid and deft, but in jealousy she began to clash the dishes, and interrupted David's report on Alida's nephews with a demand that he help her serve the coffee and pastries. These were noteworthy, and David's and Alida's family talk disappeared before the hostess's boast of a new bakery that had opened in the area—she called it "The Point"—on the remodeled premises of a nineteenth-century commercial bakery. "I wish you could see it. The old brick ovens are epic."

"And so are these éclairs," said Morgan.

"I thought the napoleon was rather poignant," said Guthrie, "heartrending in its subtlety."

"I wish you wrote reviews," said David.

Morgan took his second cup of coffee back to the gallery. He looked at the pictures for a while, came back, and said, "They'll go in the front room nicely. Will you call me when you've got a moment and make a date to come in one day soon?"

He put down his cup but remained standing, signaling that it was time to go, and managed their departure with few words; Morgan's extrication from "must you go?" and "won't you stay?" was as deft as stage magic.

"God, it's hot," he said on the street. The car, which had been standing in the sun, was stifling. "Turn on the air conditioner, Alida, will you?" And then, buckling his seat belt, he asked, "Guthrie, why?"

"Pity," Guthrie said. "She'd have eaten Hardman alive if we hadn't taken the show. She'll probably eat him anyhow. She's a user. A bitch. But she has something."

"I know all that," Morgan said, "but why should we let her use us?"

"Because she's a comer. She'll do something someday. She has a devil." Guthrie grimaced. "And then I figured Alida got us into this and she can get us out of it. She won't have any trouble selling to Lady Mary or Janet Cameron. Lady Mary will look at that vicious odalisque and the Cameron woman will look at that voracious Virgin, and they won't see anything wrong. They'll think they're looking in a mirror."

"*There's* a funny couple," Morgan said, idly. "The Camerons."

Guthrie nodded. "But they both love our Alida."

Morgan continued. "Andrew couldn't be nicer. He's smart, too,

253

and sensitive. But I suspect weakness. Only a weak man would put up with a woman like that. I feel sorry for him, but there's nothing you can do for a weak man." The association in his mind was evident when he asked, "Alida, what was Hardman's first wife like?"

"A pretty girl."

They arrived at the station with almost an hour to spare, and the men bade Alida show them the urban-renewal downtown, but their expedition became entangled in a local traffic jam, the breakup of the town's Memorial Day parade.

"Give up," Morgan ordered.

Guthrie saw a cart selling Italian ices, and asked Alida to pull over to let him buy some. They sat in the car licking ices while bits of the disintegrating Memorial Day ceremonies drifted by. The sight of a Cub Scout reminded Alida of Amelia. She hated to have her child learn about death and war, and that her grandfather had died in war. Yet of course she would have to learn, and to take pride; she, Alida, had been taught that her father's death had ennobled them all.

Was that sensible? She wondered what Andrew thought. She wished she could ask him. She wished he had been with her on today's outing. She would have liked his opinion on everybody. A uniformed bandsman bearing a tuba stopped at the cart and bought an ice, and Alida wondered if Andrew had seen a parade. She wondered what he would have thought of Miss Kinsky's paintings. Alida was uneasy about borrowing; she appreciated that it was a common practice, a vogue, in fact, and she remembered how Hugo used to lecture on the folly of pretending to originality, arguing that "original" and "authentic" were the language of dense critics. He maintained that Stonehenge was very likely as derivative as Brighton Pavilion, because humanity shared basic experiences and fundamental needs and borrowed to meet them, though rarely paying interest on loans or acknowledging its debts. Even so, Alida felt Kinsky was overdrawn.

Guthrie was rolling his tongue around inside the paper cup. "Sticky," he said. "I love raspberry. Anyone want another?"

Nobody else did. Guthrie, checking his watch, decided he had time, and left the car to buy a second ice.

"Penny," Morgan said.

"I was thinking about derivativeness generally."

"Guthrie may have something," Morgan observed. "You *are* odd. You must have had a wretched afternoon, and you escape by thinking about 'derivativeness generally.' David was thankless, considering what he owes you; you'd never know you got him his show from the way he ignored you, and that bitch owes you a lover and a show both, but she never said thanks."

"They're in love," Alida said.

Guthrie, who had just opened the car door, asked, "Who?"

"David and Francesca," Alida answered.

"I know," Guthrie replied. "Two painters in bed. Two scorpions in a bottle. It's time to go."

After their train left, Alida took a back route home that meandered through slightly rolling land. Slowing as she approached a gentle curve, she saw a white house on a rise, with a lawn that was marked off from the road by a white rail fence with a profusion of old-fashioned pink rambler roses. They were an intransigent pink, pink the color of adolescent girls' romantic dreams, but real nonetheless. The pink was so emphatic in its sweetness, the roses so insistent in their sentimentality, that they seemed to swear to the truth of the story in which they existed, the simple love story with a happy ending. Morgan and Guthrie did not know everything. Love in a loft might be as genuine as love in a cottage, or, as Andrew and Alida had known it, among the ruins of the Cameron estate.

When Alida came into her mother's house and approached the sitting room, she heard the rumble of a man's voice—Father Peele. Then her mother spoke, and Alida heard her say, "On Memorial Day, I envy graves. It's foolish, but even after all these years, and believing what I do, it hurts me not to know where he is."

Roses are not omnipotent. David had found Francesca. Alida had found Andrew. But Gertrude had found nobody, only flowers. Amelia ran down the hall. Alida bent and kissed her daughter, Gertrude's treasure.

July Fourth

When Alida and Andrew had parted on Saturday morning, they had agreed that she would call Mrs. Southern on Thursday, for he would let his office know his plans as soon as he himself knew them. If he was lucky enough to return by Thursday, they could meet at the Cameron house. Alida's Friday would be occupied by Amelia's last day at school, when Flat Rock Country Day mothers called for their children late in the morning, collected the possessions they had accumulated in their desks and lockers during the past year, stayed to lunch, and attended a summer-farewell program of student performances, at which Amelia was to recite. Andrew accepted Alida's yielding Friday to her daughter just as he was giving up x number of days to his son, but he could not tolerate the prospect of waiting to meet until the following Monday. "I have to see you by Saturday," he insisted. "No later. Even that's a whole week."

She promised that, if Mrs. Southern had not reunited them sooner, she would be in her apartment by noon on Saturday, and wait for him to telephone—"from around the corner, I hope," he said.

On Thursday morning Alida left the house before Andrew's office opened. She hoped to call from school before class, but when she entered the lobby, all the public phones were in use. From what she could overhear, students about to graduate were hunting jobs. Miss Kinsky truncated the last class of the term. She was uncharacteristically complimentary. She told them they were all superior. Returning final papers, she singled out a few, among them Alida's, as outstanding. She announced that several students had already found work, and promised to help others if she could. She would be in her office during her regular hours the following week, and her advice would be available during the summer: if a student wrote, the school would forward the letter. She asked for questions. None arising, she dismissed the class. The students gathered their folders and portfolios but chatted very little with each other. Alida's sense of being alone in this group was true for all the rest; the class regarded itself as a utilitarian, not a social or sentimental, assemblage, and closed itself down with perfunctory farewells. As Alida hurried down the halls to the telephones, she did not stop to reflect that she might never see any of her classmates again, and, when she found the telephones downstairs not only in use but each trailing a line of waiting students, she left the building and heard the door close behind her without a moment's thought that her departure marked a conclusion.

She drove home, and went to the telephone in the cloakroom. Mrs. Southern was out to lunch. Alida penetrated more deeply into the house and learned her mother was lunching out. News of her arrival reached the kitchen, and she was asked whether she would be wanting lunch. By this time she was in a frenzy of anticipation that had destroyed her appetite, and besides, she was used to skipping lunch, but she thought she had better accept an omelet in the breakfast room. She tried to slow herself, to appear decorous and to allow Mrs. Southern, who was presumably not in a rage of haste, time to eat her lunch. Alida lectured herself on her folly; since she and Andrew had promised each other the rest of their lives, a few moments or hours or even days should not matter. But she kept looking at her watch, and left her coffee when she judged it time for Mrs. Southern to have returned. The line was busy. Alida went up to her room, waited, and dialed again. Again Mrs. Southern was busy. Alida recalled her frantic efforts to reach Andrew during Easter week: the memory was almost pleasing, as a recollection of a particular despair she could never feel again. Her pink wallpaper recalled the rambler roses. Alida dialed once more, and this time allowed herself to be put on hold. Eventually Mrs. Southern came on. The sound of Andrew's name, "Mr. Cameron's office," was sweet. But after Alida announced herself, Mrs. Southern did not connect her. She said, "There's been an accident. It's not certain when Mr. Cameron will return to the office."

Alida felt her insides turn white. She was too stricken to speak.

257

"Are you there?" Mrs. Southern asked. Alida made a kind of gasping noise, and Mrs. Southern amplified: "His daughter's been in intensive care since Tuesday morning."

Alida found the courage to ask, "And how is he?"

Mrs. Southern said, "Oh, Mr. Cameron's all right. The only person injured is Miss Cameron. She smashed up a car."

"Little Janet? How? I didn't think she could drive."

"That seems to be what went wrong." Mrs. Southern's dryness conveyed her assessment of the Cameron daughter. "Is there anything I can do for you? Pardon me, but as you can imagine, I have been rescheduling and—"

Inspiration came. Alida said, very firmly, "I need the address of the hotel or motel or hospital. My mother will want to send a note and flowers."

Mrs. Southern seemed uncertain. "He asked me not— And one doesn't send flowers to intensive care."

"My mother will know what to do."

Alida's invocation of the goddess succeeded; she extracted addresses, and gained a means of contact with Andrew. She did not sit very long, stunned and solitary, before her mother came in, and, just as she was beginning to tell Gertrude what Mrs. Southern had told her, Amelia joined them. The child was even more appalled by the news than the women: she was frightened for herself. She remembered little Janet as the queer girl who had sat with them at Alida's birthday party, and though she had not liked her, she had appraised her as belonging to her own category—young girls, people's children, to whom bad things did not happen. Within the limitations of her experience, she felt assaulted, exactly as Alida had at the news of Fred's death. Alida tried to comfort her and promised that little Janet would recover—"Young people always get better." She appealed to Gertrude. "Isn't that a fact?"

Gertrude agreed but, seeing that Amelia was not responding to their efforts at consolation, tried distraction: "School's out. You don't have any more homework, either of you. So come with me to find James, because I promised to meet him this afternoon and talk about our plans for June."

That evening, over cocktails, Mrs. Waterman asked Alida whether she had thought of a summer companion for Amelia. Jenny was adequate during the school year, but she could not give the child all her time; she had duties in the house and, besides, she could not drive. They might not need a nursemaid, only a young woman who could drive Amelia to the Club and to play with her friends—a student, perhaps, someone like an older friend. Amelia asked, "What about my daddy?"

Alida was taken aback by how time had escaped her. She had been expecting to hear from Larry before now, for he had talked about Hugo wanting Amelia from the first week of June—and June was here. "I'm not sure what we should do," Alida said.

She had just mentioned to Amelia her father's plan to take her abroad, thinking that, after Hugo had worked out the details, he himself would explain them to the child. Apparently he had not; Alida began to describe a project she did not wholly understand. She began, and Amelia broke in with questions: for example, would Alida come, too?

"No, I have to work this summer."

But many other questions (who was coming with them?) Alida could not answer. One question assailed the plan itself: "Do I *have* to go to Europe?"

"No, you don't *have* to go—it's not like school. But I think watching your father make a movie would be exciting. And Europe's thrilling. Lots of different countries."

"All foreigners. Speaking funny languages."

At that moment, dinner was announced, and after the trio had regrouped around the table, Gertrude suggested that Amelia telephone her father and speak to him directly. Alida was angry at Hugo's lack of consideration for her summer plans—she expected to work in the warehouse every day until she finished the job, and then concentrate on her apartment—and angrier yet because his negligence intruded irritation and rescheduling and conceivable extra unwanted activity at a moment when Alida was grieving for Andrew. As she had observed earlier that year, modern life seemed to allow no time for sorrow; she had to steal a second even to feel. She was glad when dinner was over, and Amelia went off to telephone. Gertrude and Alida went out on the terrace, and presently Amelia joined them and said, "Daddy's sending May."

"May who?"

"You know, May, my old nurse."

"That May? When?"

"He said he'd wire you."

"I don't know whether I'm coming or going!" Alida exclaimed.

"Funny. That's just what Daddy said: 'I don't know when I'm coming and I don't know whether I'm coming or going.' "

But Hugo was as good as his word: a night letter arrived in the Friday mail, saying, "Situation fluid," and giving the flight number and arrival time of May's plane, which was due at Kennedy late Monday afternoon.

On the Saturday, Alida lied to her mother and went into the city, and just before three in the afternoon the telephone rang in her apartment. Andrew said, "I wasn't sure you'd be there."

"Where are you?"

"At the hospital." He explained that the family sat outside the intensive-care facility all day and took turns eating lunch. He had just left the cafeteria. "What did Mrs. Southern tell you?"

"Not much. What happened?"

"She stole a car and crashed it."

"I don't understand. That's—that's criminal."

"Not out here. They call it joyriding."

"Can she drive?"

"No."

The brevity of Andrew's responses was disturbing. "Is something wrong?"

"Everything. It's hard to talk about it on a pay phone."

"Do you know when you'll be back?"

"I'll have to come in for a few days. Perhaps next week. Call Mrs. Southern starting Tuesday or Wednesday. I'll tell her she can make the arrangements—we can have lunch if you can be free—"

"Andrew! Of course I can be free. What's come over you? I know you're going through hell, but I'm *yours*, don't you remember?"

"I don't know how to talk to anybody," he said. "I'll explain when I see you."

The coins dropped.

"Good-bye," he said.

"I love you," she cried.

But he had hung up.

Constant company—her mother, Amelia, Father Peele—demanded control on the Sunday, and on Monday Alida took Amelia to the city with her. The plan was to put in a day working at the warehouse and then drive to the airport to meet May's plane. The working part of the plan had barely started when it failed. Alida had hoped to impress Amelia with the importance of her job, but after they arrived at the warehouse, and Alida put on her smock and tied a bandanna around her head, Amelia said, "You look just like Bertha."

The reference was to a husky woman who, back in California, occasionally helped with heavy housecleaning, and it was clear that Amelia, observing her mother and Johnny, thought they were some sort of domestics. They were going to tackle an upstairs area devoted to every kind of display cabinet and shelf. These were crowded together, and crowded beside and between them were heavy cartons in which their contents had been placed. First Johnny and Alida had to try to clear a space where they could put the cartons and open them one by one so that she might see if any contained a treasure. Their joint efforts took thought and readjustments. They made several false starts that convinced Amelia that her mother, who normally seemed assured and not given to mistakes, was indeed unaccountably working as a menial. The child, bored in any case, and inevitably in the way, was momentarily mollified when Johnny told her, "It'll get more interesting when we open the boxes and find what's in them."

The first box they opened held a service of gold-rimmed crystal stemware from perhaps the first decade of the century, probably German, valuable, but not, as of June, 1976, stylish. It had been meticulously wrapped, and Alida and Johnny examined each piece, ascertained that the set was complete in all its expensive dowdiness, and rewrapped each glass. They were starting on another box when Amelia asked, "May I go outside and play?"

Alida was horrified. Outside was a dirty street filled with heavy trucks loading and unloading, with open cellar trapdoors in the pavement, and dominated aurally by the clank of industrial activities that would drown out any warnings called to a curious child. "Of course not."

Johnny said to Alida, "Look, school's out and she isn't having any fun."

"What do you suggest?"

Johnny's expression suggested he thought she knew the answer. His wide eyes, arched brows, hands on hip implied she was not as dense as she seemed. When he saw she was, he said, "We're six weeks ahead of schedule."

"Who told you that?"

"The bosses were talking about it. They looked at the last list I took up and couldn't believe it. They asked me if it was all true."

Alida was enraged. "They never told me," she said.

"They wouldn't."

The words "slave driver" popped into Alida's mind. All year she had been self-conscious in only one respect—no one must know about Andrew. It did not occur to her to wonder how she looked to others unless, like Morgan and Guthrie, they made their grievances known. But now she thought of how she appeared to Johnny: polite but not really friendly, undistractable because of her infatuation with objects and her drive to complete something every day. "I've been slave driving," Alida said at last. "I think you're telling me this is a day to take off."

"Yes," Johnny said, "and not a word to uptown."

"But we have no plans," Alida said, undoing her bandanna. "Will you come with us?"

He agreed. He was the indispensable guide to wasting time with a child. On his advice, Alida left her car in the garage where she had parked it, and they made their way through downtown New York by bus and on foot. They went to Chinatown for lunch and wandered in and out of curio shops, and visited the Seaport and clambered over a giant sailing ship and ate ice cream in the street. Their truant day ended with Alida and Amelia hot, dirty, and a little behind schedule.

In the car on the way to the airport, Alida said, "We're so dirty, May will be ashamed of us."

"I don't mind." The child delivered her judgment: "I don't think May's very intelligent, but she's a good driver."

The contrast was greater than they had imagined, for May had dressed up to travel and was more rigged out than Alida had ever seen her. She was wearing a blue silk dress with a matching coat and a wide-brimmed straw hat, and carried a large straw handbag to which she had tied a blue silk scarf. She had on large sungoggles and long, dangling earrings, and looked, Alida thought, like someone trying to disguise herself as a movie star in disguise, and she seemed like a teenager instead of a woman nearing thirty. She greeted Alida respectfully but not effusively, kissed Amelia, and asked, "Aren't you glad to have your May back?" And then, seeing that the child was dirty, gave a little mincing step back to preserve her immaculate self and garb, and asked, "My goodness, what have you been doing? There's dirt all over your face. And hands. And shirt."

She stopped: the implied criticism of her employer had been made but was not harped on, and they moved to the luggage carousel to wait for her baggage to appear. There was constraint or reserve that Amelia could have broken, but she chose to watch the baggage tumbling out of the chute. Alida asked if the flight had been comfortable, and May assured her that it had been, but neither could think of much to say, because they had given very little thought to each other in their months of separation. May's gear was six pieces of brand-new matching air luggage. "So much?" Alida questioned.

"It's for Europe."

May's return took getting used to. She intruded on the self-sufficient trio, Gertrude, Alida, Amelia. The girl assumed that they wanted to hear the details of how Hugo had run into her when he came for cocktails to a house where she had brought the boy she was tending to a birthday party. "He asked, 'Don't I know you?' " the girl related. Hugo's wit enchanted her. "Wasn't that funny? I asked after you, Amelia, and he told me he hoped to take you to Europe, and I said, 'How wonderful!' It really is wonderful, you'll see."

The story of their conversation, of how Hugo had asked if she was happy in her job, and how she had told him she liked caring for girls better than boys because boys were wild, and the negotiation that ended with her reappearance at Flat Rock, took two nights. In fairness to May, her adventures dominated their cocktail and dinner hours because Amelia was egging her on, asking her about all the other people she had worked for; she wanted to compare her home to other children's. When May praised the children she had cared for, Amelia asked, "Why did you leave?"

The question embarrassed May. "It was the families," she said. "You should thank God for your parents and your grandmother."

"What did they do? Did they beat their children?"

In that case, May's reserve broke down, and she said, "No. Each other. That's enough. Young people shouldn't have to hear of these things, let alone see them."

There was, briefly, a lull in May's tales, but later that evening, Wednesday evening, after she put Amelia to bed, she came out onto the terrace where, since the arrival of warm weather, Gertrude and Alida often sat after dinner. She said, "I thought you would like to hear about it all."

Alida had forgotten what "it all" meant. Without invitation, May seated herself and opened her saga of the disasters she had censored in Amelia's presence. One household, as she had let slip, was violent; another was saturated with drugs; and a third was the setting for a triangle, a case of homosexual infidelity that had driven the injured party, the mother of May's charge, to attempt suicide. Alida did not need to see the girl's expression; she could

263

hear regret in her voice as May recounted that she herself had been away from the house until after the ambulance had come and gone and so had missed all the drama. May's purposes in recounting her stories were multiple. She wanted to remind her listeners, as she filled the soft darkness with her memories, that she was in demand and that the families who employed her were rich, powerful, extravagant, glamorous. Yet she could not resist the impulse to gossip, to display the misdeeds and miseries of these families, relishing her revelations and assuming that her hearers, too, shared her enjoyment of sins and sorrows.

"How terrible for you, May," Alida remarked, and rose and adjourned the little session on the terrace earlier than usual.

The next day, just before Alida left her room for drinks, May knocked on the door. She had a letter in her hand. "It came today," she said. It was a letter from the cook who still worked for the would-be suicide. "I was not sure you believed me," May said. "Read for yourself. Nothing is settled. She will try again."

The girl seemed sinister. Alida had an impulse to fire her outright, then and there, but Amelia came by. The child and nursemaid seemed at ease together, chatting as they went down the stairs, and during drinks May was quieter than usual, deferring to Mrs. Waterman. Perhaps she was not unwholesome; perhaps she had brought the letter only to assert her truthfulness. And in the days that followed, Alida concentrated so intently for such long hours at the warehouse that she came home exhausted in the evenings and was relieved to learn that the days in Flat Rock passed serenely while she was finishing her task in the city.

It was fortunate that work absorbed her, for Andrew's return was delayed by a week. Then Mrs. Southern called to say she had reserved a table at his luncheon club for a Friday on which the heat turned out to be intolerable. The warehouse was not air-conditioned, and its thick walls, which had so far withstood the worst the weather could do, could not resist the temperature; indeed, they seemed to keep in the heat and magnify it. By ten-thirty that Friday morning, Alida was wondering if she could last until lunch without fainting. She and Johnny were working in a storeroom with shelves that were partly filled with boxes that, they were discovering, held remnants of fabric. All she had to do was make certain that no bit was a treasure. In any other climate the sheer variety of textiles would have delighted her, but today she could not enjoy, she could only survive. She and Johnny took turns in the ancient warehouse bathroom dampening their faces and arms with water that seemed to lose its power to cool the moment it touched their skins. They labored slowly until some time after eleven, when Johnny closed a box, looked around, and said, "That's it."

They stared at each other. They leaned against the shelving in the heat, their minds ranging separately over the same ground, and watched each other come to the same conclusion: they had finished, finished the job, finished the whole warehouse. The event demanded a celebration or an exclamation, and they knew it, but they shook their heads, too hot even for conversation. After a moment, Alida said, "I made a date for lunch a long time ago, or I would take you out."

Johnny said, "You could do me a favor. I want to go to the beach, and take the stuff in" (he meant the keys to the warehouse, and Alida's list) "Monday. Don't tell my cousin."

"Your cousin?"

"Didn't you know Guthrie was my mother's cousin?"

Alida was glad to learn why the decorative young man, uninterested in decoration, was working at the Galleries, but as she set out to meet Andrew in the heat, her pleasure in this little insight and her sense of accomplishment at finishing the warehouse were tainted by an appalling sense of her dishevelment. Nothing could restore the bedragglement the heat imposed, not even the Club's air conditioning, which felt as if it froze limpness, wrinkles, and creases. She wondered how she looked to Andrew—not as incoherent as Janet, she hoped—when they met outside the dining room; then all her self-consciousness was focused on trying to greet him as if they were lawyer and client, on not kissing or touching him. As it happened, restraint was enforced by others. From the moment they were seated at their table, other lunchers began coming by to visit, inquire, condole. Alida had only to sit and listen. From Andrew's answers to their questions Alida learned that little Janet had come out of coma; that the effects of the concussion seemed to be wearing off; that she was in traction; that estimates of her stay ranged from a month to six weeks; that full recovery was expected . . . All his news was good, but Andrew's telling sounded forced. When they were momentarily left to themselves, he blurted, "I'm certain she was trying to kill herself."

"How terrible!" Alida said. "But what does she say? How does she explain? What did she do?"

Andrew began the painful narrative of the morning of Andy's

265

graduation. Since his arrival in New Mexico, Andrew had been wholly devoted to his boy, trying to learn what alternative to college, if any, he had in mind, trying to understand if he was up to anything except rebellion for the sake of rebellion. "I promised myself I would make a new start with Andy. I would be patient and open . . . But I wasn't at my best, coming from you into that nest of nuts. Janet got on my nerves. I couldn't understand Andy. I told him my feelings about having everything planned for me when I was young, but he wouldn't even admit to feelings I could share . . ."

Andrew sighed. He ordered a drink; though neither felt like eating, they asked for salads. He went on, after two more stop-by-the-table visits, to explain that he realized afterward that he had been so preoccupied with Andy that he had scarcely looked at or spoken to little Janet, and had thought nothing of her excusing herself from the breakfast table Tuesday morning. She did not go to her room to finish primping for the graduation ceremony, as they assumed, but instead wandered around the motel grounds. Another guest, packing or unpacking or merely careless, had left his key in his car's ignition, and little Janet had gotten in and started to drive. Later Andrew and big Janet heard she had weaved through the parking lot and gone out onto the road, into traffic, where, by some miracle, she contrived not to run into another car. The motel was a semiresort on the town's outskirts, so that it was not a long way before the traffic thinned. She had been seen accelerating on an empty road.

The first Andrew and Janet heard of any disturbance was when, leaving breakfast, they passed the car's owner complaining at the motel desk. They went into their room while the manager notified the state police, who soon found the missing car rammed into a telephone pole with an unconscious girl at the wheel. The police ordered an ambulance and phoned the manager to say they had located the car. By this time, Andrew and Janet had finished dressing and were ready to leave; they knocked on little Janet's door and were surprised she was not in her room. They strolled around the grounds looking for her; they asked passing guests if anyone had seen her; one said, looking oddly, that they should ask at the desk. Janet decided to wait in little Janet's room, and Andrew went to the desk and learned that an unidentified young woman had been found in the missing, or stolen, car and taken to the hospital. At that moment, of course, he did not know that it was little Janet, and did not see how it could be, but he went back to their room and told Janet to go to the graduation. He went to the hospital in a taxi.

Their salads came. Alida began to make the gesture of eating, but since her throat was choking and her stomach knotting, she took a small crunch of lettuce from her fork and merely chewed it like a cud. She wished she could close her ears to the medical details that Andrew felt impelled to share with her. He was trying to tell her everything, but the images that came to her mind replaced little Janet with the child she loved—Amelia. She appreciated all the more keenly Andrew's sufferings. Something must have been happening on her face. "Am I distressing you?" Andrew asked.

"Oh, darling!" she exclaimed.

He seemed to flinch at that expression. She added, "I hate to think of what you went through."

"It was rough. But it was very distracting, too, at first, with the police around. People running everywhere, and asking questions. Was she allergic? Did we have insurance? They keep you bewildered. And then Janet came and started screaming. Howling. And I had to try to calm her. Andy helped. He changed. Just like that. That day, that first day. He grew up. But what's troubling me is little Janet."

"Naturally."

"No, I mean what I think she was trying to do. She didn't drive. She had no interest that I know of in cars. Janet can't remember her even looking at them. She thinks it was a prank. An impulse. Or, Goddamn that idiot woman, 'an experiment.' "

"What do the doctors think?"

"Alida, they're all cowboys out there. They're astonished by one thing—that a sixteen-year-old girl hasn't got a driver's license. They can't imagine not driving. So they think that stealing a car is natural. And so is cracking it up. It's another world, and I can't make them see . . . They look at her and look at us, and they judge she's not a professional car thief, so they think she's just another playful kid . . . They can't imagine walking. They can't imagine Manhattan Island. She's always walked to school. Even to kindergarten. I remember. Sometimes on the nurse's day off, I would take her. I'd see mothers and nannies and fathers like me, with their children, all walking down the street to the school. I remember holding her hand and teaching her about red lights and green lights. She was very little as a child. She didn't really reach her proper size until she was seven or eight. But she was very active. I remember she used to love to run, and she liked me to let go of her hand and let her run the last bit of the way . . ." Then he said, with surprise, "That wasn't very long ago."

His memories took him where Alida could not follow, except by analogy (Amelia's hand in her own), for she had only seen little Janet as a problem, someone between a disgrace and an embarrassment. But once there had been a little girl as hopeful as any other, running down the street to kindergarten.

Andrew recalled her to the present. "There's one surgeon, a little smarter maybe, a little more worldly; he listens. He begins to see what's troubling me. He thinks it's possible she was envious that her brother was getting so much attention—all my attention besides his graduation—and that she wanted to do something to show off."

"That makes sense," Alida said.

"Not entirely." Andrew was arguing with her. "You know she was doing all sorts of odd things. I'm not sure you could call them all showing off."

"Perhaps not." Alida was at a loss. It was not only that she did not understand Andrew's daughter: she thought of him as her lover, not as little Janet's father. Other lunchers were beginning to leave, and many came by the table for a visit of sympathy. Andrew and Alida ordered coffee. "When will I see you again?" Alida asked.

Andrew planned to return to New Mexico the next day; he was staying the night because he had promised the evening to a brother. That hurt Alida; he should have chosen to stay with her. "I'll be up again," Andrew said, "though I'm not sure when. What is your schedule now?"

Alida told him that she had finished the warehouse that very day and would start work on her apartment on Monday. She felt her voice plucking at him, trying to detain him, as he hailed the waiter, who brought the check. She said, "I need to talk to you before I talk to Hugo." Andrew nodded without conviction. "I feel guilty troubling you now," she went on, "but you've always talked about our settling our affairs—Hugo's and mine—ourselves before proceeding to the law, but I need a consultation first . . ." Andrew's silence was making her struggle. That was a new experience, and it frightened her. "Andrew," she asked, "do you remember what we talked about before you left?"

He rose, and looked down at her with an expression she could not read. "It seems a dream," he said at last.

* * *

The heat outside oppressed Alida anew, and she hated having to drive while thinking about an automobile accident or a suicide attempt. She came home and showered, and, cool if not happy, noticed a message in Jenny's handwriting beside her telephone. "Call Mr. Weinstein," it read. The number was his country house.

"Good news," Larry said. "Hugo's doing the play after all." Alida's first thought was that Larry had not really accepted her dissociation from Hugo, and she would have blurted, "Why tell me?" except that Larry's next sentence followed without pause and answered her unasked question. "He isn't going to Europe."

"That leaves me with a problem."

Alida briefly explained about May, who hated Flat Rock and looked forward to Europe. Larry broke in, "But surely that's not serious. The point is, Hugo's headed for a triumph. I can tell. He was ready to throw away some of his finest work on a cockamamie tax-shelter movie until I persuaded him to reread that play and keep rereading it until he saw what he had." Larry grew more ebullient as he recounted how he had cajoled Hugo into "taking his talent seriously," and Alida realized he had no interest in the fact that Hugo's talent created Alida's domestic difficulties. She asked, "Will he want Amelia to visit him in California?"

"Oh no. He's coming east. He's spending the summer here, upstairs in the playhouse. And he wants to see you alone. He'll be here by the weekend of the Fourth."

"But what will I do about the Fourth?" Alida cried, "My mother's—"

But Larry, of course, was only the messenger; he could do nothing; so Alida said good-bye without telling him of Gertrude's plan to close the house on the Bicentennial Fourth of July weekend. She was going to Rhode Island on July 1, to stay with those cousins who used to come to Thanksgiving years ago, and, with them, to attend the celebrations at Newport; then, on the Fourth, she would bring them to New York City, where her brother-in-law, whose offices overlooked the harbor, was giving a party to view the tall ships by day and the fireworks by night. She would not return to Flat Rock before the fifth. Alida had decided to move into her apartment for the weekend—she wanted the feel of living in it as a clue to decorating—and she would meet her mother and cousins at Uncle Arthur's party. Both women had taken for granted that Amelia would be off in Europe. While Alida dressed after her shower, she decided that she would not let Hugo's instability ruin her mother's holiday. She would not even mention the news until she had made up a scheme for Amelia for the July Fourth weekend.

At cocktails she told about finishing at the warehouse. Gertrude was the first person she had spoken to all day to whom she could impart her achievement with any expectation of it being appreciated. "I'm proud of you," Gertrude said, "and I'm sure Morgan will be."

Gertrude was working on Alida's tapestry, and Alida asked her for samples of the threads so that she could begin to place them beside each other and think of paints and fabrics. Gertrude mentioned the difficulty that one often failed to get a sense of color from such small samples. "I wish I were further along," she said. Alida got up and leaned over her mother's shoulder to see what was visible. "I had an idea," Gertrude said, "that since this is for a city apartment I ought to think about flowers in the city, and I—"

The telephone rang. Sally came in and said that Mr. Kelly wanted to talk to Amelia and May.

"Himself again!" Alida said, after they had departed.

"Do you know what this is about?" Gertrude asked.

Alida told her mother what Larry had told her. "The problem, as I see it, is that May will quit again, and it may be too late to get a student, as you suggested. I know I need someone for the summer, but I'm not sure about the fall . . ."

May and Amelia returned. Amelia was delighted. "Daddy's going to be here, right here, all summer," she cried. "And we don't have to go to Europe."

May was struggling against her disappointment, bracing herself when she sat down in her chair, fighting tears. "I know you're upset," Alida said. "What did Mr. Kelly tell you?"

She slightly accentuated the "you" to imply that Hugo had spoken confidentially to her. May brightened as she repeated Hugo's plea. "He told me about the play. He said it was an emergency and he counted on me."

So Amelia had a nursemaid for the time being, and Alida could get on with her summer's work. That left only the Bicentennial to solve, and over the weekend Gertrude began to solve it. She telephoned Rhode Island and ascertained that her cousins could find room for Amelia and May, if she wanted to come. "It's something she'll remember her whole life"—Gertrude, of course, was talking about her grandchild—"and I want her to see it all. But I don't think Jane can put them up," Gertrude went on, for her sister was housing her own children, the Rhode Island cousins, and Gertrude in New York City.

"Why don't you all stay with me?" Alida asked. "It has to be rough and ready, but we can have breakfast there, anyway, and I'll buy some folding cots. Amelia can use them later, when she has sleepover parties."

Thus all the knots were smoothed away, with only one more rearrangement via another call from Larry. Hugo wanted to see Alida as soon as possible, preferably the day after his arrival. He would reach the Weinsteins' late on the third and was asking if they could meet anywhere on the Fourth. Alida fought her impulse to delay the interview. "Tell him to come here to lunch on the Fourth. That way I can still get in for the fireworks."

She was troubled afterward by her curtness with Larry, but perhaps he was used to the disadvantage of playing middleman— receiving the blows the parties intended for each other. And Alida was troubled because she wanted Andrew's advice and did not know how to get it. In the end she wrote a brief note addressed to Mr. and Mrs. Andrew Cameron, expressing her concern, saying she wished for news, and mentioning that if either needed anything done for them in New York, she could be reached at her mother's or at her apartment. Her love and slyness were rewarded. Andrew wrote her at her apartment, and fixed a date to meet her there at the very end of June.

Once Alida began to work on her apartment, she came by the Galleries several times to check their files of contractors, fabric houses, and the like. She glimpsed Guthrie, looking preoccupied, and Morgan, who greeted her twice, saying he had to talk to her immediately but had no time. He called her at the apartment the day she was to meet Andrew and asked her for drinks. Luckily he set the hour early and was prompt. He apologized for not choosing a more gala place than the horsy bar to celebrate her finishing at the warehouse, and ordered champagne. Then he said, "Guthrie and I went over your lists together carefully, and I went to the warehouse and made a spot check, and I can't tell you how pleased we are with you."

"Thank you. I enjoyed it." She *had* enjoyed going through the warehouse; her curiosity about objects was limitless, and she added, "I feel I lived through generations."

"Now then," Morgan said. "Guthrie wants me to talk about the

271

fall. He's very enthusiastic about you. So am I. We want you at the Galleries. You have to do what we say, but we also want your ideas. Guthrie's got a Pygmalion thing for you. He plans to mold you, form you, make you perfect. That may be hard on you. He doesn't really distinguish between things and people. He thinks you have a lot to learn, but you can learn from us and go to school, and Guthrie will pick your courses."

Alida remarked that she was learning already. She recalled that, early this past spring, she had despised Miss Kinsky's—"I can't call her Frannie"—teaching, but when she looked at her apartment as a job, she could see the need for compromise, disguise, tricks.

"You don't despise perspective. That's a trick. Or *trompe l'oeil* painting. Fooling the eye is a legitimate procedure. Nothing's perfect. The trick is to make it look perfect. That's art. Imposing order. Hiding the mess. The mess is always there, of course. The mess is life." He ruminated over his profundity, and said, "I just realized we haven't thought about salary. We'll get to it. When do you think you can start? When are you moving in?"

Alida had no date in mind, except Amelia's school opening, sometime in September; she could not remember the exact day, and was embarrassed to be vague; and then, in the middle of her vagueness, said, with amazement, "I'm thrilled."

"You should be," Morgan said.

He hurried away to change for a dinner party—"the very last of the season, thank heaven"—while she stopped at a delicatessen on her way to the apartment because their meeting left her no time to cook for Andrew.

She turned on the air-conditioners, hurried upstairs to primp, and gradually began to appreciate how good—how great—her news was. Being Guthrie's protégée would be hard, but supremely instructive. Then her mind scrambled to Morgan's notion of art as disguise, and she wondered what he made of such critical compliments as "honesty." She went downstairs, wandered into Hugo's old workroom, the room she thought of as Andrew's library, and asked herself where he would display his silver. Would he like to put it into a cabinet? Her habit of arranging and fantasy-arranging asserted itself. If one wall of the bookshelves came out ... Which one? Opposite the door? Or opposite the window? Black lacquer would set off silver, but a whole black wall would sink the room. The outside would have to be light. Applewood. Applewood lined with black ... But then, she reflected, she had no idea of the size of the collection. The doorbell rang. "How much silver have you got, Andrew?"

"What are you talking about?"

"You know, the silver you collect."

He came into the living room and asked why she asked. She explained her plans to display it, guiding him to the door of the library and gesturing. He listened with concentration, as if to a foreign language he had studied only briefly, and at last translated: "You're designing my place here."

"Where else? Don't you like this apartment?"

"It seems unreal."

"What seems unreal?"

"What we talked of. My getting free."

Alida was perplexed. She realized she had come at him unexpectedly. When she turned to look at his face as he stood in the doorway to the library she saw how worn he appeared; he was wearing a hospital face, not a silver-collecting face. She began to babble, "Oh sit down, darling. What do you want to drink? Let me fix it. You're exhausted. I'm sorry I nagged you with my plans. My obsession."

Andrew sat where he always sat, with his back to the window, and asked, "Which obsession? Me or furniture?"

Alida responded to his effort at lightness: "I love you both equally."

She leaned over and kissed his cheek, and that started something in him. He became as violent or desperate as he had been on the stage of the playhouse. They never got upstairs, and it was a long time before, half-dressed, with drinks in their hands, they began to talk. Alida told Andrew she would be seeing Hugo on the Fourth. He sighed, and asked, "Might you have gone back to him if I—if we—hadn't . . ."

"I doubt it. And, anyway, we have."

"But look, when I asked you to marry me . . . It was less than a month ago, but it seems so long ago . . . I expected then that it would be hard for me to get free. Janet isn't in this world at all. I've seen that repeatedly this month. But I thought I could do it, and in a measurable time. Now I don't know. The difference is, I think little Janet is crazy. I used to think she was a brat who needed discipline her mother wouldn't give and wouldn't let anybody else enforce. But now that I've been with her, day in, day out, she seems so genuinely bizarre, so uncomprehending. She isn't hallucinating and she doesn't talk to herself, but when she talks to me, answers me, she never seems to be *with* me. I asked her what she was doing when she took the car, and she said, airily, whimsically, as if I had asked why she was eating soup with a teaspoon, 'I don't know. I felt like it.' And there sits Janet, who doesn't believe in misfortune. That's why she's so charitable; it's all pretend. She can't believe her daughter is off the wall, and the only sense she makes out of it is that we should give her driving lessons . . ."

"Poor Andrew," Alida said. "What can I do?"

"Nothing. I need a consultation, I think, but no psychiatrist can help much without seeing the patient. Still, I've heard enough from clients to realize that everybody would agree that this was not a time for me to leave, and destabilize, you might say, the surroundings of this unstable child. I promised you I would leave them this summer, but now I think that, if I do, little Janet will either kill herself or end up in a locked ward."

Alida could see the sense of what Andrew was saying, and didn't blame him for her disappointment. She said, quietly, "I do think you ought to have a consultation while you're in New York, even if it doesn't clarify much."

"I know," Andrew said, "but I'm talking about us. I'm concerned about you. That's why I wonder, now, if I wasn't right before Easter, and wrong to come back. I got in the way . . ."

"Of what?"

"Of your going back to Hugo."

"Why do you think I would?"

"It was a respectable alliance, in the old phrase. And he's good to Amelia."

"Let's eat."

They ate delicatessen out of cartons and off waxed paper in the kitchen. "If my mother could see me now!" Alida exclaimed.

"Do you worry what your mother thinks?"

"Not the way I used to. I've learned to admire her. I love her, and I see that we're closer than I used to suppose, but I don't feel I have to do exactly what she would do, or want me to do. She wants me to go back to Hugo, even though she doesn't like him much."

They ate some more and drank beer. Alida began to feel the staleness of air conditioning. It reminded her of a subject that had come to her mind intermittently: the country place New Yorkers need in order to survive the city climate. She asked Andrew if he thought she should try to buy her mother's guest cottage and turn it into their weekend house, and he said, "You still plan for us."

"I can't help it."

After they showered and dressed, he was sober. "I have to offer you your chance, release you, set you free. Of course you *are* free, but I mean morally free. I don't want you to feel bound to me, because I've no idea what will happen. And if I were only your lawyer and not your lover, and you came to me with your story, I'd advise you to break off. I'm a bad bargain."

"I don't bargain in people."

"All right, then. I don't know where I'll be all summer, and if you need ordinary legal advice, talk to Hooper. I've mentioned him. I'll try to write you here. And we can phone each other about business sometimes, I guess. But I wish I . . ."

After they kissed at parting, Alida said, "Andrew, I don't want to be another burden. I don't want to add to the load, but remember, I need you, too."

Alida had rarely been entirely alone in a house for any length of time. She felt strange, waking on the morning of Independence Day with no family, company, or servants on the premises, but the pretty morning invited her to take her coffee to the terrace and watch the sun light the world like a play. As the shadows subtly shrank and the colors gradually affirmed themselves, she realized it was time for her to begin the action. Her bedmaking dissatisfied her, as it had her camp counselors years ago, but she had confidence in her cooking. She was giving Hugo cold poached salmon for lunch. Perhaps it was being alone; perhaps her sense of freedom came from not being helped or surveilled. For whatever reason, she was cheerful, almost hilarious, reveling in solitude or independence, not fearful of Hugo, on Independence Day. She had prepared for their meeting by telling herself she must be dignified and remote and never stoop to reproach. That attitude reflected her feelings—she could remember as a fact of history that she had been humiliated by his affair, but she could no longer summon up any anger about it, and she was in danger of forgetting her shock when he had slapped her. But she had been uneasy because she knew that people can provoke each other inadvertently and she did not want to lose control. The sunshine of Independence Day dissipated these fears, and she felt strong and merry as she entered the kitchen.

In her mother's house, the servants' bedrooms were up on the third floor, but there was a downstairs staff room beside the kitchen, with a television set that Alida turned on along with the cook's radio in the kitchen. While she explored the closets and shelves, their competing racket brought her a sense of a country transformed into a festival, unself-conscious and exuberant in gaiety, exhibitionism, and sentimentality, with possibly a core of seriousness. While she looked for pots, the instruments brought her music and cheers and speeches and descriptions; parades and presidents and bands and crowds. And those ships, those magnificent, anachronistic sailing vessels.

Starting the court bouillon and watching it simmer, she began to feel herself, too, coming to a boil of excitement. Alone, she was nonetheless with her countrymen. Watching and hearing them, she felt herself part of them and of the nation. Wrapping the salmon in cheesecloth, she asked herself what being American meant. What had her country done for her besides killing her father? Of course, that was not the way to put it: one said, or thought, or believed that he had given his life so that . . . So Gertrude and Josiah and Alida might be who they were. Independent. Free. Democratic. She was not emotionally independent of Andrew or legally free of Hugo, and, while she was sure democracy was good for her, she was less sure that she had made much of a contribution to its workings in her country, nor, given Guthrie's plans for her, that she was likely to do so. Inconsequently she regretted her youthful scorn, not entirely outgrown, of overfamiliar Colonial Revival. Still, while she peeled and sliced cucumbers and jumped at cannon going off over the radio, she argued that democracy entitled her to vote against spinning wheels. By the time she left the kitchen to go upstairs to dress, she was trying to imagine what she might have been like if she had not been American. Alida English or Alida French was not Alida. She tried to imagine Amelia a foreign child. Like herself, Alida thought, Amelia had wider hopes, greater expectations, than any of the European females she had encountered. Filled with wonder at herself, her national identity, her emotional outpouring for her country, she whistled "Yankee Doodle" and patriotically assembled navy blue linen slacks, a white silk shirt, and a red belt. She hummed "Columbia, the Gem of the Ocean" when she went down to recheck the kitchen. She felt rueful about giving Hugo a better meal than Andrew, but perhaps the pains she was taking for her husband marked the extent to which he had become a stranger with whom it was unthinkable to share the slovenly intimacy she had just known with Andrew.

She was so absorbed in television—boom! went an artillery salute—that she did not hear Hugo arrive. His first words were "Are you thrilled by it, too?"

She motioned him to sit beside her and offered him a bloody Mary. They watched together in silence, in the room where she sat evenings with her mother and child, until a station break, when he said, "I love it. It's so American—sloppy, lowbrow, high-spirited. Disorganized but working."

Hugo was all eagerness. Like Alida, he yielded to an unexpected surge of patriotism. Even when the cameras merely scanned the crowds, they were fascinated. "Look at us! Look at us!" Hugo exclaimed.

Alida remarked, "If I'd known I was going to feel like this, I'd have cooked hot dogs. My mother knew all along how it would be. Amelia's seeing everything."

"She'll remember it the rest of her life and tell her grandchildren about it, the way old-time Californians boast about earthquakes."

"Did you listen when you were little? I didn't."

"I did. Indeed I did. My mother told me all the family stories. Pioneers and cowboys. She made my family, on both sides, sound like movies. And I suppose they were. Or what they made movies out of."

"Not mine. Bankers and lawyers and lawyers and bankers as far as memory goes."

"Stuffy fellows but solid," Hugo commented. "Dependable. Not like yours truly." Relaxed and affable, Hugo did not mean his comment on himself to be envious or invidious or false modesty in hopes of evoking a denial; it was a matter-of-fact prelude to his explanation of his changed plans. Hugo did not have a great deal of revision left; he had been working with the material for several months. He was settled at Larry's country house in expectation of going into production in August for a September opening. Hugo went into considerable detail both about his own work and about Larry's contributions. Alida, listening, thought he had not lost the habit of marriage, for he spoke of himself as he had always used to do, assuming her interest. He was particularly expansive telling how much Larry had done—how he had put together most of the elements, as a producer is supposed to do—but had intended to step back and hand them over to a producer he had found. Hugo had insisted on Larry's co-producing. Hugo's report eventually wound its way to a point that did concern Alida: "So it'll be hard for me to see much of Amelia before she goes back to school." Alida nodded. Hugo went on, "It's not easy to be a separated parent when your work doesn't jibe with the school year."

Alida nodded again; she said, "I felt bullied by holidays all year and suddenly I'm excited by one. But this summer, May can drive Amelia over when you like—that is, if she stays."

"I'll have to make it up to her," Hugo said. "I promised May Europe. She never told me why she left last year."

"She was bored. We weren't glamorous, we weren't scandalous, and she hated the nurses at the Club. I'm not crazy about May, and I'm not sure she likes me. She isn't rude or defiant, but she gives me the feeling I disappoint her. Still, Amelia is used to her and I have all this work, and perhaps I want her to come to the city when we move in. I'll be working every day."

Hugo knew no more about Alida's plans than Amelia had told him, which was not much, and asked about her job. Alida described what she had done at the warehouse and what she expected to do in the fall, explaining that Morgan's offer was only a few days old, and she was not certain what it would entail except that Guthrie was sure to be demanding. "So you see," she ended, "I'll need someone, and Amelia knows May. But I fear that even in the city May will feel let down. I'm not a celebrity and I don't know any celebrities and I'm not snappy or snazzy and I don't deal in drama. She was very excited telling me about an attempted suicide at one of her jobs this winter. She didn't sound sorry until she told me she had come home after the ambulance left."

"I'll try to help you keep her if you want her," Hugo said, "but I draw the line at suicide." He spoke more seriously: "I don't like any of this." A brass band drowned out Alida's reply, and Hugo continued, "You know I don't. Larry's told you I made a mistake and I want another chance. When I really face it, a divorce seems horrible, impossible, sickening. If we were together this summer, I can imagine Amelia coming in and interrupting me working and my yelling at her, but she'd be my child, and I'd see her."

"It takes getting used to, I suppose." Alida was companionable in discussing the problem. "I was disturbed when I thought of her being with you in Europe this summer. Not that I expected anything to go wrong or to *be* wrong—just her being away. And I was furious about Thanksgiving."

Hugo looked down at his hands and let the sound of cheering wash over his regret. "I don't suppose I can ask you to forget," he said at last. "I wish I could. Larry says there's an attraction to junk women like junk food, and that it often comes out when there's a setback, but still I'm ashamed."

Alida was consoling. "We'll both forget."

"Do you mean you'll try again?"

Hugo put his proposal of reconciliation casually, without emphasis, as astute negotiators try to slip in controversial clauses unnoticed. Alida realized she must be unmistakable and firm. "The opposite," she said. "What's past is past." As if to stress her decisiveness, she rose. She needed to stir. Being firm was an effort—she had been trained to compliance—and she thought a moment before she said, "You remember how you always used to say that clichés record nature, and that every proverb is a plot? And that there's no point in trying to be original because if you are you don't have to try, you can't help it? I'll answer in clichés. I went home to Mother to lick my wounds. They healed and I'm ready to let bygones be bygones. I can't be triter than that."

Hugo rose, too, not wanting to play the scene at a disadvantage. "Including our marriage?" Alida nodded. "You're willing to turn it all over to the lawyers?"

"Whenever you say. Although actually mine's not around."

She gave Hugo an abbreviated account of Andrew's plight, mentioning that he had told her who else in the firm could advise her, but that, since his disaster was recent, and she did not know when he would return or what Hugo would ask, she had begun nothing. Hugo was moved by the news of the Camerons' misfortune. "A daughter strikes home," he said. "Let things stand for now, if you will. I mean to win you back." Alida refrained from telling him he was starting on a script in which she would decline to act, but she could not help smiling when he added, "As soon as the play is on."

She laughed, and said, "That's American. Our Puritan heritage. The job comes first."

Hugo looked worried. "I've put my foot in it, haven't I?"

"Never mind. Where shall we lunch?"

"I hate to leave the television. Can we eat in here? Can we have another drink?"

"Yes to both."

Alida set the old round coffee table while Hugo mixed drinks. As they stood there, first far away and then louder and then as if bursting over their heads, the sound of church bells pealed. Alida began to cry. Then she wiped away her tears, and said, "It was so majestic," and sat down and thought that drinking friendly bloody Marys while watching television with your future former husband was very American, too.

While they ate, Hugo stole glances at her, as if covertly scouting a target. But he had the sense, the judgment or intuition, or perhaps just the familiarity with Alida, to understand that he should not push her at this moment. During the rainstorm that beat down for an hour, he drew her into gossip, telling her about people they knew. His talk was entertaining, like a performance. Alida mentioned seeing Tom Frank and asked what Tom was doing. Hugo told her he was thinking of going into his play and added that he, Tom, had mentioned seeing her, and Alida said that Andrew had been very helpful in starting her working. Hugo commented, "Cameron is my real enemy. He made your life interesting. It would be easier for me if you had remained a sleeping beauty."

Alida, appalled that Hugo came so close to the truth, said her life was interesting to her, not *interesting* interesting, reminding him again of how she bored the nursemaid, and then, trying to match his lively gossip, told him about David and Francesca, and about Morgan's theory of art disguising the mess.

"*Substituting* for the mess," Hugo corrected. "Replacing it. No, your job *is* interesting. I can see you've met some people with interesting minds. I'll have my work cut out for me making you interested in me." He rose to go, and Alida suddenly thought of him as a friend—a nice, bright man, who was talented, entertaining, quick-witted, charming, and informed. She walked Hugo out to the car, and they stood beside it for a moment after Hugo asked, "Will you see the fireworks?"

She told him that she was going to drive into the city and meet her mother and Amelia, and May, too, at her uncle's party. She was a little sorry to mention her uncle because he made Hugo uncomfortable, as Arthur used to make her, and she had never told Hugo how she learned that Arthur was loving as well as difficult. She did not know why she was so concerned to spare Hugo's feelings, or so attentive to his expression, which seemed momentarily to lose the crispness, the chipper charm he had so resolutely maintained. Was it possible that Larry had been right, and Hugo was afraid of her? But all Hugo said was "I wish," before he caught himself and told her that he, too, was going to the city, where Larry had arranged a fireworks party. "This is not the way my stories end," he said, "with a handshake instead of a clinch."

She waved as he drove away, and for a moment felt what she had expected to feel—sadness at the ending of a tie—but it was combined with a relief that was almost elation at her own firmness in asserting her will to separate from this gifted man who, she could now admit, had taught her more than he had hurt her.

III

ON
HER
OWN

Alida loved working on her apartment. Using only what was at hand—furniture already there, pieces that had caught her eye at the warehouse, and family things, heirlooms or hand-me-downs— she discovered that placing, as much as evaluating or selecting, enthralled her. Putting diverse articles into a proper relation was an exercise in millimeters and a study in perfection. It was also an assumption of power; she became the arbiter of the objects she admired, and in this domination she recognized a kinship to her mother's gardening. Neither woman made her raw material; both arranged it. That realization might explain her mother's worship of a—or the—Creator. Alida, however, felt differently. At the very beginning of July, when she perceived herself obsessed by precision, she remembered the saw "God is in the details," and, moving a mirror higher in the upstairs hallway, said aloud, "No, *I* am in the details." The prospect of working on her own had somewhat intimidated her, but almost immediately she began to rejoice in the clarity of solitude: the risks were all hers.

Yet of course she was never alone. All her ideas owed something to almost everyone she had known, and, day after day, workmen and craftsmen taught her possibilities and limits—for instance, how closely colors could match each other in fabric, paper, paint. Technique ran through everything, and when she found time to talk to her mother, she learned that Gertrude took for granted that expertise underpinned esthetic purpose. Her tapestry was coming along; true to her promise that it would reflect the city, she had designed a large, free rendering of a florist's display case as it might be in

283

spring. Her imagination thrilled her daughter; Alida learned that her mother could be entertaining or unexpected. One evening, when they were sitting on the terrace after dinner, Alida began to discuss what she had been doing that day. Her ruminations stimulated Gertrude to talk of designing flower borders, and she observed that some textures were "inherently naive."

The word startled Alida, and she asked what Gertrude meant.

"You know what I mean," Gertrude said, almost testily. "Everybody knows that buttercups are like calico."

Alida commuted from Connecticut, where she slept, to her apartment, where she worked and, sometimes, saw Andrew. In July he flew to New York once a week, and went from the airport to his office. Mrs. Southern crammed his day with business, and he spent the night at his brother's on Long Island; the next morning his brother drove him back to the airport. That left only the brief time between the office and the Long Island train for Alida. Andrew would arrive at her apartment tired, harried by the timetable, and greedy for her body. He would briefly and drily impart medical bulletins, and she would try to call his attention to the progress she had made—for every week brought change—and so remind him that her apartment, at an unspecified time in the future, would be his home. One tactic was to ask his opinion: what did he think of the dining chairs? He shrugged, put down his briefcase and overnight case, and said, "I need a drink, Alida."

He drained it, asked for another, and, glass refilled a third time, began to go upstairs. On these visits he was inarticulate, as he had been before they admitted their love after Easter. When she asked him about the brother with whom he stayed, Andrew once more gave an inexpressive shrug. She did learn his brother's address, and informed him that his brother lived on the same road as her cousin Paul, but Andrew seemed to consider her cousin as dull a topic as his brother. When she drove home that evening, the comfort his body gave her was tinged by uneasiness at his reluctance to admit that one day they would share their relatives. The painters had been at work the next week, and, when Andrew came, Alida remarked that so much of their love affair had been bound up with the building trades that she had begun to regard a stepladder as a lewd object. His brief smile resembled a grimace. Did he resent her attempt to divert him or to remind him of their delicious hours on his great-aunt's property? At the end of the month, he told her that he would not be able to see her the following week because they were bringing little Janet east to recuperate in Maine. Janet, his wife, had inherited a share in a family camp that was crowded with cousins every summer. The Camerons rarely went there because Andrew found it too remote, but now that drawback had become an advantage. "There isn't much little Janet can do to herself up there, surrounded by relatives. There's no privacy, and no place to wander off, except the woods, which are so thick and wild you can't even get into them. She needs a nurse who knows physiotherapy. Mrs. Southern's looking for one who's willing to imprison herself in the wilderness. I'm supposed to settle them in and come back to the city, but I worry about leaving little Janet with her mother. I never had time to see a psychiatrist in New York—nobody could fit me in—and nobody out there takes me seriously, but I'm convinced there's something wrong with her."

"What is she like?"

"Quiet. I think she's angry. I think she hates me. She *can* talk—she's polite to the doctors and nurses. Not forthcoming, not friendly, but correct. But with me—with us—she gives an impression of glowering, of biding her time. And . . ." They were lying side by side on their backs staring at the bedroom ceiling in the waning light that filtered through the venetian blinds. During the pause he seemed momentarily to become physically stiller. When he spoke, his voice lowered and his tone flattened: "Sometimes I feel her hatred so fiercely I hate her back before I can stop myself. But of course Janet feels nothing."

He sighed, sat up, and went in to shower, leaving Alida rejoicing that she had obeyed a rule she had imbibed heaven knows where—wives might nag, but mistresses must never complain. Her unexpressed grievances—missing him, envying his brother; resenting his lack of interest in the apartment and his refusal to refer to their future—would have made unspeakable demands, had she expressed them, on a man so emotionally drained. After he came out of the shower and started to dress, he suddenly asked if she had seen a lot of Hugo. Andrew was bending down putting on his shoes, so that she could not see his face. She wanted to know if he was jealous—that would have been a kind of reassurance—but she did not ask. "Not since the Fourth," she said. "When will I see you again?"

"I don't know. Perhaps by the third week in August, if all goes well, but . . ."

He did not have to complete the sentence; it was obvious that he had a presentiment that all would not go well. She said, "I feel you're terribly alone."

He looked at her with such gratitude for that morsel of understanding that she was more deeply moved than at any moment since they had become lovers, but the train to his brother claimed him before they could speak another word except "good-bye."

Occasionally Alida thought she should be spending more time with Amelia. When they met at breakfast (less often at dinner, for Alida frequently came home late) the child seemed perky. She took to lecturing her mother about current events—the political conventions, the Mars landing. Alida was grateful as well as amused, since she had no time for newspapers. May seemed less scornful of, or perhaps more resigned to, Flat Rock this year. She betrayed her longing for drama only by insisting on showing Alida every letter she received from the would-be suicide's cook. Alida did not know, until Betsy told her, that May and Amelia had been going to the Weinsteins' almost every day. Hugo would call whenever he foresaw a pause in his work, and May would drive Amelia over. Amelia, tactful or wary, had not mentioned her visits to her father to her mother. Luckily, Betsy, who stopped by the apartment on a scorching afternoon, was still adjusting her eyes from the sunshiny outdoors with sunglasses to the comparatively muted light of the apartment, and so did not notice Alida's expression of surprise. (If she had been asked where she thought Amelia and May spent their days, she would have said that they went to the Club.) Alida gave Betsy iced tea and took her on a tour of the apartment while Betsy told her how greatly her much older children and much younger grandchild and Larry and she herself enjoyed Amelia. She said that she had come by specifically to invite Amelia to continue her visits after Hugo's play went into rehearsal and he left the country for the city: that would be any day now. Betsy mentioned that Tom Frank had backed out, but that they had another male lead about whom Larry was more enthusiastic. Alida had been struggling with her indecision about turning Hugo's workroom /Andrew's library into a parlor and had started to interview housekeepers, and could not spare much thought for Hugo's cast. The women finished walking through the apartment at just about the same time that Betsy finished imparting her invitation and her news. Alida asked her to stay for more tea and chat, but Betsy declined—she was really due back in the country, and had called up and come by, she said, on impulse. She took her iced-tea glass into the kitchen, where she put on her sungoggles, and said, before leaving, "Amelia's such a lovely girl. No wonder Hugo adores her."

Alida went back to work. She extracted from Betsy's call only the notion that Amelia was pleasing. Betsy's visit also reminded her to prompt her mother and May to start outfitting Amelia for school, but Alida herself did not really look at her child until a Saturday in August when May was off, and Alida went to Amelia's room to take her to the tennis lesson that had been a regular and pleasurable part of her routine for the past two summers. She found Amelia lying on her bed staring at the ceiling. Alida assumed she had had an attack of dreaminess and asked, sympathetically, "What are you thinking?"

Still staring at the ceiling, the child replied, "How I hate tennis."

"Hate it? You're very good at it. Isn't Jackie" (the assistant pro who taught children and beginners) "proud of you?" No response. "Anyway, it's time to go."

"I'm not going."

This was so unlike Amelia that Alida asked, anxiously, "Are you sick?"

"Sick of tennis."

"What would you like to do instead?"

"Nothing."

"Then you'd better go today. They're expecting you. I'll cancel the rest of the lessons unless you change your mind. There aren't many more, anyhow, before we leave for the city."

"I don't want to leave for the city."

Alida wanted to go on being understanding, affectionate, supportive, and companionable, but she was bored by Amelia's schedule and regretted time away from her apartment. The words she spoke were kindly—"I don't understand you. Tell me what's wrong"—but she might have uttered them at a pace too speedy or in a tone too dry, for the response was an explosion, a stream of tears, legs flailing and fists beating the bed, and, through the sobs, "Everything's wrong. I hate my life."

"That's very dramatic," Alida replied, "and I don't believe it."

"You'd better."

That threat frightened Alida, who could not help remembering Andrew's recollection of his daughter as a tiny, joyous kindergartner. Might her child, too, turn into a nightmare? But she mastered her fear, and, using the only resources she could command,

287

belittlement and common sense, said, "You're very angry. Come along and beat up the ball. We'll talk about the rest later."

She succeeded in jollying Amelia to tennis, and after the lesson and their own game and a swim, the child seemed to have forgotten her tantrum. But that night, around eleven, Alida came in from the terrace, where she had lingered a few moments after her mother had gone to bed, and found Amelia, in her nightgown, sitting halfway up the staircase. She said she was not sleepy.

On Sunday night Alida mentioned Amelia's odd behavior to her mother. Gertrude had not yet noticed anything out of the way, but promised to observe and report. On Monday Alida was distracted from worrying about Amelia by a new worry. Morgan came by the apartment, inspected it, and told her they expected her to give an after-the-opening party for Francesca's show on the Thursday after Labor Day. When Alida objected that the apartment would not be ready, Morgan said, "It's coming along beautifully. Fresh, merry, unpretentious. Cheerful. Original, but not so anyone notices it. The colors work like magic. The only thing behindhand is this room." They were standing in Hugo/Andrew's room, which Alida had painted pale green, with curtains and carpet to match. At the moment the bookshelves were bare and there was no furniture. "You won't need it for the party. We're thinking of a buffet for thirty or forty, and you could handle it in the living room, dining room, and entry hall."

Alida felt bullied, pushed—slave driven—at the prospect of a party so soon after a move, but Morgan, without giving her time to organize her complaint, said, "It's like a furnace out there. What can you give me to drink?"

"What would you like?"

"Iced coffee."

Alida gave the order to Silvia, her newly hired housekeeper, and rejoined Morgan in the erstwhile library. His eyes ranged as he talked. "This is a nice space here," he said. "Remind me how you used it."

"It was Hugo's workroom."

The housekeeper brought the coffee, and Morgan sipped it, still standing in the library, and said, "Of course. Hugo reminds me. Do you know Larry Weinstein? The accountant? Hugo's producer?" Alida admitted she did, and Morgan said, "I want you to ask him to the party."

"Why? You don't think he'd like Francesca's—"

"Probably not, but he collects, and I haven't met him."

"I like him. I like his wife. But they're Hugo's friends—"

"This is business. For business purposes they're your friends." Morgan was conclusive: "We'll get the caterer."

Alida grumbled, "Business before pleasure. I suppose you want me to ask Hugo."

"Not a bad idea. He may need a decorator."

Morgan left, and Alida devoted the week to the library/parlor; she knew he wanted it finished.

On May's next Saturday off, Amelia had acquired the technique of dumb insolence. She did not object to playing tennis, but played badly; she did not refuse to swim, but thrashed in the water and stumbled around the edge of the pool dripping on somnolent tanning adults. She did not argue about lunch, but did not eat it. She projected listlessness and dejection so grandly that they appeared theatrical, almost fraudulent. But late in the afternoon Alida, passing Amelia's room, thought she heard crying. Did she cry to *be* heard? Alida pushed open the door and found Amelia squatting on the floor with the doll and doll clothes Aunt Jane had given her for Christmas. Her face was covered with tears, but seemed to harden when her mother appeared. "Go away," she said. "I'm playing."

"You don't seem to be enjoying yourself."

Amelia gave a teeth-baring rubber-face grin. "I was playing sad."

That night on the terrace, Alida told her mother about Amelia's latest scenes. Gertrude agreed that Amelia seemed less happy recently, and suggested that, since the school medical form had just arrived and Amelia would have to see Dr. Dunne, Alida should take the child to see the doctor and talk to him about her nerves. Gertrude added, "She's been so good, she may have spoiled us. She's only a child, after all."

Dr. Dunne examined Amelia the following Monday, listened to Alida, and sympathized in his youthful-pompous way. He stated the obvious: This was a period of change. Anxiety was normal. "She'd be queer if she wasn't worried." He recommended a policy of wait-and-see and prescribed a mild tranquilizer. "Keep it in your bathroom," he warned. "I don't like any medication, not even aspirin, kept where a child can find it. And don't hesitate to call me." He finished filling out the school form, and when he looked up to give it to her, he said, "You look tired. Is something the matter?"

"I'm working hard."

"Don't overdo. And call if you need me."

She thanked him. There was a mirror in the waiting room. Her features seemed to have collapsed. She took Amelia home, went into her room, and called Andrew's office. Mrs. Southern told her that Andrew had not returned, and offered to connect her with Mr. Hooper. Standing in her bowknot-rosebud bedroom, Alida felt totally alone. Deserted. Abandoned. Andrew had vanished as if he had stepped through the door in *Galaxy Guards* that opened into antimatter. This was a device Hugo used to write an actor out of the show. But who was writing Andrew's and Alida's life? She began to tremble. Then the caterer rang from the city with a question about Francesca's party. Alida was not deserted; she was beleaguered.

The next day, her mother came into the city with her, helped the housekeeper organize the pantry, bought a new vacuum cleaner, and did some mysterious checking that enabled her to tell Alida that James and his boy could start installing the fernery in the master bath, the garden in the dining-room windows, and flower shelves in the former library/future parlor.

Until Morgan's visit, the ghost of Hugo and the hope of Andrew had inhibited Alida's planning that room. The remembered placement of Hugo's desk and sofa acted as a mental barrier to new placements of new furniture; so did the competing vision of arranging Andrew's silver and the partner's desk and tall clock that she recalled as standing in the Cameron library. When the painters were working in the apartment, she had had the room painted green because it had been mostly blue when it was Hugo's, and then she tried putting her own desk where Hugo's had been. Hers was too small for the space, and went upstairs to her bedroom. The library refused to become a boudoir; it remained obstinately—in her mind, anyway—a husband's room. Making it a parlor called for resources of ruthlessness that came, ultimately, from Morgan and Guthrie and what Alida recognized as their determination to push her and use her as far as she would let them. Their toughness mobilized hers. She was not sure whether she was committing exorcism or symbolic murder, but she decided to try a suite of Louis XVI furniture made, she judged, about 1880, that she had seen in the warehouse. It was in excellent condition, having very likely sat unused in a front parlor before it had gone to the warehouse. McKinley's file produced a team who polished the gilt wood frames and cleaned the upholstery, a tapestry with tiny roses scattered on a beige ground. The suite—a sofa, a loveseat, and two armchairs—looked unresolved until Alida, walking down the street, saw a round

Directoire table in a dealer's window, and bought it for the center of the room. The table's three round legs were connected by stretchers whose curves provided the certainty that the reproduction furniture lacked, and its ormolu trim made the gilt wood more credible. Her mother agreed to line the bookshelves with pots of flowers in brass planters, the easiest of her installations; the fernery was the trickiest.

While Gertrude and her staff worked in Alida's apartment, Gertrude observed her daughter and thought her tense, overwrought—agitated and suppressing agitation that nothing Gertrude saw explained. She was distressed that her daughter as well as her granddaughter seemed on edge, and purposefully praised Alida, hoping that appreciation would tranquilize. Since the vocabulary of solace is limited, Gertrude found herself saying much the same thing over and over, with no effect, until, after she repeated how impressed she was with the way Alida had harmonized flower colors, Alida snapped, "You said that."

James was driving them home and his boy was riding with them, so that Gertrude did not feel free to confront Alida's rudeness. The mother repeated that everything looked beautiful and—a last stab at comfort—added that everything was just about done, and it was only the last week in August.

"Yes, Mother," Alida said.

The sound of her fury startled herself. Gertrude's reference to the last week of August spoke aloud of the second week in which Alida, every day, had wakened with the hope that Andrew would come or send word, a hope disappointed every day.

Hugo, however, did telephone, the day after they moved into the city, the day after Labor Day. Amelia was exploring Alida's bedroom and took the call there, standing beside her mother's desk. "Daddy!" she screamed with joy, "Daddy, where are you?"

Alida watched her child's face brighten as she listened to her father; she looked as if she were hearing news too good to be believed, and nodded and grinned while he spoke. When he ceased, she asked, "When will I see you?" eagerly, possessively, and, Alida thought, anxiously. Amelia was too elated to restrain her demonstration of feeling for her father, and Alida realized how contained Amelia had been about Hugo only at this moment when the child burst the emotional confinement she had apparently imposed on herself. After she hung up, she said, "Daddy's been in the city, working hard on his play, just like he said." Had she feared her father was deceiving her? "He said to tell you he's coming to see me at your party on Thursday."

On Thursday morning, Hugo sent a bowl of roses. Alida placed it on the table in the parlor like an offering on an altar whose god had disappeared; for a moment—a moment only—she thought of Hugo's memories of his room. But the day had its demands, and Alida went out to meet them.

Everybody liked the parlor and liked the party, which was a mix of painters and patrons. The Weinsteins and Hugo made up a theatrical delegation, for they brought along the Nortons. Matthew Norton was their play's star; his wife, Georgia, was a quiet, self-possessed blonde whom another guest recognized: soon the whole party knew that she was a highly regarded young concert violinist. As for Francesca Kinsky, on the night of her triumph she was principally concerned with keeping David at her side.

Alida had scarcely any connected conversations. Hugo sought her out before he left and promised to call California and send on the art books, antique books, and catalogues she had been collecting since her student days. These had been shelved in the entry hall where her mother's tapestry now hung. After all the guests had gone, Alida wandered back into the parlor. She found she disliked it; it was, at best, clever. The wall of flowers imparted all the life it had. If she replaced her mother's flowers with her art books, the whole room would die. She would have to send back the warehouse furniture and start again. What sort of room would she make? A study for herself? A setting for a single working woman?

Morgan phoned the next morning to extol the party. He offered a persuasive collection of secondhand compliments as well as his and Guthrie's flattering observations, and tendered their thanks. "We knew you could do it without trouble, but we're grateful anyway. Did we tell you that you start work—we expect you—at the Galleries on Monday?" They had not, but Alida said she would be in. "By the way," Morgan asked, before he hung up, "did you hear anything from the Camerons? We invited them, but they didn't come."

Alida's job devoured her days, and, starting with his play's opening, Hugo began to surround her. He invited Alida and Gertrude as well as Amelia and May to the opening: "The whole family," Amelia said, gleefully, as the four women set out together.

Gertrude had brought her station wagon down from Connecticut with James at the wheel. The play more than fulfilled Larry's predictions. Though Matthew Norton was not as strikingly handsome as Tom Frank, he was a better actor, with an unnoticeable technique that gave depth, spontaneity, and sincerity to his lines. Hugo had written him a wonderful part. Norton played an old-fashioned hero, honorable and chivalrous, brave and tender, called upon to combat an unparalleled evil whose source, supposedly extraterrestrial in the first act, was revealed in the second as terrifyingly sinister because entirely human. Gertrude was impressed: when the final curtain fell, she said, "This work is about Original Sin."

Alida liked the play, but she did not like the persuasion that brought her to the Weinsteins' party afterward. Gertrude betrayed her. "I've never been to an opening-night party," she whispered to Alida, and went on to second the Weinsteins' argument that James could drive May and Amelia home, and call for Gertrude and Alida later. Alida wandered through the Weinsteins' familiar rooms, attempting to detach herself from the gathering, which was not difficult during the anxious wait for reviews, when everyone was muted in anticipation, absorbed in suspense. Presently radio and television and then newspapers transformed the room's restraint into exuberance, as critics reinforced each other's praise, and the group's elation at having worked well was aerated by gaiety at having worked successfully. There was an outbreak of hugging and kissing and quoting—accosting the bar with "Once more unto the breach, dear friends"—and the villain pursued Alida in a tipsy fog of flirtatious goodwill. He took her elbow and steered her to the buffet, claiming she had a "lean and hungry look," and asked who she was. She pretended to be awed by the splendor of the feast—"Is that *lobster*?" she asked Betsy, who was standing nearby—in order to avoid identifying herself.

But the actor was persistent, and asked Betsy, "Do you know this dazzling damsel?"

And Betsy said, "Of course. She's Hugo's wife, Alida."

For the rest of the evening Alida received a wife's congratulations upon her husband's achievement.

And Amelia ensured that her parents were thrown together. She arranged for them to attend the first parents' night at school in each other's company, and Hugo took Alida to dinner afterward on the pretext that they needed to discuss Amelia's education. They barely did so, for, like lunch with Andrew, dinner with Hugo became a reception. Hugo was recognized in the theatrical restaurant he had chosen, and a procession of old friends; acquaintances promoting themselves to the rank of old friends; well-wishers; and hopeful actors and actresses came to their table. Alida believed their attentions were less genuine than those Andrew had received, for these visitors, paying tribute to fortune rather than misfortune, were courtiers, and courtiers never seem sincere. Yet though she belittled them, she enjoyed them—she always enjoyed the heightened presence of theater people. All she minded was their deference to her, their desire to please the playwright's wife.

Hugo's next step was the weekend. He understood that Amelia wanted to be with her grandmother, so he stayed at the Weinsteins' country house and called at Gertrude's; went to church; had Sunday dinner with Father Peele; and walked the grounds while they talked of preparing for the fall and frost and winter. Alida thought he fitted in better than he had in the past; he no longer tried to define himself, in a host of uneasy little ways, *against* his mother-in-law and all the Clarks and Watermans. After that first weekend, Mrs. Waterman told Alida that, at Amelia's insistence, she would ask Hugo to stay at her house. Hugo began the second weekend by taking Amelia to her Saturday-morning tennis lesson. Alida stood on the front doorstep to see them off. Hugo was both cavalier—carrying his daughter's rackets and bag—and father—reminding her that he could not help her in the ladies' changing room. She looked up at him, turning her head sideways and shaking it a little, pursing her lips, and protesting, "Oh, Father, you know I'm not a child anymore . . . ," before they moved out of earshot.

Again Alida was haunted by Andrew's recollection of his agile young daughter on the way to kindergarten. Never having experienced the tie between father and daughter, Alida had not thought much about it until this past year, when it all too often exhibited itself in desperation: baffled David and screaming Teeny; queer little Janet, dressed up by her father, saying "Cheese" at Alida's birthday party; Amelia's hysterics when Hugo's play went into rehearsal and he left the Weinsteins'; even Debby's obedient return to her husband at her father's command. But, at the end of that Saturday, Alida saw that there was much more to the tie. She was sitting on the terrace with her mother when Hugo and Amelia returned. They looked like a pair of lovers as they came through the house door. Their stances and their faces changed just before they greeted Alida and Gertrude, and Alida could almost feel the effort of will by which Amelia and her father relinquished the delights of their twosome. They looked at each other one last time, and Alida thought they had to unclasp their eyes.

Every time she opened her medicine cabinet and saw the bottle of Dr. Dunne's now unnecessary tranquilizer, Alida was reminded of the good Hugo's attentiveness did Amelia. But his presence tormented Alida. Finding Hugo where she wanted Andrew, she felt herself the victim of a malicious practical joke.

Where was Andrew? He should have been in the city weeks earlier. Mrs. Southern would only say that he was still "out of the city" and that his daughter was "as well as can be expected"; she offered to transfer Alida to another member of the firm. Alida tried the Camerons' apartment. If she reached Janet, she would tell her how much Amelia liked Fanny Burney. The first time Alida called there was no answer; the second time, a woman with an accent said, "No home. No peoples home," and hung up. So Alida waited. She was fearful that some new misfortune had struck, and perplexed because Andrew had not found a way to write or call. She had moments of anger that he could forget her need for him, and moments of guilt at the selfishness that made her angry, but mostly she simply longed for Andrew, and it was a horrid mockery to see Hugo at her mother's table, asking Gertrude about bulbs.

Alida decided to spare herself some hours of painful sham intimacy by taking the next Saturday in the city for herself, sending Amelia up to Connecticut with Hugo in the morning, and following at the end of the afternoon in time for dinner. She was not lying when she telephoned her mother and told her she needed the day; she really had to buy clothes for work, and she wanted to try a new city hairdresser. Alida's day proved successful but tiring, and when she came back to the apartment to change and pack a bag for the country, she was tempted to call her mother and defer her arrival until Sunday. She stood beside her desk, with her hand on the telephone, and balanced her duty to Amelia against the pleasures of a bathrobe-and-television evening alone at home. But she was not alone. She heard footsteps in the hall, and someone at her door. May burst into Alida's bedroom and surveilled her mistress like an officer of the law.

May was free every weekend after seeing Amelia off for Connecticut, and Alida had not expected to find her lurking in the apartment on a pretty, sunshiny Saturday. Alida was irritated, besides, because May had been badgering her ever since they moved to the city. The girl was overhelpful, insisting on learning along with Silvia how to tend their indoor gardens, and going through the mail before arranging it on Alida's desk, so that she could announce, when Alida came home, "No letters today, Mrs. Kelly, only bills."

295

Sometimes she seemed to be trying to be Alida's nursemaid: when she gave Alida a telephone message, she often nagged until Alida returned the call. Alida was not certain what May intended or hoped by dogging her; today, though, the girl's presence was unmistakably invasive. Alida said, sharply, "What are you doing here? Why aren't you out?"

May was taken aback by her mistress's annoyance. She said, "I *was* out, but I came home to nap. Then I heard someone come in. I thought it was a burglar after your jewelry." Her tone became less defensive after her explanation. "I see you had your hair done differently. It looks beautiful, Mrs. Kelly."

Driven from her apartment by May, Alida went to Connecticut. She found her mother had invited the Weinsteins to dinner. From almost the moment she arrived, Larry began to question her about her job. Alida was pleased by the attention, but Larry gave too much. At cocktails and on through dinner, he forced her to monopolize the party talking about herself. He would not let her abridge. She told him generally about her first assignment, finding or designing the fittings—handles, hinges, keyholes—for the paneled closets of an apartment playroom/bar/TV room/hi-fi center, and when he insisted upon detail, she explained that the client was a very old woman who had just moved into the apartment from a house done years before by Mrs. McKinley herself, and that the point of Alida's task was to undo Guthrie's native understatement with garishness, for their client, they learned belatedly, was losing her sight, and needed to be surrounded by shiny things. She did not understand why Larry made her go over every aspect of that commission and describe her own work on it almost minute by minute, and he was equally exacting in asking her to recall her hours talking to a writer who was preparing an article about Francesca Kinsky for a feminist magazine, and going over the Hardman-Steins' first consignment: Morgan was training her to deal with decorative-crafts workers. The two men had crammed her days, competing with each other in tutelage and teaching her more than she had ever suspected there was to learn. The party had reached dessert when she told them that Lady Mary, back from Europe, had just telephoned a request that Alida come over to consult about some rooms.

"Will you do Lady Mary's rooms by yourself?" Larry asked.

"I suppose I'd work with Morgan and Guthrie. Under their direction."

"Could you do a house?"

"The firm could," Alida said.

"Of course she could," Hugo answered. "What's on your mind?"

"I'm thinking about Georgia Norton."

"What a marvelous idea!" Hugo exclaimed, and, turning to Alida: "They're enchanting people. You'll love working with them."

The Weinsteins agreed with his estimate, and the conversation moved from delight with the Nortons to the high fortunes of the play, which was casting a national company and negotiating a London production. Gertrude began to ask, and the men to answer, several textbooks' worth of questions about theatrical production. These lessons continued when they moved out onto the terrace for coffee. Gertrude was fascinated by their lore, and occasionally referred to plays or performances that had affected her. She and Larry were exchanging rapturous recollections of the Lunts when Amelia came out in her bathrobe to say good-night, and their memories of Ina Claire were interrupted by a census for brandy and liqueurs. But Larry did not forget the Nortons. "We've decided they must buy a house," he told Alida. "There's nothing like a mortgage to keep people steady. They've never had a penny before, and they must learn to save. Is your firm too dear for them?"

"Come off it, Larry," Hugo said. "You know you'll set the budget and see that they keep it."

Larry told Alida that Georgia Norton would call her, and after the Weinsteins left, Hugo entertained Gertrude with stories of Larry's fatherly concern for his protégés. He recalled Larry persuading him to do the play as if the drama of persuasion *were* a play, acting out both characters, his depressed and reluctant self and the confident, persistent Larry, whose pet phrases—"genuinely gifted," for example—Alida recognized. Hugo was charming and Gertrude was charmed, but Alida was uncomfortable in this threesome in the dark. She rose, saying that her day had been long, and went up to bed, where she lay awake for hours before she slept. When she slept, she dreamed, with every moment of the action reproduced as if on film, of Eliot on the night of Labor Day. She woke in shock, half-expecting to find her torn pajamas on the floor beside her bed, and fell back in relief, but also in disgust. Alida lay in the dark and told herself that she had no reason now or ever to remember Eliot Jones, but the moment she closed her eyes, the film began again. This time it started at the beginning, when she came downstairs into the cottage parlor. May was talking to Eliot, and they both stared at the woman who entered in bare pajamas, wearing too much makeup.

How queer she looked! How tasteless and provocative! And then, how complaisant and flirtatious her manners were! She was a terrible actress, false in every note, but what part was she playing? The memory troubled her; the dark menaced her; she turned on the lamp beside her bed and sat up, staring at the bowknots and buds on the wallpaper until she understood at last that, to Eliot, she was a stock character in the modern commedia dell'arte, the divorcée desperate for sex. But why was she thinking of that now, when she wanted to sleep? Enviously she counted all the sleepers in the house—Cook, Jenny, Sally; Gertrude, Amelia, Hugo. That was it: Hugo was keeping her up. His presence was disturbing her sexually. Eliot had been wrong; last year she was too numb to desire anyone. But this year, after Andrew, she expected passion and consolation, the erotic and supportive; she needed the relief from isolation and uncertainty that Andrew's body afforded her, and in his absence she was weak; pathetic; pitiably lonely. Hugo's insinuating presence was undermining her; she could imagine a moment of discouragement or anxiety in which she might drop her guard, or a moment of sexual need in which she would offer herself to him, not out of desire for Hugo but out of desire. The dependence Andrew had created had transformed her into the woman Eliot had mistaken her for—the hungry female of masculine folklore, like the women who went upstairs at the old Inn.

On Monday Alida eluded the distress of her personal life by overworking. Georgia Norton called, and they agreed to meet for lunch on Thursday; Morgan reminded Alida how right he had been to insist that she invite the Weinsteins to the Kinsky party. During the next days, he counseled her how to behave at a first meeting with a prospective client. "Don't talk," he advised. "Listen."

He also warned her against making firm promises or commitments. Larry telephoned Alida twice to assure her how much she would love Georgia and to adjure her to be careful with the Nortons' money. So much coaching intimidated Alida, who encouraged herself by having her hair done again and by wearing a suit she had bought the past Saturday, a mannish-jacketed, narrow-skirted "executive" suit that made her look more businesslike than she felt. When she presented herself for Morgan's inspection before leaving for her debut—her first interview with her first client—he said, "You'll terrify her," as he patted her shoulder. "Good luck."

The women met in an overdecorated restaurant near the Galleries. Georgia scanned the pretentious menu, and ordered scrambled eggs. She said she was about to start on a tour and wanted to prepare herself for the diner meals and coin-machine food that were her frequent fare on the road. She also told Alida that she and Matt had never owned anything except her violins, their clothes, and, sometimes, a secondhand car. She understood why Larry wanted them to buy a house; she had no objections, but no interest, either.

Alida asked, "When you were a little girl, what kind of house did you want to live in when you were grown up?"

"I didn't think about houses. I was practicing."

Alida tried again. "What does your husband like?"

"He sees everything as sets or props."

By the time lunch ended they had revealed themselves as women so different that neither could have imagined the other—Alida dedicated to place, object, substance, Georgia to the impalpable constructions of sound—but they felt like friends because they responded to each other's honesty. Georgia confessed, "I was terrified of this lunch because I didn't know *what* you'd make me do."

Alida replied, "And I didn't know what I was supposed to do."

Georgia asked, "Could you or your firm fix up a house without forcing me to decide what I like?"

And Alida answered, "I'm not supposed to promise anything, but I will."

Morgan forgave Alida for promising. He was intrigued by her description of Georgia, an artist with no interest in their art. "I can see how you got carried away," he said. "You must have been a girlish twosome."

At the end of the afternoon Alida went to meet her aunt Jane for tea at her aunt's club. They might form another "girlish twosome," but Alida looked forward to a little modest boasting about her job, for she cherished the absurd hope of some day convincing her aunt that she was a grown-up.

Jane was waiting for her on a sofa in a lounge. "Sit for a moment," she said. "First we'll chat and then we'll look around and see who's here, and I can introduce you. You're looking well. What have you been doing?"

"Lunching with my first client."

Aunt Jane was nonplussed. Although she admired Alida's apartment and remembered that Alida worked for the McKinley Galleries, she did not think of her niece as working in the same way as her husband and sons or, for that matter, as Morgan and Guthrie. When Alida explained about Georgia Norton, her aunt picked up the connection with Hugo, an aspect of Alida's life that Jane took seriously: marriage. "Your uncle and I were talking the other day," she said, "and we decided we misjudged your husband. Underestimated him, perhaps. Your mother feels that way; she told me so. She likes his play very much, and so do I. I saw it at a matinee. Arthur is too busy for the theater, though sometimes he has to go to a benefit, but it is a very good play and, as your mother says, really profound. She says Hugo is very nice nowadays, and wonderful with Amelia. He's quite the gentleman, I understand, and Father Peele finds him interesting." Alida said nothing at all. Aunt Jane chattered on. "I was wondering if you were going to move back to California, because the Club is not very enthusiastic about out-of-town members." Seeing how blank Alida looked, Jane explained, "Their dues are lower, and of course they can't work on committees."

"Aunt Jane, I've settled in New York. I have a job here."

"Oh yes, we used to think it was wrong, taking the bread out of the mouths of married men." She continued more briskly, "But that was a long time ago, and I expect you will tell me this is 1976." Jane rose, and said, "In that case, let's go into the dining room and see who's here."

They strolled out of the lounge and crossed the main hall to the arched entry to the brightly papered dining room. No more than six or eight women were scattered at tables. Jane was disappointed. "We usually have more people at tea," she said. "Are we early?"

They looked at their watches in the doorway and Jane lamented the absence of influential friends drinking tea. Alida heard someone call, "Is that you, Alida?"

She looked up. Janet Cameron came toward her down the hall. To her normal appearance of physical disarray, Janet had added a new air of emotional fragmentation, an expression beyond despair in the pale eyes in her ashen face. She said, "I had to get out of the house." Her voice was hoarse. "Let me sit with you."

Aunt Jane regarded the powerful Janet Cameron, however distraught, as a potential sponsor of her niece before the membership committee, and said cordially, "Of course you must join us. We were just about to have tea."

The three women sat at a table, and Janet burst out, "How glad I am to see you! I didn't know where to go. The way he talked to me!"

"Who?" Jane asked, but immediately, as the waitress approached, changed her question: "Tea?"

"Scotch, please," said Alida, "with a little water on the side."

"A good idea!" Janet exclaimed. "I'll have what Alida's having."

Aunt Jane studied the menu, and wrote down her order. The moment the waitress left, Janet rasped, "Your precious Andrew, that's who. Everybody's always telling me how wonderful he is, but they don't know what he's really like. He's leaving me. Not that I mind. But now, just now, after what happened . . ."

The waitress brought their drinks, poured Jane's tea, and told her that, because some people had found the scones a little dry today, she had brought extra jam and honey. "Thank you," Jane said. "I like scones crumbly."

"What happened?" Alida picked up the questioning.

"We lost little Janet, and he's leaving."

"Where is he now?"

"At the apartment. Packing."

"I must go to him," Alida said. She stood up abruptly, and apologized for jarring her aunt's tea. "I must talk to him."

"That's very kind of you," Janet said. "Perhaps you can make him see reason. I don't think you can change his mind, though. He's very self-centered."

"Don't you think—" Aunt Jane began.

Janet interrupted. "Don't stop her, please. Let her try. He's always liked her, and perhaps he'll listen to her. Nobody can reach him, not even his darling brother. Maybe he'll trust Alida."

Alida found Andrew, in his shirt-sleeves, sitting at the desk in the Camerons' ugly library. She was filled with tenderness at the sight of his masculine deshabille. But he did not greet her tenderly. He stood up and seemed angry as he asked, "What are you doing here?"

"I met Janet at my aunt's club. How long have you been in the city? Why haven't you called me?"

"I called you at home this morning, but you had gone. I was busy at the office because I'm leaving and I was talking to the men who'll be taking over. Henry Palmer, one of the senior partners, will be handling your affairs, yours and your mother's. Hooper's too young. I tried the Galleries before I left the office, but you were out. I was going to call you at home this evening."

Andrew stopped after producing his account of a lawyer's efforts to reach a client. He sat down, picked up a paper, and placed it on a pile to one side. His hand trembled slightly. Alida's hands were clammy. As far as she could tell, the room was unchanged since January, but now it seemed more than ugly: cruel. The red was

301

blood; flames; hell. The lumpy furniture was deformed, like a freak show. And the clock ticked like a telltale heart.

"Andrew, are you leaving me?"

"I don't know."

It occurred to Alida that she was the second woman who had asked him that question today. She was doing only slightly better than Janet. She said, "Tell me what happened."

"You know little Janet committed suicide. She was locked up, but Janet insisted on taking her home."

"I didn't know."

"It was in the newspaper as 'fell.' "

"Why didn't anybody tell me? Did my mother go to the funeral?"

"It was only a tiny item. The doctors said it was a dizzy spell. That's what Janet believes. There was no funeral."

Alida remembered what she should say. "I'm sorry, Andrew, very sorry."

Then there was no sound except the clock ticking. A host of questions sprang up in Alida's mind like weeds after rain, but she did not know which to ask. Her eyes began to fill, less in sorrow than in horror; her tears were not for the child she had known but for madness and death and Andrew's grief. After a few moments, she caught her breath and spoke. "I don't want to make a spectacle of myself. I can't bear to think of what you've been suffering. Why haven't you come to me?"

"There was no time."

"But you've been in the city."

"Not long."

Their lives, hers and Andrew's, had diverged so widely in recent weeks that Alida had no words to bring them together. She rose and leaned over him as he sat, putting her arms around him, kissing him on the side of his face, his neck, his ear—for, instead of returning her kiss, he pulled away, unclasping her embrace. "Don't," he said. "Don't tease me."

So far their conversation had been slow and low, suitable for mourners; his rejection, though not loud, was quick. At Easter, she remembered, he had begged her not to tempt him. Yet she did not see herself as a temptress but as a loving woman, a promised wife. "Andrew," she said. "I love you. I came to—to console you."

Andrew rolled down his shirt-sleeves and tightened his necktie. He got up, picked up his jacket from the arm of the sofa, and put it on. His dressing was distancing them, and that made Alida angry.

Her eyes followed him as he sat down again at the desk, and she noticed the paper knife and paperweight she had given Janet. They greeted her like a couple of cynical old friends. They had been in her guilty love story from the beginning—she had bought them for Janet on the day when she first went to bed with Janet's husband—and they said, in effect, We are all liars and all losers. While she stared, the clock struck six, and Andrew said, "I have a lot to do before I get away."

Alida picked up the paperweight and threw it at the clock, smashing the glass and knocking off one hand. "You owe me time," she said.

Her violence had been ineffectual: the mutilated clock went on ticking, and its single hand continued to creep across the dial like a worm.

"I owe you," Andrew said, "but I can't pay you now. I'm empty."

"But what about me? Don't you care how I feel?"

"I failed my child. Do you know how *I* feel?"

"I can guess. That's why I know you need me, need someone who loves you." Alida hated to hear herself pleading, but could not help it: "You can't bring your child back."

"I can remember her. I want to remember you, too, but not crying or begging."

"*You're* making me cry and beg," Alida screamed. Andrew put his finger across his lips, and Alida shouted louder, "Damn you. Don't jilt me and correct my manners."

"I'm thinking of you. You'll be ashamed of yourself."

"And you won't be?"

"I am." He picked up her handbag, and gave it to her, saying, "I'll see you out."

She asked, "Is that all?"

He nodded. Without thinking, she picked up the paper knife, raised it high, and, with the frenzy of frustration, stabbed him in what she hoped would be his faithless heart. The blade tore his suit and then skidded against another texture, not flesh. Alida had knifed the wallet in his breast pocket. Andrew looked at her with wonder, and said, "I didn't know you loved me enough to kill me."

"What am I doing?" Alida cried. "I must be mad."

"No," he said. "Upset. I can't help spreading misery. But you'd better have some brandy."

Alida gulped the drink he brought her. Andrew had been right: she was ashamed of herself, and wanted to flee. She had been there far too long; the cracked clock struck seven. She put down the empty brandy glass on the desk, and Andrew said, "Don't blame yourself. Don't think I blame you."

He sounded like a father, an exhausted father trying to make a child feel better, but his effort at reassurance desolated and infuriated her. Of course he blamed her. He did not see her as his beloved, the center of his life, the hope of his future; he saw her as his accomplice in adultery, the temptress who had seduced him from his duty to his unhappy daughter, an accessory to the death of his child. Her anger frightened her. She did not trust herself to stay, and left without saying good-bye.

It had rained while she was indoors, but the air remained oppressive with rain still undischarged. Walking was not refreshing, but she walked without plan or direction. She was stupefied by the suddenness with which the end had come. Or was it sudden? she asked herself. Had Andrew given her up weeks earlier? Had he never . . . ? But she was too distraught for consecutive thought. Sometimes she felt only bleakness and sometimes rage at the injustice of which she was the victim. Once in her anger she did not notice that the traffic light had changed, and was almost run over by a truck. She tried to steady her nerves by stopping in a bar for another brandy, but she did not linger. No one else was there alone; all the drinkers were couples or parties, and the sight of companionability in her loneliness was intolerable. She went out and walked until it started to rain. Then she went home.

May leapt at her in the entry hall and told her that a man had called in the morning without leaving his name, and that her aunt Jane had called an hour ago and wanted her to call back the moment she came in. May stared at her. Alida realized why as soon as she consulted a mirror; she was wet, and she had wept away all her makeup. She poured herself a glass of whisky, went up to her room, and called her aunt, who was inquiring on Janet Cameron's behalf. Jane had taken Janet home, and they wondered if she should stay the night. "I don't think he's dangerous," Alida said. "Andrew wouldn't hurt her. But he's in a strange mood. I don't understand him. Perhaps she's better off with you."

Her aunt thanked her. "I'll tell Janet. I'm sure she'll be grateful."

After Alida hung up the telephone, she sat at her desk, unable to remember what she was supposed to do next. She sensed someone and turned. May was there.

"What is it?"

"We left dinner for you in the oven. Shall I bring it up?"

"What time is it?"

"Past ten."

That was certainly time to eat. "I'll go down," Alida said. "Thank you. You may go now."

Alida found shriveled hamburger, desiccated spinach, and caked mashed potatoes in the oven. She refreshed her drink, and sat at the kitchen table ruminating on the incalculable behavior of men. Verses came into her head: "Sigh no more, ladies, sigh no more. / Men were deceivers ever." The mashed potatoes tasted like paste. Alida refilled her glass and sipped. After a while she scraped her plate, rinsed it, and bent over to put it in the dishwasher. "When lovely woman stoops to folly, / And finds too late that men betray, / What charm can soothe her melancholy?" Where was all this good advice when she needed it, this evening, when she went to Andrew, expecting to find him and keep him forever? She poured herself some more whisky and went up to her room. While she looked over the mail on her desk, she began to hear a fruity theatrical voice reciting, "*Ariane, ma soeur, de quel amour blessée, / Vous mourûtes aux bords où vous fûtes laissée!*" and, accompanying Phèdre's verse, she saw a painting of a drowned young woman with long blonde hair floating in a stream, and presently Ophelia's reedy voice began to sing, "Before you tumbled me, / You promised me to wed." Alida could not tell whether the voices and visions were inside her head, or outside, in the real world. She blinked her eyes and shook her head, and they stopped for a moment. Then Ophelia went on, "So would I ha' done, by yonder sun, / An thou hadst not come to my bed."

Alida thought of washing the voices off in a warm, perfumed bath. She would like whisky to sip while she soaked. She went downstairs and came back up with the whisky bottle; she poured some Scotch into her glass. It was very good, and she liked it, but perhaps it was too strong. She did not want to get drunk. She went into the bathroom to add water to her drink, and the sight of her bathroom enraged her. Every plant in her mother's fernery was out of line. All the pots on the ledges set into the tiled walls were off center, and the hanging baskets listed. She was infuriated at whichever silly woman could not water her plants without disorganizing her room. The askew, lopsided mess was like a rape. Her anger grew until she felt herself slipping out of control. She remembered Amelia's tranquilizer. There the bottle was, on the top shelf of her medicine cabinet. She took the pill bottle down and set it beside the whisky glass on the edge of the sink. The more she looked at the room, the more impossible it was to leave all the plants crooked overnight. She started to step into the bathtub to straighten the pots on the wall above it. Her high heel caught in the hem of her narrow skirt, and she lost her footing. She fell backward, hitting her head against the basin and knocking over the whisky and the pills.

May found her, called an ambulance, called Hugo, and waited for congratulations and, perhaps, her picture in the papers.

As Alida was leaving the lunchroom, she was asked to go to the west lounge to help decorate it for the Halloween party. Before half an hour had passed, the others were taken away to their classes and therapeutic hours. There was no one left to stand on the ladder and hold up the swag of orange paper ruffle while Alida stepped back to see the effect. She held up a black cardboard cat against the window to see how much light came through its orange-cellophane eye, but her arm's length was not long enough for her to judge. She put the cat on the table with the other decorations, and wondered what they wanted her to do. She assumed she was being observed; she had been under observation ever since she woke in a hospital bed with a pain in her head. A nurse was sitting in the room. Alida asked where she was. The nurse told her.

"Why?"

"That's for Doctor to explain."

When the doctors explained, Alida countered with her explanation: May, with her passion for tawdry drama, had concocted one. They did not believe Alida. She was up and about in no time, for she had only fallen when drunk. The staff came at her in relays, presenting May's little playlet—her rescue of her suicidal mistress—as a fact, and telling her that the first step in getting better was to admit that she had been ill and had wanted to die. They meant "crazy" and "suicide." Alida was angry. She was angry not to be believed; she was angry to be locked up on the word of an idiot nursemaid; and she was angry at herself for having gotten drunk. Her anger reinforced her custodians' judgment that she was not fit to be released; they thought her sullenness was a symptom of resentment, and her wish to be let out was "denial," a defective grasp of reality.

Alida spent an hour every day with a resident, a rangy young man, almost too leggy for the small cubicle where they met, who was developing a professional "ahem" and developing, too, a not-very-well-concealed dislike for the obstinate woman who would not cooperate and "work through" her reasons for trying to kill herself. His supervisor, shorter, fatter, and older, had attained more detachment. He said to Alida, "You're like a mistreated dog that snarls at the ASPCA."

"He knows they plan to put him to sleep."

Alida's visitors astonished her. No one could conceive of her as an angry woman who had gotten falling-down drunk, and no one suspected her connection with Andrew. No one was interested in her story, the story she repeated to the doctors: she had slipped by accident, and May had invented the suicide. Her mother merely looked confused when Alida accused her of taking the word of a melodramatic nitwit instead of her own daughter. "I saw how tired you were last summer," Gertrude said. "You were overworking. I wish I had persuaded you to stop. You're here to rest. That's all you need, a rest."

Aunt Jane agreed with her older sister, and added that "Arthur says this is the very best place in the whole country."

Guthrie now regarded Alida as a spiritual kinswoman. "I gave up these existential gestures before I was thirty," he said, "but I know that feeling of absolute isolation: no one understands you, no one sees what you see. That's bad enough. What comes next is worse: you understand that you'll never be able to realize your vision. But you have to learn to struggle on in a world full of strangers. No, aliens." He paused, and thought for a moment. "It's not so bad."

Morgan would not visit. "You know how he is—always interested in appearances. It's 'unseemly,' he says." Guthrie coughed or hiccupped what was meant as an ironic laugh. "He'll never understand anguish." Guthrie looked around the lounge curiously. "No one ever sent me to a place like this. No one had the money." The lounge was another chintz-covered furniture-strewn room. Alida had been performing on the same trite set all her life. "What do you do here, anyway?" Guthrie asked.

Could she have told him she passed her days resisting? That, greatly as he respected her suicidal impulses, she refused to admit them? "I rest," she said.

It was Hugo on whom her freedom depended: in law he was her next of kin. He was tender, but she sensed triumph beneath his concern. That puzzled her. If she could have read his mind, she would have thought *he* was crazy. He had found himself another junk woman, an understudy in his play whose pretentiousness entertained him. He was convinced that Alida had found out, and he was thrilled by his belief that she had tried to kill herself for love of him, love she had not admitted, love she fought against, love she could not conquer. Hugo had no intention of giving up Alida; she was exactly the wife he deserved—an ornament and a lady whose fragility, demonstrated by her pathetic, lovesick gesture, made her all the more valuable. But now he felt he really did belong among Larry's "genuinely gifted" and was entitled to many women. Sometimes he thought he would like to father a bastard. To Alida's complaints about May, he replied easily, "We'll worry about that when you come home." Hugo had moved into the apartment to be with Amelia. Alida was jealous when he reported that she missed her mother, but was getting along. "She sends love, but I think it would frighten her to visit."

Betsy was the only visitor who talked to Alida normally, because she was, as usual, so harassed by her household that she forgot to be soothing. Her children were in eruption; the contractor had made a mess of the interior of Larry's playhouse (Larry sent love); and George, their houseman, had developed high blood pressure. "It's strange, how you come to depend on people," Betsy said. "I thought George would always be there for me, like my father." And, after a moment, "I suppose it *is* like my father, after all; we're taking care of him."

They recalled the days when they had studied art history together, and Betsy confided, "It sounds funny now, but then I thought the kids were growing up and I'd better prepare myself for a job or I'd have nothing to do."

When Betsy rose to go, she asked, as if Alida had been staying at a resort, "When will you be coming home?"

They walked through the lounge to the lobby, and, while they waited for an attendant to unlock the door to the outside, Alida repeated her story that she had only fallen by accident. "Don't they tell you here that there are no accidents?" Betsy asked.

That was exactly what they had been telling Alida, and Betsy's matter-of-fact tone (she might have been inquiring about a kindergarten's policy on reading readiness) made their nonsense plausible. For the first time, Alida understood that she was being punished by people who did not think they were punishing her, who loved or trusted or admired her but did not know her. She could not recognize herself as the fatigued, sensitive woman her mother saw, as the overrefined esthete Guthrie thought he understood, and certainly not as the naughty girl the institution was trying to discipline for her own good. Who was she? Surrounded by people who were brittle, cowed, or ashamed, and whose responses were erratic, she could not gauge herself. She began to ask herself, Who is the irreducible Alida? And concluded, Probably a decorator. So she had agreed to join the communal work of decorating for Halloween. It was her first gesture of obedience or conformity, and it had ended with her desertion by her fellow inmates.

She went to the window of the empty lounge and stared out at a gray afternoon, all steel and lead, with the light, such as it was, streaming through clouds uncomfortably low over a river whose surface looked like chain mail. The Seine flows under the Mirabeau Bridge and takes our loves with it; and the Hudson flows under the George Washington Bridge and the Tappan Zee Bridge and bridges at Poughkeepsie and Rhinecliff and who knows where else. And all the rivers flow into the sea. All those gray waters meet and slap each other, heaving mindlessly. They develop white rims that disappear, reappear, heave, swell, slap, break forever and ever. Uncaring, purposeless, the tomb of fathers, not even knowing it is a tomb, obeying a ball of stone in the sky, which, itself dead, has no idea that it tugs murderous waters. Beneath the moon, the earth, a bare ball barely disguised by vegetation, operates as a machine for making orphans. Man-made decorations—Hugo's plots, Guthrie's rooms, her mother's gardens—disguise this truth but do not change it. Alida felt proud to have grasped ultimate reality, even though her unique wisdom suggested that her romance with Andrew might have been just another pretty story, another decoration as valid or ephemeral as Art Deco or *Galaxy Guards*. She leaned her head against the window, yielding to the seduction of melancholy, and then came alert, for she heard steps. Father Peele had come to visit, wearing his full clerical outfit, as he never did in the country, and carrying a prayer book.

He smiled at her slightly, and said, "Your mother doesn't know I've come."

"Why are you here?"

"To help you get out, of course. We will sit down," he suggested, "and I will give you spiritual comfort." He looked around the room, choosing their setting. "That will do nicely," he said, and led her to a loveseat somewhat apart, set between windows rather than in the midst of other furniture, and opposite the open double door, so that they were visible from the hall. "They like to see us," he said, and repeated, as they sat down, "I've come to help you get out."

"How?" Alida asked.

"You must do as I say," he said, "and you must do as they say. It's the only way. If you don't like to tell them the truth, you must lie. If you don't like to lie, think of it as acting."

Alida was astonished at his assurance. "Do you know the whole story?" she asked.

"I doubt it," Father Peele answered, "but I used to work in places like this when I was young, when I believed that the words of Christ and His healing power could, through me, have an immediate effect . . ."

"You don't believe that now?"

"Not as I did then. Then I did not understand that I was expecting to work miracles. It took me some years to realize that my demands on God were outrageous."

Alida was moved by his confession, and wondered if he expected her to confess in return. She said, "I wish you could work a miracle for me."

He said, "When I was a hospital chaplain, my medical colleagues used to refer, in a tolerant way, to 'the Christian myth,' or, sometimes, 'the God hypothesis.' When my feelings stopped hurting, I understood that they believed in a therapeutic myth. They had their bible—their ideal narrative—and their rituals. You are in their country, so you must conform to their religion. You are living their story."

Alida said, "If that Goddamn (excuse me) bitch hadn't . . ."

Father Peele said, "You mean the nursemaid. They tell me she saved your life."

That was a new idea to Alida, but she could see how her mother and Hugo might believe it. "Let me tell you what really happened," she began.

"We don't have time," Father Peele said, "and it doesn't matter. You must lie or act. Act. For instance, can you think—think very hard now, live the feelings all over again, let them possess you—can you think of something you did that you're terribly ashamed of? Think of it. Hold the feeling."

Alida remembered Andrew's wasted expression as he said, "I failed my child," and she recalled her fury when she tried to stab her grieving lover, and, as Father Peele had counseled, she let the feeling of shame wash over her. He watched and said, "That's it, that's beautiful, that's right. Now, as you begin to say what they want you to say, keep whatever that thought is in mind, and you'll look perfectly genuine—I coached a youth drama group. And, if you can, let it

310

come out bit by bit. Don't let it happen all at once, or they'll call you 'unstable.' A sign of coming around is beginning to blame yourself. Then you build."

Alida said, "How smart you are!"

"No," he said, "I'm only beginning to be humble. There's somebody in the corridor. Would you mind very much if we knelt in prayer?"

When they got up, he left her a tract. "I'll be back," he said.

"One moment, Father. Tell me, before you go, is art a lie?"

"Everything that isn't a fact isn't a lie, Alida, but you mustn't worry about that now. First decide to live; then find out why. Oh, one more thing. Don't try to be funny, but if you must, do it badly, as if you're trying to cover your embarrassment at what you have to admit. That's very hard."

Alone again, Alida went to the table piled with crepe paper and cardboard emblems of festivity. She picked them up and put them down. Another holiday, another set of rituals, symbols, and myths; every holiday was about ghosts. She was alone with the livelong furniture: the print mingled a harsh mustard with a rusty orange and an acid blue. And with the eternal river whose waters visited her father. She thought about Father Peele's instructions. Father Peele. Whose Father was he? Was her life, *her* life, a story about fathers? Never mind. Her intern was coming for her, and he was not fatherly. She went to the window and assumed her pose for the next scene.

When Alida hears the doctor enter, she takes two beats and then turns. She remembers to underplay and does not hurry.

ALIDA: I love the river. I never tire of the view. (*She shows some tension now. One hand clenches and unclenches.*)

INTERN (*sternly*): We're not here to discuss the scenery.

ALIDA (*drops her eyes, ruefully*): You're right. I guess I've been here long enough. (*She raises her eyes, smiles timidly, and speaks that genuine work of art, a true lie or a lying truth.*) I am afraid, Doctor, I have been very foolish.